Praise for *Rites of*

ignant, both from a musical and personal perspective. The
ce builds powerfully to a dramatic and ultimately very moving
onclusion. Completely gripping!' Tasmin Little

Duchen paints a vivid and utterly bleak picture of modern
amily life, poignantly depicting Liffy's increased isolation
as the people around her become so preoccupied and alien-
ated from one another . . . A sensitive and thought-provoking
ovel that will resonate all the more for those with musical
eanings.' Femke Colborne, *MUSO*

Jessica Duchen has crafted a riveting drama set within the
arts world . . . The neatly-composed plot charges to a climax
as steadily as Ravel's Boléro, with Duchen capturing well
he inner world of the pubescent girl and the London
assical music scene. For fans of Joanna Trollope and
Russian composers alike.'

Anna Britten, *Classic FM Magazine*

Duchen skilfully enlists our compassion and understanding,
nd her not-inconsiderable achievement was to make me
mpathise, as well as sympathise, with the central characters.'
Barry Witherden, *BBC Music Magazine* (5 star review)

Praise for Jessica Duchen

'Everything she writes is worth reading' *The Times*

'It is an intriguing life story . . . Jessica Duchen's highly
readable new biography, the first comprehensive book on
he man in English'
BBC Music Magazine on *Erich Wolfgang Korngold*

'Lucid an   rngold

About the author

Jessica Duchen was born in London and grew up with music and writing as twin passions. She has written for publications including the *Independent* and *BBC Music Magazine* and as a music journalist has interviewed most of today's greatest musicians. Her books include biographies of the composers Gabriel Fauré and Erich Wolfgang Korngold. She lives in south-west London with her violinist husband.

JESSICA DUCHEN

Rites of Spring

HODDER

First published in Great Britain in 2006 by Hodder & Stoughton
A division of Hodder Headline
This Hodder paperbacks edition 2006

A Hodder paperback

1

A CIP catalogue record for this title
is available from the British Library

ISBN 978 0 340 83931 7
ISBN 0 340 83931 7

Typeset in Plantin Light by
Palimpsest Book Production Limited, Polmont, Stirlingshire

Printed and bound by
Clays Ltd, St Ives plc

Hodder Headline's policy is to use papers that are natural, renewable
and recyclable products and made from wood grown in sustainable forests.
The logging and manufacturing processes are expected to conform to
the environmental regulations of the country of origin.

Hodder and Stoughton Ltd
A division of Hodder Headline
338 Euston Road
London NW1 3BH

To the memory of my mother, father and sister

'Olivia.'

She opens her eyes into the darkness that is never dark. She strains her ears in the silence that is never silent. Street-lights, a sound-soup of traffic from the South Circular, the groaning planes passing overheard. And a voice, a still, small voice.

'Olivia.'

A friend at primary school had once heard voices. She'd called them 'the pixies in the wall'. Liffy knows enough about the world to be sure this isn't a pixie. She doesn't believe in pixies. She can hear her own breathing and the heartbeat accelerating within her developing breast. The house around her seems suspended in time and motion.

'Coming, Olivia? With me?'

Liffy sits up, rubs her eyes and switches on the lamp under her Pooh Bear poster. The voice has gone, sucked away into the pool of pale light.

I

It's the day after the funeral. April sunshine slants into the house, thinned inside by pale muslin curtains and outside by concrete-grey and ghost-white clouds. Liffy is first up, as usual. She likes to get up earlier than the rest of the family: she enjoys the only quiet moment of her day, settled on the sofa with her legs tucked under her, still wearing her purple pyjamas patterned with zebras.

The garden beckons, the daffodils loud and luminous, the apple tree taut with heaving buds. Spring has startled Liffy this year. All she remembers, before, is liking it, but never loving it, not so much that she wanted to run to the grass naked and throw herself face down in it to embrace the earth. It is a peculiar impulse and not one that she'd like to admit to anybody, least of all her parents. Certainly not the day after her grandmother's funeral.

She makes herself breakfast: a cup of weak tea with plenty of milk and two teaspoons of sugar, a bowl of muesli, a banana. Sometimes Dad makes scrambled eggs for them all, but Liffy doesn't wait around in case because she can't bear watching the twins eat. They go about it with the clamour and gluttony of tiger cubs at a kill. At the party – if you could call it a party – after the funeral, they'd stuffed their faces with so many sand-wiches that Alex had been sick in the car on the way home. In any case Liffy prefers, twins or no twins, to eat alone, but – without knowing why – she doesn't like to say so. It's another of those impulses that have started this year and don't quite make sense in the context of family routine. She presses a button on the remote control and watches a perky, attractive girl who looks no older than herself reading something disheartening about school results on the breakfast news.

Upstairs there's the rumpus of her father trying to get the twins out of bed. The trouble with the twins is, first, that they share a little world of their own, which makes them super-resilient to outside interference; second, that they hate school; third, that they pick on Liffy. She doesn't mind if they get up late – there's more time for her to breathe and just . . . just *be* before the onslaught begins. But they have to get to school and each day it's the same, with Dad hauling out one and then the other from under their car-patterned quilts, trying to be jolly and laugh them into wakefulness, only to crack as they protest or ignore him. Liffy listens, bored, as Dad's voice rises to outstrip the two little rebels – 'Matt, I *won't* tell you again!' By the time the twins appear on the stairs, one after another, they will be fuming, tearful or both. It is as if none of them can start their day without this ritual that leaves them tense and coiled like springs in a clockwork hamster.

Mum, in the big front bedroom, is still asleep. She's lying on her back, mouth open, snoring. Liffy glances in on her way to the bathroom. Mum, when she's awake, is striking – charismatic. Everyone is impressed by her, in one way or another. At school, other girls tell her, 'My mum says your mum's Sasha Wood and she's really famous.' Margaret, Liffy's ballet teacher, says it's a shame Mum had had to stop dancing because she'd been so beautiful on stage; they'd once been in the same company. Miss Carroll, the English teacher, wants to know why Liffy's English composition isn't better than it is, since her mother is such a wonderful writer. All of them watch Mum on *The Weekly Review*, on which she speaks as cultural critic at least twice a month.

Liffy never saw her mother dance – she was the reason she'd stopped; she can't read her book (too difficult and grown-up); and when *The Weekly Review* comes on, on Fridays at eleven o'clock at night, she has generally been asleep for over an hour, though sometimes she watches a videotape of the programme the next morning, only to find she understands nothing as it's all about new films, plays and books that she doesn't know. At breakfast time, Sasha has been asleep for too few hours; she is not often up early enough to see her family off, and nothing can wake her, not even the aeroplanes overhead. Liffy can't help feeling that everyone else knows her mother better than she does.

Liffy puts on her uniform – dark green – and brushes her long hair, which, like Auntie Lisa's, is the colour of clear honey. She checks her rucksack for books, lunchbox (which she has prepared herself the previous evening) and the full complement of homework, plus well-concealed mobile phone; says goodbye to her father and brothers, who respectively kiss and ignore her; and walks up Somerset Road under the light, drifting petals of cherry blossom towards the bus stop.

Adam, ushering Alex and Matt through the routine of bathroom, school uniform, shoes, schoolbags and lunchboxes, wonders how Sasha can sleep through the racket. He knows better than to challenge her for, after thirteen years of marriage and – he realises with a lurch – nearly twenty years together, on and off, she has never been any different. She applies the same intensity to sleeping as she does to writing, speaking or making love. That's one of the things he has always loved about her; he can't question it now.

He walks the boys to school on automatic pilot – it's not far, just ten minutes through pretty, garden-decked side-streets – and deposits them with mingled anxiety and relief at the gates. He watches the two mop-headed little figures charging through the playground to meet their footballing friends for a game before school. They always run; they never walk. Adam turns his attention to his journey to work.

The station; hazelnut latte and croissant from Claudia, the

Mexican girl who runs the coffee shop; late train; twenty-two minutes, twenty-five in rush-hour, to Waterloo. Carriages vacuum-packed with sharp-suited women, students with studs through their eyebrows, plump, self-satisfied men older than him, younger, thinner, anxious-looking ones with trendy rectangular glasses. The variety of languages and colours increases as the train approaches central London.

Adam's gaze falls on an Asian youth in denims, carrying a wide, flat black case of the type Adam recognises only too well as an artist's portfolio. The boy has dark, serious eyes; his gaze meets Adam's for a fractured second and Adam senses at once the inner transformation, the artist's instinct that breaks up everything it sees into line and form and essence – not intention, but second nature. The youth is deconstructing him, perhaps turning him into an abstract form, a pattern of fierce yet fading colours and shattered outlines, entitled *Desperate Father Commutes*. Adam wonders whether the boy can see – in that sliver of time on an overcrowded train – how much he longs to switch places with him.

At the back of his brain, a rhythm is beating. *Mum. Mum. Mum.*

His last image of her is branded behind his retinas: laid out flat, arms by her sides, eyes closed never to open again, skin grey, awareness gone. All the times she had cooked and scolded and punished and embraced and fussed and despaired and hoped for him, her only son, her only child, she his only mother, and it had all to end there, in her bedroom with the spring breeze lifting the chintz curtains and the cruel sun shining on and on, an icy stillness spreading through the house as if its own soul had breathed out and gone away. Adam's heart is screaming and screaming for her to come back – it's like his three-year-old separation anxiety, left in the car while she nipped into the Summertown grocery for a minute to pick up cornflakes, milk, bread and Marmite, and he knew she was never, ever coming back . . . and now, forty years later, he sees he'd been right after all. It is not yet twenty-four hours since he watched her coffin being lowered into the grave and heard the rabbi intoning her name in the middle of the Hebrew prayers, pronouncing it 'Marta' rather than the anglicised 'Martha'. He can still see his father's blank, anguished face beside him, still hear the ghastly dull thud of the first clod of earth on the lid, still feel Liffy's cold little hand jerk in his own with shock at the sound.

He casts his gaze across his fellow commuters. Death amid modern life takes place behind screens and locked doors, under fluorescent light or in the dark, in places smelling of disinfectant and the putrid, rotting stems of abandoned flowers in plastic vases. Death today is not to be looked in the face. Most of Adam's carriage-mates, he knows, imagine death simply as the closing of a box – if they imagine it at all.

At Waterloo, Adam is carried with the crowd down the stairs to the Waterloo and City Line. Underground, the train is cramped and grimy. Adam holds on to a scarlet metal pole during the five-minute journey to Bank; as always he's relieved to be out of the Tube and plodding up the sloping travelator towards the open air. Another few minutes on foot – the quietest time of his day, in which he can mull over the twins' impossible energy, Liffy's inscrutable workaholism and the unwakeability of his wife – and he arrives at the Bishopsgate offices of Forrest & Burns Magazines where his place waits for him on the third floor at the head of a bank of desks, all similarly adorned with state-of-the-art flat-screened computers and a system of in-trays and out-trays containing magazine job bags tracking the state of each feature for the next issue of *Fifteen*.

'Look, mate, at least you'd be using your skills and getting paid properly for it.' Those words had drawn him into this bizarre, unnatural world – words from Nick, his oldest friend from art-school days. Nick works upstairs at Forrest & Burns, which owns ten of the most successful magazines in the country. He's art director on a different kind of monthly and when Adam had phoned him in 1994 with the news that he and Sasha were having twins and he needed to find a better-paid job PDQ, it was a good word from Nick to Terry Forrest that had fixed things. Not that Adam had wanted to admit that to Sasha – her much-vaunted liberalism stopped well short of encouraging contacts in top-shelf magazines – but he hadn't had much choice.

On the days when Adam and Nick, each up against endless deadlines, unreasonable demands from Editorial, even more unreasonable ones from Advertising and problems with the printers, slope off at six for a drink before heading home, they sometimes sit over their beer remembering their younger selves and laughing at their old dreams of being the next David Hockney.

'We still had to learn painting,' Nick reflects, when the Turner Prize rolls round again. 'Nobody bloody paints any more. It's all film installations and pickled sharks and filthy beds now.'

'Ever do any these days?' Adam asks.

'Not bloody likely. You?'

'Sometimes.' Adam prefers not to tell his old mate that he couldn't live without the release that is a blank canvas, a palette, the tray of oils and the brushes that lie somewhere in the broom cupboard, waiting to tempt him back into the only world that is all his own. Certainly not during these years in which he controls the look of double-page spreads targeted at girls just a few years older than his daughter, articles about pitfalls to avoid when trying to colour your hair at home, how to achieve the right school–life balance, how to choose the right bra and, most frequently, such matters as what to wear for a first date with a boy. Some lunchtimes he bounds upstairs to the fifth floor to find Nick and go for a sarnie; and Nick will be working on his own mag's spreads, fitting breasts to page edges, airbrushing underarm shadows or crows' feet around the models' eyes, designing front covers with coloured lettering that picks up the shade of the girl's eyeshadow, G-string or nipples.

Over the Friday beer, Adam listens to Nick's problems. Nick's wife, Mary, has run off with a merchant banker, taking their three-year-old daughter with her. Adam doesn't like talking about himself at the best of times, but he doesn't know how to explain to Nick the dismay, the terror he often senses, looking at the bright, defiant, trendy teens in his magazine and the sex objects in Nick's, about what the future holds for his beautiful, innocent, ballet-obsessed twelve-year-old Liffy.

Lisa Wood, her hair wound up and pierced through with a mock-ivory hairpin like a dinosaur tooth, is pacing the lecture theatre waiting for her students. They're often late – although, to be fair, it's not always their fault since most are at the capricious mercy of the London transport system. There are just forty first years and they drift in in groups. Some carry a case concealing a violin, flute or oboe; the cellists deposit their hefty burdens at the side of the room. The lecture theatre has no windows. They can't be distracted from Stravinsky's *Rite of Spring* by the sight of the real spring that brings out all the urges to do – well, many things other than listen to Lisa's lecture.

She allows them three more minutes, then gives up on the absentees and begins. 'When Stravinsky described the origin of *The Rite of Spring* – who can tell me what he said?'

A startled moment of silence: the students are shocked out of their dozy state, as she'd intended, the onus on them to respond. A hand goes up to the right of the theatre.

'Edward?'

'He said he dreamed it,' says the youth, a compact fellow with a public-school voice and hair gelled into spikiness. He likes answering questions. 'He said that he saw in a dream the image of an ancient tribe performing a ritual in which a young girl dances herself to death to propitiate the god of spring.'

'Very good, Edward. But actually it was the sun god, Yarilo. And you know how we know that?'

Silence. No student has heard the name Yarilo before.

'Because,' Lisa says, 'if you look at the *facts* – not the fictions drawn up by various people including Stravinsky himself – they tell you that there is only the very slenderest chance that Stravinsky could take as much credit for the idea as he wanted to. These days we tend to look at art, dance and music as three separate entities. We're losing out, because Diaghilev, who commissioned this ballet, certainly didn't separate them. And if you look at who the designer of *The Rite of Spring* was, the artist Nicholas Roerich, you see that his interest in Russian folklore meant that he probably provided a substantial part of the idea and knew the name of this god. What does this tell us?'

Silence. Lisa sighs inwardly.

'It tells us,' she says, 'that creation doesn't happen in isolation. For every creative baby, if you like, there has to have been a creative sperm – no sniggering, please! – to spark it into life, and a creative womb, a creative environment, to nourish it and enable it to grow. It tells us that if we want to understand the miracle of artistic creation, we have to look at the *whole* picture. This course is called "The Origins of Twentieth-Century Music, 1880 to 1925", which is as general as it comes. Who has read Debussy's letters?' A few hands go up. 'Who has read Tolstoy?' Five people admit to it. 'And who has read a history of the Russian Revolution? Who has read Karl Marx?'

The room falls into shocked stillness. Lisa can't help remembering that when she was at university people still read Marx, and believed in his work, and she is only thirty-three. Nobody reads Marx any more.

'The Russian Revolution,' she says, 'took place eight years before the official end of our course. Unless you know why so many Russian composers were living in exile, you won't begin to understand what made them tick . . .'

Even while she lectures, Lisa is preoccupied with her own Russian in exile. Vladimir had phoned her at almost midnight the evening before. She'd talked to him for half an hour, told him about Adam's mother's funeral, told him her anxieties about her own mother and the difficulties in her sister Sasha's family and the way her downstairs neighbour keeps having his doorbell rung in the middle of the night and how she sees shady characters going in and out. Vladimir told her about the new record producer he is working with, about his chamber-music colleagues for the CD, about a delayed plane and lost luggage and how he hates German food. 'I bought you some beautiful shoes in Berlin,' he added. 'They are purple suede, very elegant.'

'That's sweet of you, darling,' said Lisa, even though it is Vladimir, rather than herself, who gets a kick out of beautiful shoes. 'Vovka, I miss you so much.'

'I miss you too.'

'When can we see each other?'

'Darling, we'll work something out. I will call you *very* soon.'

Lisa knows that this is a sure indication she won't hear from him for at least a fortnight.

Vladimir's problem is not his busy schedule, his broken marriage, his reluctance to commit or even his musical stardom. It runs deeper than any of those. Vladimir's problem is Stalin. He'd spent his early childhood constantly on the move because his parents, who were both academics, had been denounced in Kiev years earlier by a jealous neighbour. Two years in Tashkent, two in Siberia, two in Georgia, eventual calm amid faceless Soviet concrete tower blocks in the Ukraine, where his father had walked out. It's the fear that has stayed with him since he 'defected' – pre-*perestroika*, with much fuss in the press. It's the deep-seated, unconscious fear of staying anywhere for too long, in case it leads to indefinite incarceration or violent, premature death. How can she explain the effect of the Russian Revolution to a roomful of spoilt eighteen-year-olds in designer jeans? It's hard enough to grasp the implications herself.

After the lecture, as the students pile out, she notices that Edward has left behind the piece of paper he's been sharing with his neighbour – writing scribbled asides to one another. She couldn't be bothered to stop them, not seeing much harm in it. At least they'd turned up to the lecture: many others had not. She walks up the stairs and retrieves it.

On the paper, the outline of a woman's body is drawn in black ink, topped with a swirl of hair pinned up with something resembling a gigantic tooth. Beneath it is scribbled the following exchange:

32D?

11/10.

What's a nice girl like her doing in a crap job like this?

How about: can't find a man?

Lisa Wood. If she could. But she can't.

Wouldn't mind righting her spring . . .

Lisa scrunches up the paper and deposits it in the nearest bin. Then she fishes it out again, smooths it and stows it in her briefcase.

Later, on her way out from her office, down long, bare flights of Victorian stone stairs, she passes the student canteen where she spots Edward tucking into a plate of chips topped with half a bottle of tomato ketchup. She pushes through the glass doors and comes up behind him. He is so busy holding forth to the girl opposite him that he doesn't notice her until it's too late.

'Hi, Edward,' she says. He turns round and guilt flashes over his face. Lisa pulls the piece of paper out of her bag and slaps it down on the table in front of him. 'You left this behind. Oh, and you were wrong about one thing: it's thirty-two *double* D. See you tomorrow.' She saunters out, leaving her stunned student speechless over his chips.

*   *   *

Liffy's school bus collects her and a gaggle of other girls from the stop opposite the tandoori restaurant. Then it crawls along like a giant sloth, past the supermarket, past boutiques selling novelty gifts and sports equipment, past the garden centre, and stops again to pick up a crescendo of occupants. The noise inside the bus increases by many decibels with every intake. Liffy, sitting with feet tucked under in her favourite seat exactly half-way down the bus, talks to Charlotte, who clambered aboard beside the pub. She tries to ignore the noise. She hates people who giggle. Charley says she has decided to be vegetarian because of all the antibiotics that are pumped into farm animals.

'Cool,' Liffy says, wondering why she hadn't thought of it herself.

The bus accelerates, halting once half-way up a long road lined with expensive historic piles and again at the top just before Hammersmith Bridge. WEAK BRIDGE, says the notice. Gazing at the lapping grey water of the Thames at low tide and the ornate, green edifice of the bridge, Liffy tries to dispel the image that always rises in her mind of the road buckling, the bus tumbling off, the water claiming them all.

The other side of the river is like a different city. Gone are the wide streets, the generous trees, the Italian delis and pretty clothes shops. In their place stand Victorian terraces several floors high, their window-frames begging to be painted, the steps up to the front doors sprouting stray dandelions. Some doors are patched with wood where glass should have been. The newspaper hoardings bear sensational headlines: 'Bomber's connection with Bin Laden'; 'Scores dead in flood disaster'; 'No to Euro, says former PM'. A stream of cheap hotels with names like Roxana, Demetrios and Hellenic line the street and she almost always sees the same red-bearded tramp foraging in the dustbins and the same half-crazed man in threadbare tweeds wandering along, shouting and singing at the passers-by. Legend has it that the girls used to make their own way to school on public transport, but such was the outcry among the parents about the danger and the expense that the school began to lay on its own buses, which Liffy is certain cost far more per term.

Liffy tries not to show it, especially not to Charley, but she feels afraid every morning and every evening. She'd feel afraid in between too, if the stream of lessons paused for long enough to let her. It's a fearsome, unbalanced world, drawn with skewed angles and double standards and inside-out priorities: its geometry makes no sense. Why do people sleep rough in Hammersmith? Why do scarlet-faced alcoholics linger there? Why does nobody help them? Why are so many people dying of AIDS in Africa? When will the next crazed suicide bombers strike, and when will they pick London to strike at? Why is global warming being allowed to continue unchecked? Why does nobody care? Because nobody does. In her year nobody, except her and Charley, seems to care about anything except how fat they are and who wins *Pop Idol*.

Obesity is the fastest-growing health problem in the UK, scream the headlines. Children don't get enough exercise. All they do is sit and eat crisps and hamburgers in front of video games and the TV. They don't play in the street, they don't run in the park, and instead of walking to school, they are driven there by mothers in 4WDs. Liffy cannot match the news headlines to her own experience.

They have four compulsory sport sessions every week and she loathes them all: they are bussed down to the games fields and stand in the freezing cold in their short gym skirts and short-sleeved blouses while the wind flays their knees and gnaws at their young bones. She's never played a video game: she doesn't have time, what with too much homework, too much practising (she has to do all her ballet exercises every day), too many parties at the weekends, too much to do, no time to do it all, no time to close her eyes and – well, just *be*. As for obesity . . . On the noticeboard in the school entrance hall is pinned a piece of paper giving the extension number you should ring if you think your friend has anorexia.

At lunch, Liffy looks around the crowded school dining room, a hive of green bees with hands and feet and buzzing, droning voices. Almost everybody is eating chips or burgers or both. The school lets them choose whether to buy canteen food or bring their own lunch from home. Some have been given sandwiches by their mothers. A few have sloped out of school (illegally) to investigate local fast-food outlets instead. Charley, who's in love, doesn't want to eat at all.

'He's never going to love you,' Liffy says, feeling it best to tell her straight. 'You're a kid.'

'But if I wait . . . Seven years isn't so long. Not really. I'll be twenty in seven years' time and he won't even be forty yet.'

'You don't need to wait until you're twenty, nitwit,' says the superior-toned Sophie, who sits opposite them. 'You'll be legal in three years. And who waits *that* long anyway? Nobody waits to lose their virginity until they're sixteen.'

'You'd have to stop having flute lessons,' Liffy says. 'Otherwise he could get sacked for – what's it called?'

'Gross moral turpentine,' Sophie declares – and looks bewildered as all the girls around her choke, laughing, on their lunch.

'I'm useless at the flute anyway.' Charley sighs. 'I can't cope with him looking at me.' She scrapes the remains of her sandwiches into a nearby black-lined bin.

'You're not useless,' Sophie says kindly. 'You're really good.' She's the only other girl in the class who has flute lessons – another reason why Charley despises her. Charley snorts and looks the other way.

'God, I feel fat,' announces Leila. 'I went shopping on Saturday because I can't get into my jeans.'

'Come on, Leila, you're a size six!' Sophie challenges.

'Not any more I'm not.'

Leila is a tall, exquisitely beautiful girl with coffee-coloured skin much envied by the others; she's half Persian (she always says 'Persian' rather than 'Iranian'). She's so exotic and elegant that the plain white English middle-class girls who make up the majority of St Catherine's School would have crowned her queen at once, if given the chance. Sitting beside her, Liffy feels too short, too pale and far too plump. She glances down at Leila's backpack by their feet, its top flap open. Inside she can see what looks like a packet of pills bearing the word 'Sennolax'.

Liffy and some of the other Jewish girls in the class once tried to argue that they were a trendy ethnic minority too, but got laughed at. 'You don't even have funny noses,' Sophie had tried to explain. 'You look just like everyone else. Anyway, Israel's horrid. You don't want people to associate you with *that*, do you?'

Liffy, Sarah and Katia all have cousins or family friends in Tel Aviv or Haifa; they all lost relations in the gravel-hued background to something called the Holocaust that they know only through faint tales from reluctant grandparents. The three stared at Sophie in silence. Sophie gave a nervous giggle and hurried away, looking embarrassed. Liffy wonders why Sophie always puts her foot in it but never knows what she's done wrong.

The ground under Liffy's feet sometimes does not feel solid. She imagines, as she walks, that the ground is not earth but paper: her foot might go through it at any time and she will dangle by one leg, suspended in space over an infinite dark universe. If she were to walk too close to the edge of the pavement, she thinks, she'd fall off and instead of landing in the gutter she'd fall and fall and keep on falling and she'd suddenly see the earth in the distance as a hollow blue ball bouncing among predatory stars that might gobble it up in one gulp. She always walks as far inland from the kerb as she can.

'You're half Irish anyway, aren't you?' someone had asked her, after the Sophie débâcle.

'No,' Liffy sighed for the thousandth time.

'Then why are you called Liffy? That's the river in Dublin, isn't it?'

'It's short for Olivia.'

'Well, Olivia's not a specially Jewish name, is it? Why are you called Olivia?'

'Apparently,' Liffy announced, nose in the air, 'I was conceived under an olive tree on a Greek island.' That shut them up and had the advantage of being true.

Deciding what to call Olivia for short had been a tricky family matter. Adam and Sasha, thirty-one and twenty-seven, gazing besotted at the tiny, pink prawnlike being they had inadvertently created, thought of 'Olivia' almost as a joke – to find that it stuck to the baby girl like a second skin. Over the next several years they tried transforming it into Olly, but Gerald said they couldn't call a girl Olly, it sounded like Laurel and Hardy. They tried 'Liv', but it just didn't work for a baby or toddler. Liv Levy sounded ridiculous anyway, according to Martha; she wasn't going to have her granddaughter made a laughing stock. They tried Libby, the strange confluence of V and B suggesting itself as a possible exit route, but Olivia was a V girl, not a B girl: she was so light that there might have been tiny white wings fluttering on the back of her heels. She'd pattered on her feet rather than thumping when she learned to walk; she never walked when she could run (the one thing she had in common with her brothers), or stood still when she could dance. She needed a name that flew, that was not held down by the lead plumb-line of a letter as solid as B. So Liffy she became and now everybody thought she must be Irish.

'Ah, Adam. Sorry about your mother. Lousy business.'

'Thank you, Terry.'

Adam is sitting in the MD's office on the tenth floor. Terry Forrest – fifty-something, five foot six, with small, astute eyes – sits opposite him behind a wide cherry-wood desk.

'I've asked you to pop in for a little chat because we've got some good news,' Forrest says. 'We're buying ourselves a new toy.'

'Oh yes?' says Adam.

'It's a kind of spinning top.' Forrest sits back in his leather chair and folds his hands together over his paunch. 'The principle's easy. When it spins, it generates money. It sells like hot chestnuts. And it badly needs a new home. Its daddy's been run in for . . . shall we say, financial irregularities?'

'And what name does it answer to?'

'*Trafalgar.*'

'You have got to be joking.'

'I kid you not. *Trafalgar* is ours, with *Trafalgar*'s hundreds of thousands of readers and hungry companies slavering at the chops at the thought of advertising in it. Now, Adam, you're our best designer and our best manager too. I'm impressed with the way you look after your team. They trust you and they respect you. You'd be surprised how rare that is. So. I'm offering you the art directorship.'

'The art directorship?' Adam feels as if he's in a lift that's stopping too quickly.

'Big raise. Big raise for big responsibility. A bit snazzier, too, than the teeny-boppers. *Very* glossy. Major quality-control issues. High pressure, with high rewards. How does it grab you?'

'A big raise,' Adam echoes. 'Can I ask how much, exactly?'

Forrest utters a figure. Adam's mouth almost falls open.

'What do you say?' Forrest sits forward and fixes Adam with his little eyes.

Adam can't speak for a second. 'Thank you, Terry,' he says finally. 'It's a great opportunity. Can I have a day or two to think it over?'

Forrest's eyebrows rise. 'If that's what you need,' he says. 'Come back to me about it by Thursday.'

Adam gets up to go, wondering whose life he's stepped into by accident. It certainly doesn't feel like his own.

Sasha sits in her study, tapping her fingers on the desk as she watches her list of new emails appearing on her computer screen, bold letters on a white background. She agrees to let her email address appear at the end of the column and people do insist on writing to tell her what a terrible person she is. You have a column in a newspaper? You get emails. Your job is to provoke, to be opinionated, to goad people into using their grey matter a little, and all that happens is that they write to you saying you are provocative, opinionated and an intellectual snob. Now and then she gets a handwritten letter, forwarded from the office, from one woman somewhere north of Watford cheering her on, but on the whole people prefer to write negative responses, just as bad news is always bigger than good.

The trouble is that she can't get going today. She has deadlines, as usual, and she has nobody to blame but herself. She could have phoned her editor to explain that her mother-in-law had died and she'd been to the funeral and that writing about the lack of charm among New Labour women MPs could not have interested her less at this moment. But she hadn't. How can she let life stop, just at the time when life has to go on? Missing the column for a week, or pulling out of *The Weekly Review* on the coming Friday, would have been a triumph for Martha over her, from wherever it is that Martha has gone, and if she could triumph once in death she could continue triumphing into eternity, for she has become an immortal with nothing better to do than keep an ever-watchful eye from another world over her son, who happens to be Sasha's husband. Sasha decides she is damned if she is going to let that come about.

Sasha is not accustomed to writer's block.

Once, when she was eleven, Liffy had brought home a ques-
tionnaire – the sort that little girls love, the answers to which
are supposed to tell you something profound about yourself.
Liffy had begged her to fill it in and Sasha had come up with
the following:

NAME: Sasha Jane Wood

DATE OF BIRTH: 3 April 1963

ELEMENT: Fire

FAVOURITE ANIMAL: [Sasha had agonised over this one, torn at
first between friendly shaggy dogs and fierce wild cats.] Dolphin

FAVOURITE COLOUR: Blue

FAVOURITE FOOD: Mediterranean, preferably on a Greek island

FAVOURITE DRINK: Rioja

FAVOURITE SOUND: The sea

THREE QUALITIES: Determination, idealism, grace

THREE FAULTS: Stubbornness, anger and [um] vanity

ONE REGRET: Not being a dancer any more

ONE DREAM: To live fully

NUMBER: [Sasha didn't know why you were supposed to have a
favourite number, but she wrote down the one that meant the
members of her immediate family, excluding Martha, excluding
Gerald, excluding even her mother and Lisa.] 5

WHO OR WHAT IS THE GREATEST LOVE OF YOUR LIFE?
My children [She'd thought of writing 'my husband', but just at
that moment he wasn't.]

HOW WOULD YOU LIKE TO DIE? Not today, thank you. [Liffy
and her odd little friend Charlotte had laughed and laughed at
the twisted meaning, to Sasha's satisfaction.]

Liffy and Charley had examined the answers, then embarked
on a personal ritual, clapping their hands and intoning a rhyme
like a modern adaptation of an ancient spell. Then Liffy had
drawn a piece of paper out of a felt pouch they carried around
with them, and read it out: '"You are ambitious, passionate

and a dreamer. You have much to give to the world. Do not neglect your friends and family in your quest".'

'Quest?' Sasha echoed. 'This sounds like something out of *Lord of the Rings*. People don't have quests any more.'

'Ah,' Liffy said, 'but maybe *we* do.' She wouldn't elaborate.

Liffy has a quest and Sasha knows what it is. Every time they walk or drive through the park, Liffy's eyes stray to the quiet road up the hill, past the white notice forbidding through traffic, the road that finishes in a copse of oak trees beyond the acres of long, dry grass: the copse that conceals the ballet school.

Liffy wants to go to the ballet school. She'd auditioned, two years before, and hadn't got in. The letter declared that the competition had been tough and the standard exceptionally high, and they regretted that Liffy had not been in the final selection. Liffy, though, wants to try again and, as she tells her mother all too often, there's no reason why she shouldn't. Perhaps the competition might be less severe next time.

Sasha has not the slightest intention of letting Liffy become a dancer. She attends one of the best schools in London and hence in the whole country; she will have a fine education and she will not be permitted to fritter away her youth on something that will cause her nothing but heartache.

'I'm going to dance,' Liffy hissed, when Sasha tried to encourage her to spend more time doing homework and less on *pliés* and *battements en cloche*, 'and nobody is going to stop me.'

Sasha's email emits a ringing sound: a new message tells her that her companions on *The Weekly Review* will be the usual presenter George Urwin, the poet John Castleton, who has a new volume out with Faber, and the theatre critic Cindy Smith, who's just finished a book on black history reflected in white theatre. Sasha loves Cindy, tolerates George, hates John. Each appearance (twice monthly being her usual quota) puts another cog into the mechanism for selling her next book and the chances of some publisher buying it for what she knows it is going to be worth when she gets round to writing it. *The Weekly Review* is her most crucial activity, because underneath her fire-laced words lies a faint, irrational terror that some day someone is going to expose her for the fraud she knows she really is.

The phone rings and Sasha reaches out to answer it. From the receiver comes – nothing. There is a distant breath, then silence and a click. Sasha pushes back her chair, strides to her answering-machine and switches it on with one swipe. She has too much to do to be bothered with heavy breathers today.

In the office, Adam hangs up on his wife. How can he tell Sasha, professional latter-day feminist, judgemental liberal, mother of his three children, newly turned forty, that he's about to become art director of an upmarket men's magazine – including all that that implies?

Sasha abandons her desk to fetch her twins from school. They come hurtling through the playground like rocket-launched missiles and grab at her from two directions, yelling at the same time.

'Mu-u-um, did you get any sweets?'

'Mu-u-um, can we have some ice-cream?'

She's infuriated by them at every moment, yet loves them with an animal ferocity she hadn't known she was capable of until she gave birth to them. She hugs one with each arm, moved by their still babylike body warmth to a sensation that is grand and protective and makes her feel like some kind of fertility goddess. She remembers when the doctor held the ultra-sound scanner to her burgeoning bump, gazed at the screen and exclaimed, 'Sasha, there are two. You're having twins,' and she'd howled, 'Twins? My life is over!'

I don't half think some daft things. She smiles, saying no, she has no sweeties and, no, they can't have ice-cream until after dinner, marching them down the hill towards the main road. She can tell them apart, though few can: Matt's grin is the more lop-sided, Alex's hair the more disobedient. Matt's temperament is pragmatic but stubborn, with interests pointing towards a future career in business; Alex is less witty but more imaginative and she can't predict what on earth he will do for his living.

They have much more homework than any eight-year-old boy should have. At their little desks, side by side in the window of their room, they sit together writing, Alex biting his lip as he concentrates, Matt wriggling beside him. Later, she'll quiz them for their forthcoming spelling test. They attend the finest prep school in the borough – paid for, she's ashamed to remember, by Adam's father; it has a ninety per cent success rate for getting its pupils into the best private secondary schools. It's against all the principles that Sasha fought for and marched for and yelled for twenty years ago – but somehow, since she's had children of her own, those principles have steamed away over the relentless heat of real life.

She still doesn't approve. Children should be taught in a single stratum of state schools, paid for by the government, with everyone receiving the fine education to which a civilised society should entitle them. And so she says in her column from time to time. Nice idea, said Gerald, giving her a copy of the financial paperwork, but that's not how things are. Wish they were, but there you go: you've got to do what's best for your children as individuals. Moreover, Martha had insisted: 'I won't have my grandsons put in one of those bloody zoos,' she'd announced. Eventually, gritting her teeth, Sasha admitted defeat and the boys, like Liffy, went private.

Around five o'clock, Sasha hears a click of the latch – no footsteps to speak of – as Liffy comes in from school. The energy in the house shifts like sand into a new pattern: Liffy, wings on her heels, lightens the prevailing sensation of muddy little football boots and mini-macho maleness. She slips up the stairs and changes into a scoop-necked, fuchsia-pink top and flared jeans that trail to her toes. The air softens with the fragrance of clean hair and girlish floral perfume. Alex and Matt squabble over the last biscuit on the plate that Sasha has given them to spur on their homework; Liffy watches them, pulls a face and disappears into her room to work. She's been told that her target for this term should be to improve her maths and Sasha has promised that she'll help her with ballet practice later if the maths gets done – *properly* – first.

Bill, the big ginger tom, clatters through the cat flap into the kitchen and Ben, a smaller, slower, black-furred animal, gives him a slanted green gaze from the couch in the corner where he has been sleeping for most of the day. The cats don't like each other; they eat side by side at their bowls only under duress. Ben pads upstairs in pursuit of Liffy and settles down on her bed, paws tucked under. The sycophantic Bill avoids the twins, winds himself round Sasha's ankles and miaows on the off-chance that it might be suppertime.

After she's given the children cold drinks and biscuits and fed the cats, Sasha marinates chicken pieces ready to cook later, answers the phone to a double-glazing salesperson, changes the kitchen rubbish bag, which never wants to come out of the tall thin designer bin (what a daft way to design a bin), empties the dishwasher of clean plates, rings Lisa to make sure Lisa has called their mother, Sally, to see if she's OK (she has and she is), stops the twins killing each other in a fight over a red felt-tip pen, tests them on their spelling and at last sends them into the garden to play football while she goes upstairs to the loft, which they'd converted first into a play-room and then a ballet studio complete with barre, to help Liffy as she'd promised.

Liffy has changed into her ballet gear and stands straight, slender and poised in a perfect fifth position, feet turned out and stacked one against the other, a light hand resting on the round wooden barre. She sinks upright towards the floor in a full *plié*, knees to the sides, heels rising at the last minute; legs straight again, she folds her head and upper body in towards her knees, stretches forward and then up, lifting her free arm above her head and finishing the movement with a backward arch. Sasha praises the line of her arm, the tilt of her head, the open shape of her shoulders. Liffy's knees don't turn out as far as her feet do, though.

'I can't,' Liffy says. 'I am trying.'

Sasha knows there's nothing Liffy can do about it: her joints aren't built that way. If she lies on the floor with her legs bent up and drops them outward, feet together, to make a diamond shape, her knees cannot and will not touch the floor. The ballet school in the park will want them to. They won't. It's nobody's fault.

'I *will* get there,' Liffy says, straining for the turnout at her hip joints. 'I *will!*'

'You're tensing up,' Sasha says. 'It won't help. Relax into it.'

The more Liffy tries, the more tense she becomes and the less her hip joints want to co-operate.

Sasha knows she won't get back to her desk before ten o'clock that night, and she has to finish a column of which she's written just 232 words. She sighs. It never occurs to her that Liffy, hearing the sigh, might think her mediocre balletic ability had caused it.

Adam arrives home and hangs his raincoat on the wrought-iron stand near the front door. Sasha pours gin and tonic for him and herself, calls the children for supper – which involves prising the twins apart in another fight ('Matt, I *won't* tell you again!') – and asks her husband whether he's had a good day. He looks pale and exhausted, but she attributes that to the continuing after-effects of the funeral.

Adam mutters something about delayed trains. He props up on the Welsh dresser in the kitchen the card his colleagues have given him: it pictures a bunch of yellow flowers, roses and daffodils, cheerful and at odds with the content. The print reads: 'Thinking of you in your hour of need.' His colleagues have added: 'We were so sorry to hear about your mother.'

Sasha looks at Adam, permanently tired yet not sleeping, working himself into the ground yet not on the work he'd have loved, the passion drained from his spirit by paying for the house, the car, council tax, school uniforms, the twins' PlayStation, designer trainers, ballet lessons, holiday football coaching and food for all of them, plus Hairball Control Reduced Calorie Formula for Bill and Ben. Is this her husband? Is this her Adam?

This isn't where we started out. This isn't what we wanted or intended. How did we come to this?

There's silence in the children's rooms. Adam and Sasha switch off *Newsnight*, lock the back door, put the chain on the front door, brush their teeth in their white en-suite bathroom, get into bed under the white linen-covered duvet and turn out the lamp. Adam takes a breath. He's spent the entire evening thinking out the wording. But even as he begins to say her name, Sasha says, 'Night night,' curls up with her back to him and falls asleep.

Adam longs for the comfort of her body against his. He reaches out an arm, without hope. Sasha, semi-conscious, makes a gentle, protesting noise, wriggles further away and begins to snore.

Adam slides out of bed, pads downstairs to the living room and opens the low walnut-wood cupboard in the corner. It conceals several bottles of whisky, a large flask of Spanish brandy and some fruit liqueurs that he can't stand. He pours himself a dose of Talisker – the muskiest, peatiest of the whiskies – and puts the TV on, mute, to read the news on Ceefax while he sips. There are problems out there in the world: the Israelis and Palestinians are blowing each other up in the most brutal exchanges, George W. Bush and Tony Blair are blasting Iraq to pieces, Saddam Hussein may or may not be dead. Compared to such devastation and danger, he's comfortable. He has a beautiful house in a quiet cul-de-sac, three adorable children, a wife who – well, a wife at any rate – and they still live together as a family. The country is full of fears: desperate refugees escaping from war and torture amid resentful locals, gang warfare with guns in parts of north London, everywhere drugs and sickness and crumbling infrastructure; but here his family lives safely in a privileged, cocoon-like world spun round them as if by a silkworm. His job is to keep them safe – and safe they are, thanks to the money he earns for them. He's been offered one of the biggest jobs in his business. So he shouldn't complain. He really should not complain.

Mum, Mum, Mum, beats the rhythm in his head.

The night, in the south-west London suburbs, is never quite night: the sky – empty at last of planes at this hour – is the colour of burnt tobacco. The north wind carries a yeasty whiff from the brewery nearby. The neighbours' houses are dark and silent. Adam sits awake and stares into the night that is the only night he is permitted to live.

2

The music thunders through Lisa. It thrashes at her brain, tears her limb from limb, bone by bone, rips her apart at the fragile seams.

She's heard it a hundred times, maybe five hundred; she knows every note of it as intimately as she knows her mother and sister, maybe more so; but beyond the point where she knows it backwards, she knows it not at all and its power still has the upper hand. It knows her better than she knows it and can twist its knife through her guts while she lies defenceless, sacrificing to it her peace of mind and soul.

Sitting next to her in the cramped velvet darkness that is the upper amphitheatre of the Royal Opera House, warm and padded and crimson as a womb, Liffy sits forward, slender hands clasped tightly together. Her gaze follows the Chosen Maiden's every move on the stage below. They are watching the original *Rite of Spring* in its latest reconstruction: choreography by Vaslav Nijinsky, designs by Nicholas Roerich, dancing by the finest ballet company in the country, the one that Liffy longs to be part of. The Chosen Maiden is dancing herself to death. Paralysed by terror, she holds a stylised pose, hand against her cheek, then flings herself, as if against her will, into the jerky, ungainly, possessed movements that Nijinsky assigned to her in 1913.

What in the name of fuck, Lisa thinks, makes any human being write a piece of music like this? How could any otherwise sane person in the run-up to 1913 – and Stravinsky, whatever his shortcomings, seems to have been pretty sane – create something that depicts, with the cracking of the ice floes and the violent, irresistible Russian spring, the killing of a maiden by her own tribe? And how can that resonate, with all its fury and terror, in people living in numb, suburban, Western comfort ninety years later?

That's the eternal question that drives Lisa. That's why she is where she is; that's why she does what she does as a junior lecturer in music, a job that to her mother seems ill-chosen ('You'll never make any money'), to her sister irrelevant ('You've got a brain, why waste it?'), to her eight-year-old nephews uncool ('Classical music? Sad!') and to Liffy mistakenly glorious ('How wonderful to spend your life studying ballet music!'). Adam approves and constantly tries to spur her on ('Lee, when are you going to write that book? How's the cello? Don't stop practising, you play so well!'), but his encouragement has the side-effect of making her feel guilty: the fact is that she is doing what she loves, albeit at a threadbare salary, while he is not, because he's had, of child-supporting necessity, to sell out. As for Vladimir – well, Vladimir wants to answer her question too. At least, he says he does.

With a soft rush of air on the flute – death rattle, orgasm or both – the Chosen Maiden falls to the ground. A moment of silence that lasts for ever; then her tribe rushes forward in one final surge and on the last chord hoists her lifeless body triumphantly towards the sky. Lisa feels weak and drained. Liffy, next to her, claps as hard as she can when the ballerina comes forward – alive after all – to take her bow.

'Ice-cream?' says Lisa. Liffy nods, her eyes very bright. They edge across the narrow seats to the stairs and out into the amphitheatre foyer. From there they sail down the escalator into the Floral Hall and saunter over the shiny wooden floor towards an ice-cream seller, the great glassy Victorian structure arching black, white and gold above them.

'Do you understand it?' Lisa asks her niece.

'Yes, of course I do. The Chosen Maiden gives herself to save her tribe. Right?'

'Spot on. Even though she doesn't want to.'

'She does want to.'

'You think so?'

'Yes. Because she does it. She's terrified, but she does it anyway. It's an honour.'

Strange, thinks Lisa, handing over a handful of pounds for two honey and stem-ginger ice-cream tubs, how Liffy – children generally, for that matter – can accept as natural things that to adults are horrific. Liffy, eating her ice-cream slowly, is moving her feet and her fingers. Lisa notices, to her astonishment, that she has remembered the complicated rhythm of the Sacrificial Dance perfectly first go.

'You're very quiet,' she says.

'Trying to remember it all. I can't decide which I liked better – *The Dream*, or this one. And they're so different.' Frederick Ashton's classic to Mendelssohn's *A Midsummer Night's Dream* had begun the evening.

'I'm not sure about fairies with wings,' Liffy goes on, 'but I did like Oberon. He's quite creepy, isn't he?'

'He had a very good stage presence. So much of the time he's almost camouflaged in his brown and green against the woods, but you know he's there because that dancer really has the most incredible eyes . . .'

'Yes, to hold the stage like that without doing anything is something special,' Liffy agrees, and Lisa wonders how she knows.

'How come your mum doesn't take you to the ballet more often?' she asks.

'She doesn't have time,' shrugs Liffy. 'Besides, the twins won't go, and the tickets are expensive, so it's not fair.'

'It's not fair on you either, *not* going, when you want to be a dancer. And these seats upstairs aren't so expensive.'

'I don't think Mum wants me to be a dancer.' Liffy sighs.

'She keeps saying it's a horrible life.' She puts down her tub of ice-cream on the counter of the Floral Hall bar; she's only eaten half. Lisa wonders whether the talk of her mother's attitude to dancing has put her off her food. She can understand why Sasha wouldn't want her daughter to follow her into ballet. Things hadn't exactly worked out for Sasha, even if that was partly her own fault: gadding off to Greece for an entire summer and coming home pregnant hadn't been the best way to ensure a continuing career in dance. Lisa loves taking Liffy to the ballet – especially as her treat for her forthcoming birthday, when she will become a teenager – but she can't help reflecting that if she had a daughter of her own, she'd want to take her out to things she enjoyed all the time.

'Isn't it amazing,' says Liffy, gazing at a photo of Darcey Bussell, slender, long-legged and radiant, on the wall, 'that a human body can turn into something so incredibly beautiful?'

A bell rings somewhere high above them and the milling audience turns in the direction of the auditorium doors like shoals of tropical fish towards sunlight. Liffy and Lisa settle in for the finale, a lively, abstract ballet to a good piece of Poulenc.

Back at home in West Hampstead later, Lisa gives Igor, her black and white cat, a little extra supper, then sits in her kitchen – the nicest room in the flat, yellow and white with a pine table overlooking the back garden – to drink some camomile tea. Liffy's image hovers in her mind: slight, passionate, perfectly young, painfully beautiful. How would she see Liffy, she wonders, if the girl were her own daughter? She doesn't like sending Liffy home, mainly because Liffy's home encloses many intangible elements that Lisa dislikes. Sometimes she longs to spirit away her niece and keep her; sometimes she even imagines the delicate negotiations with Sasha.

The phone rings. It's Adam, who'd driven into town to fetch Liffy after the ballet. 'Thanks for taking Liffs out,' he says.

'She's going to bed now, she's got school in the morning, but she'll phone and thank you herself tomorrow.'

'That's OK. We had a great evening. How are you getting on?'

'OK.' Adam doesn't sound it. 'Bearing up. What are you doing this weekend? It would be nice to see you.'

Tourist maps in small resorts sometimes show up a flashing red light at the touch of a button, telling you where your hotel is. Now, somewhere in the remote areas of the map that is Lisa's mind, a small red light begins to blink. Lisa doesn't hear that her sister and brother-in-law and their children would like to see her. She hears, instead, a cry for help. 'It would be nice to see you.' It would be nice to be distracted from themselves, to have somewhere else to look other than inward, to have the presence of an outsider to tap off the steam from the boiling pot that is their stifling household.

Lisa, who had been looking forward to spending her pleasant, quiet, lonely Sunday pleasantly and quietly alone, resigns herself to the inevitable. She doesn't have a car, so it means a journey of an hour or more across town from West Hampstead to Mortlake; then another hour back again in the late afternoon. It means the whole day gone.

'How about coming over for Sunday lunch?' Adam says, with a brightness she knows he doesn't feel.

'All right.' Lisa is rendered powerless by Adam and Sasha's need of her. 'How's Sash?'

'She's fine. She sends her love. She has to read a new book before the *Review* on Friday, so she's busy with that at the moment.'

'Well, have a good few days and I'll see you Sunday.' Lisa is glad to hang up and make her tea in temporary peace.

Five minutes later the front door slams and she can hear, downstairs, a violent duet taking place: her neighbours, Andrew and his girlfriend Melanie, arguing as they arrive home from some outing.

'Andy – *Andy*! Just listen to me, can't ya?'

'I don't want to talk about this. It's crazy. I've had enough.'

'Andy, just *listen*—'

'Why should I? What's there to listen to? You yattering on?'

'Fucking bastard!'

'Stupid cunt!'

'*Fucking ba-sta-a-a-a-rd . . .*'

Every furious footstep downstairs shakes the walls of Lisa's first-floor flat. The house was converted in the mid-1980s, done in haste for a fast profit, and she sometimes thinks the walls must be fixed on with Blu-tack. Her nostrils curl and dry up as acrid smoke from Melanie's Gauloise assaults them, rising on the hot air from below to above through no fault of its own: that's what smoke does. Andrew and Melanie would hardly know she was there, but for the skittering of Igor's paws on the carpet when he pounces on his catnip mouse and the occasional blast of loud Stravinsky – which to them isn't loud because they go to so many clubs that they must be half deaf by now. She, however, has to hear their every move, every spat, every plate or window-pane smashed during their fights. She tries not to complain, since Melanie is kind enough to feed Igor when Lisa is away visiting Vladimir in Paris.

They've gone into their kitchen, out of Lisa's immediate earshot, and at least she can't hear the exact words any more. She pulls a pair of wax earplugs out of her bedside drawer, softens and inserts them and hopes they'll be strong enough to cut out the rest of the rumpus. The wax takes hold, bringing her blissful, golden silence. Igor comes out of his litter-box, which stinks of cat pee but which she puts up with because it means she can have Igor. He curls up on a favourite chair and begins to purr. The phone does not ring again.

Vladimir, says Lisa's heart. Vladimir.

She can't phone him because that would be chasing him. She can't allow herself to do anything that will push him further away from her than he already is. He isn't due home for another two weeks. She knows that the moment she sees him again, she'll take one look at him and forgive him for every day he hasn't called, every call when he hasn't asked about her work or her family, every moment when he hasn't been there for her when she longed for him; she can't help wondering whether he ever longs for her. She suspects that he doesn't.

Lisa's mobile phone gives a sudden buzz and emits an electronic twiddle.

'Thank u SO MUCH 4 1derful ballet,' she reads. 'C u v soon, nite nite, lol Lif xxxxx.' Lisa presses out a quick reply – 'U2 sleep tite, love u lots, Lis' – and finds, as she prepares for bed, that she's smiling again.

Sasha rolls over in bed, opens one eye and says to her husband, 'Make love to me.'

Adam has wanted to do nothing else for weeks. He shrugs his pyjamas on to the floor and Sasha, who still has the neck of a swan and the arms of Margot Fonteyn, or so he fancies, lifts off her long blue nightshirt with a movement as graceful as those she made twenty years ago when he saw her for the first time. Adam dives under the duvet and gathers her silky, bony, gorgeous, brittle, soft body to him, burying his nose in her marvellous hair. Here at last is the escape he needs – no ill mother, no dead mother, no funeral, no bereaved father and no Terry Forrest to tell him that being art director on something that pretended to be for aspirational men but was really a porn mag was the best thing that could ever happen to him . . .

'Ad, is something wrong?'

'No – no – I'm just a bit tired. It's been a tough week.'

'We haven't had a bonk for months – and you're too tired?'

'I'm fine, Sash. Give me a minute.' Adam tries not to give in to despair: this has happened many times before, since his mother's illness. A long-forgotten line of a Hebrew prayer floats across his mind. '*Shema yisrael, adonai elohainu . . .*' He has barely heard it since he left school, except at a wedding or two . . . The image of his mother, lying silent and dead in her bed, after she'd been alive and talking to him minutes before, flickers behind his retinas.

'Nothing's happening, is it?' Sasha says.

'Let's get some sleep, shall we?'

Sasha's dark eyes in the lamplight give him an unfathomable look that strikes him in the solar plexus – no, Adam thinks, let's be honest here, it hits him clean in the balls.

'We've hardly done it since your mother got ill.'

'Sash. I'm sorry. I'm so sorry. Don't you remember, when your father had his heart attack, when we were on the island—'

'That was years ago. That was completely different.'

'Sash—'

'Have you gone off me?'

'No, of course I haven't!'

Sasha, yawning, wriggles back into her blue cotton. 'I wonder,' she sighs. 'Night night, then.' She turns over with a brisk whump.

This is insane, Adam's mind screams at him. All I need to do is open my mouth and say the words. Perhaps she'll laugh. Perhaps she'll be pleased, especially with the money. What the hell am I afraid of? That she won't understand? That she'll leave me? That she'll take the kids and move to Australia? That she'll go off with somebody else and take him and his kids and my kids to Australia and farm kangaroos? It is the void beyond 'what if' that locks his jaw, shrivels his penis and paralyses the last slice of his brain.

Sasha is asleep in less than thirty seconds. Adam lies awake for what feels like half an hour before, for the second night running, heading downstairs for a whisky, a reality check with Ceefax and a cuddle with Bill, who is most likely to allow someone to stroke his orange fur at length when taken unawares, half asleep.

★   ★   ★

On the outside of Liffy's door is pinned a lopsided drawing
of a skull and crossbones bearing the words:

OLIVIA'S ROOM
NO ENTRY
ON PAIN OF DEATH

Inside, Liffy is in bed, with Ben, the black cat, on top of her
patchwork quilt, a warm, feline lump of life next to her feet.
She hears a murmur of voices from her parents' room, followed
by silence; then the soft footfalls of her father going downstairs. She can't sleep either: her head is too full of the ballets
she's just seen, the violent rhythms of *The Rite of Spring* and
the image of the tribal girl sacrificing herself to the sun god
hammering inside her temples. To make matters worse, her
period is coming on and her abdomen is tensing in protest at
the idea of the imminent bloody onslaught.

When Liffy had gone to the loo at school and found blood
in her pants for the first time seven months earlier, it had been
a source of great pride. 'I've caught up with you,' she'd told
Charley in delight, and several of their friends had come up and
congratulated her. But it wasn't long before reality bit. Five days
of agony every month. Blood flowing and flowing and flowing,
her life force ebbing away from her, uncontrollable, ruthless,
beyond what her mother likes to call 'mind over matter'. Her
stomach sticks out and spots erupt on her forehead, chin and
nose. Mum has bought her some antiseptic facewash, some
deodorant and several months' supply of sanitary towels, which
Liffy hates wearing in case anyone can see them under her ballet
leotard. She doesn't want to miss her classes or her practising
because of these dreadful few days, or else she'd lose five days
every month, which means five times twelve which is sixty days
per year, nearly *two months*, sacrificed to the complaints of her
idiotic body – but sometimes the pain is so bad that the blood
drains from her head, she feels dizzy and has to be sick. She
can't dance if she's going to be sick.

'Mum, how did you cope?' she'd asked. Mum made sympathetic noises and brought her a hot-water bottle with a fuzzy pink cover: it seemed to be the only thing that helped. Liffy had hoped for some sensible, practical advice – a chapter of a book on 'How To Train As A Dancer While Suffering Period Pains' – but all Mum said was, 'Oh, sweetie, it's hard, I know it is. Mind over matter, remember. Have a Nurofen and a nice cup of herbal tea . . .'

'I *hate* it,' Liffy mutters to Ben the cat. 'If only you knew how much I hate it.' Ben blinks at her through green slit eyes; she wonders whether he understands any words other than 'Ben' and 'suppertime'. She is almost a teenager now; she is supposed to be rebelling. But how can one rebel against one's own body?

'If men had period pains,' Mum said, 'the world would be a very different place.'

Liffy isn't sure that her imminent period and over-excitement from the ballet are the only reasons she can't sleep. Something in the air isn't right. Something is skewed off centre. Everything in her room is where it should be: her small pine desk stands by the window overlooking the garden, laden with homework and a few toys that serve as her exam mascots – two grey squirrels from the shop at the zoo, bought when she was seven, and a miniature koala that Charley brought back from Australia for her after a family trip. Her biggest poster hangs on the wall behind her bed – Pooh and Piglet holding hands – and the springy armchair is strewn with soft toys so numerous she's lost count of them. Her favourite thing, however, is her blue frosted-glass vase – she'd fallen in love with it at IKEA and Mum bought it for her. Now she intends to keep it filled with fresh flowers all summer. The scent of daffodils – as yellow-gold as a scent can reasonably be – hangs, gleaming, in the air. But even that can't stand the world upright again. The twins sense it too, she imagines; they've been too quiet, using their mysterious inter-twin communication system in preference to speech to anyone else.

She hasn't seen either of her parents smile for weeks, and now Dad is up in the middle of the night.

The daffodils on her desk seem to glow in the dark. Daffodils aren't meant to be fluorescent. They stir of their own accord. Flowers don't do that. Liffy rubs her eyes. Perhaps she is imagining it.

By her feet, Ben the cat shifts and, in one swift arc, leaps from the bed, tail abrush. He crouches on the floor, nose down, gaze fixed unswerving on the vase of daffodils.

Liffy sits up, one hand over her abdomen, and looks from cat to vase and back again. And she hears the voice. 'Olivia,' it says. That is all.

Ben, crouched low against the carpet, half runs, half crawls from the room, silent with terror.

If it was just me, Liffy thinks, Ben wouldn't be doing that. And before she knows what's happened, she has jumped out of bed and is running after the cat, down the stairs to where Dad sits in his pyjamas sipping something golden, reading the news on TV and stroking Bill. 'Dad?' Liffy says, noticing how tired he looks.

He reaches out an arm and gathers her on to his lap. 'Oh, sweetie-pie,' he says. 'What happened? Did you have a bad dream?'

Perhaps that's all it was, Liffy hopes, forehead on her father's warm, striped-cotton shoulder. She begins to return to earth.

'The cat,' she says. 'The daffodils.' She doesn't know how to tell him. He'll think she's going mad.

'What about them, love?'

'Look at him,' Liffy says, hearing paws padding into the kitchen. But there comes the sound of the cat eating, metal nameplate clonking against his bowl; a moment later he passes the lounge door. His coat is smooth, the tail upright like a flag, and he makes a happy-cat chirruping noise in greeting.

'He was scared,' she says. 'His fur went on end and he did

that sort of low-running thing he does when he's frightened of something.'

'What was he frightened of?'

'There was – the daffodils were – it's like they were, like, glowing.'

'That's how daffodils look in the dark, darling.'

'And I thought I heard this – like – a voice? Saying my name?'

'It must have been the telly coming on. I switched it on a few minutes ago and I forgot to turn the sound off straight away. It probably wasn't your name at all. Poor old Liffs, you've had a bad dream. Better now?'

Liffy stares up at him with her big brown eyes and nods.

Her face is pale and scared – unconvinced, Adam knows. He hugs her and kisses the top of her head; her wavy, honey-coloured hair is soft and childlike and smells of clean, warm little girl. He doesn't want to let go of her. If this girl of his should ever be in trouble, he swears to himself, he'll give his life to protect her. 'Hush, now. Everything's OK. Everything's going to be fine. Go back to bed, there's a good girl. It's very, very late.'

'OK.' Liffy seems resigned. She climbs off his lap and trails back towards the hall and the stairs. Adam watches her: his bright, beautiful, talented, sensible daughter, half him, half Sasha, yet someone else, someone separate in her own right. *God*, how he loves her. She's been herself since the day she was born: brown-eyed, perceptive, loving, sensitive, perhaps too brainy for her own good. She's never changed, only grown a bit bigger. But now she isn't quite a child any more: under her pyjamas, patterned with a kiddies' parade of bright orange and pink animals, he can see the first experimental swelling of breasts, and where her straight, thin child's body had no waist, one is beginning to indent a subtle presence. He wonders how much longer she'll sit on their laps. Kids grow up so fast these days, everybody says. And poor Liffy, not quite thirteen years old, is expected to do likewise even though she hasn't, even though she is just a kid.

She, at least, is worth living for. She is his greatest work of art, better than any painting. When he remembers that she and the twins were the reason he'd given up painting and got a proper job, he is not sorry: he is proud.

Adam downs the last of his whisky and goes back to bed.

'What I can't stand is the way people on trains put their feet on the seats,' says the man sitting opposite Lisa.

'Yes,' Lisa replies. To either side, her friends Lindsey and Paul are watching her while pretending they aren't – looking, no doubt, with the best of intentions, for signs that she and Paul's colleague Steve are getting along well over their fruit salad and ice-cream.

'It's about lack of respect,' Steve declares. 'Nobody in this country has any respect for public property any more. No wonder things don't work. It's endemic inefficiency and lack of basic courtesy, from top to bottom.'

'Can I help you clear the bowls?' Lisa says to Lindsey.

'No, no,' Lindsey insists. She's a freckled, young-looking woman with long fair hair held back in an Alice band. 'You sit and relax.'

'How did you say you know each other?' says Steve. It's the first question he's asked Lisa since before the starter. Lisa explains, aided and abetted by Paul, while Lindsey fusses quietly in and out of their large, stainless-steel-adorned kitchen.

'Lindsey and I were at college together – and you know what a superb pianist she is? She met this nice investment banker here, who wanted a wife who could play his Steinway.'

'I play a lot,' Paul interjects, laughing through his beard, 'but my big dream was always to find a wonderful wife who would play my piano to me in the evenings. And even then I never dreamed of finding anybody quite as incredible as her.'

'The age gap didn't bother you?' Steve asks.

Lisa gives him a frosty glance, but Paul, some fifteen years older than his wife, laughs it off: 'What do you think?'

Lisa watches Paul's gaze follow Lindsey to the kitchen – still full of longing and tenderness after six years of marriage. They are childless after three failed IVF attempts, but surround themselves with friends and promising young music students, some of whom Paul's bank sponsors through a foundation he's set up for the purpose. They hold regular musical evenings in their Hampstead house, where their friends can meet and talk and play and eat and where new chamber ensembles are plucked from the air and given life. Lisa's heart, as she watches her dearest friends together, twists into a strange-hued salad of pleasure, sympathy and pain.

Then she looks over the table at Steve and feels depression about to encroach as he restarts his favourite topic, the lack of discipline in modern London life. She wants to blank out this tactless City bore's bland features and replace them with Vladimir's high cheekbones and wide mouth; to paint over his pallid, sun-free skin with Vladimir's dusky complexion; to paste over his piggy blue eyes with Vladimir's big, dark grey-green irises. As if it's not bad enough that she can't stand the man that they want her to like, Lindsey and Paul are the only people among Lisa's many friends who know Vladimir – what was worse, they had introduced her to him. In the garden beyond the tall french windows, birds are going crazy with joy in the warm spring evening. Spring is the worst time of year to be unhappily in love and have your friends try to set you up with someone else.

'I mean, where are the policemen today?' says Steve. 'When did you last see a bobby on the beat here in Hampstead?'

'I'll help with the coffee,' Lisa mumbles and slips out of her chair towards the kitchen.

'Well?' Lindsey whispers, cafetière in hand.

'He's perfectly pleasant,' Lisa whispers back, 'but he's got to be the most boring man on earth.'

'Darling, come on . . . He's not that bad, is he?'

'The whole thing – these set-ups – it just makes me miss Vladimir even more,' Lisa confesses, a lump in her throat.

Lindsey looks into her eyes and Lisa sees the dismay strike her as she understands. 'Oh God. You're really in love with him, aren't you?'

Lisa's whole self, body and soul, aches for Vladimir day and night, like a magnet pulling towards its opposite field yet unable to clamp against it. But she can't explain that to anybody – not even her best friend – certainly not to Vladimir. Nobody believes in a love like that until they discover they're in the middle of one.

Lindsey envelops Lisa in a big hug and says softly, 'Lee, I'm sorry.'

'I'll give you a call some time,' Steve suggests, back at the dinner table, 'and maybe we can go to an exhibition. Have you ever been to the London Transport Museum?'

'I'm a little busy marking coursework right now,' says Lisa.

'This is bloody incredible,' Nick declares, handing Adam a pint across a steaming ashtray. 'I'd have given my right arm for that job, if I hadn't needed my right arm to do it. Have you told Terry you're taking it?'

'Nope.' Adam takes a long swallow of beer.

'Treat him mean, keep him keen.' Nick downs half his pint in one go. 'Maybe he'll tempt you with even more pound signs.'

'No, that's not the reason.' Adam sits back on the pub bench and looks with some longing at Nick's cigarette. He hasn't smoked for thirteen years. 'I don't know that I really want this job.'

'Ad, you're off your head. I know it's a bad time, with your mum passing on, but you've got to seize these chances with both hands, you know? Carpe the diem.'

'But is this the diem I want to carp?'

'Are you saying you're too intimidated by your wife to take a job on *Trafalgar*?'

'It's not that I'm *intimidated* by her . . . but I think if she told me I was selling out, she'd be right.'

'But she hasn't told you.'

'Because I haven't told her.'

'Fuck.' Nick puffs on his cigarette and blows a smoke-ring towards the low pub ceiling. Adam used to do that too; he wonders whether he'd remember how. 'With Mary gone, I'd already begun to forget what it's like,' Nick remarks. 'Jeez, how do any of us manage to bloody get on with our other halves? What do you think she's going to say, Ad?'

'She'll hate it. She might like the money, but she'll absolutely fucking hate how I'm earning it.'

'And if you turn it down, you're still sitting on the third floor brushing up the bows on the teeny-boppers.'

'You said it.'

'Tell me something.' Nick leans over the wooden table and Adam remembers, looking at his sharp gaze and knowing the intelligence behind it, how Nick had won the college award for life drawing twenty-three years ago and how beautiful his nude sketches had been. Wonderful sense of line, with the sureness of a Matisse, said the college principal, handing over the prize.

'How is it worse?' says Nick. 'How is it selling out more to take a better-paid job on *Trafalgar* rather than a magazine that tells teenage girls how to kiss boys for the first time? Because presumably, when you talk about selling out, you're talking about not being an artist any more. Ad, it's not selling out, it's called real life, it's called making a living and supporting your family. We all have to do it.'

'Do we?' Adam thinks of his mother, thin and shrunken and dying, staring semi-conscious into his eyes. 'Because this is all we've got, Nick. It only comes once, it goes faster each year and it's not a rehearsal.'

'That's exactly what I mean. That's why you've got to grab your chances while you can. Because there aren't any second chances. There's no such thing.'

'And that is exactly why I'm going to turn down the job.'

'Ad, you're bloody insane.'

'Maybe,' says Adam. 'Maybe I am.'

Nick drains the rest of his pint and puts the glass down with a thump. 'And you know something else?' he says. 'I wish I had your guts.'

When Lisa has finished her Friday morning lecture, she strolls out of college and up the Strand to meet Sasha for lunch in Covent Garden. It's a beautiful spring day, unseasonably warm: what birds there are in central London sound high on sunshine. Men are walking around without shirts; women expose winter-white flesh for the first time that year.

Lisa is dressed for her job, in a caramel-coloured knee-length skirt, long boots like Sasha's and a cream cotton shirt, with a silver necklace gleaming at her throat. Sasha is waiting for her at an outside table in Covent Garden Piazza. Everything about her is long and flowing, dark and bright – she's swathed in dark blue and purple cotton, her abundant hair forced back under an unwilling slide. Apart from their choice of boots – Lisa's determined by Vladimir's taste for high heels – nobody would take them for sisters.

'Sash. Sorry I'm late.'

'Good lecture?' Sasha jumps up and hugs her.

'When my students aren't busy eyeing me up instead of listening to what I tell them.' Lisa laughs.

'Hm,' Sasha says. 'You should be so lucky to have students eye you up!'

This is such an extraordinary statement coming from Sasha Wood – arch-feminist celebrator of the female body in motion, author of *The Dancer and the Dance: The Instinct of Feminine Power* – that Lisa thinks she's misheard. 'What's up?' she asks. 'Did something happen?'

'Lee, Adam's lost interest in me. We never, ever have sex. I honestly think he doesn't love me any more. And just as I hit

forty.' Sasha smiles and adds, 'You have to laugh, really, otherwise . . .'

'Oh, come on, Sash. Martha died just after your birthday.
I'm sure it's that. He's upset. He would never stop loving you.'

'You know, you can write and theorise and pronounce and
reclaim your power all you like, but you still can't keep a man
when you're past forty!'

Lisa glances down the menu. Sasha in melodramatic stage
mode is best taken with a pinch of salt, probably a dash of
pepper too – especially as it's self-evident that the problem
has nothing whatever to do with her age. Lisa tolerates her
sister's theatricality, occasionally indulges it, but knows better
than to believe in it. It's always a mask for something else,
something splintered and painful that Sasha does not want
anybody to see.

'Sash, you and Adam are among very few people I know
who've married the love of their life,' Lisa tells her.

Sasha sips her mineral water. 'Here's an idea, Lee. Do you
fancy switching places for a few days?'

'What?'

'You're lucky. You're completely free. You've had hundreds of
boyfriends. You've got a wonderful job doing what you love. You
don't have to slave away feeding hungry children, or contending
with a husband who'd rather be with his father than you.'

'Oh Sash, I'm sure it's not that bad. What shall we eat? Are
you hungry?'

'I am hungry,' Sasha says. 'I'm hungry for *life*.'

'Sash, big sister, I promise you, you do *not* want to be me.'
Lisa pictures her messy flat, the smell of cat litter, life on the
brink of – well – something dangerous with Vladimir, and,
completing the heady mix, Andrew and Melanie throwing
crockery at one another downstairs. 'If you knew how much
I'd have liked to be where you are . . .'

'No, you wouldn't. You'd never live as far out of town as
we do.'

Lisa has come to loathe West Hampstead with its thin walls, its overcrowded Victorian terraces and its snarled-up traffic. To her, marrying the love of your life, even after a long period of waiting and wondering, then settling in a beautiful house with a conservatory and two cats and bringing up three intelligent, personable children sounds like heaven on earth. She knows, of course, from Sasha and Adam, that it isn't – but it is at least preferable to her current situation.

What's more, people buy and read Sasha's book. Lisa's own effort – a revamping of her thesis, an academic analysis of *The Rite of Spring* full of music examples and graphs and pie charts – had sold about fifty copies in its first year, most of them to university libraries, about twenty in its second, mainly to music students, and so far this year just nine. Nobody ever invites her to comment on the latest artistic goings-on on television; nobody would dream of asking her to write a column in the *Independent*.

An Australian waitress with a stud in her nose brings their salads and the sisters eat – Sasha devouring hers as if trying to ingest the whole world. Lisa watches as the tuna, lettuce, eggs, olives, beans, potatoes, tomatoes and onion vacate the bowl at twice the rate she can put away her own lunch. Is Sasha comfort-eating? Food and Lisa's elder sister have never enjoyed the easiest of relationships.

'Are you on tonight?' she asks.

'Yup. A spot of detective fiction, a new TV series about unconventional sex and a book-length poem by Laurence Kingston. I don't know why they ask a feminist ex-dancer to comment on detective fiction, but that's TV for you.' Her plate is as empty as the day it was made. Lisa chews a mouthful of her salad, a mountain of ingredients in primrose yellow, rose pink, carnation red and plentiful green – attractive, but too copious.

Sasha helps herself to a forkful of Lisa's lunch. 'Are you off your food?' Sasha asks. 'Are you missing Vladimir?'

'Of course I miss him.' Lisa tries not to sound defensive. 'But I'm not off my food. This salad's big enough for four!'

'You know, it's high time you got rid of him.'

'Get rid of Vladimir?'

'Lee, he's not good for you. He's taking advantage of you. He comes to see you when he's got a few days off and fancies a quick bonk. He never even acknowledges that you have any emotional needs – because he doesn't have any himself. And the shoe thing is ridiculous.'

Lisa counts to ten before she answers. Sasha is not to know – having never met Vladimir – that his emotional needs are five times as great as hers; that she couldn't care less if he prefers beautiful shoes to beautiful underwear; or that he has never been one for a 'quick bonk'.

'I don't know why you stay with him.'

'We get along. We're good companions.'

'When you see him, that is. Don't your friends help you meet other men? What about Lindsey and Paul? Don't they know anyone to introduce you to?'

'They try.' Lisa does not add that they try far too often. 'But I haven't met anyone else I like.'

'That's probably because you don't want to. You have to get rid of him before you can turn on to someone else.'

Lisa puts down her fork. 'I don't want to break up with Vladimir,' she says.

'Don't tell me you're in love with the bastard!'

Damn it, thinks Lisa, and aims for the jugular.

'Sash.' She leans forward and lowers her voice. 'Vladimir is spectacular in bed. I don't mean good. I mean *absolutely incredible*.'

Sasha recoils. She opens her mouth and shuts it again. 'In terms of – what? Er – duration?'

'Not only that. He's an artist. And his livelihood depends on his sensitivity of touch.'

For once, Sasha is lost for words.

'So don't tell me to get rid of him,' Lisa says quietly. 'If I decide I can't cope any more, then maybe I'll give him some kind of ultimatum. I've thought it all through, you know. But at the moment, I can cope.'

'Good sex, then . . . Is that really enough?' Sasha shifts in her chair.

'Sash, I do love him. It may not be a conventional relationship, but I love him and I don't mind waiting for him. He's worth it.'

Lisa's description has punctured a nerve centre. Sasha has lost her train of thought, thrown off course by two things – one being that she and Adam never have sex these days and the other being that she knows, according to her own book, she should approve of exactly this kind of freedom and individuality in a relationship, but that because it is her little sister's she doesn't. 'I've always thought he was – hm . . .' she begins.

'A sort of fairy-tale prince?' Lisa finishes the sentence for her. 'Yes. Perhaps he is. But how many people ever meet a fairy-tale prince? Look, for all I know he might turn back into a frog at any moment. But until he does, I am sure as hell going to appreciate him while I've got him. You don't live for ever. And even if it all goes pear-shaped and I end up losing him, I'll still have had the experience and I'll never lose that. Do you understand?'

Sasha feels her lip threaten a tremor. She is remembering herself and Adam, aged twenty-six and thirty, on their Greek island: herself dancing naked on a hilltop at dawn while Adam sketched her; and the most wild, beautiful lovemaking, the like of which they have not imitated for the past nine years as mostly they're too tired. 'I know, Lee,' she says. 'I do know that.'

It's all gone, all of it; but, unlike Lisa, she doubts whether there was any point in ever having had it if you were only to lose it. If life has become so joyless that she'd wake up in the morning wondering what would happen if she announced that she was never going to get out of bed again. She exists on automatic pilot most of the time; she's hit forty with a terrible bump; and she can't confess to her effectively single, mildly broody sister that the only time she feels she's herself is in the full flood of a fight with her fellow critics live on TV. Nor can she tell Lisa that some remote part of her is terrified of ending up like their mother, who, widowed long ago, lives alone in Queen's Park, walking neighbours' dogs for a little money to supplement her pension and occasionally lapsing back into the alcoholism that had blighted their childhood.

'You're coming to lunch on Sunday, aren't you?' she says. 'It would be nice to see you.'

3

The Irises land in a heap in front of Adam at five fifteen, covering his computer keyboard. On his screen is a spread showing two teenaged girls, plastered with glittery makeup, their mouths open as if screaming in fun. THE PARTY LOOK: HOW TO GET IT, says the headline. Adam has been playing about with fonts for the word PARTY, not really seeing the results.

'Ad, can you cast an eye over these?' says the deputy editor, who doesn't look much older than the girls in the pictures.

Clarissa is an ambitious woman, in her thirties though she tries to appear younger, and Adam knows she hates him because he can see straight through her – the way she's cropped her hair and wears short skirts, just like Henrietta the editor, modelling herself on her so that everyone will think they are conveniently interchangeable. Henrietta's hand is adorned with a bright new wedding ring and each month Adam watches Clarissa's eyes stray towards her flat stomach, waiting and praying for it to bulge: were Henrietta absent on maternity leave, Clarissa would step straight into her shoes, her office and ultimately her job. Adam can disconcert them both any time he wants to, with one glance from his dark eyes. The staff joke that he must have X-ray vision. 'Sure, Issa,' he says. 'Leave it with me.'

'I need them back PDQ.' Clarissa puts her hands on her hips and hovers.

'I'll get back to you in a minute. I must just get this spread over to the subs so they can start work on it, OK?'

'Ad, these pages have got to go to print tonight, if I may remind you . . .'

'OK, Issa, keep your hair on. I know all about it.'

'Well, are you going to get on with it or *what*?'

'While you're standing there with your whip, I could be doing my job,' says Adam. 'What's the problem? PMT?'

'You know, I don't have to put up with you. I can complain to Henrietta any time I like.'

'So can I, Issa, so can I.'

Simon and Magda, Adam's team of designers, have stopped what they're doing and are glaring up at Clarissa in her short skirt, Adam sitting back at his desk facing her, the tension between the two hissing like a burning fuse.

Adam can hardly believe he's just accused the deputy editor of having PMT. But, hey, he's leaving anyway, going upstairs to the fifth floor.

Or isn't he?

'Get on with it, Adam, *now*.' Clarissa turns tail and marches away as determinedly as her tight little skirt will permit. Tight little cow, thinks Adam. Strange how, in the magazine world, power hunger and incompetence so often go together – as if the ability to do a job well is deflected by the inflation of the ego that lies beneath.

Adam leafs through the Iris proofs one by one. Half-way through, he does a double take. 'Christ,' he says.

'What?' says Magda.

'Look.'

Magda looks. 'Christ,' she says.

'How the fuck did that happen?' says Simon.

Adam strides towards Clarissa's desk. Henrietta is away at a meeting with some advertisers.

'Issa, we've got to get them to redo this. This page has the wrong strap on it.'

Instead of BEAUTY TIPS, the page strap reads BOYS. Someone in Editorial should have spotted this long ago.

'Who passed this page?' Clarissa demands.

'You did, if you remember, when Henrietta was on her management course.'

As Clarissa begins to yell, part of Adam switches off. Only his shell is left standing in the office, Irises in hand, Clarissa's shrill voice attacking him. His real self is in a dance studio in Clapham in 1983, his charcoal an extension of his fingers, his fingers an extension of his soul as the drawing takes form: the long legs, the exquisite arms, the curved, supple body, the wild dark hair and great intense eyes of the most extraordinary woman he has ever seen. And as she appears line by line on his cartridge paper, so her image fixes itself, line by line, on his own body. She's his soulmate, he knows that at once, but he doesn't know her name yet. He hears it for the first time as the choreographer says, 'Sasha, on "three-and", spin and fall . . .' and he feels himself spinning and falling with her. As he feels the fall again, nearly twenty years later, he sees the image behind his retinas, the one he can't expunge: his mother, grey, haggard, cancer-ridden, at the point of death.

'All right,' says Adam's shell in the office to the odious Clarissa. 'If that's how you feel, do it yourself.'

He walks back to his desk, picks up his jacket and makes for the door, heedless of the shouts of his name from Simon and Magda. He doesn't know where he's going, but he knows, as the fresh air beyond the revolving glass doors beckons, that he isn't turning back.

He walks for ten minutes, then takes out his mobile phone and calls Terry Forrest.

'Adam, wait a minute. Don't be so hasty,' says Forrest. 'You've just lost your mother. Take some time to think it over. Take some unpaid leave. As much as you need. Don't throw it all away.'

'Thanks, Terry, but I've had all the time I need. As of today, I'm out. Give Magda my job, she's talented and very capable.

And as for *Trafalgar*, Nick's your man for that one. Not me. Thanks for everything.'

He presses a button and is free. And unemployed.

When he reaches the next pub, he goes in and orders a whisky. He is still spinning and falling, but now he's going to have to tell Sasha he's walked out of his job for no good reason except that a tidal wave is gathering itself into a vast jade green watery coil above his head, preparing to crush him. He downs the drink and puts his head into his hands, wondering how he got into this pub, into this street, this city, this mess.

He doesn't want to go home. He wanders out to the grey-brown of Bishopsgate and walks on and on. From the sleek glassy edifice of Liverpool Street station, trains depart for Cambridge, Peterborough, Stansted Airport . . . If only, he muses, he could just walk through that shining, impersonal, shop-lined forecourt, step aboard the express to the airport, take to the open skies and a few hours later find himself in another country, another time, another life. What will he do now? What on earth *can* he do?

The answer, at least for the moment, is simple: he goes home and makes supper for his kids. Sasha is out, meeting her *Weekly Review* colleague Cindy Smith for a coffee before they head for the BBC. Adam, half alive in his shell, going through the motions, makes sausages and mash – easy to cook and comforting too.

'Liffs. How about some more mashed potato?'

'I don't want any more, I'm full.'

'Come on, Liffy. You've hardly eaten anything.'

'Alex, stop it,' Liffy hisses. 'Dad, he's kicking me!'

Adam spots Alex's foot swinging in Liffy's direction under the table. 'I saw that,' he says. 'Go and do your homework. Good boys.'

'Homework's *sad*,' says Matt.

'Homework *stinks*,' says Alex.

'You've got to *do* it, whatever you *think* of it,' says Adam.

The twins exchange an inter-twin telepathic moment and announce together, in perfect, poised unison: 'Piffle, piffle, piffle!'

Adam can't believe his ears. 'Where on earth did you learn that?' he exclaims. Liffy is rolling up the leg of her too-long flared jeans to examine the patch where Alex has kicked her.

'The tape of Mum's programme,' Matt declares. 'That guy last week said a film was *piffle!*'

'Look, Dad,' Liffy whines. 'Look what he's done to me.' A big, plum-coloured bruise is beginning to darken the pale skin just below her knee.

'Alex, there's no excuse for that.'

'She started it.'

'I did not!'

'Did too. You poked me in the ribs.'

'Did not.'

'Did too.'

'I didn't mean to!'

'Piffle! You poke me in the ribs, Liffy Levy, you get kicked, and there's two of us and only one of you! So there!'

'*Dad!*'

'Homework, boys, NOW.'

'Homework's—'

'NOW, THIS MINUTE,' Adam explodes at the little boys. 'GET OUT OF HERE AND DO YOUR HOMEWORK.'

It doesn't seem to be him doing the yelling, but some alien who has taken possession of his mind and body. He glimpses his face in the mirror above the mantelpiece: he has turned scarlet. His head feels like a pasta pot spilling over. The boys, shocked into submission, get up and go.

Liffy, her long hair and big hoop earrings gleaming in the lamplight, sits opposite him, mouselike, staring down into her unfinished food.

'Come on, Liffs. Eat up.' Adam sighs.

'I'm not hungry. And I've got homework to finish too. I'd better go and do it.'

Liffy collects all the plates, empties her own into the bin, rinses each one for ten seconds under the tap, stacks them inside the dishwasher one at a time in a tidy row and walks away up the stairs.

When the children are finally in bed and all is quiet, Adam switches on the TV to hear the tail end of the news and to watch his wife strut her stuff on *The Weekly Review*. There she sits, to the right of George Urwin, John Castleton opposite her, her friend Cindy Smith beside her.

'And now we come to the massive four-hundred-page poem by Laurence Kingston that's just hit the bookshelves,' George announces. 'Four hundred pages, John. What are we to make of such a publication in the year 2003?'

'Well, George, a poet of real stature, a Ted Hughes or a Philip Larkin, could get away with it.' John Castleton crosses his legs briskly as he speaks. 'But what we have to ask ourselves is this: is Laurence Kingston actually worth reading for four hundred pages? After all, this is a poet whose reputation to date has been built on his performance work and his education projects in prisons. Is this someone whose written poems carry enough personality without his presence to project them? Or is he simply capitalising on the familiarity of his face? I mean, let's face it, these days it's a positive advantage to be of ethnic origin in the arts . . .'

Oh boy, thinks Adam. Sure enough, the Sasha-and-Cindy air-force team is ready to swoop and destroy on its Mission Castleton Storm.

'John, how *can* you say such things on live TV?' Cindy is black, born in Manchester to parents who'd come from Barbados. 'Laurence Kingston's achievement is absolutely immeasurable! What this one person has done for the self-esteem of black poets by producing this book, in what is still very much a white man's world, will go down in history as

one of the great moments of early twenty-first-century literature! I simply don't understand how a poet of your skill and
intelligence can fail to see the greatness of this poem.'

'The extended poem may be a dying form,' Sasha adds,
'but I truly believe that Kingston is bringing it back to life.
Look at the story: it's highly contemporary, it's vastly moving,
it's beautifully and passionately written. It proves how relevant
poetry can be to our society, while elevating us with the
expertise of its language . . .'

Adam watches the pair of harpies demolish the pale little
man in his salmon-and-cucumber Garrick Club tie and can't
help feeling the tiniest bit sorry for him, odious though his
political views are. *The Weekly Review*, as Adam sees it, isn't
so much a chance to promote the contemporary arts as an
invitation to the world to observe pretentious people tearing
each other apart. What other reason is there to watch it?
Nobody with a genuine love of the arts would give such
posturing windbags the time of day.

Does he, then, consider his own wife a posturing windbag?

'I mean, *listen*!' Her eyes are flashing with fury. 'Aren't you,
John, expressing exactly the attitude that Laurence Kingston is
absolutely lambasting at the heart of this book? He blows
Establishment stances sky high, and he does so with such wit and
flair that it's completely irresistible! No wonder you don't like it!'

Adam watches Sasha's passion rise, his heart, as always,
swelling with pride. That is the passion that had made him fall
in love with her, that had made him take all sorts of silly risks
just to be near her. He couldn't look at anyone else, not really,
not seriously, because those fiery eyes held everything he'd
ever wanted.

Why does she not look like that at home any more? Why
does she only come alive on television? He imagines he is
watching someone else acting the Sasha he had once known
and loved. She exists only in a digital dimension: transmuted
into glittering particles of light speeding down cables and

across satellites orbiting in space, then metamorphosing into myriad spinning numbers that form themselves into a flat-screen TV picture, made utterly of light, not warm, living flesh.

There's a commotion on the other side of the ceiling. He takes the stairs two at a time. The twins are together outside Liffy's door, pushing. Liffy, in her room, is pushing back, shouting, 'Go away! Leave me alone!'

'We're gonna get you, we're gonna get you,' sing the jubilant twins.

'Get out! Get *out*!' Liffy fights. The door sways on its hinges between the warring children.

Adam grabs a twin with each hand by the scruff of the pyjama collar.

'I don't know what the hell you think you're doing,' he yells at them. 'Get back to bed now – this instant! If I hear one more squeak out of you, there's going to be big trouble. Understand?'

'Piffle,' Alex grunts, as Adam marches him and Matt towards their room.

'It's not piffle. I won't tolerate any more of this. Do you know what time it is? It's a quarter past eleven! Go to bed, leave your sister alone and be quiet. I *won't* tell you again.'

Adam bundles each twin into bed, switches off the light, shuts the door. A faint sob drifts from Liffy's room. Of course her 'keep out' notice is a provocation to the boys, but if she takes it down, she insists, they'd never leave her alone at all.

Somehow when Sasha is home there is less trouble. Adam remembers their ideals, the system for living that they had promised each other when they got married.

We will always put our love first.
We will never hit our children.
We will never shout at our children.
We will be nourished by our art.
We will be supportive of each other's needs.

We will help each other and depend on each other.

We will love each other for ever.

We were young then, Adam reflects. The art has gone west, at least for him – and, he supposes, for Sasha, who no longer dances although her writing compensates for that. They help and depend on each other – but for practical matters, like shipping the children to parties, school and weekend courses in cookery, football, tennis or puppetry; doing the shopping, preparing the food, changing the lightbulbs, unblocking the dishwasher. They try to put their love first, but with a house full of screaming, fighting, irrational children it is not as easy as it was thirteen years ago. They have managed not to hit those screaming, fighting, irrational children, but shouting came into the equation long ago, with the exhaustion and exasperation. Sasha shouts less than Adam: his temper is hotter, his temperament more open, more craving of expression. Sasha expresses passion on live TV but at home, under stress, she shuts herself into her study and works while Adam stews, needing her to come out and talk it through, knowing that she won't.

Well after midnight, Adam hears the scuffle of Sasha's key in the lock and the clack of her boot heels on the wooden hall floor. The Beeb provides her with a taxi home after the programme. She is still glowing with the thrill of the kill.

'Hi,' Adam calls.

'Did you see it? Wasn't it great?' Sasha, eyes bright, hair wild, marches through the lounge door.

'Shall I pour you a drink?' He reaches for the Scotch.

'That revolting little man!' Sasha takes the glass in her left hand, gesturing with her right. 'What a reactionary little shit! Did you hear what he said about Larry Kingston? And he calls himself a poet!'

'It's interesting that some of the greatest creators in history have been people you wouldn't want to have round to dinner,' Adam remarks. 'What about T.S. Eliot?'

'Eliot – oof! Horrible!'

'And Wagner.'

'And all those drug-crazed pop stars. Imagine having Jimi Hendrix round for a meal . . .'

Adam and Sasha laugh together over their Scotch until Adam asks, 'Sash, is it really any good? Kingston's poem?'

'The book? Oh, sure. It's OK.'

'Just OK? You and Cindy made it sound like the hottest thing since Shakespeare.'

'Well, of course it's a great achievement. As far as I know, no Afro-Caribbean poet has produced a book like this before. It's not as good as Vikram Seth's *The Golden Gate*, but that was inspired by Pushkin's *Eugene Onegin*. Kingston's found a sort of rap-stroke-reggae-inspired rhythm that's very much his own.'

'Doesn't it get a little – well, isn't it kind of heavy going to read a book in reggae rhythm all the way through?'

'Well, I wouldn't write it myself, naturally,' Sasha says. 'I suppose that for someone of our background it might start to get on your nerves after a bit.'

'But you still have to make out it's the greatest thing since—'

'Ad, don't take it so seriously! We have to get John Castleton, don't we? He's a right-wing pig and we can't let him get away with all his cynical stuff about how Larry's too politically correct to be any good.'

Adam decides it's better not to tell Sasha that he'd had a good leaf through Larry Kingston's four hundred pages and thought it read like an Old Labour manifesto in rather obvious rhyme with a few contemporary spellings (or, to Adam, misspellings) thrown in for good measure. He doesn't want to spoil her fun.

Instead he tells her about Liffy's battle with the twins. As he talks, he sees her deflate, shrinking back from her larger-than-life television self towards her tired-out housewife self – and at once Adam knows he's managed, after all, to prick the bubble that so elevated her.

'Ad, there are times when I just don't know what to do with those kids,' she confesses. 'Perhaps we shouldn't have had any.'

'Oh Sash. You know you wouldn't be without them.'

Sasha is silent for so long that Adam's mind shifts into freefall.

'They weren't exactly planned,' she admits eventually.

'I for one have no regrets,' Adam announces. God, that sounds pompous, he thinks.

'Good,' Sasha snaps.

Silence. Upstairs, the twins slumber. Downstairs, Adam and Sasha drink whisky, perched at the top of a house of cards that, separate and silent, they know needs just a single tap from outside to come fluttering down. And Adam knows that telling Sasha he's walked out of Forrest & Burns at this moment would be not a single tap but a cardland earthquake. He keeps quiet.

Liffy is lying awake, oblivious to her parents. She hadn't been asleep when the twins launched their invasion: she was on her computer, having an online instant-message chat with Charley. Now she can't sleep for thinking about what is happening to her best friend. She'd found Charley crying in the loos at break and, for once, her friend refused to tell her what was wrong. In silence, on the computer screen, it all came out.

– Robin kissed me [Charley wrote].

– Really?

– At the end of my lesson. It wasn't on the lips – but it nearly was. I mean, he just kissed my cheek, but he sort of caught the side of my mouth and I don't know whether he meant to or not.

– Does he usually give you a kiss when you leave?

– No, but I've sometimes thought he wants to.

– What did you do?

– I kind of hugged him. And he hugged me back.

– So what are you going to do next?

– I don't know. I've got another lesson next week, so I've got six days to think about it.

– Do you want him to kiss you again?

– YES, OF COURSE I DO, I'M IN LOVE WITH HIM, TWITFACE.

– Don't call me Twitface. You can't be in love with him. You're 13. He's 26.

– Juliet was only 14.

– Juliet's a fictional character from the 16th century. [Liffy was amazed at how worldly-wise and mature she could sound when she wanted to.]

– I don't care. I only know I'm in love with Robin.

– Get real, Charl. Get over it.

– But maybe something's going to happen?

[Liffy sat staring at the instant-message screen for a few minutes, wondering what to say next. All kinds of strange questions were skidding through her mind.]

– What does it feel like, being in love?

– Weird. It's, like, sort of light inside. It's like you live every second three times over before it's finished. You want to hang on to every single moment you're with him and not forget a minute of it ever.

– But, like, what do you want to do?

– You want to, I don't know, you kind of want to be with him and have him put his arms around you.

– When he does, is it as good as you thought it would be?

[There was a long patch of visual silence here, until Liffy wondered whether Charley's mum had come up and packed her off to bed. But the computer told her Charley was still on line. Finally a reply appeared.]

– I think so.

It was just then that Liffy realised the twins were ganging up outside her door; she'd signed off with 'Gotta go, c u Monday,' and leaped up to defend herself.

She is lying on her back now, in the dark, imagining Charley and the flute teacher locked in an embrace. She pictures Robin's mouth against Charley's, his groin pressing against her slim body, and the image makes her feel nauseous. She knows she would loathe it if it was her and not Charley. How horrible. Some of her friends, and the twins' friends, have elder brothers and they all have horrid spots but still think they're God's gift. She can think of nothing worse than being kissed by one. On the other hand, Robin is a man, not a boy – he's twenty-six, exactly twice Charley's age. And perhaps that's different. But of course he shouldn't be kissing her at all, not for at least another two or three years and certainly not if he wants to keep his teaching post.

Charley is almost a year older and further 'developed' than Liffy. She'd got her period when she was eleven and had made much of her advanced status before Liffy and their other friends had 'caught up'. She's taller too – five foot five – whereas Liffy burns up all her energy dancing (says Mum) and is still a petite five foot one. Charley has larger breasts and a slender, obvious waist. Most people think her older than she is. Charley thinks Liffy is jealous. She's anything but. She doesn't want to be part of it.

She understands that hormones happen to you, beyond your control, having everything to do with your body and nothing to do with your mind or your free will. Boys will come after you whether you like it or not and you have to make sure you are slim and wear good clothes so that they will want to, even if you can't stand them. How unfair. And they'll put their thing inside you and God knows what that will be like, it's bound to be painful and horrible, and then you might have a baby, and it's nothing to do with you as an individual person, it's just because of hormones and instincts that you never wanted in the first place. Liffy presses her hands against her eyes to shut out the images. She doesn't want to be part of something as base, vile and brutal as that.

Feeling something on the bed beside her, Liffy reaches out and, for one lurching moment, thinks that what she touches is a hand. But it's only Ben's tail brushing by as he settles in a feline curl close to her waist. The cat's presence makes her feel better. I wish I was a cat, thinks Liffy, falling asleep.

Sunday morning, everyone habitually sleeps in – even the twins. Sunday is an oasis. Adam and Sasha watch political interviews on TV; Liffy does her homework, sipping fresh orange juice that tastes like molten sunlight; the twins make a dash for their PlayStation or trot round the corner to play with their friend Julius ('Who calls a child Julius these days?' Sasha protests). If they are alone for the day, they have a big brunch with lots of scrambled eggs and slices of smoked salmon and a frizzy salad full of delicious green, red and olive-dark bits and pieces. If Lisa comes over, with or without her and Sasha's mother, Sally, they have a normal muesli breakfast and then Adam – who is a better cook than Sasha – roasts an organic chicken, popping half a lemon inside the cavity, rubbing the outside with butter, sprinkling it with tarragon and roasting it whole, which perfumes the house with a citrusy, herby aroma. He makes the traditional Levy family's perfect rice – fried lightly in sunflower oil, then boiled with two cinnamon sticks, twice as much water as rice, for twelve minutes; and maybe roasted root vegetables and salad, or fresh spinach, which Sasha insists her grumbling sons must eat. If Lisa is there without Sally, or with Adam's parents (well, Adam's father), they have some wine; if Sally is there, they don't.

Next in the ritual is a walk in Richmond Park if the weather is fine. The twins tear about in their football gear, Liffy casts longing gazes in the direction of the ballet school and Lisa wraps a scarf round her throat to block out the wind in the exposed grasslands. They parade through mud and long grass, or dodge bicycles on the paths, walking in alternate forma-tions: Lisa with Liffy, Adam and Sasha handling the twins and/or a parent, or Adam with Liffy, Sasha and Lisa dealing with their mother, the twins careering off after a frisbee or a football and clamouring for ice-cream in the car park. Adam and his sons hanker for a dog to walk (Sasha does too, but knows that nobody would have the time to walk it); often they spot a magnificent retriever or a silky-eared spaniel and Alex or Matt bounds up to hug it, to which owners respond in a variety of ways. Back at the house after an hour or two, they have tea and cake and then Lisa goes home, Sally with her, and for the twins the over-excitement ends in tears and tantrums, while Liffy removes herself to her room with a good book or to the loft for ballet practice. She does not eat the cake.

Lisa, at home on her own at last, wonders how people who are individually so bright, so intelligent, so nice, so creative can collectively paper over all their problems, and takes two painkillers to deal with the inevitable headache.

This Sunday is the day after Liffy's thirteenth birthday. Saturday afternoon had been a major production number: Liffy had invited Charley, Sophie, Leila, Katia, Sarah and two girls from ballet class to lunch at a world-foodish café on Richmond Hill, after which they all went to the cinema, then back to the house for a long, late tea. This morning the family should all be exhausted.

Standing on the Somerset Road doorstep with a bottle of Australian wine in her hands and Liffy's present wrapped up inside her shoulder-bag, Lisa understands that what she's seeing is worse than exhaustion. She stares, distressed, at Adam's pallor and the shadows under his eyes. 'Ad? What's the matter?'

She knows she's said the wrong thing: Adam can't stand anybody, even her, greeting him with such words.

'Nothing,' he barks. 'Nothing at all. Come in, come in, let me take your coat.'

Lisa wanders into the house, which is going about its usual business: the twins are playing with a ball in the garden; Liffy is not in evidence, but must be in her room doing homework since her purple trainers are in their place on the shoe rack; Sasha, stirring something in the kitchen, is yakking into a portable telephone perched between her chin and her collarbone, and Gerald, who had driven over from Oxford the day before and stayed overnight, sits motionless on the leather sofa watching a political programme on TV. None of them seems inclined to stop what they are doing and greet Lisa, although she has travelled for more than an hour to get to them.

'Yes, I'm on next week,' Sasha is saying into the phone. 'You too, I hope?'

'Cindy,' Adam says to Lisa.

'Fabuloso,' Sasha declares. 'The Fall and Fall of John Castleton, Part the Second!'

'Boys,' Adam shouts into the garden, 'come and say hi to Auntie Lisa.'

'Hi, Auntie Lisa!' The twins wave hard but don't leave the lawn.

'And mind my rose bushes!' Adam yells. 'That's a garden, not a football pitch!'

Lisa thinks her ears are playing tricks: did one of the twins really utter the word 'piffle' under his breath?

'How are you, Gerald?' she asks Adam's father, who stands up and gives her a kiss.

'As well as can be expected, thank you, my dear.' Gerald is poised and professorial as usual; the only outward sign of his grief is that the soul Lisa sees in his dark eyes is only half there. Sally has not been invited today because Sasha thought Gerald, in his current frame of mind, would find her too trying. Lisa wonders whether their poor mother has guessed.

Sasha glares out of the kitchen. She has enough to contend with in the house already – the twins wilder by the day, Liffy

more and more the sulky teenager, Adam in a constant irri-
tating, short-tempered mood and utterly uninterested in sex –
without Gerald coming to stay for weekends. And now he's
glooming about, pretending all is well, yet staring at pictures
of Martha – which have been elevated to sacred status, complete
with candles and little vases of flowers – while Adam waits on
him hand and foot. Perhaps she should rent an office somewhere, or convert the garden shed into a studio. She needs
quiet if she's going to work. And she has to work, because life
is too short not to say the things you need to say about it . . .

She calls Liffy, who doesn't want to come down. 'Liffy, come
here this minute!'

'I'm working,' protests Liffy's voice upstairs.

Like mother, like daughter, Sasha reflects, turning to vent
her anger on the innocent cucumber, which is soon split into
a hundred pieces.

Lisa wonders whether she should just go home. She doesn't
like the air in her sister's house. While she would be hard
pressed to explain what it is, some atmospheric demon there
gets straight under her skin, presses on her temples, constricts
her breathing. Tension emanates from Sasha and something
more than tension from Adam; grief from Gerald; sulkiness
from Liffy; and blithe indifference to the lot from the twins,
crashing around outside.

'Alex! Matt! I said, keep *away* from my roses! I *won't* tell
you again!' Adam yells.

Liffy appears at last, trailing downstairs in jeans and a scoop-
necked purple top that shows off her thin, bony shoulders.
She gives Lisa a kiss on the cheek and asks, 'How's Vladimir?'

'OK, I suppose. Happy birthday yesterday, sweetheart.' She
pulls a small parcel out of her bag.

'Oh, thank you, Auntie Lisa!'

Liffy unwraps the deep green paper, revealing a ballet DVD
that includes the original *Rite of Spring* as they'd seen it at

Covent Garden. Liffy hugs Lisa and puts the DVD on top of a pile in a corner of the lounge that Lisa realises consists of the presents she received yesterday – scarves, handbags, books and more DVDs, including the Royal Ballet in *The Sleeping Beauty* and the Bolshoi in *The Firebird*.

Lisa feels trapped, caged in some kind of cat-carrier basket – comfortable yet inescapable – that transports her to her sister's house on Sundays, college on three or four weekdays, the British Library when she is lucky, and Vladimir's home in Paris in moments of supreme good fortune. In between, she is its prisoner. A pang of missing Vladimir hits her so hard that she wants to sit down on the stairs and howl – which, of course, would do nothing to help a recently bereaved household. She glances at her watch. In three hours and five minutes it will be four o'clock and she can make her excuses and leave. She watches an aeroplane on the Heathrow approach, wondering where it has come from, where it will fly next.

She goes to the kitchen where Adam, between peeling carrots, is frowning out of the window at his sons.

'Look what they've done,' he exclaims. A branch of his best rose bush has been struck by the twins' newest football and the fresh spring leaves are already dangling towards the ground, half dead. 'They just don't listen.'

'Dad, let me do the vegetables,' Liffy pleads.

'Watch yourself with that knife,' says Adam.

Liffy begins to slice carrots, parsnips and a butternut squash into even pieces, with the attentiveness of a quality barber.

'Oh for heaven's sake, give me those.' Sasha grabs the knife from her daughter. 'It'll take for ever and a day if you do it like that.'

Lisa is losing her appetite. She walks back into the lounge where Gerald is sitting alone sipping something with soda in it, gazing at the picture of Martha in its ornate silver frame on the mantelpiece.

'I still can't believe she won't just walk in and sit down,' he tells Lisa.

Not one of them, other than Liffy, has asked Lisa anything about her life. And even Liffy is more interested in Vladimir, whom she has never met but who fascinates her, at least in principle. Lisa has noticed her examining Vladimir's CD boxes and his photo on her desk whenever she's been to West Hampstead. He's a good-looking man and Lisa can't blame her niece for being intrigued. But now Lisa, bereft of reflected glory from her exotic, absent lover, feels spare and unnecessary. She sits down next to Gerald and leafs through the *Independent on Sunday* so that she has something to do with her hands.

Nobody sees the ball coming towards the kitchen until it's too late.

The football, red and green, new, glossy and thick-skinned, lifts in a great arc from somewhere in the middle of what was once the lawn, rising with a life of its own away from Matt's foot, watched in awe by the open-mouthed Alex. It sails above Adam's rose bushes, above Sasha's terracotta pots of herbs, above the bench on the patio that Gerald and Martha gave Adam and Sasha as a moving-in present nine years earlier, and makes prompt, unavoidable contact with the kitchen's big window. As plastic strikes glass, propelled by the full force of Matt's fresh, elemental, eight-year-old energy, the kitchen shakes with a noise like the fury of a provoked house god. The window trembles, blisters and collapses inwards; and Sasha lets out a shriek as flying glass scatters around her and Liffy where they stand by the worktops. Outside, the twins freeze, wide-eyed, not knowing whether to laugh or cry. They decide to laugh, and by the time they realise this is a mistake, it is too late to stop.

Adam stands on the kitchen doorstep staring at the guilty little boys, the wrecked window and the glass shards that now line the floor. His father's gaze is on him, judging. Sasha, Lisa and Liffy stand together, a female trio of outrage. He is the man of the house. It is expected that he do something. And what can he do? What can anyone do against a fate that propels people into and out of hated jobs, an energy that forces small boys to behave like small boys, the power of time that forces them to change and grow up, and made his mother fall ill and die and makes him grow older and turn grey and useless?

His heart cracks apart. Someone who does not seem to be him paces out into the garden where he seizes his small son Matt with a strength he didn't know he possessed and half drags him into the house where the neighbours can't see them, while the boy squeals like a piglet in distress with his brother leaping alongside shouting, 'Dad, get off him! Get off him!' and Sasha, seeing what he is about to do, calling, 'Adam, no!' and Liffy pale with horror and Lisa hunting for the broom, and in the quiet of the lounge, in front of the picture of his mother on the mantelpiece and his grandparents' wedding photograph on the wall and the Prime Minister speaking on the television news, he lays Matt over his knees, pulls down his tracksuit bottoms and begins to wallop his backside until his hand hurts with the repeated impact and Matt is wailing like a creature in mortal torment and Alex howls in sympathy with his twin who is really part of himself. And the more he wallops Matt, the more he cannot stop: some kind of blood lust is releasing itself within him, some need for power over something so much smaller and weaker than himself for which he should hold responsibility, and he goes on and on hitting the child, whose pain is the sacrifice that can absorb all the guilt and terror and hurt of the past weeks and months and years—

'Adam! Stop it!' His wife seizes his wrist, pulls at Matt and half flings him across the room, and her hand flails into Adam's face and strikes him with pistol-whip force across the cheek. That pulls him up short at last. *'How dare you hit my child?'* Sasha screams.

Adam's shoes and socks are damp and an acrid smell fills the room – poor Matt has wet himself in the shock of what would once have been a commonplace domestic incident called 'a hiding' but is, to the twins' generation, an alien act of barbarism and betrayal. Matt, face scarlet, mouth wide open, is no longer howling but gasping; Alex, at once terrified and furious and relieved that it wasn't him, is whimpering beside him. Gerald stands in the doorway, arms folded, looking on.

Adam sinks down in his chair and puts his head into his hands.

Lisa, who has been sweeping up the glass, comes in and gathers Matt into her arms.

'Hush now, sweetie, it's all over. It's going to be all right.'

No, it isn't, Adam's mind tells him. *Nothing is ever going to be all right again.* He feels Sasha's eyes, white hot with fury, flaying him alive.

'I'm going out,' Liffy says. She takes her trainers off the shoe rack and puts them on, making sure the laces are the same length on each side before she ties them.

'Where are you going?' Sasha demands.

'Charley's,' she says, without looking at her, without looking at any of them. She pulls her coat, purse and keys off their hook and slips out of the front door.

'Mattie,' Adam groans. 'God, Mattie. I'm sorry.'

Matt, in the depths of Lisa's ample embrace, glowers at him with reddened, resentful eyes.

'Come on, guys,' Sasha says, her voice flat. 'Let's get this mess cleared up. Matt, go and put on some clean clothes.'

Alex reaches for Matt's hand and the two slink upstairs together. At least they've got each other, thinks Adam. He has never felt so alone in his life.

Gerald fetches the carpet shampoo from under the sink. 'A good hiding never did anyone any harm,' he says. Nobody answers.

Lisa takes a vacuum-cleaner to the last remaining glass splinters in the kitchen, while Adam pulls on some rubber gloves, gets down on his hands and knees and tries to rub the pee out of the carpet while Gerald sprays Alpine Grove air-freshener around the room. Upstairs, the twins are unnaturally quiet in their room. Sasha, smelling burning, dashes to the oven and tries to salvage the blackening chicken and the rice, which is thick and charred at the bottom of the saucepan.

By the time Adam has phoned an emergency glazier, the carpet is clean again and the house has settled around them into some semblance of tranquillity, lunch has proved inedible.

'Never mind,' Lisa declares, courageous. 'Why don't we get a takeaway from the Indian place?'

Adam looks around for what is left of his family and wonders whether anyone will ever agree to eat anything with him again.

4

Liffy walks along the main road, putting one foot in front of the other.

Her body seems to be on automatic. Her heart is so numb with fright that she feels disoriented and her hands are freezing. Is her father going mad? Dad is so gentle, so kind, so sensible – and of course there've been times when she's wished he would teach the twins a lesson and make them leave her alone, but now she can hardly recognise him. The thing is, will he do it again? If he can do it once, he can do it twice; if he can do it to one child, he can do it to another. She would never kick a football through the kitchen window, but she knows her brothers well enough to understand that they hadn't meant it to happen. It wasn't naughtiness. It was an accident. Why couldn't Dad see that? Normally he would have sliced off his own hand rather than hurt a child.

She stands at the bus stop outside the supermarket, watching the traffic. Buses are less frequent on a Sunday; there's no sign of a friendly red façade with a yellow 33 smiling from its forehead. On the pavement, her foot has just avoided someone's discarded chewing-gum. People are pigs, she thinks. Pigs are nicer than people.

She's left her mobile phone in her schoolbag, so she can't call Charley to ask if it's OK to come over, and now it occurs to her that if she turns up unannounced on Charley's doorstep, she'll have to explain why. And if her family is obsessed with the necessity to 'be together' for Sunday lunch, maybe Charley's is too. Unlike her, Charley has numerous aunts and uncles and about a hundred cousins ranging in age from zero to thirteen. They'll all be clustering round, wanting to know what's wrong – because she's been crying and they'll notice – and then they'll phone her parents and ask whether they can help by bringing her home again.

Liffy turns away from the bus stop and begins to walk. She reaches the crossroads where a stone war memorial bears the names of dead soldiers plus the legend HYDE PARK – 8 MILES. She crosses and turns right, heading uphill towards the park. The street's narrow lower stretches are lined with terraced and semi-detached Edwardian houses much like her family's, their front gardens adorned with daffodils, forsythia and contented-looking cats; higher up, the road widens, the houses are newer and bigger, some encased behind high walls or spiked fences. Ahead of her looms the black wrought-iron frame of the park gate and beyond it the welcoming expanse of Richmond Park, pond to the left, car park to the right, ballet school straight ahead. A flock of fallow deer grazes on the open meadow beneath the copse. Liffy walks on towards the grass and the trees and the deer.

The park is at its Sunday busiest, full of cycling couples, families with dogs and toddlers in three-wheeled buggies, pensioners strolling along, taking the air, and little boys – just like Matt and Alex – playing with footballs. A spring wind, full of the soft, green scent of April sap, strokes Liffy's cheeks and hair. She takes lungfuls of its freshness, letting it comfort her. A dachshund and a spaniel are sniffing and barking at each other while their owners pull on their leashes and make weak apologies with watery half-smiles to one another. Liffy longs to get away from all these people and dogs and things with wheels, to be alone with the grass and the trees and the sky and the earth. She strikes out across the field, leaving behind the paths and the roads, taking a diagonal route up a hill that will bring her into the trees close

to the ballet school, her Mecca. To dance, never more to
weep . . .

She finds a quiet patch, free of dog mess, under an oak
tree. She loves the strength of oak trees. She takes off her
coat, spreads it on the ground and sits on it, her back against
the trunk. Overhead, birdsong rises into the spring sky. She
is surprised to see bluebells under the bushes a few metres
away. The trees around her meld into a deep background of
green-brown air. She unleashes her hair from its grips, which
reduces the tension round her head and helps her relax. She
lies down under her oak and feels the whole earth behind
her, supporting her like a superhuman, godlike dancing
partner.

Liffy daydreams.

She lets her mind go where it wants, creating for her. She
watches it, enters it and lives in it.

She imagines that she can hear a light, silvery sound and
recognises it as if it were part of her: long forgotten, missing,
presumed dead. The bluebells are ringing. It seems to her that
she'd always known they would, sooner or later. She lies,
watching them sway on their stems, and behind them the grey-
green-brown earth darkness forms itself into a figure: the figure
of a man. As she watches, living her dream, the figure moves
towards her. He is the same green-brown as the woodland
background, his eyes are deep grey-green and he wears a
garland of leaves in his midnight-brown hair and a tunic of
leaf shadow, branches and flowers. He is young and handsome, though a man rather than a boy; perhaps, she fancies,
about twenty-one. His shoulders are broad and strong, his legs
long and athletic. His gaze fixes on hers, sympathetic, wise,
tender. He steps through the bluebells – which are ringing in
his honour – and sits down beside her.

Liffy has to come up with a name for him.

'Call me the Earth Prince.' She can almost hear his voice –
it's beautiful, as soft as the leaf-mould on the ground. 'I am

the forest spirit. I am the prince of the earth kingdom, the lord of all you see in nature.'

Liffy likes this dream. It's the best she has had in a long time. Though she seems to know this voice.

'I've been watching you, Olivia,' he seems to say, 'and I have plans for you, which I will tell you about one day. Now, I want you to do three things for me.'

'I will. Tell me?'

'First: the vase in your room. Always keep flowers in it. I can only appear to you when plants are present.'

'I will.'

'Next, stop eating meat. Your energy will be better if you don't eat meat. You will feel lighter, less weighed down.'

Liffy is surprised. But sometimes, the part of her that remains earthbound tells her, you learn things in your daydreams that you didn't know you already knew.

'And finally,' the Earth Prince adds, 'you must tell nobody that you have met me. As long as you are true to me, I will protect you. But if anyone else learns that you've seen me, I will never be able to appear to you again. Do you understand?'

'Shake on it?' Liffy says.

A shiver goes through her as she feels his earthen hand, weirdly warm, envelop hers.

The sound of a dog barking nearby rouses Liffy. She sits up on her coat. Nobody. Nothing resembling the Earth Prince of her dream; not even the bluebells that she's certain were there a minute ago. She has no idea how much time has passed. On her right hand she notices a browny-green smear where she has brushed against some lichen at the base of the tree. She could almost imagine that it was a mark from the Earth Prince's handshake, but that would be silly. Of course it would. Wouldn't it?

She walks down the hill, feeling light, feeling safe at last. She will give up meat as from today. She'll feel better if she eats less, lighter and less weighed down, as the Earth Prince had put it. What a marvellous idea he was. She wonders how her mind had managed to come up with something so original.

Liffy finds she is at her own front door. She walks in, lost in her dreams.

In the hall, Gerald is clutching the phone in one hand and Mum is pulling on her boots. Dad is nowhere to be seen. The twins hover inside, pale-faced, holding hands.

'Liffy? Liffy! Where've you been?' Mum swoops down on her. 'We've been worried sick! And don't try to tell me you've been at Charley's because we phoned them to see if you wanted to be fetched and they said they hadn't seen you . . . And now Dad's gone out to look for you!'

'Why? What's the time?' Liffy asks.

'Five o'clock,' Mum says, accusing.

Liffy blinks. She'd gone out at lunchtime, amid the chaotic aftermath of the football incident, and she's eaten nothing in the interim. She'd thought she had been asleep in the park for an hour or less. She feels light-headed, dizzy.

What on earth has happened to her?

She gazes at her mother, torn with fright and unspoken questions, remembering her promise to the Earth Prince and wishing she had never made it. But she would rather die than break her word, even to an imaginary creation of her own.

'Where's Auntie Lisa?' she asks instead.

'She went home ages ago. She had work to do.'

Fat chance, thinks Sasha: Lisa had just wanted to get the hell out of this crazy home, and who could blame her? They'd had some excellent Indian food from the Lal Bagh restaurant, words of forgiveness had been said, and Lisa had left as soon as curry container hit bin-liner. Meanwhile the glazier had arrived to put a new pane of glass into the kitchen window, and football in the back garden had been banned. She looks at her errant daughter and shakes her head. Liffy turns to go upstairs, a peculiar expression on her small, frightened face – as if she has never seen her mother before, as if she has come back from a very long way away.

In West Hampstead, Lisa, her heart breaking for her niece and nephews, swallows 400 milligrams of Nurofen Plus and dials Vladimir's number in Paris. Sometimes her resolve breaks down and she phones his answering-machine just to hear the sound of his recorded voice. But, to her astonishment, he answers.

'Darrlink!'

Lisa's knees buckle under her.

'Darling, I miss you!' Vladimir exclaims.

'I miss you too! I didn't even think you'd be home.'

'I am just back from the airport. Five minutes ago! Listen, Lisa, I am supposed to play in Italy next week, but the concert is cancelled.'

'Why? What happened?'

'They lost the sponsors – you know, it's probably the Mafia! But I am free now, until the end of the month. Would you like to come and spend some days with me?'

'Would I like to?' The colours of the world deepen and brighten around Lisa.

'Can you arrange your teaching?'

'Yes. I'll find a way.' Lisa's mind spins. In the week ahead she is supposed to prepare some lectures and write a book review for an academic journal. She can do all this in Paris . . . but if only she had a bigger place in London, with the real family piano, not just her tacky hired upright – long ago her mother boarded out their grand piano with a friend of Martha's in Oxford, who seems unlikely ever to give it back – then Vladimir could come to stay with her . . . and if only they were really together, they could live together . . . But there is no point in pursuing this line of thought and she stops herself. If Vladimir misses her so much, why doesn't he even have a mobile phone? Why doesn't he call her when he's away from home? There's no point in thinking like that either. A few days with Vladimir is all she can have, but it's still an unexpected taste of heaven.

There is nothing more guaranteed than an afternoon at Sasha's house to dispel all of Lisa's inclinations towards marriage and children. Alone for too many evenings at a time, she'd find herself longing for a real home, not just a glorified office with a bedroom attached; for real companionship, not just a voice on a phone from across the Channel; for children who need her and only her, not just Igor the cat, who purrs for anybody who is kind enough to feed him. Then she'd walk into her sister's house and all those images would soon vanish in the harsh light of What It's Really Like. And so she would go back to her Russian in Paris, luxuriate in his expert physicality, watch him play the piano to sold-out concert halls, and store up the experience to live on by replaying it in her mind until the next time their paths cross, however many months away that might be. Somewhere in her life, she feels, a record has got stuck; the needle can't move beyond the blemish.

Darkness. The children are asleep – at least, Adam hopes they are. Sasha turns out her bedside lamp and lies on her side, well away from him.

'Sash.'

'Go away.' She has said no more than two direct words to him since he smacked Matt, and they were 'Where's Liffy?'

'Sash, please talk to me.'

'I don't want to. If you don't like it, you can sleep in the study.'

'I don't want to sleep in the study.'

'Then go to sleep and leave me alone.'

'Sash, this won't help anything.'

Sasha throws back her half of the duvet into his face.

'Right, then,' she says. '*I'll* sleep in the study.'

When Adam goes after her, she glides away, closing the study door behind her. He hears the sound of the lock turning and, a moment later, some faint thumps as she unfolds her sofa into a bed.

5

'Mum,' Liffy says in the morning, 'I want to be vegetarian.'

'OK, Liffs.' Sasha does not look up. She's still in her dressing gown, fingers flying over her keyboard as she writes an email to a correspondent objecting to her latest column. Liffy hovers, wondering whether she was really listening. Still, she's agreed, even if she wasn't: that's the important thing.

Liffy picks up her school-bag and sets off for the bus stop. A rustle in the air as she walks makes her feel that the Earth Prince is beside her. She's pleased that he has not vanished back into the depths of her imagination: he's too good an idea for that. She feels that he is a companion, someone to hold her hand when the going gets tough. In the absence of more substantial, human support, it's good to think that someone who might have magic powers is there for her, even if nobody else can see him.

Charley, flute case in hand, flops down beside her on the bus.

'Is it today?' Liffy asks her.

Charley nods.

'What are you going to do?'

'I've made up my mind,' Charley declares. 'If he kisses me and I like it, I shall kiss him back. Why not? It's what he wants.'

She's lying to you.

Liffy's shoulders shudder at the voice. It is just a whisper in the back of her mind, but it's the whisper of the walls at night, the whisper of the daffodils in the blue vase.

'I want to know what it's like,' Charley says, her voice low and excited. 'I can deal with it. I can!'

Liffy watches the river flowing under Hammersmith Bridge. The school bus is a symbol. I am carried forward on a path not of my choosing, towards a place not of my choosing, and I am powerless to stop it. I have no control over my own life.

Yes, you have. Be watchful. Be light.

'How was your weekend?' Charley asks. 'Mum said your mum thought you were at our house. What happened?'

'Oh, nothing. I went out for a walk.'

With all the stress of the day before, she'd forgotten to prepare her lunchbox, so she finds herself facing the school canteen at one o'clock. She refuses something dry and brown that passes for roast beef and takes a veggieburger and salad instead. She by-passes the chips: she's seen something on television about how deep-frying food produces a substance in the oil that can cause cancer. The burgers are labelled organic, however, and after she has removed the bun, she doesn't mind eating one.

Charley bounds into the dining room, a bright pink patch across each cheek. She has come from her flute lesson. 'I'll tell you about it later. Internet,' she whispers to Liffy.

Liffy looks sideways at her and wonders abruptly whether she can believe what her best friend says.

Sasha, alone in the house, sits in front of a blank computer screen. Her mind is clouded with anger, which makes her angrier still. She is trying to rationalise away the idea that when Adam spanked Matt he had smashed their marriage vows.

Their wedding had been a quiet, register-office affair, with only family present to witness them signing their names across the protruding bump that was to be Liffy. Their real vows, beyond declaring that they were free to marry and that they wished to marry each other, were the resolutions they had made in private, determining the ideals by which they would live and raise their children. Adam has breached the one about shouting many times – to be fair, so has she – but to strike a child is something so brutal that she feels she barely knows the man who has done it. When they first met, Adam had been gentleness itself; usually he still is.

She well remembers her first glimpse of Adam, the day he came to the rehearsal studio with a pad of A3 paper and some charcoal, wanting to draw the dancers. The door opened and a stranger appeared and it was him. There'd been a time in her life before she knew him and, after the door opened and he came in, there had been the time since. Before and after the opening of a door. He'd come to the studio because he happened to live in the same street, in a bedsit, and, walking by, noticed that a ballet rehearsal was taking place inside.

He'd settled into a corner, sitting cross-legged on the floor, and she saw him first almost upside-down while she bent her body in two, warming up at the barre. He had dark hair as unruly as her own, and a bushy beard; and his deep brown eyes were the most piercing she had ever encountered. As her partner hoisted her into the air that day, she had felt the young artist's gaze branding her with its brightness, magnetising her. She couldn't stop looking at him. She was twenty years old and although she had had an affair or two – and found them disappointing – she had never been in love. She hadn't believed in all that love nonsense.

Yet although she didn't believe in it, after the rehearsal he asked her out for a drink, and she packed up her gear and left with him. They'd had a drink and then another, then some food – Adam had had pizza, Sasha a green salad – and went back to his room together. She left at dawn the next morning while he was still asleep, terrified by the speed and intensity of her feelings; he'd had to come back to the studio to find her and make her see sense, which took some doing. Then she had become ill – an episode that she prefers not to think about these days – and wound up in hospital. He had come to sit with her there every day while she recovered, making her keep on eating to gain the weight she lacked, insisting on taking care of her, determined that she should give him and their relationship the chance he knew they deserved.

It was a long process, after all, their coming together, but when they did, when she discovered that she'd given her soul to him along with her body, she experienced an elation that, at the time, seemed way beyond the bounds of possibility or probability. She imagined their hearts were so closely blended that they were becoming one soul, one searing expression of art and idealism, whether in dance or painting, politics or love.

Back in the real world, however, Sasha had had problems of her own, among them lack of money. Her wage from the small touring company covered little more than her rent in the flat she shared with two other girls in Clapham. Her father, whose fortunes had gone up and down over the years, at first refused to help, telling her that she had to stand on her own two feet. Meanwhile she was becoming too much a rebel for classical ballet: she was beginning to hate being told what to do. For a dancer, submission to the ballet master and the choreographer was not part and parcel of daily life but the essence of it. She couldn't move in with Adam, in whose bedsit there wasn't room to swing a ballet shoe, and although she shared his politics in principle, she felt alarmed when he joined Militant Tendency. The claustrophobic atmosphere of his parents' house depressed her when they went to visit, especially the tension that crawled through the spaces between him and Martha and Gerald. And Martha unnerved her. She was not used to being unnerved by anybody.

Sasha needed time to learn, to grow, to find herself. And so she negotiated a loan of some money from her father, booked herself into a training course in Paris at a school of contemporary dance for mind, body and spirit and excused herself abruptly from Adam's life.

She loved Paris, where she lived in the Latin Quarter in a room she could cross with four steps. She learned to speak fluent French, kept a diary, discovered that she loved to read books and fancied the idea of writing one, wondered whether to apply to a university. Outside the dance studio waited a world of which she had experienced too little; in her mind lurked the thought of Adam and the thrill of the heightened awareness he had brought so violently into her life. She missed that intensified, energised existence; without it, the days seemed to slip by for no reason. Life without passion seemed no more and no less than a waste of time.

Back in London two years later, stuck in Queen's Park with her choleric father, quavering mother and academic sister, she felt bored and only half alive; the eating disorder that had landed her in hospital threatened to return. She agonised over whether to contact Adam. She was about to lose her resolve and phone Gerald and Martha to ask where he was, what he was doing and if he was married – when, in some nonsensical twist of fate, she bumped into him in a dance bookshop off Charing Cross Road. He walked in without seeing her, carrying a portfolio of his drawings of dancers that he was hoping the shop would exhibit and sell for him. They stared at each other, speechless, for at least thirty seconds.

Over a toasted sandwich in a nearby café, it didn't take them long to find out that neither of them was seeing anyone else and that they had never forgotten each other; soon, that they might still love each other. Several weeks later, they knew they did. Adam had abandoned Militant and Sasha her dreams of being a rebel Fonteyn. He was teaching art in a private school in north London and she was busy writing to local education authorities, trying to persuade them to accept the French contemporary dance method that she was now qualified to teach.

Adam had bought a small flat in Edgware. Sasha was living at home in Queen's Park, worrying about her father's blood pressure and her mother's drinking, and being encouraged by Lisa – who was doing four A levels – to apply for a grant to go to university and take a degree, perhaps in French, or women's studies. Adam encouraged her too. He had come into some money, left to him by his entrepreneurial grandfather who had died while Sasha was in France, and he had a decent job. And so she moved in with him and let him support her while she studied and tried to keep dancing and while he taught and tried to keep painting. There were high moments in their mid twenties. Adam had an occasional exhibition; Sasha made friends, joined women's groups and consciousness-raising sessions and declared marriage an outdated institution. She and Adam were partners, not 'husband', a term better applied to the care of farmyard animals, and 'wife', the word for ever associated with screaming infants, laundry and vacuum-cleaners.

In Queen's Park, Sally drank herself unconscious and had to be hospitalised overnight. In Bloomsbury, Lisa put on her glasses, pinned up her hair, decided to learn Russian, and buried herself in the university library. In Oxford, Martha looked Sasha up and down, listened to her feminist ideals ('Women have to reclaim their power,' Sasha told her passionately), heard about the state of her family and pursed her lips.

Sasha graduated. The day after Adam's school term ended, they took a cheap flight to Athens, boarded the first ferry they could find and disembarked on a small island where they rented a room over a taverna, intending to have two months of painting, reading, writing, dreaming and sex. They made love in bed at sunrise, on the floor in the afternoon, at two a.m. on the beach by moonlight and one lazy lunchtime in a grove of olive trees on the other side of the island, when Sasha hadn't put in her cap but was certain her cycle was not yet into its dangerous days.

Soon afterwards, thunder from heaven and hell: a phone call telling them that her father had had a heart-attack, a chaotic, terrified retreat to London too late to see him – for he never regained consciousness – and, a month after the funeral, a positive pregnancy test. Gerald and Martha had sat them down in the Oxford drawing room overlooking the walled garden and explained to their son and the pregnant girlfriend whom they regarded as neurotic and unsuitable that they were happy to help them put down a deposit on a house, but in return Gerald and Martha had to have a hand in choosing that house, and Adam and Sasha had to get married, because if something were to happen to one of them, the UK's archaic inheritance-tax laws would leave the other financially ruined and launch Martha and Gerald's first grandchild into life with a massive and unnecessary handicap. Adam and Sasha were too upset and frightened to object; and that night, for the first time, they imagined that the child would be the essence of their two souls combined, the physical incarnation of the inseparable union that their younger selves had craved. And they became, if not exactly happy, at least happier. The baby, though, had been the nail in the coffin of Sasha's fast-fading career in dance.

They couldn't depend on Grandpa's legacy, Adam's scant money from teaching and Gerald's help for ever; and when the twins decided to be conceived, the relatively carefree days of Liffy's early childhood came to a rapid end. Twins meant three children to support. Adam loved art but hated teaching; Sasha, with a few academic papers about dance, womanhood and society under her belt, realised in horror that she was to be chained to two screaming infants as well as the enchanting but highly demanding small person that Liffy had become – and that she could not afford to pay someone else to help look after them. 'Well,' Gerald shrugged at Adam, 'you'd better find yourself a proper job.' And Adam, knowing he was right, forced his hand to dial Nick's number so that he could ask his friend about design jobs at Forrest & Burns.

The journey from angry young artist to designer and thence

to art director on a magazine for the ghastlier kind of little girl was one that Adam Levy had neither expected nor desired to make.

As for Sasha, she tried to laugh off the fact that she and Adam had settled in the suburbs (specifically, one that boasted the best state primary schools in the country – ironic, given that Martha wouldn't let her send the children there) and were living lives that both of them would once have despised.

When you're young, Sasha thinks, you have ideals. You don't know that life is going to deliver a great many things to your door that you never ordered and can't send back.

Sasha picks a blank, lined index card out of a box on her desk. She seems to be surrounded by blanks: blank screen, blank card, blank marriage. She writes:

I BELIEVE IN . . .

And wonders what to write underneath.

> Freedom of the individual.
> *Liberté, egalité, fraternité.*
> The right to choose.
> Existentialism. You make your own life through your choices.
> [Not that her own life is an example of any such thing – with the sole, fabulous exception of her book.]
> Being kind to children.
> Free, high-quality education and health care for all.
> Banning alcohol.

She reads the list, then tears up the card. You can't simultaneously believe in the freedom of the individual and the banning of alcohol. Except that she can – even without wanting to give it up herself; perhaps it should apply only to her mother.

How many of her ideals is she living? She's a feminist who fell in love. She's a career woman who's had three children by mistake. She was a dancer, is now a writer; instead of physical, non-verbal movement, she now expresses herself through non-physical, verbal eloquence. She's an existentialist whose high-flying plane has been hijacked by the terrorists of fertility, instinct and time.

Does she still believe in the dancer as a symbol of feminine power? She once wrote a tome on the subject, fuelled by frustration and fury, a tome that people still read; now she can't remember how she did it. That thought is more depressing than the rest of her musings put together – except the one that asks where the magic that had once been her and Adam had gone when they weren't looking.

She stomps downstairs, puts some coffee into the cafetière and takes out the video of the art movie that she has to watch before *The Weekly Review* on Friday. She and Cindy will round on John Castleton again; at least she has that to look forward to.

Adam – who has come home at the usual time but not called her from the office all day – makes salad with chicken livers for supper. The twins try to outdo each other in declaring it yucky and Liffy refuses to eat it: 'I'm vegetarian, Dad.'

'Since when?'

'Since this morning. I told Mum.'

'Nobody told me.'

'But I told her before I went to school!'

'Well, one extra day of meat-eating isn't going to hurt, is it?' Adam groans. 'You can be vegetarian from tomorrow. Eat up.'

'I don't want to. I'm vegetarian now.'

'Find yourself something else in the fridge, then,' Sasha snaps.

'I'm not hungry, thank you,' Liffy says. 'Can I go and do my homework?'

Sasha and Adam are too tired and depressed to argue.

'Mum, can we have chocolate ice-cream for pudding?' Alex demands.

'Dad, can we watch James Bond?' says Matt.

'Mum, why can't I have new trainers? Like, everyone else has them.'

'I want some too! It's not fair!'

'Life *isn't* fair,' says Adam. 'Get used to it.'

Sasha slinks away to the bathroom to find a headache pill. The stripped-pine door under the skull and crossbones drawing opens a crack as she passes on her way back. 'Mum?'

'Yes, love?' Sasha stops, surprised by the vulnerable, honest look on her daughter's pale face.

'Can I – do you think I could – audition for ballet school again? It's not for ages yet, but Margaret said that maybe I could try . . .'

'We'll see, Liffs.' Sasha wonders how she can tell her daughter that she is never going to be a ballerina because her build is wrong and her joints aren't loose enough and it isn't her fault. 'We'll see.'

Liffy has just been having an instant-messaging exchange with Charley about how Robin had kissed her at the end of her flute lesson and how it was *indescribably incredible*. Liffy's stomach had churned up and she feels a little sick and dizzy now. She wants to leave her school and go somewhere where people want to do the work and think about that and nothing else.

She glares at the blinking cursor on the computer screen. It exerts some kind of tyranny over her, this machine, pulling her back as if by force, coercing her into more typing when her wrists are aching and all she wants to do is sleep. Charley has just asked her another question, about who she'd voted for on the latest TV pop-star-hunting show.

'Switch it off,' she feels the Earth Prince telling her. 'Make yourself do it. You can. You're in control.'

Liffy knows that she will see Charley on the bus in less than twelve hours' time. All she has to do is type 'C u tmrw' and log off. He's right: she's in control, after all. It would be so easy not to be, not to feel in control of anything, as she feels so often; not to be able to assert her own will as strongly as everyone else around her. She feels her jaw stiffen with new determination. She won't knuckle under. She won't be controlled by her parents, her brothers, her teachers, her schoolfriends, the limits of her body, the pressure of the turning world about her. And if the Earth Prince controls her, at least he is imaginary and therefore her own.

She raises her hands to the keyboard and does it. It isn't so difficult. Not really. She moves the mouse to 'Shut Down'; the screen darkens and the whirring stops.

She lies in bed, switches off the light and waits for sleep, wondering what was missing. What has she forgotten? Homework? Packing her ballet stuff for class tomorrow? No, she's done all that . . .

Then she realises that something, or someone, isn't there. The top of the duvet is vacant. No paws are kneading at the cotton; no warm, dark fur is brushing against her elbow. Ben has not come up to join her. Where is he?

Liffy gets up again, puts her head round the door and calls him. 'Ben! Benny! Bedtime, Bennypuss!'

A pair of green eyes stares back at her from the landing. The cat wants to come in, but won't. Something in her room is frightening him. And she wonders, not for the first time, whether cats can see some things that people can't, and what it is, new to her life, that scares him. Something he can see that even she, its creator, cannot?

6

If there is one thing better than being with Vladimir, it is the few hours beforehand, when Lisa can relish the insane joy of anticipation without any of the associated anxiety.

She arrives at Waterloo far too early, as always. She paces about the departure hall, past the coffee shop and Boots' travel accessories. The terminal is heaving with Easter holiday-makers – backpacking students, American tourists 'doing' Europe with six suitcases each, families coping to varying degrees with ballistic toddlers. She eyes the backpackers to make sure none of her students is among them, hoping that she will be in a quiet part of the train. Aboard Eurostar, she settles by the window with book in lap and, once the train is gliding southwards, fetches herself a large cup of coffee from the bar.

Lisa intends to use her time on the journey to practise her speed-reading. She's been learning how to do it for several months. Apparently it should be possible to achieve over two thousand words per minute. Lisa doesn't much like the idea in itself – she prefers to take time to savour words and language – but there's no denying that faster reading would be useful for her research, not to mention marking student essays. She sweeps the tip of a pencil diagonally across a paragraph, following it with her eyes, then up in a loop for a few lines and down again in the opposite direction. Then she tries to read a whole page in stages the same way. It's starting – slowly – to feel easier than it used to. But it is not long before her attention lapses while her coffee grows cold. She gazes out at the Kent orchards sliding by, counting the hours, the minutes, until Paris.

At some point, in transit, she locks herself into the toilet and changes her image. She's never dared to do it in London, although she couldn't have said why. Superpersonlike, she comes out of her chrysalis, morphing from prim, classic lecturer to great musician's mistress. Out comes the toothlike grip from her hair; she lets it loose so that it tumbles around her shoulders, then brushes it until it shines like burnished brass. On goes the makeup: rosewood lipstick, full-lash waterproof mascara, powder to take away the shine of travel sweat. On goes her lowest-cut top. Off come her sensible loafers and on go her latest birthday present from Vladimir – brown mottled snakeskin shoes with straps that criss-cross her ankles, an unthinkable designer label lurking under her soles.

The tunnel is past in just twenty minutes and, once through it, the train gathers speed – the French, unlike the British, had bothered to build a proper track for it from the start. It hurtles through the sprawling fields of northern France towards the Parisian suburbs. As the Gare du Nord nears, Lisa can see, in the distance, the elongated hump of the Sacre Coeur standing sentinel above Montmartre. Soon she will cross the full length of the platform to the concourse; and there will be Vladimir, waiting for her. Her heart thumps under her ribs.

But when she reaches the end of the train, walking carefully in her less than comfortable shoes and pulling along her small suitcase on wheels, there's no sign of him. She stops, wondering what to do. The Gare du Nord, milling around her, is all opaque globe lights and arches, chrome and brick and what feels like half of Paris in manic motion. Lisa's heart sinks back to its normal speed. He is often late – he'd assured her that this was quite usual in Russia and that, honestly, he always does his best – but when he comes to London and she meets him at Waterloo International she is always there half an hour before the train comes in, as if that could make it arrive any faster. Now she's looked forward to seeing him for more than two months and he can't even be there to meet her?

Lisa stands still, thinking. Should she set off and head for the house? Has her mobile clocked into a French network yet? Should she just take the next train home and write off Vladimir as a bad job? And then she sees someone running down the glass-framed stairs, someone with dark curly hair and a leather jacket, and her heart soars as she goes to meet him and feels his mouth fasten on to hers.

You're not really supposed to find romance in musical academia. When Lisa had arranged to interview a Russian pianist, an acquaintance of Lindsey and Paul's who was making a speciality of Stravinsky and knew some of the composer's surviving friends, she had not expected anything more than an interesting afternoon. She had arrived at Vladimir's hotel at two thirty as arranged, and when a tall, sultry-looking fellow in his forties, wearing jeans and a leather jacket, approached her in the lobby, she was about to tell him to get lost, having expected someone (a) older, (b) duller, (c) less attractive. After a minute at cross-purposes, she'd understood that this was indeed her quarry and startled him by speaking Russian. They settled at a table in the bar and ordered blueberry cheesecake for two; he surveyed her cleavage and, oddly, the curves of her ankle and instep with eyes alight, and she realised that this was going to be a longer meeting than she'd anticipated.

Vladimir had just recorded a CD of a recital programme including two pieces of Stravinsky's piano music ('The Genius of Vladimir Vasilevsky,' declared the box). He finished it with the composer's arrangement of three dances from *Petrushka* – everyone who wanted to show off their virtuoso technique played those – but also he played the Serenade, little known but a favourite of Lisa's. Yet never had the composer for whose sake she'd spent so much time in so many libraries felt so dead and distant to her. For once, she didn't want to talk about him, or even about her thesis, which she'd all but finished. She wanted to find out who Vladimir really was, what his tastes were in music, food, art and, surreptitiously, women – and soon they'd requested more coffee and another piece of blueberry cheesecake and he'd invited her to his concert the following night. When she left, it was five o'clock; they laughed together about that as they said 'See you tomorrow', and when she glanced back across the hotel foyer on her way out, he was still looking at her.

The next evening, Vladimir sat at a piano below a gold and turquoise pre-Raphaelite mural of the Soul of Music, playing the roof off the Wigmore Hall. The queue at the box office had stretched out into the street. Lindsey's husband's bank's name was prominently displayed in the programme as principal sponsor. Lisa alternated between watching every move of Vladimir's beautiful hands and closing her eyes in an attempt to sense his soul through the music: ethereal Schubert and elemental Beethoven in the first half, mystical Scriabin and pounding Stravinsky (to promote the disc) in the second. Backstage in the green room afterwards, he stopped talking to a terribly important agent in order to talk to her. He gazed at length at her curves, offered her a glass of wine, asked her if she'd like to come out to dinner with him and some friends at Sofra in St Christopher's Place. She looked into his eyes and her head spun, and so she went; she sat next to him, impressing with her linguistic ability and academic credentials his current agent, whom he wanted to leave for a better one, and a gay critic who looked sorry to see her. She drank far too much from sheer nerves, ate little of the mixed mezze for the same reason and ended up walking him back to his hotel round the corner where he said the Russian equivalent of 'I've got some of my CDs upstairs for you . . .'

Lisa had watched Sasha and Adam falling in love, years ago, and never quite believed it. She is seven years younger than Sasha, so she was thirteen when Adam came to the house for the first time, looking scruffy and disreputable under his beard until his very nice public-school voice emerged. At first she'd been starry-eyed at the thought that her sister was in love, until she remembered that Sasha's habitual theatricality meant that her emotional overdrive was perhaps predictable and therefore not guaranteed to be genuine.

Lisa had always been academic, consistently getting top marks at school, and she played the cello passably. Although she loved the expressiveness of her instrument, it was finding the way to set down her ideas in words that fascinated her, analysing those ideas, locating their source and taking them apart like a clock to see how they worked. Through her twenties she had four successive boyfriends – who had hurt her by (1) dumping her on his mother's instructions, (2) lying about everything from his schooling to the grocery shopping, (3) belittling her intellectual ability and bad-mouthing her to the faculty out of jealousy, (4) emigrating to California and chucking her by email once there. After all this, she'd become wary of emotional involvement. She neither expected nor wanted to be swept off her feet. She wanted instead to bury herself alive in the British Library.

Or so she had thought, until she went into the hotel with Vladimir and he hadn't seduced her or even tried to. Instead he'd given her a Waterstone's carrier-bag containing copies of all his CDs and told her he had to leave for Switzerland at five in the morning. Then he asked if he could call her and she said, 'Yes, yes, of course,' feeling too prim and way too academic.

'And call me if you come to Paris. Please,' he added. 'You won't forget?'

'Forget?' Lisa exclaimed. Her enthusiasm was all he needed to lean forward and kiss her cheek, and on that fraction of contact she felt part of her spirit whirl away into the night sky.

'Come and visit me in Paris,' he said. 'So. Goodnight . . .'

'Goodnight,' Lisa echoed. She wandered down the hotel

passage in the wrong direction. Most other men would have tried to jump on her; how typical that the one she wanted was the only one who wouldn't.

He'd called the following week, once he was home from his tour. They'd pencilled in three days in three weeks' time; and when she found herself in Paris, wondering what on earth she thought she was doing there, they ate oysters together, then went up the Eiffel Tower to admire the lights of Paris by night, and Vladimir put his arms round her in the lift.

She couldn't understand why he was single; but, of course, it turned out that he had been married for ten years and was now separated, pending divorce. It wasn't simple, he said, although there were no children. Not acrimonious, but painful nonetheless. Eighty concerts a year, recording sessions, rehearsals, chamber-music collaborations – all over the world. It didn't make a good basis for domesticity. His wife had worked for a leading firm of artists' managers and had to be in the office by nine every morning, but Vladimir was of necessity a nocturnal creature, taking several hours to wind down from his hyperactive concert mode; and he liked to practise at night, when the phone didn't keep ringing. Maybe, suggested Lisa, he needed to be with someone whose working hours were less fixed and demanding; maybe, Vladimir said, yes, maybe. But an artist's life is difficult: you're only as good as your last concert; you have to practise. That must always come first. It's hard to ask your partner to accept music as a rival that must always win. And Lisa knew, as he closed the shutters of his small courtyard house and slid her jacket off her shoulders, that he was trying to tell her something.

She quickly forgot about it. He led her up the narrow, winding staircase to where a dark red Indian bedspread and plenty of pillows lay in wait on the bed. Then he undressed her slowly, garment by garment, until all that was left were her black high-heeled shoes, which he wanted her to leave on temporarily. Soon she was making discoveries about her own sexual abilities that none of her former lovers had induced her so much as to imagine. She possessed muscles she hadn't known about; her body proved more flexible than she'd ever suspected; she found new sensations to experience, different touches to explore, a level of desire and demand that was new to her and desperately unEnglish. The communication of touch was stronger than any words between them, whether in Russian, English or French; he let her know that he was in charge, changing position without disengaging from her, arranging pillows beneath first her, then him; she showed him, with motions and kisses, where and how to caress, only to find that he already knew that better than she did; he showed her, to her astonishment, that she was entitled to, and capable of, more than a meagre single orgasm at a time. When the first light of dawn struck the curtains and they finally subsided into sleep, she calculated that they'd made love for almost six hours. Closing her eyes, she asked Vladimir to pinch her wrist to make sure that she wasn't dreaming. He'd obliged, laughing, kissed her one last time, then put some foam earplugs into his ears and a mask over his eyes and turned his back.

'Have you brought something nice to wear?' Vladimir asks her now, waiting for the Métro.

Lisa is breathing in the Paris Métro scent: dust, tar, garlic. The question surprises her. 'I've got my black dress – why?'

'Because tomorrow my friend Yasha is getting married and I said I would play at the reception – so we go to a wedding in the Russian church!'

Lisa wonders why he hadn't bothered to tell her before. 'But I can't wear black to a wedding!'

'It's fine. Lots of people wear black, it's not a problem. Don't worry about it.'

Lisa does worry. She tells herself not to be superstitious, but the idea fixes itself like a red weal at the back of her mind.

Vladimir's little house is tucked away behind a block of nineteenth-century flats, ten minutes' stroll from the Eiffel

Tower. Downstairs he has a kitchenette and one large room, which doubles as lounge and studio, with three tall, elegant windows, triple-glazed, shrouded with fine muslin curtains. Upstairs are a bedroom, study and bathroom. Each time Lisa walks through the little courtyard into the house she feels as if she had left it just the day before – but it would have been weeks or months ago and in the intervening time he would have had something painted or bought a new picture or retiled the bathroom. Something is always different. This time the downstairs walls have changed colour, from beige to a subtle off-white.

'I like to keep changing it,' he says. 'It's always better, just step by step . . .'

Always changing, thinks Lisa. Always changing.

In the bedroom, she hangs her black dress in Vladimir's cupboard. On the bed, perched on the pillow that will be hers, is a shoebox wrapped in red paper with a gold bow on top. She unwraps it: it's the purple shoes from Berlin, extravagantly expensive, idiotically beautiful creations that don't match her black dress or much else in her wardrobe. When she tries them on, they fit, mysteriously, as if made especially for her. She wonders when she'll ever have occasion to wear them. Stroking the suede, she replaces them in their box with care.

She looks out of the window, luxuriating in the quiet; there in the courtyard, you'd never know you were in the middle of a great capital city. On the wall opposite grow pink climbing roses that pour out fragrance in the summer; now there are tulips in the flowerbed, nodding in submission to the relentless rain. Vladimir stands beside her and gazes at them and the darkening sky overhead with his wide, grey-green eyes.

'Isn't it beautiful?' he says.

A lump rises to Lisa's throat.

The next day they take a taxi through miles of Parisian suburbs to the Russian church, which Vladimir regards with almost proprietorial affection, although he, like Lisa, is technically if not committedly Jewish. The church is like a small slice of Russia that has been lifted whole, carried westward and deposited on an incongruous little hill behind someone's back garden – complete with onion domes, a gold and ochre interior and an invisible choir singing *a cappella* chants behind a carved wooden screen. Vladimir knows everybody: guest after guest embraces him and casts a curious glance at Lisa, whom Vladimir presents as 'a friend from London'.

Congregations do not sit in a Russian church, so two hundred wedding guests stand in their trim suits and watch as the bridal couple, Yasha and Elena, take their places for the ceremony. Vladimir is one of the group of chosen male friends who take turns to hold a heavy golden crown over Yasha's head; Elena is similarly attended by women. The priest, in full white and gold regalia, bearing a magnificent beard, intones in archaic Russian. Elena is a gorgeous blonde girl with wide Slavic cheekbones and a generous smile. She sits radiant in her ivory silk gown on her throne next to her bridegroom, and when Vladimir and Lisa go up to congratulate them at the end, in line with everyone else, she gives Lisa a big hug although she has never seen her before.

Weddings, said Sasha some time around 1980, were a waste of everyone's time and money. It's an excuse for the girl to dress up, not realising that she's a sacrificial lamb. It's not about love. It's about property. 'Who gives this woman to be married to this man?' and 'With all my worldly goods I thee endow . . .' It's formalised male chauvinism. If you want to make a real commitment to the person you love, you should be able to do it without this bloody rigmarole. The pretty white dress, moreover, was all very well when most brides had been nineteen or so, but today many middle-class brides are over thirty and it looks ridiculous. Seven years later, Sasha declared her own wedding the biggest non-event of the decade and her obvious pregnancy rendered the whole thing surreal.

Elena, like Lisa, is thirty-three. She does not look ridiculous. She looks happy.

Lisa, as a teenager, used inevitably to soak up some of the viewpoints that her confrontational sister let fly. She'd always thought them correct – in principle. But that bears no relation to the pain that slides through her stomach at the idea that this may never happen to her. Vladimir has been married once and doesn't want to do it again. Once burnt, twice shy. He has many such platitudes, convenient phrases, clear, uncomplicated ways of maintaining the status quo that permit him to take nothing any further than he wants to.

The wedding reception is in a faded mansion close to the Seine that during the day is a small music college; the basement houses a Russian restaurant where Vladimir and Lisa had eaten borscht and drunk aromatic vodka during her first visit. The guests take their seats in the main hall and Vladimir bounds on to the stage and plays for half an hour, selections of Elena and Yasha's favourite music: Tchaikovsky, Rachmaninov and the three dances from *Petrushka*. Afterwards, around the buffet table, he attracts almost as much attention as the bride and groom.

Lisa leans against a piano in the reception room, sips champagne and watches and listens, the languages – Russian, French and several others – melding into a musical wash around her, like the fairground scene in *Petrushka*. She wonders how the young Stravinsky would have composed this reception. It would be a far cry from his austere music for the ballet *Les Noces*. A strong ceremonial theme, perhaps, for the buffet table – laden with trays of oysters, Russian salad, rye bread, blinis with sour cream and caviar and, at the centre, a French-style wedding cake, a tall pyramid of profiteroles covered with golden caramel and spun sugar. He'd write graceful, faux-Baroque music for the French women guests in their perfect suits and matching hats, maybe pastiche Couperin; and an energetic Russian dance for the Russian men, knocking back vodka and clapping Yasha on the back.

A student from the music college comes in, wearing Russian peasant costume with a loose, embroidered shirt and holding a balalaika. He begins to play a folk song: Elena lifts her trailing silk skirt away from the floor and dances. Vladimir's gaze fixes on her graceful feet and ankles, clad in simple ivory satin slippers, while an old friend from Moscow engages him in vigorous conversation. Someone refills Lisa's glass and a woman in a turquoise Yves St Laurent suit, one of the faux-Couperins, comes up to talk to her, having seen her standing on her own.

'*Vous êtes une amie d'Elena?*'

'*Je suis une amie de Vladimir,*' Lisa tells her.

'*Et vous êtes aussi russe?*'

Lisa explains who she is and soon finds herself adopted by Marie-Françoise, her husband and daughter. Vladimir, when he looks round for her later, seems surprised to find her chatting away in French with neighbours of Yasha's whom he's never met.

At one a.m. they take a taxi home.

'It's funny,' Vladimir says, holding her hand, 'but I've known Yasha longer than anybody. We lived in the same block in Stalino, after all the – all the trouble we were in, and my mother was finally able to settle. We used to play together outside and get into mischief all the time. I remember once when Yasha's father caught us writing on a wall and he gave Yasha a – you know, with the belt – but of course he couldn't punish me. And I was pleased I wouldn't get punished, but really all I could think of was that I didn't have a father any more.'

Lisa squeezes his hand, wishing she could wave a magic wand to heal his pain. Somehow she finds she's thinking distantly of Adam and the twins.

'Then we both got into the Moscow Conservatoire and travelled up there together by train,' Vladimir goes on. 'Yasha was very talented, you know. Fantastic violinist. He should have been somewhere better than second fiddle in the opera orchestra. He never worked hard enough, that's the trouble. I was practising nine hours a day, but Yasha was always out, drinking too much, always one girl or another girl, and one minute he'd be crazy happy and the next down in some terrible depression. It's taken him a long time to find Elena, but I think this time he really is happy.'

'And you?' Lisa says. 'Will you ever be happy, Vovka?'

'It depends what you mean exactly. I am not sure that happiness is part of my nature. I am not sure I *should* be happy. Because if you're happy, perhaps you don't have the drive always to improve.'

'Isn't that because if you're happy you don't need to improve?' Lisa suggests.

'But always you need to improve. As a musician, once you stop improving, you are dead. It's simple.'

Lisa looks down at her feet next to his on the taxi floor. She is not sure she will ever get through to this man. And she's tried. She's tried for so long.

Back at the house, she pulls off her black dress, puts on the purple suede shoes and parades across the living room towards him. It doesn't take him long to pounce. Making love makes her forget, at least for the moment, the understanding that has been stalking her all day.

But later she lies next to him, staring upwards. Vladimir senses something wrong. 'What are you thinking about?'

'Lots of things.'

He nods gently. Strange, she muses, how he can be so sensitive and so obdurate at the same time. A tear escapes her eye.

'Darling, don't cry. Let me hold you.'

That makes her cry more.

'What's wrong? Tell me?' He strokes her hair.

'I don't know what I'm doing here,' Lisa manages to say. 'I can't live like this. I just can't do it any more.'

She doesn't know what she hoped he'd say, but whatever it is, he doesn't say it.

'I always knew you would want something more,' he says instead. 'I was always afraid that would happen.'

'It's enough for you, then – meeting every couple of months, never looking ahead . . .'

'I'm happy this way. I'm happy with you this way. I don't want to lose you. But I have my concerts . . . I can't change my life.'

'Vovka, I know you won't. I'm not asking you to. But I think that I have to change mine.'

In the morning they take the Métro to the Gare du Nord and linger upstairs by the Eurostar check-in. Lisa should have been staying two more days. She looks into Vladimir's quiet, accepting face and thinks for a moment that she will never reach home alive if she has to leave him. He kisses her on both cheeks and says, 'Call me whenever you like.'

'You too,' she says, not certain she means it.

She hands her passport and ticket to the Eurostar official, turns away from Vladimir and walks out of his life.

7

Sitting in the taxi on the way to Television Centre, Sasha takes deep breaths of the fume-filled air of Shepherd's Bush and feels liberated.

The home of which she has always been so proud, with its bright chenille cushions, its cream-coloured walls, its conservatory abundant with well-fed plants, has tipped off kilter, sliding away at a dangerous tangent and taking with it her work and her peace of mind. Adam has clammed up since the football incident: it's as if he's sent himself to Coventry, if only because nobody else has punished him as hard as he feels he deserves. Liffy has retreated into a teenaged shell, picking at her food, saying little other than 'yes' or 'no' – usually 'no' – and the twins are running riot over the lot of them, as if sensing, without knowing the terminology, that they've won the moral high ground and can do whatever they like without fear of reprisal. The BBC studio is an escape, a blessed little refuge in which Sasha can live for her mind and not her family, in company with her kindred spirit, Cindy: twin Valkyries, singing out against evil in praise of the worthy.

This week they've been sent a neo-feminist book by a young woman journalist to review, as well as a sci-fi film and a TV costume drama, and Sasha knows what will happen. John Castleton will huff and puff in his Garrick tie and she and Cindy will laugh him off the face of celestial live TV.

She chats to the bare-midriffed assistant who comes down to the lobby to fetch her. Following her through the corridors towards the studio, she rehearses her best comments in her mind – 'A brave and very beautiful first effort' for the book, 'Simply pandering to the lowest common denominator' for the movie and 'Excellently acted, of course, but missing an unconscionable amount of the original's subtlety and meaning' for the costume drama.

'It's a pity that Cindy can't be here today,' the assistant remarks. 'She phoned this morning – said it was something she'd eaten last night.'

'Cindy's not here?' Sasha says, thrown off course. 'Who's coming instead?'

'Well, John's still on, but we've got Jeremy Leigh instead of Cindy.'

'Jeremy Leigh? You have *got* to be joking.'

'No, it's him all right. Why?'

'Oh, nothing. Nothing. Nothing.'

The studio door ahead swings open and she sees them sitting there by someone else's desk and computer, two pompous male critics with matching bulging bellies, sipping glasses of water and chortling together, probably over old times when they were both students in Cambridge. Jeremy Leigh and John Castleton are indeed the best of friends. The would-be Valkyrie almost freezes in her tracks and wonders whether there is still time to turn round and go home.

'Ah, Sasha, how excellent to see you,' George says, bustling up to her and pumping her hand. At the far end of the studio, in front of the cameras, the newscaster is in full flow: house prices have rocketed still further, a mix-up in an IVF clinic has given triplets to a woman who had not consented to risk them, a politician has been making controversial comments about the justification for the war in Iraq. Sasha allows herself to be led to the makeup hot seat where a stronger lipstick is applied to her mouth and plenty of powder patted over her face to soak up the nervous sweat that is starting to break out on her forehead. It isn't that she needs Cindy. She can make her points alone. But she knows all too well what the programme's subtext is. The problem is that normally her side outnumbers the opposition.

Jeremy and John greet her with warm enough handshakes and Jeremy jokes that he's only been invited on to the programme because they couldn't get hold of anybody black, Asian or from Hoxton. Sasha protests that, being Jewish, she is, of course, a member of an ethnic minority, but Jeremy laughs and says that that doesn't count because it's the wrong kind of minority – like the wrong kind of snow on the railways, ha ha ha. Sasha presses her lips together, determined to save her vitriol for the camera.

It's five to eleven. Most people, by five to eleven on a Friday night, have had enough for one week and are heading for bed. For once, Sasha wishes that she could, too.

'Hello, hello, everyone, please come through,' exclaims a voice she's never heard before. She looks round, and then up.

The producer is new. He is six foot four and has sandy hair and a smile the width of the Thames. His eyes are the bright, clear blue of remote Irish lakes. He has long limbs and long, fluttery hands and is wearing a designer cotton sweater in a lilac shade that sets off his eyes. 'I'm Richard Byrne,' he says. 'Everyone calls me Rick.'

'"Everybody goes to Rick's,"' quotes Sasha, thinking of *Casablanca.* But this Rick does not resemble Bogart. This Rick seems to have dropped straight off the planet where irresistible men are manufactured specifically to torment long-married women having a bad patch.

He takes her hand and she hates the quicksilver way he beams at her as if he's known her for ever. She realises that her palm is sweaty. She wants to let the studio floor swallow her. She straightens her shoulders, lifts her chin and strides to her usual chair at the *Weekly Review* coffee-table.

The cameras roll and focus on George. 'Good evening,' he declares, 'and welcome to *The Weekly Review*. This week my guests are the author and journalist Sasha Wood, the literary critic Jeremy Leigh . . .'

Sasha tries to let the words float over her and takes deep breaths to steady herself. First they tackle the costume drama: an extract of it is shown, with doe-eyed young actresses in Empire-line dresses aching after suave actors in red uniforms. 'So, what did you think of it, Jeremy?' George says.

Jeremy talks about slicing up the classics into bite-sized pieces for a modern audience with no attention span. John has a brief rant about the unpoetic nature of television that purges all the beauty from one of the great works of English literature. Sasha says, 'It's excellently acted, of course, but it does miss an unconscionable amount of the original's subtlety and meaning.'

Next they demolish the latest multi-billion-grossing sci-fi movie. Jeremy finds the special effects impressive but empty; John decries the lack of originality in movie-making today and points to the impact of the great sci-fi movies of the past, while today all the film studios can do is churn out doomed clones; Sasha protests at the male-oriented story in which on the Good side women are only there to be fancied or rescued, or on the Bad to be evil, controlling and criminally unfeminine. 'Simply pandering to the lowest common denominator,' she declares.

'This brings us on to our book, *Like, Come On, Get Real* by Zoë Macklow,' says George. For the benefit of the viewers, he adds, 'Zoë Macklow is usually termed a neo-feminist and in this, her first full-length book, she argues that feminism must descend from its ideological and philosophical standpoint and root itself first and foremost in the everyday experience of modern women. So, Sasha, what do you make of it?'

'Well, I think it's a brave and beautiful first effort,' Sasha says. 'Zoë Macklow is very young and she argues her case so coherently and convincingly that it's clear she's got a great future ahead.'

'Well written, then,' George says. 'What about her ideas? How do you feel they carry the feminist question forward?'

Jeremy Leigh snorts. Sasha ignores him. 'There's a lot of good sense in there,' she says. 'In many ways, I feel she's right. To base feminist theory too intensely in academic thinking and philosophical tracts is to deny its precepts to the vast majority of women today who still desperately need it. It shouldn't be academic and élitist: it's about basic human rights. And, yes, the experience of women in the modern world proves all too clearly that theory and reality don't meet. I mean, look at the way even most middle-class women live now: they have to have jobs to support their children whether they like it or not because the cost of living is so high, while this government is the only one in Europe that does not recognise and back up with real support the value of family life early in children's lives. It's the same old story, family versus career, and it still doesn't work because nothing practical, based on people's real, day-to-day experience, has ever been done about it at state level, at least not in this country.'

'John, what about you?'

'Well, really! I couldn't possibly comment!' John Castleton laughs. 'I mean, this kind of polemic that suggests a man should have no say over whether a child of his can be aborted, that suggests laws for women's rights should be made by women alone with no input from men – who, if you remember, are also people and also have rights – that suggests men are inferior beings in some way because we are apparently genetically incapable of seeing past the end of our own noses. Well, really. I'm just a man, so who am I to object?'

Across the table, Jeremy Leigh lets out a leonine roar of laughter. Sasha feels something resembling a pressure cooker steaming inside her head. 'If men hadn't treated women as inferior beings since the beginning of time,' she cuts in, 'there might never have been a backlash against them, might there?'

'But, Sasha, the blessed irony of the whole thing,' Jeremy

expostulates, 'is that you feminists have brought the whole thing upon yourselves! Isn't that obvious?'

'The whole what, exactly?' Sasha growls.

'Oh, come *on*. You're a reasonably intelligent lady, you should be able to follow some simple thought processes!'

An 'ooof' sounds from George and John, and, she thinks, from most of the surrounding cameramen (and they are mostly men).

'I can't believe I'm hearing language like this,' Sasha says.

'But look!' Jeremy is undaunted. 'What exactly have you achieved? Tell me! "Wimmin are powerful!" "A woman without a man is like a fish without a bicycle"! All the little platitudes and affirmations that gave us so much fun and games through the seventies and eighties. And where are you now? Aren't all you Powerful Wimmin right back where you started? No, you're not. You're worse off than ever before! Because you insisted on having the right to careers and jobs, the right not to get married, the right not to have hordes of screaming babies. Fair enough. I'm all for that. As you say, it's basic human rights, at least in the Western world. But look what's happened now. The upshot is that you have to work. It's expected of you, you have to support your families – and meanwhile you've discovered, to your chagrin, that some of you do still want to have male partners and a few babies. So now you want the right *not* to work. As a literary critic, I find it deeply depressing to see a whole generation of what should have been talented women writers producing nothing but fluffy chicklit about how all they want to do is have a white wedding with a romantic hero for bridegroom and then produce lots of babies! The right to do this and that and then, oh whoops, we got it wrong, now we want the right to do *that* instead! Rights, rights, rights. Did any of you ever think about your *responsibilities*? Did any of you ever think about what it takes to raise children properly? Would any of you have been on your high horses in the first place without the input of mothers who took good care of you and did everything for you when you were small children?'

'I object!' Sasha exclaims. 'You know nothing of our families. Every family has problems, hasn't it? You're assuming some rosy view of motherhood that bears no relation whatsoever to the reality!'

Her own mother had been less than perfect. Jeremy's words have cut into her, reminding her of days in her teens that are best forgotten.

'Yes, yes, yes.' Jeremy sighs like an impatient headmaster. 'But just think about it. Just think what you – yes, Sasha, *you personally* – have done for the feminist cause. The celebration of the female body and feminine power through dance! Come *on*! Every dog has its day, all that rot is over and done with. It's been and gone. It's old-fashioned. It's outmoded. It is, indeed, as dead as a dodo in the reality of modern society. We've got more important things to worry about. In a world with Osama bin Laden, Saddam Hussein and George W. Bush in it, my dear, you've got to face the fact that you and your disciples like little Miss Zoë are has-beens. If you're going to build a fairer world for women, you're going to have to do a darn sight better than this.'

Images flash through Sasha's mind of her mother sipping gin beside the kitchen sink; of Lisa aged six asking again and again when Daddy was coming home; of herself aged fourteen going to her ballet school and loving every moment of it because while you dance you can't think about anything else. To her horror, she feels tears gathering in her eyes. Oh no. She can't cry on live TV.

'So in your view, Jeremy,' George says, clearly amused, 'what are the more important things that young writers should be concerned about today?'

'The breakdown of society, for a start. Without a strong society, anarchy will rule. And you can lay the blame for that fairly and squarely at the feminists' door.'

'No, you cannot!' Sasha is horrified to hear her voice emerge thin and choked. 'You can lay the blame first of all at the door of Margaret Thatcher, who, if I remember rightly, was the person who said, "There is no such thing as society," and second, more alarmingly, at the door of the drug-pushers and the criminal gangs associated with them, much of which is the result of idiotic government ideology about drugs.'

'Fiddlesticks! Poppycock! Piffle!' Jeremy cries, fired up for his final onslaught. 'There won't be any progress until you feminists admit one thing: *you got it all wrong*. Reason versus instinct, nature versus the rationale of personal choice – you've set them against one another from day one. So you have to rethink. You have to start all over again. Back to the drawing-board, Sasha. Rethink the battle lines. Get real!'

'Which,' George says, into the camera, 'is exactly what this book tells us to do. On that merry note, it's time to say good-night from all of us in the studio, and have an excellent weekend. Goodnight.'

'Goodnight,' chorus Jeremy, John and Sasha, as they have to. And the lights go out.

Sasha doesn't know how she has got from the chair to the studio door. Her knees are watery, her blue silk blouse is drenched with sweat under her arms and she can't seem to get her breath. Out in the corridor she leans against the wall, cups her hands over her nose and mouth and breathes through them. It doesn't help. How could it? Two members of the Garrick Club have just thrown her life's work into the dustbin, and there was nothing she could do to stop them.

She knows she's in the right. Her ideals are true and her world vision accurate. She spent hours, days, weeks, months, years thinking about the ideology that went into her book, reading all the texts she could lay her hands on, sitting near the swings in the park with one eye on the page and the other on little Liffy playing nearby. Once it had taken shape in her mind and she had begun to write, she'd wake up early every morning itching and impatient to get to her Amstrad and continue. Writing the book changed her life. Oh yes, you can be a visionary, your words can change your life and other people's too, but what if nobody can be bothered to listen?

'Sasha? Are you OK?'

The voice, with an Irish lilt to it, comes from somewhere above her head. Sasha looks up into the blue, blue eyes of Rick Byrne. 'I've been better,' she admits. Rick's gaze is too direct to let her lie.

'Come into my office. I keep something there for emergencies.' He brushes a hand against her shoulder and leads the way down a long corridor between innumerable closed wooden doors. Eventually he stops and opens one. Sasha's inner reservoir of energy seems to have drained away into dry soil; when Rick opens a cupboard in his office and pulls out a bottle of Irish whiskey, she is more than happy to see it. 'I think you'll find it better than Scotch,' he declares, pouring.

'Right now, I'd be happy to swig meths. God – those two men!'

'Yes, that was one of those rare occasions that someone must have dreamed of when they set up this programme. I know it's cruel. But it makes fantastic TV, don't you think?'

Sasha thumps her glass down. 'I'm going home,' she explodes. 'I've had enough! Destroying someone's work like that isn't what television should be about!'

'Ah, Sasha, come on. Don't leave, I didn't mean to upset you. Think about it: you and Cindy normally win, don't you, now? Sometimes the other side has to get a look in! Don't take it all so seriously. Don't let the bastards grind you down.' Rick sits on his desk, long legs crossed. 'Look,' he goes on, 'you're a marvellous, strong, idealistic woman – more than that, a marvellous, strong, idealistic human being. We need more people like you around here.'

Sasha casts a cautious look at him. His eyes keep drawing

her gaze back to them – they are so intent, so intelligent, so interested in her. She can't remember when anyone last looked at her like that, if indeed anyone ever has. She picks up her glass again and lets the whiskey slam into her brain. 'So, tell me,' she says. 'You're new here. Where were you before?'

'News. I'd been there seven years, and it was time for a change. I'm very happy, it's a good injection of energy and it's good to meet new people and think about something different.'

'News must be pretty stressful.'

'Ah, just a bit!'

'Where are you from? Dublin?'

'I studied in Dublin, but I was born in Galway. Have you been there?'

'I haven't. I hear it's beautiful.'

'It's exquisite. The coastline, the lakes, the air – it's magic. You must see it yourself some day. It does rain, though. Rains a lot.'

'Do you miss it?'

'Sometimes. But I left more than twenty years ago for the bright lights and the big city. It's two extremes for me – complete peace and quiet and beauty or complete excitement and activity and stress. I like them both. What I don't like is the compromise between them: a little activity that's never exciting enough, and a quiet that is never quiet enough. Which, I guess, is how most people live. It's how I live now, for that matter. Have done for years. It's fine, of course. I can't complain.'

'Where do you live?'

'Not too far from here. We're in Barnes, close to the pond.'

Sasha takes a long sip of whiskey. 'Then we're neighbours,' she tells him. 'I live in Sheen. Speaking of which, my taxi's waiting. I should get going.'

'Oh, we can cancel the taxi. Let me drive you home – it's no distance. As you say, we're neighbours.'

'Thank you,' Sasha says. 'That's kind.'

'It's my pleasure,' Rick says. Sasha almost kicks herself for being impressed with his gallantry.

They walk out of Television Centre into the grimy, threatening gloom of Wood Lane, W12, at midnight – not a place anyone in their right mind would choose to be, thinks Sasha. In the car park, they climb some concrete stairs to level one, where Rick unlocks a shiny new Merc.

He is wearing some kind of sandalwood aftershave and the scent reaches Sasha's nostrils along with a faint aroma of sweat, male yet strange, subtly different from Adam's. With the car's interior, which smells of new-minted luxury, the combination is unfamiliar and heady. A door swings open in Sasha's mind. Although it seems extraordinary, she thinks, there are other worlds besides the one she knows. Parallel universes do exist. Perhaps this car, on a bleak, run-down west London road in the middle of the night, is carrying her through an eleventh dimension into an unseen bubble of existence that's only half a millimetre away. Sasha's pulse has increased. The bubble beckons. She wonders what kind of world spins within it.

'You've got kids, haven't you?' Rick says, circling Hammersmith roundabout and turning off towards the bridge.

'Yes, my daughter's just thirteen and my twin boys are eight.'

'Twin boys! That'll be a handful.'

'You could say that.' Sasha sits back in the leather seat, enjoying the smoothness of the car.

'My son's fifteen. We caved in and gave him a drum-kit for his birthday.'

'I've that to look forward to . . .'

Bowling along towards home, Sasha finally lets herself admit it: she *fancies* this enthusiastic Irishman with the direct gaze. She fancies his decisiveness, his kindness, his ability to think on his feet, the impression that he lives in and for the moment. She fancies his broad shoulders, his bright, enticing eyes, his big, long-fingered hands. She looks at him and knows she shouldn't compare him to Adam, or Adam to him. 'Is your wife in television as well?' she asks.

'No, no. She's a housewife, these days. You and Adam must come round – we'll have you over for dinner. What's your email?'

Sasha tells him.

'I'm just Richard dot Byrne with the usual BBC format like all the others. So, we'll be in touch. And I'll see you in a week or two, next time you're on.'

'Do I get asked back after today?'

'Good Lord, of course you do! You were fantastic. Really fantastic.'

Rick pulls up outside Sasha's house and looks into her face. He doesn't smile. 'I'm a big fan of yours, Sasha,' he says. 'I know you weren't happy with what happened today. If you decided you didn't want to come back, we'd understand, but I hope you'll do the opposite. I hope you'll be back in two weeks' time, fighting your corner with all the flags flying. Trust me?'

'OK. Yes . . . I trust you,' Sasha says.

'Good. So, see you in two weeks?'

'Yes, I'll be there. Thanks for the lift. Thanks for the whiskey. And thanks for the moral support – I appreciate it.'

'My pleasure.' Rick shakes her hand. The contact with his palm, warm from holding the steering-wheel, pleases Sasha too much. She turns away fast, opens the car door and walks into her house without looking back.

8

As the sun streams in the next morning, Adam looks at his sleeping wife's solid form under the duvet and tells it that he is going to Oxford to see his father and does she want to come too? They can take the kids if they leave later.

'Uh-uh,' Sasha mumbles.

'Is that a no?'

'Yes. I mean yes, it's a no. Are you going now?'

'If you're not coming, then yes. I'll phone you.'

'Mm-hm. Night night.'

It's ten o'clock: the twins are in the garden with the badminton set Adam has just bought them, and Liffy has gone to her Saturday ballet class. They'd watched the videoed *Review* over breakfast.

'Fiddlesticks!' Matt shouts, batting the shuttlecock into the air.

'Poppycock!' Alex shouts, batting it back.

'*Piffle!*' they chorus in delight.

Adam backs the car away from its port in front of the house and turns out of their street on to the South Circular. He'd cross Kew Bridge, wiggle round the back-streets to the M4, then swing up the M25 to the A40 and on towards Oxford. He's relieved – after a long and fearful week of lying, evading and keeping his phone switched off – that it's the weekend and he doesn't have to pretend to be going to work.

The car is the only place he is ever alone. He switches on the radio for comfort. Anonymous babble, news or music can stop him hearing the protests inside him, usually muzzled by domesticity or work but crescendoing as soon as that rare solitude resumes. Guest commentators are talking about a suicide bombing in a Jerusalem shopping mall, and Adam lets the words wash over him, blanking out his mind. In transit there are no cares.

The traffic is heavy, but even so it is just an hour and ten minutes after leaving home that he pulls off the ring road on to Banbury Road and turns right into the familiar, tree-lined level stretch of Davenant Road. The view is almost identical to his earliest memories of it, aged around zero, except that today there are more cars, and more locked gates in front of the driveways. Opening his father's gates with his copy of the electronic fob, he feels the usual mixture of welcome home-coming and trepidation over his mother's absence, the posi-tive and negative jostling for space in his overloaded mind. He parks. Crunching across the gravel to the front door, past the walled garden, he can see the upper branches of the cherry tree that arches over the bench where Martha had loved to sit. The leaves are new and growing. The bench is empty.

'Ah, Adam. I've just made some coffee,' his father says.

Gerald – unlike Sasha or the kids, Adam feels – is glad to see him.

Father and son fortify themselves with coffee and then, with a glance of agreement passing between them, they set about the task for which Adam is really there. Armed with a roll of black plastic sacks, they open Martha's cupboards.

How cruel it is that when a human life is extinguished the material objects associated with it are not extinguished too. Martha's clothes hang where she left them, like a row of patient passengers waiting for a bus that will never come; her sweaters lie folded in the drawers, while her tights and socks and nightgowns muddle together in another.

Gerald stares into the depths of the wardrobe.

'I don't think I can do this,' he says.

'Dad, it's got to be done some time,' Adam encourages him, although his own instinct is to recoil in horror from the dead arms that no longer fill the blouses, the dead feet that have moulded the shoes, the dead heart that's vacated the woollen jerseys. He steels himself. 'We should get it over with.'

Gerald turns away.

'Dad. Go downstairs. I'll deal with it.'

'No, Ad. I don't want you to have to do it on your own.'

'You shouldn't have to do it. And who else is there to help? I'd rather do it alone.'

His father gives a silent assent and removes himself.

Adam begins to take out the clothes and pile them on to the bed. Handling them feels like touching part of another person – forbidden and frighteningly intimate – and bundling Martha's favourite suits, skirts and jerseys into black bags seems the ultimate in disrespect. Adam remembers his days as a political rebel, when finding the ultimate disrespect to the state and all its flaws (actually Martha and Gerald, although he hadn't realised that until later) had seemed a justifiable goal. Oh, youth.

On the mantelpiece above Martha's bedroom bookshelves, in the alcove of a one-time fireplace, stands Adam's favourite picture of the two of them: Martha with an arm around his bearded young self on the day his first exhibition opened.

They'd made up by then, at least on the surface. Adam's dropout phase lasted only as long as dropping out remained his primary desire. When he found that his longing for expression via paper and charcoal, canvas and paint was stronger than his urge to defy authority, Adam had had a miniature crisis that propelled him into what was then a brand new psychobabble organisation. This organisation, in a few dynamic evening sessions, persuaded its entire audience of several hundred people to swallow its pride and set about healing its life. In Adam's case, this entailed going home, taking his mother a bunch of flowers, helping with the washing-up and telling her he loved her. After that there was no going back.

If only, thinks Adam, packing the clothes into plastic sacks. There's no less productive thought in the world than 'if only'. Yet if only he had done it properly instead of taking short-cuts and papering over the cracks; if only he had talked through the problems with his mother instead of repeating to himself mantras about love and forgiveness. Repeat something often enough, the theory went, and it becomes true. Fiddlesticks. Poppycock. Piffle. He'd tried to be a free spirit. But at what point does a free spirit become a lost soul?

He'd found himself, or so he thought, only when he fell in love with Sasha – and there was no New Age solution in the universe that would solve the problems that that had created. It's too late now to right the wrongs. Perhaps it always was. Perhaps it was true that his mother would never have accepted any woman he wanted to marry.

'She's tense and neurotic,' Martha had said, when Sasha, who was still a dancer then, came to tea for the first time and refused to eat the home-made cake. It was the first of many such arguments.

'She's a bit of a snob,' Sasha had said on the way home to Edgware, referring to how Martha had turned up her nose when she'd said her father was in the construction industry.

'These dancers have no education – they don't learn about anything intellectual,' Martha had grumbled later, until Sasha enrolled for a degree in women's studies and gave up performing, at which point Martha said to Adam, 'Shouldn't she be out earning her share, instead of living off you like some kind of parasite? How self-centred, trying to go to university at this stage of life, when she's already got a perfectly good career.'

'She stifles you,' Sasha had said to Adam in the car, escaping after one Sunday lunch in Oxford. 'She always has and if you let her she always will. Because you're all she has in her life that she thinks is really hers. She has totally unrealistic expectations of you. She'll never be satisfied.'

'Tell me about it!' Adam had exclaimed.

'Look at all that stuff she has in the house. All those things she collects. She's completely out of touch with her feelings and she's acquisitive as hell, probably because she's so insecure. No wonder you decided property is theft.'

'Good of you to try and understand her,' Adam said.

That didn't last long.

'Pregnant? Couldn't she have been more careful?' Martha had yelled at Adam after he gently broke to her the news of Liffy's imminent arrival. 'I hope you're not expecting *the grand-mother* to come over and help out all the time.'

'Other people's mothers are only too glad to come and help with the grandchildren now and then,' Sasha had groaned, alone with the three tinies while Adam was at work six years later. 'I know she had a terrible childhood, I know you've always made allowances for her, but that makes it even more impossible to understand how she can make herself so objectionable.'

Adam did love his mother, deep down – they'd had such an interdependent relationship when he was small that it was physically impossible not to. He had kept hoping that she and Sasha would come to understand one another – each had problems that were perfectly logical if the other were only to think them through sympathetically – but no doubt the unspoken competition between them, over him, was too great to let them. So, to steer the most diplomatic course available between his mother and his wife, he had resorted to saying as little as possible to each about the other.

Adam ties the plastic handles into reef knots. Around him, on every surface, on every stretch of wall, on every floor of this ample Victorian villa and all along its fine central staircase, are Martha's things. Little bronze sculptures and bits of pottery from craft shops, lithographs (some, fortunately, by

Braque and Miró), carpets from a long-ago trip to Turkey, books new and second-hand, read and unread, shells from beach holidays, photographs of distant cousins ('They were all the family she had,' says Gerald), notebooks, felt-tip pens and biros, ancient tapes of plays, talks and symphonies that she'd made from the radio, several shelves full of shoes that she hadn't worn for decades, and a drawer crammed, mysteriously, with empty egg boxes. Gerald cannot take one step in that house, move his head a quarter-turn or lift his hand three centimetres without encountering some inanimate *thing* that is there because of Martha's inability to throw anything away.

Nowhere in the house is any painting by Adam displayed. Those he'd given them for safekeeping – in the secret hope that one day they'd put them up somewhere – were confined to the cellar, where Gerald and Martha thought they'd be safest because it was cool. Dropping out of Cambridge and entering art school had not been Adam's most popular decision at home.

Adam phones the Oxfam shop and fixes a time for them to bring a van and fetch the bagfuls of clothes. Then he turns to the task of distracting his father. 'Come on, Dad,' he encourages, in the cheery voice he sometimes uses to try to prise the twins away from their PlayStation, 'let's get out of the house. Let's go into town, have some lunch and go for a walk.'

'If you like,' Gerald says.

Adam drives and Gerald sits, passive, beside him; they inch along through the Saturday traffic until the grey-gold stone of the first college building comes into view. Adam negotiates the one-way system and, after much spiralling through a multi-storey car park, manages to find the last space.

From the car park they walk down into the centre of Oxford. Adam still loves his home town: the upturned ochre bowl of the Sheldonian Theatre, the graceful chapel spires, the heavy-doored college gateways, the gaping bookshops and the cafés that spill out on to the tourist-thronged pavements. Compared to the chaotic stresses of his London life, Oxford is an enchanted land. It restores Adam's faith in man-made beauty.

His roots are in every paving-stone. Every college brick and every peaked, red-tiled, mossy roof still whispers its memories to him as he walks by. A shadow at the side of the Sheldonian Theatre marks the spot where he had his first kiss at fourteen, with a girl called Camilla. There's a café where he used to meet politically oriented friends to grouch about Thatcher and Reagan and create, in words, Utopian societies on Thursday evenings, but it's had several facelifts, the latest featuring ivory paint, pots of pussy willow and light birch tables. Relatively unchanged is the pizza joint into which he and Sasha had virtually collapsed after he'd taken her home to meet Martha and Gerald for the first time. They'd laughed so loudly, from stress release, that the couple at the next table had asked the waitress to get them to tone it down a bit.

Gerald grumbles as they go, about traffic, tourists, lack of parking. Adam lets him. He is still a vigorous walker: they take a brisk pace along the paths past Merton College and Christchurch Meadow behind it. They stroll on to the towpath by the river and slow down to watch the first punts of summer go past under the hawthorn blossom and fresh willow leaves; they feel the spring sun warming their faces and the exhilarating sense of renewal rising from the scent of new sap. Gerald asks Adam if he's read any good books and begins to talk about how interesting he has found a recent tome on the fall of Berlin.

Adam would find it difficult to admit out loud that he prefers Oxford to London, the Cherwell and Isis to the full-blown Thames, the colleges to the City. If Gerald should ask him whose company he prefers, his father's or his wife and children's, he'd deny any preference. But just at the moment, he might have thought, in private, that he is more than happy to have an excuse to come to Oxford to spend a day with his widowed father. As long as they keep away from personal discussions, he enjoys Gerald's company and conversation:

Gerald, every inch the retired professor (his letterhead reads, 'Emeritus Professor of Modern History, University of Oxford'), has an objective way of talking about anything from college politics – which he is glad to have left behind on retirement – to the latest historical literature and the troubles in the Middle East.

Adam finds his attitude refreshing. Unlike Sasha, Gerald isn't a critic: he is a teacher and his role, as he understands it, is to analyse, clarify and communicate without passing judgement. Discussing books, politics or history with Sasha tends to leave Adam feeling as if he's been hit over the head repeatedly with a large metal spoon. In any case, these days his reading matter consists solely of bedtime stories for the twins, when he is home in time. Among his favourite activities are reading, gardening and sex with his wife. But for months now he has been almost always too tired, too worried or, more recently, too depressed to do any of them.

Adam and Gerald turn away from the river and meander down a narrow side-street, past ancient walls of golden brick and a few students, who glide along on bicycles. They soon come to Gerald's favourite restaurant, a tiny, family-run establishment with apple-green tablecloths and curtains, sprigs of lilac blossom in jade-coloured jugs, and food that is almost as good as home-cooking.

Adam looks down at the menu. He can't seem to focus on the meaning of the words. He feels exhausted.

'Adam,' Gerald says, 'forgive me if I'm wrong, but I wonder whether something is bothering you apart from everything I've made you do today.'

'You didn't make me do anything, Dad. I wanted to help.'

'You're not answering my question. That makes me certain you're worried about something.'

'It's nothing, Dad.'

'Are you sure?'

'Just a bit of trouble at work.'

'Tell me about it. It would do you good to get it off your chest – and I may be able to help.'

Adam takes a deep breath. His father used to examine *viva voce* exams. He can read a face as others would a book. 'You have to promise me that you won't say a word to Sasha,' he answers in the end.

'I give you my word. Now, what's going on?'

Adam begins to speak and as he explains the situation he watches Gerald's face darken as it used to when he had a bad mark for his homework or had transgressed by daring to switch on the television on a Saturday. The darkening used to put the fear of – well, the fear of he didn't know what into Adam's spirit. At least Gerald should be on his side now, after their mutual bereavement.

'Sasha doesn't know?' Gerald exclaims.

'How can I tell her? She'll be furious. She'll blame me.'

'How can you not tell her? You can't keep going off in the morning pretending to be at work! Doesn't she phone you?'

'She uses the mobile,' Adam points out. 'The company never allowed personal calls on its lines. I'll work something out, Dad. I know I have to.' Adam is well aware that he doesn't sound convinced.

'At least you've had time to start looking for another job?' Gerald prods.

Adam says nothing.

'If I were you,' Gerald says, 'I'd start phoning round some other magazines and find somewhere else to take my talents.'

'Dad, I don't *have* any talent for it. It was never what I wanted to do. And those are the kind of magazines I don't want to be a part of. I can't sell out any longer.'

'Adam, your kids need support, and support needs paying for. Now, I don't know how you got yourself into this situation in the first place, but can't you see you've got to do something about it? Or are you *completely* mad?'

A chirpy waitress with an Eastern European accent comes to

take their order, and Adam, smarting with pain as he'd known he would sooner or later, chooses the warmest and most filling soup on the menu: a chowder full of yellow and orange root vegetables and pale green slivers of leek.

Adam savours it, because it is teaching him something he could never have learned at Cambridge or art school. You can fill your stomach with nourishing, warming, organic food that will give you energy through the day, or you can fill it with junk that is deep-fried in much-used oil, or ground together out of the remnants of unfit cattle: things that pretend to be nourishing while they poison your system with substances that may kill you some day. You have a choice. This is why it's impossible for him to walk from the job he has abandoned straight into another that will lower the cage round him the moment he sets foot in its office. The question is where, in the world of paid work, he can find the colourful organic roots that he needs.

He doesn't tell Gerald this. At work, Gerald is non-judgemental. In his family, the outsized barrel of his critical capacity habitually spills its entire contents over Adam's head.

At the same moment, Sasha is trudging through Waitrose with Liffy drifting along beside her and the twins taking turns to go careering up and down the aisles pushing the trolley. Other shoppers make tutting noises as the boys race by, but avoid Sasha's gaze when they near her. Sasha, grinding her teeth, wonders, as she often does, why the British public cannot be more honest and upfront. They'll grumble in private and write letters to the supermarket and the local paper, but they'll never say, 'Control your kids!' straight to your face, let alone grab a twin and shout, 'Stop that, you little monster!' And she will not do that either, because aspirational suburban mothers like herself simply don't. Instead their haloes shine round them at the shops while they begin every sentence to a child with 'Oh, *dar*ling . . .'

Sasha picks a big tub of apricot yoghurt off the chiller cabinet shelf, swipes the barcode with the do-it-yourself scanner and places it in a bag in her trolley while she has the chance. The system is designed to make shopping quicker and easier: you scan the barcodes yourself and pay at a special check-out without having to queue for too long. In company with Liffy and the twins, though, the words 'quicker and easier' aren't especially appropriate.

'Mum,' Liffy protests, 'that's full fat. Can't we have this one instead?' She takes the yoghurt out of the trolley, swipes the barcode again using the scanner's 'subtract' button and puts it back on the shelf.

'Liffs, this is ridiculous. You've grumbled about everything I want to buy. This is too fattening, that's bad for you, beef has BSE, fish has mercury in it, vegetables and fruit are full of pesticides – if you worry about all this too much you're never going to eat *anything*.'

'Liffy's too fa-at! Liffy's too fa-at!' Alex and Matt intone in unison.

Sasha rounds on them: 'Liffy is not too fat and you know it. You're menaces! Both of you!'

'Well, I don't want to get any fatter,' Liffy argues back, taking the twins' part for once. 'I don't want to be the wrong shape for ballet.'

'Liffs, I've told you a million times, your shape is something you're born with. The amount of meat on your bones doesn't change your proportions,' explains Sasha, who is tiring of this.

'It doesn't help—'

'Mum! Mum! Can we have jelly beans? Can we have chocolate muffins?' the twins exclaim, watching a trolley go past packed with sweets and topped by a two-year-old in the baby seat.

'No,' Sasha says.

'I'd just like to put this broccoli back and get some organic instead,' Liffy says.

'No, Liffs. Organic costs almost twice as much.'

'Mum, when we've finished here can we go to the sports shop and look at the trainers, cos Julius's mum just bought him these cool new Nike—'

'No!' Sasha's temples start to hum as her neighbours push past, annoyed with her family for blocking the aisle. Where the hell is Adam when she needs him? Visiting his father. How selfish of Gerald, taking away a father from his children . . .

Matt has grabbed a big pack of chocolate muffins from the cake shelf.

'Put that back,' Sasha demands.

'No,' Matt says.

'Now, Matt.'

'But I *wanna*—'

'I want, I want, I want, I want, *I want*!' Sasha's fury spills over. 'Can't you do *anything* except *want things*? Can't you see that when you get what you want, you forget about it and just start wanting something else? Can't you see that there's more to life than wanting things?'

'Like what?' Alex plants himself in the middle of the aisle.

'Like enjoying a good story or some music. Like sunshine in the park. Like your family. Like your friends.'

'Our friends want things all the time too,' Matt says. 'And, Mum, those muffins are on special offer.'

Somewhere a pair of eyes is staring at Sasha, fixed and unblinking. It takes her a moment to realise that she is being observed scolding her children in the supermarket. And then she hears: 'Sasha! Hello! How lovely to see you!'

There, behind an overloaded trolley, in company with a skinny blonde woman and a boy of indeterminate teenage years, is Rick Byrne, gazing at her from those bright, foxy, I'm-very-pleased-to-see-you blue irises.

'Hello, Rick,' she replies, her mouth moving into an automatic smile. She wants a giant chiller cabinet to rise up and conceal her and her impossible daughter and beastly little boys, and her total inability to cope with them, from this intelligent, friendly, handsome BBC producer and his too-perfect wife. At least his child doesn't look any easier than her own: he is on the pudgy side and in their trolley is a plastic bag of ten smaller plastic bags containing artificially flavoured potato crisps.

'This is Marjorie, and this is Basty – Sebastian.'

'Liffy, Matt and Alex,' Sasha says, indicating.

'Gosh, you really are identical.' Blonde Marjorie smiles at the interested twins. And to Sasha: 'It's so nice to meet you. I'm a great fan of your stance on the programme.'

'Thanks. I'm glad someone is.'

'Do you watch it, Liffy?' Marjorie asks.

But Liffy isn't listening. She is standing beside the adults, motionless; her eyes have turned blank. She often does this now and Sasha has come to think of it as 'going off somewhere': her soul doesn't seem to be present in her body. It is as if she is listening to another voice, living a separate inner life, going through the motions of shopping in Waitrose without engaging spirit or mind. Not that mind or spirit *would* engage in a super-market if given the option . . .

'Liffy, Marjorie asked you something,' Sasha says. And Liffy starts, as if returning from miles away; she apologises and answers at once that, yes, of course, they video the programme and she watches it the next morning before going to ballet.

'I can see you're a dancer,' Rick remarks. 'You've got the posture.' And Liffy has: the long neck, the upright back and open shoulders, the duck feet. Whenever a group of young girls from the ballet school passes her in the street – as they often do – they give her a second glance, wondering if she might be one of them.

'You must come round some time soon,' Sasha says to Rick and Marjorie, though more to Rick than Marjorie. 'I'd say come over for coffee now, but Adam's gone to see his father in Oxford and to be honest everything's a little chaotic.'

'Of course, of course, don't worry, we have to be getting back. But I'll see you Friday week, won't I?' Rick says.

'You certainly will.' A thread of warmth zips between Sasha and Rick.

Marjorie's smile is fixed in her perfect makeup, but the brightness in her eyes dulls for a moment.

'Who's that, Mum?' the twins demand, as Rick and his family melt into the Saturday throng.

'The producer of *The Weekly Review*. They live up the road. Come on, guys, let's get finished here and then we can go and do something more fun. OK?'

Back at home – her brain still turning over what Rick might have thought, encountering his Amazonian reviewer as a frazzled lone mum in Waitrose – Sasha sees the light flashing on the answering-machine. While Liffy unpacks the shopping, examining each item in turn and finding the single most perfect spot for it in the fridge or cupboard, Sasha presses the button and hears her sister's tearful voice declaring that she has come home early from Paris because she and Vladimir are going their separate ways and can she come round for the evening because she doesn't want to be on her own?

'Oh God,' Sasha says aloud. 'That's all we need, Lisa having an emotional crisis.'

'Mum? I'm going upstairs to practise,' Liffy says behind her. Sasha, pressing out Lisa's number, nods and waves her away.

It hasn't taken Liffy many days of experimentation to discover that the less she eats the more energy she has. She hadn't believed Leila and her group at school when they'd told her, but it's true. Her body feels lighter; her mind feels clearer. She can even hear the voice of the Earth Prince with greater clarity than before. And clarity is all to the Earth Prince at the moment.

'Think clearly, see clearly, stay in control,' he whispers, while she winds the pink satin ribbons of a ballet shoe round her ankle, ties a reef knot and tucks in the ends. 'Stay in control.' He whispers to her while she practises, encouraging her: leap higher, aim for the sky, shine out like the sun. She has plundered her parents' modest CD collection for music to improvise to, and whether she uses familiar Tchaikovsky, unfamiliar Bach or some dated pop music, the Earth Prince is her dancing partner. She imagines him as he might look beside her: rather like Oberon in Frederick Ashton's *The Dream*, dark and forbidding and romantic all at once, clothed in brown and green, a wreath of leaves on his head. He keeps her going; he spurs her on when she is tired, reminding her that every minute of work is a minute well spent, that every move and every bend and every stretch burns up more energy and will keep her shape from expanding into unsightly bulges. She knows that that night she will be exhausted; and she will lie in bed and hear him whispering to her there too, imagining him holding her, warm and close. She doesn't know why, but to be warm and close is what she longs for and somehow a cat is not enough any more.

'When the world tips over,' the Earth Prince says, inside her head, 'you need to balance yourself. When the world has gone mad, you must stay sane. Keep your control, keep your strength. When you're strong you can cope with everything.'

But at night Liffy can't sleep. She's seen too much of the news. Dad would have comforted her by saying she'd been watching too much television, but this is the news, this is real. Terrorist bombs and shootings in the Middle East; starving children in Africa, their eyes huge, their bones and swollen, bloated, empty stomachs sticking out, their parents dead or dying of AIDS, themselves to follow soon; in Australia drought and forest fires; in the American Midwest a student shooting his classmates in school; in South America the economies of entire countries falling apart. And at home her little brothers want expensive new trainers, her friends worry about their music exams and she wants to get into ballet school and it all seems so pointless because the world has unbalanced itself, probably through global warming and government corruption and cruelty and war and animal testing. It's all jumbled up in her mind and she can't make sense of it. Her head is spinning and she feels too light, too insubstantial; she feels giddy and sick.

Holding the banister, she makes her way downstairs to the kitchen for a glass of water with just a dash of lemon squash in it, for some extra glucose.

Mum is sitting at the kitchen table with Lisa, who'd arrived after the twins' bedtime. Lisa's eyes are scarlet-edged. Mum is in lecture mode. Liffy hears her say, 'Lee, Vladimir is a prize bastard, we always knew that. He's never going to think of anybody but himself. You can't let him trample on you.'

'*I* left *him*,' Lisa says.

'Well, for Christ's sake, don't feel guilty about it.'

'I don't feel guilty. I miss him.'

'Don't miss him, then. He doesn't deserve it. He didn't deserve you.'

'It's funny,' Lisa says, mopping her eyes with a tissue, 'but up to a point I felt I knew him so well. We had all these strange things in common, things about a shared background a hundred years ago, more than about where we are now. Stupid things like washing our hair on its own, not when we're in the shower. And yet sometimes I didn't seem to know him at all – but I always felt he could see exactly who I was. I feel I've failed him.'

'You haven't. He's failed you.'

'Just because he wants a different way of life? I don't want to blame him. I don't think he's to blame.'

'Of course he's to blame! He wants to have his cake and eat it. And he can't. Simple.'

'Nothing is simple.'

Liffy makes a soft coughing noise.

'Hello, Liffs!' Sasha exclaims. 'What's up?'

'I wanted something to drink,' Liffy says, almost in a whisper.

'I love the zebra pyjamas.' Lisa smiles at her niece through her tears.

Liffy trots across the kitchen and gives her a kiss. 'Don't cry, Auntie Lisa,' she pleads. 'It'll be all right in the end.'

'Sweetie.' Lisa hugs her. 'You're so sensible. I sometimes can't believe you're only thirteen.'

The front door opens and shuts with a soft clump. Adam is back, at last, from Oxford.

'Ad?' Sasha calls.

Adam is pale and quiet as he walks into the kitchen. He sits down opposite his wife and her sister and pulls Liffy to him for a hug. As he begins to speak, Sasha understands what he is going to say before he says it, and knows that she'd known somehow that this was coming, that she'd guessed without ever admitting it, and that he'd deceived her by saying nothing about it before, and that now their whole future isn't going to be what they'd thought it would be, and that the walls are tumbling down between the Levy family and the outside world.

'What do you think, Sash?' Adam says at the end.

She says nothing. She is looking at him as if she has never seen him before.

'Sash? Have you been listening to a word of this?'

9

In all the world, Lisa thinks, there can be no food as comforting as the iced cinnamon twists in Louis Pâtisserie in Hampstead Village. She's sitting in its olde-worlde, wood-panelled tea room with Lindsey, drinking Lapsang Souchong and indulging in the cakes, as they often do.

'I still think it's a good thing, even if you feel awful,' Lindsey encourages, pressing Lisa's hand. 'You had to make the break before you could move on.'

'But can I move on? It's been weeks now. I think about him all the time, and the more I try not to, the worse it gets.'

Lindsey sighs in sympathy. Lisa knows how hard it must be for her friend to share her feelings – she knows of nobody happier with her partner than Lindsey.

'And now Adam's showing no signs of trying to find another job and Sasha is going completely nuts. Anyone would think she never earned a penny herself!'

'Is it the first time she's been the chief breadwinner?' Lindsey asks. Lisa reflects and realises that it is: years back, before the kids, Adam had supported Sasha while she studied. Was it possible that Sasha, feminist principles or none, had perhaps got used to that? That, as a result, she felt more insecure than she needed to?

'So the power base has been turned upside-down,' Lindsey suggests.

'Either that,' says Lisa, 'or something worse. I'm worried about Adam. His mother's death has really knocked him . . . He's just not himself at all.'

'Oh God, Lee. The poor kids.'

'That's what really gets to me.' Lisa finds her fists are screwed up and her nails hurting her palms. 'They haven't done anything, but they're the ones who have to suffer. Liffy's already too thin, I don't know if she eats properly and I'm scared for her. I don't like what I'm seeing, but there's nothing I can do about it.'

'Why not?'

'Because when I try to talk to her, all Sasha does is yell at me and say, "What do you know about bringing up kids?" And she's right, of course, because I don't know a damn thing.'

'Just be there for them.' Lindsey pours out second cups of Lapsang for them both. 'Let them talk to you when they need to. That's sometimes the most helpful thing of all. Now, Lee, we're having a chamber-music evening soon and I've got this nice singer I'd like you to meet—'

'Oh, Lin. Please don't. Not now.'

'You're right. Maybe you need some time on your own.' Lindsey pats her hand.

'Maybe.'

Lisa picks up her fork and puts it down again. She feels uncharacteristically as if she can't swallow the last of her cinnamon twist. A heavy blanket of exhaustion seems to be sweeping across her, to the point that she feels almost nauseous; the rich, sweet, heavy cake is more than she can stomach. She wonders if she's getting ill.

Sasha reads back over what she has just written. Then she highlights it with one swipe of the mouse and presses the delete key.

It is her fourth attempt to start her column. The mental dots are not connecting. Usually she sits at her desk and begins to type, and a few hours later there it is, a length of coherent and witty writing on a topic dear to everyone's hearts: the trains, the schools, the hospitals, domestic violence, dumbing down in the arts, public funding for regional theatre. Now the words are simply refusing to happen. She tries not to panic. She shifts in her chair, crosses and uncrosses her legs, turns the light on, turns it off again, strokes Bill, the ginger cat, who likes to keep her company while she works.

A pungent, unexpected aroma is drifting up the stairs and into her room. Sasha sniffs in disbelief. 'Adam,' she calls from the landing, 'you don't smoke.'

'Do now.'

Sasha marches down to find him. He is in the conservatory armchair, cigarette balanced between his third and fourth fingers, Ben the black cat on his knee. Beside him stand a cup of coffee and a brand new ashtray. Adam looks round at her and blows a perfect smoke-ring towards the glass roof. Sasha blinks. 'You haven't done that for a long time.'

'Too long.'

'But you don't smoke!'

'What else should I do?' Adam shrugs. 'I don't have a job any more.'

'What you do is, you go out and look for one.'

'On yer bike, is it? I never knew you were such a Tory, Sash.'

'Don't be obnoxious.'

'I can't go out and do the same thing all over again. It's not me. You know it's not me. You always knew that.'

'What you forget,' Sasha says, through her teeth, 'is that we have three children. Whether it's "you" or not is neither here nor there. It's been over a month now and all you can do is sit around being miserable.'

'It makes me realise,' Adam reflects, drawing in a long pull of smoke, 'that I was right all along in the old days. Capitalism *is* evil. We're all slaves to it. But we're only slaves if we let ourselves be slaves. We can still turn round and say no.'

'How exactly are our kids going to manage with a father who turns round and says no?' Sasha feels despair creeping up her legs like a plague of spiders.

'They'll manage. People always have.'

'Ad, *please*. Get a grip. I'm worried about you.'

'Instead of bugging me, why don't you go and do *your* work? You're the breadwinner now. Thank goodness we have a media celebrity in the family.'

Sasha turns tail and retreats to her study. She closes the door behind her and leans against it. She doesn't understand what is happening to her husband, and the less she understands, the more it hurts.

Liffy and Charley are in the school computer room at break. Charley is surfing, her fingers darting expertly across the keys. They are looking up exercises for firming the tummy, reducing the thighs and boosting the metabolism.

'Lying on your mat with your knees bent up and your feet flat, hold the small of the back against the floor. Lift the shoulders a few inches and tuck your hands behind your head to support it, but do *not* use the arms to propel you as you raise the upper body . . .'

'I didn't eat breakfast or lunch on Saturday *or* Sunday,' Charley announces.

Liffy feels ashamed that she'd cracked and eaten both, on both days. She regrets it now. Her stomach is sticking out and in the ballet-studio mirror she can see the fat gathering on her bottom. 'I go a bit wobbly if I have nothing at all,' she admits. 'I find it really difficult.'

'Just have a tiny bit of honey. It's all you need. You don't need much to put your blood sugar right. It won't hurt.'

But Liffy fears that it would.

'*You're fat. You're disgusting. You're unworthy of me.*' The Earth Prince's voice sometimes sounds loud in her head at night. '*You'll never amount to anything. You don't deserve me. You're useless. You have to lose your fat. You have to purify yourself.*' Liffy wants to protest, but she knows he's right.

★   ★   ★

Sasha walks up to the twins' school to fetch them and as a special treat takes them out for tea at Leonardo's. Matt eats the largest piece of chocolate cake Sasha has ever seen and Alex wants a croissant filled with cheese.

'They should do us a deal if we have the same thing,' Matt suggests. 'Two pieces of cake for the price of one. Don't you think, Mum?'

Sasha sighs. She sits under the white arches and the hanging plants, sipping a double espresso, letting the boys chatter and swipe punches at one another. Her column is late. She can't write about an intractable unemployed husband or an obsessive daughter, or how it feels to long to throw yourself from a great, great height into a warm sapphire sea.

Rick's image has worked itself into her brain like a splinter. The deeper she digs to dislodge it, the deeper in it goes. She can see his wide, embraceable wing span and his bright blue eyes whenever the distractions of the moment pause and leave her space. The pictures coil up, waiting to spring as soon as she lets go of her consciousness at night. The wretched man is haunting her dreams. She doesn't know how this has happened or why, or how to stop it, or whether she should even try to stop it.

Nothing like it has taken place before in all her years of marriage. She's had occasional crushes that have faded in days, weeks at the most – once a man she met on the Tube between Bond Street and Waterloo, another time a journalist who'd interviewed her about her book. She'd let well alone and resisted the temptation to get to know them better. Other men have pursued her now and then, but she has always told them where to get off. Now she's looking out for Rick's emails – two-line, noncommittal messages that arrive every three or four days. She agonises over them, wondering how to reply, how soon to reply, how not to write too much in reply. She aches to tell someone about him – but, of course, this is the one thing she can't do.

Unless her sister will listen.

She hasn't seen Lisa for ages – not since the appalling night when Adam came back late from Oxford and told them the truth. Perhaps Lisa is angry with her; she probably has a right to be, for Sasha is a tad ashamed of her reaction that evening.

She'd screamed at him, mostly because he'd told her nothing sooner. He'd not trusted her enough and she felt betrayed, kicked in the stomach; their old sexual contact had already fallen casualty to Martha's death and now this had come along to wreck the trust that had built up over their two decades together. And so she'd screamed at him, and he has scarcely confided in her since. All he's done is potter about in the garden (which looks a great deal better for it), read a few very fat books (*Daniel Deronda*, *The Corrections* and the latest Harry Potter), paint – covering canvases with blocks of violent, clashing, frightening colour – and start smoking again. Away from the canvas, he's bottling up his anger, packing it away with all the explosive potential of a carbonated drink in the freezer. He acts normally with the children, but surely they aren't stupid enough to believe him.

Oh, what a fine thing to be Lisa: unencumbered and un-committed, buried in a heap of Russian books in the British Library. Sasha imagines Lisa challenging her about her be-haviour. Lisa wouldn't, of course: she lives and lets live and expects others to allow her that privilege in return. But Sasha imagines, and hears herself explaining. *I can't cope. I can't make him see sense. I can make a whole nation read my arguments and agree or disagree with me, but I can't get through to my own husband.*

A squeal brings her back to the café – one twin has swiped at the other too hard and tears of outrage are the result. Sasha barks at them – 'Alex, Matt, I *won't* tell you again!' The silent image of the tropical sea and a high diving-board rears up, beckoning.

                    *   *   *

Adam, drawing in a long stream of nicotine from his twenty-fifth cigarette of the day, decides to take a train to Twickenham, walk by the river and sketch. It has been years since he last had time for riverside walks, let alone sketching. He digs out a half-used A3 pad from the back of the broom cupboard in the utility room, slings it into a plastic bag with a couple of pencils and wanders the familiar route to the station.

Adam does not miss work, but he misses the little details of getting there. He misses the tired people on the train, people who never speak to each other but whose lives he used to follow via their mobile-phone conversations. He misses the friendly faces at the station: Daniel, the station-master from Ghana who has a personal greeting and big smile for everyone; Claudia, the bright-eyed Mexican girl in the coffee shop who practises the guitar between making cappuccinos; the moustachioed newsagent – nobody is quite certain what his name is or where he comes from, but Iran is suspected – who only has to glimpse you to know which paper you're about to buy.

He crosses the footbridge; the train isn't due for five minutes and, as it turns out, will be another five minutes late. He wanders into the coffee shop to buy a cappuccino from Claudia. It seems a hundred years since he's last had one.

'Hey, Adam! How are you?' says Claudia. Her vivid dark eyes remind him, disconcertingly, of Sasha twenty years ago. 'Have you been away?'

Adam explains, and watches Claudia's face fill with concern. 'What will you do?' she asks. 'Will you look for something else?'

'I don't know yet. I don't want to work in magazines any longer.'

'I'm not surprised.' Claudia nods. 'You were an artist at first, weren't you? I'm sure you should get back to that.'

'I don't know.' Adam takes the steaming cup Claudia offers him. 'But I'm sure something will turn up.'

'Of course it will. Just give it time. Seriously, Adam. It's for a reason. There's something out there waiting for you to do it. There's something out there waiting for me too – I'm not going to make coffee for the rest of my life! We'll know it when it comes to us. I promise you.'

'I'm sure you're right,' says Adam. He wishes he could believe it. Why is it that he finds more sympathy at the station than in his own home?

At Twickenham, he wanders down the alleyway past the parish church to the riverside. The Thames slides by, verdigris at high tide, with a few ducks riding along on the surface; the trees are in full leaf and rustle softly overhead. Away from the four walls that should be his refuge, Adam feels he can breathe again. There's an oppressiveness in the house these days, clinging to the Edwardian bricks and the rose-velvet curtains. He can't run it to earth. He can't hunt it down and blow it up in its cave. It's hiding in the molecules of the air; it's buried in Sasha's barbed-wire words, the twins' relentless attention-seeking, the bizarre way Liffy has started to eat apples – slicing them into micro-thin slivers and chewing each one fifty times. It's elusive and destabilising, and it hurts him more at every moment.

Adam walks along the towpath beside the Georgian mansions, the White Swan pub, the walled splendour of Orleans House. How strange to think that all the years he has been sitting at a wide screen designing pages that will last a few weeks only to be thrown away, commuting on overcrowded trains, dealing with children's demands and seeing his mother die by inches, the river and the trees and the buildings have carried on oblivious around him.

Adam sits down on a bench in the sun and watches some swans diving for river weed. When they resurface, grey droplets slide down their necks and off into the water, leaving them dry, if less white than they should be. He wishes he could let the air of his home wash away from him in the same way. He lights a cigarette. He'd given up smoking when Sasha became pregnant with Liffy. God, how he's missed it. He takes out his sketch pad and a pencil and begins to draw the outline of a streamlined, diving swan.

Half an hour later he looks down at his new handiwork. When he sees what he's drawn, a sackload of depression bursts open somewhere in his mind. The diving swan is a beautiful, long, curvaceous, feminine shape, but is almost obliterated by the river around it; where there should be water there is frantic, over-intense cross-hatching, writhing coils of river weed, floating debris – a Coke tin, a McDonald's wrapper, polystyrene cups, a discarded newspaper and something that looks like a used condom. The swan swims from right to left, pointing its long neck downwards. There is no sign that it will ever surface again.

Adam closes his sketch pad and fumbles for another cigarette, wondering how much longer he can manage to be a strong man who never cries.

'Adam, please don't,' says Sasha at the dinner table. 'If you've got to smoke, go outside to do it.'

'Is this not my home any more?' Adam demands. He sounds as sulky as Liffy, maybe more so.

'Dad, it's revolting,' Liffy chimes in. 'Yuck.'

'Dad, Matt hit me,' Alex whines.

'Shut up,' says Adam. The twins freeze like rabbits on a road. Sasha thrusts her chair back and clumps to the stove to fetch the food she has prepared for the foot soldiers in the war zone that is the family kitchen. Haddock fillets, mashed potato, peas, salad. She dishes it up in silence, not looking into any of the pairs of eyes that watch her serving spoon move from platter to plate.

The twins fall on their food and wolf it down almost without chewing. Liffy spears a flake of haddock with her fork and moves it round her heap of mashed potato as if drawing an elaborate geometric pattern, then nibbles at a corner. She begins to eat her peas, one at a time. Sasha can hardly believe what she's seeing. 'Liffs, do eat up,' she pleads.

'I'm not very hungry,' Liffy says, in a low squeak. 'I had a chocolate biscuit on the way home with Charley.'

'One biscuit shouldn't have hurt, and you've been doing your ballet since then. Can't you at least eat more than one pea at a time?'

'I like them like this.'

'Oh, for God's sake, Liffs!' Adam explodes. 'Just eat it, can't you? What's the big deal? Stop making such a damned fuss about it!'

Liffy turns her big, reproachful eyes to him and puts down her fork. 'I'm really not very hungry, Dad,' she says, calm, controlled. 'Please may I be excused?'

'No, you may not! Eat your dinner!'

'I can't.'

Sasha smells burning and realises she's left the gas flame on. 'Shit,' she exclaims, forgetting the children, as she dives across the room and sees her cat-patterned tea towel, left too close to the hob, crackling merrily into red and orange fire on the worktop. She seizes a mug and flings water over the conflagration. The twins try, half-heartedly, to chortle. Sasha waits, a knot tightening in her stomach, for Adam to make a remark about the misplacement of flame in the house: he can't light up inside, yet she's nearly set fire to them all through her absent-mindedness. Absent-mindedness? Sasha has never in her life been absent-minded. She grinds her teeth. No wonder she's distracted.

She surveys her family. Adam, scruffy and angry and exhausted. The twins, confused, annoying, too young to understand. And Liffy, not eating.

Why is Liffy not eating? Liffy, so bright, so pretty, such a perfectionist, Liffy, always considered so mature for her age. She can't be getting into *not eating*. It can't be happening.

Surely not. It must just be a phase – mustn't it? Surely Liffy can't be entering the zone that strikes horror into Sasha's heart, as into the heart of every middle-class mother with a teenaged daughter. Sasha knows about anorexia. She knows too much about anorexia, coming from the ballet world. And now Liffy's not eating. But Liffy hasn't *not eaten* before, not really. Anyway, the atmosphere in the room is enough to make anybody lose their appetite at the moment. Sasha feels a little sick and wobbly herself.

'Could I have some fruit?' Liffy asks. 'It's all I feel like.'

'Yes, of course!' Sasha exclaims, almost giddy with relief. 'Have as much as you want.'

She watches, with some thankfulness, as Liffy munches her way through an orange, an apple and a large bunch of grapes, although she refuses the ice-cream the twins demand. She's eating. Eating fruit, but eating nonetheless. All's well. All has to be well. All manner of things have to be well. Haven't they?

Adam wanders out of the back door and Sasha sees him fiddling with a cigarette lighter on the patio. The twins, with her permission, head for their PlayStation and Liffy insists on helping her wash up, although Sasha tells her gently not to worry, to go and do her homework. She's never seen anyone wash up as fastidiously as her daughter. She watches Liffy's slender hands and intent, pale face and wonders at the mix of adoration, anxiety and bafflement that assails her at the idea that this dear girl is her own flesh and blood yet she has not a shred of a clue what's really going on in her mind.

Sasha retreats to her study. She still hasn't written her column. She has until ten o'clock tomorrow morning to file copy and she hasn't typed one word that she likes. And she needs to relax her frazzled brain, allow the images that rise up unbidden in it to offer her their untold, irresistible escape. At her computer, in the quiet aftermath of the ghastly dinner, Sasha closes her eyes and lets them.

Rick's face is haunting her. Her mind is full of green Irish hills and blue Irish lakes that she's never seen. Her hands are over-sensitised, longing as if on their own for his skin to touch. The images in her head are almost too sweet to swallow.

After the show on Friday, Rick had caught her eye and she'd understood and followed him down the corridor to his office, where the Irish whiskey was waiting in the cupboard. At the idea of being alone with him again, her heart had begun to race; her cheeks flushed and she hung back in the corridor, afraid he'd notice. How daft, she thought, for a woman of forty to behave like an infatuated schoolgirl. Yet how marvellous, how exquisite, to realise that she still could.

Rick poured whiskey and Sasha looked at his shoulders, wishing she could put her palms flat against them.

'How's your lovely daughter?' he said, when they'd clinked glasses.

'She's being a little strange at the moment. She doesn't seem quite – well, it's not that she isn't all there, but she sometimes seems to be somewhere else.' She was falling over her words. She didn't want to let her feelings get the better of her: she feared losing control. She breathed slowly and forced steadiness into her voice.

'Hormones.' Rick nodded. 'We're having some problems with Basty – have done for a while. Classic couch-potato syndrome.'

'Does he use his drum-kit?'

'He's bashed around on it a few times, but he's too lazy. He sits and eats junk food and watches television and messes around with his computer games.'

'What were you doing at his age?'

'Me? Let me see . . .' Rick smiled, more to himself than to her, Sasha thought. 'I was fifteen in 1970. I played LPs of the Rolling Stones too loud and annoyed my mum. I played rugby on Saturdays. I tried smoking dope for the first time and nearly got myself expelled from school, but they gave me the benefit of the doubt. Still, I was getting regular exercise. I was out with my mates. I ate like a horse, but I needed the energy because I burned it up so fast. And I didn't eat crisps. I ate them with the beer I wasn't supposed to drink at the pub I wasn't supposed to be in, but I didn't eat them all day long.'

'Food neurosis is usually a symptom,' Sasha said, 'rather than a cause. But I don't know what it's a symptom of.'

'Well. Ours is perhaps not the happiest home in the world,' Rick admitted. 'Basty might be in better shape if he had some brothers or sisters.'

Sasha thought she'd misheard – was Rick really confiding such personal matters in her? 'You never wanted more children?'

'We wanted them, but it seems they didn't want us. Marjorie miscarried three times.'

'Oh my God. I'm sorry.'

'Nothing one can do about it, but it was hard for her and somehow it seems she blamed me. I don't know why.'

'Perhaps it's comforting to blame someone, even if it's pointless.'

'Ah, who knows? I don't think she forgave me, though.'

Oh shit, Sasha thought, *is he about to tell me that his wife doesn't understand him?*

'It's not exactly that she doesn't understand me,' Rick went on, as if reading her mind, 'but we don't communicate very well. She wears – well, I call it her mask. She has to look perfect to the outside world. She has to pretend everything's perfect. Because then maybe it'll make things perfect. Repeat something often enough and eventually you start to believe it. She can't bear anyone to suspect that she doesn't have the best marriage in the country, or the happiest home, or the brightest child. Trouble is, she doesn't have any of them, and I can't right that wrong for her.'

Sasha accepted a refill of whiskey, knowing that their level was changing, not certain what to do about it. How out of practice she was in such situations. She hesitated, her nerve failing for a moment before she found enough guts to explain the state of her own marriage.

Rick's reaction wasn't quite as she'd anticipated. 'Adam sounds as if he needs a bit of help,' he said.

'Adam needs to pull his socks up and find a job.'

'It's hard when a parent dies. It happens to us all and we're never ready to accept it, however old we are.'

'My father died years ago,' Sasha told him, 'and I'm fine.'

'You are now. How were you at the time?'

She tried to remember. She could picture herself howling her head off, and Adam holding her and letting her cry. He hadn't *done* much, but he'd been there and that was all she'd needed. And although she knew that, she didn't know how to copy it. She wanted things to be done. She wanted action. She wanted rolling cameras, bright lights, directions, steps that must be danced in the proper order. She had no choreography for this situation and somehow she couldn't find the right tools to create her own.

'It wasn't easy,' she said. 'But I suspect the problem is more than that. I suspect the problem is that we don't get along the way we used to.' She hadn't meant to say it, but she'd wanted to too much. Before she'd married Adam, she hadn't been one to hang around being subtle when a man she liked was on the scene. She'd gone to bed with Adam almost at once – and with several men in Paris when she'd studied there, before she met Adam again. Either you wanted them or you didn't.

And now, she saw, Rick wanted her. Something at the edges of his eyes melted. She watched him, half disbelieving, as he came towards her; she saw his hand extending, as if in slow motion, towards her waist while the other lifted her chin and made soft contact with her neck before his lips followed suit.

For a second Sasha's knees dissolved under her; her hands reached up to hold his shoulders and her mouth to press the mouth she'd been dreaming of. It didn't feel as she'd expected.

How extraordinary to taste different lips; how peculiar to feel different hands on her back, caressing her waist and her behind; how weird to accommodate an unfamiliar tongue exploring her teeth. His hair under her hand was fair and straight and fine, not dark and wiry like Adam's. The new picture clashed head on with the old and Sasha moved away, dizzy and parched with thirst.

'It's not that I don't like it,' she said. 'It's just so odd.'

Sasha lifts her hands to the keyboard and begins to type words, sentences, lines, paragraphs, about the difference in the lives of teenagers twenty-five years ago and their lives today and why so many are getting too fat.

10

Lisa can't get her breath. She's never hyperventilated in her life before. She opens the bathroom window and gulps in oxygen, probably too much, pleading that something will jolt her awake and she'll find herself coming round from a nightmare. She paces backwards and forwards the few steps her bathroom allows her across its cork floor, half an eye on her watch, each second an eternity.

The time is up. Lisa closes her eyes and renders a wordless prayer. Then she looks into the liquid. It contains a double blue line.

'Shit,' Lisa says. 'Fuck.'

Lisa hardly ever says either word, but now she says them both again and again. She retreats to her bed and lies flat, willing herself not to cry. Crying isn't going to help.

It must have been the last time, after Yasha and Elena's wedding. Ten days into her cycle and hence lethal. The cap must have dislodged. Or maybe she'd been too distracted and upset to notice that she'd not fitted it properly.

The worst of it is that she has not stopped missing Vladimir for one minute since she came back from Paris, and the creature giving rise to the blue line is the embryo of his child. A child of Vladimir's that is also hers. Lisa flinches at the idea and tries to ban it from her mind. Turning a lump of cells into something human is the last thing she must do right now, because that's all it is, a lump of cells, growing like a tumour inside her body. Not a living being with a soul waiting for consciousness among the stars.

She's on her own now: she can't afford to move house, she has no room to have a baby here, no doubt Vladimir will have nothing to do with her any more, the college won't take kindly to her demand for maternity leave, although she has a right to it, and her research will be put on hold, possibly for ever, because she can't afford childcare on her junior lecturer's salary and she'll never see another penny from her book. There's one solution. She must tell nobody and she must go to a clinic and get rid of the lump of cells, have it vacuumed away and forget it ever existed. Lisa pushes her face into her pillow and howls, hoping her neighbours won't hear her as clearly as she usually hears them.

When the telephone sounds she is shaken out of her despair. For a second she hesitates to answer, but an irrational suspicion that it might be Vladimir propels her hand to the receiver and she forces out a greeting, wiping the tears from her face.

It's not Vladimir; it's Sasha. It's too late for Lisa to pretend she is an answering-machine. She asks her sister how she is.

'Oh, God,' Sasha says, 'it's impossible. Adam's doing nothing, being utterly useless and saying that capitalism is evil. Liffy sits in her room and sulks or practises her ballet and sulks doing that. The twins won't stop kicking each other. I don't know what to do with any of them. One has to laugh, really.'

Lisa holds the receiver slightly away from her ear. She has no intention of letting her sister know about her own problem. It had been mortifying enough to have to hear Sasha's 'I told you so' on the news that she'd left Vladimir.

'How about meeting up for lunch?' Sasha says.

'OK.' Lisa is unable to think of a suitable excuse in time.

On reflection, Lisa decides Sasha's call might have been a good thing. It's reminded her that life must go on and that she must be ready to mark exam papers and listen to the final-year students' recitals and plan something to do over the summer beyond having as rapid an abortion as possible.

'Sumer is icumen in', as the ancient song says: the temperature is soaring, the London Underground has been declared too hot for the transportation of animals, let alone people, and the students are drinking too much as their exams judder to an end. Life has to go on, and go on it will, whether she likes it or not.

Liffy, too, is sitting exams – exams for the sake of exams, not ones that will affect her future. Charley and her family have invited her to go on holiday with them in August: they are renting a villa for two weeks on a Greek island. As her own family seems incapable of organising a weekend at home, let alone a fortnight abroad, Liffy is thrilled at the idea, although the pit of her stomach feels less certain. Charley has hinted that she has secrets to tell about beloved Robin that she can't possibly speak about at school and must on no account type into her computer for fear that an instant message or email could somehow be intercepted or retrieved. Liffy makes escape plans, telling lies at home (only white lies, of course) that she's going to Charley's house and more white lies to Charley that she has to practise her ballet extra hard. She walks up the hill and into Richmond Park to lose herself amid the ferns.

They grow so high in midsummer that when she hides among them, lying flat on the prickly ground, they rise far above her, soaring surreally towards the arching sky and the fierce sun. She stretches out on her back, soaking in the rays and feeling the earth strong and limitless beneath her.

Except that the earth is limited. As she sees it, as she feels it, the earth is a living organism and, like all living organisms, it must die. People will kill it before its time, plundering it and burning it and polluting it. They will perish with their own planet and they're too stupid and selfish to stop before it's too late.

And yet it is so good, so beautiful. The sun fills her body with warmth. So often, these days, she feels chilly even during the heat wave, even during this strange, excessive summer where the sky stays unnaturally blue all day long. And the pressure of sun and earth together brings out a longing for something warm and physical that she doesn't have and can't expect for years, but that terrifies her at the same time. She closes her eyes and as she dozes she imagines the Earth Prince reaching out for her as he rises from his element below and draws her down and further down, infusing her whole self with the emerald life force of the summer ferns.

When she eventually goes home, she feels slightly sick and ashamed of herself, yet she's also annoyed by the mundane nonsense going on in the house. Dad is trimming something in the garden, Mum is yakking to Cindy on the phone and the twins are on their PlayStation. She could have been back among the ferns, back with the Earth Prince in the enchanted world that lures her so irresistibly. She could go there – and just stay. Sometimes she's afraid that she might.

She worries in case her cover is blown, in case Charley has rung or Mum has phoned her house, but nobody looks up from what they're doing. None of them seems remotely interested in where Liffy has been. If she went, if she let the Earth Prince take her away into his world and keep her there, would they even notice?

Liffy gives herself a little shake and tells herself not to be an idiot. Time to forget it: time to get stuck into ballet practice.

'I don't like that friend of hers, the one called Charlotte,' Sasha tells Lisa over salad in Covent Garden. 'She's a bad influence. I reckon she's a pathological liar. She's always come up with ridiculous stuff. The first time I met her, she said her house was a palatial interior-designed one-off. Is it? Hell, no, it's a standard semi-detached job like all the others . . .'

Lisa has been having morning sickness. She can only pick at her lunch. She nods and says nothing.

'And now she's invited Liffs on holiday with them. They're going to Greece for two weeks. Which is good, because of course we're not going anywhere just at the moment, things being as they are.'

Sasha's eyes are wandering beyond Lisa, as if she's looking out for someone who isn't there. Lisa wonders who. 'Liffy seems to have gone very quiet recently,' she says, 'and I'm worried that she's not eating properly.'

'I don't know what to do with her. Or the twins. It's un-believable, the way the world can be falling to pieces around kids' ears and they don't even notice. They're so self-absorbed that I don't think they'd notice if the house blew down.'

'That's a little harsh, isn't it?'

'You, dear sister, don't have to live with them.'

'You're frustrated,' Lisa diagnoses. 'Why don't you think about doing that other book?'

'How am I supposed to write another book with three impossible children and a useless husband to look after?'

Lisa considers an appropriate response and is pleased with what comes to her: 'As best you can. It's up to you, not them. And if it sells, it's good for everyone.'

Sasha chews her salad. Her eyes suggest that she's some-where else. She hasn't spotted Lisa's pallor or lack of appetite. To be fair, Sasha is not herself either: she's barely smiled. Lisa wonders what is distracting her so.

'You mustn't tell a soul about this,' Sasha says, as if in response to the unasked question. 'Do you promise faithfully?'

Lisa swings into a time-warp: they are children again and she is confiding secrets in the teenaged Sasha with the inevitable 'Do you promise faithfully?' – words that guarded, as if with divine power, such solemn issues as what she was going to give her best friend for her birthday.

'I think,' Sasha says, without waiting for Lisa's 'of course', 'that I may have met someone.'

'What?' Lisa's picture of Sasha's life breaks into a million

shards of coloured glass. Sasha's eyes have lit up and deep-
ened. She is fidgeting with a loose strand of her hair.

'He's intelligent. He's charming. He's a doer, not a dreamer.
That matters.'

'So, Sasha, do your home and your children!'

'Oh Lee, don't be sanctimonious.'

'Come on, Sash. You disapprove yourself. You wouldn't be
asking me to disapprove for you if you didn't.'

Sasha won't meet her gaze. 'What shall I do?'

'For God's sake, whatever you do, think first. Think about
what's going to happen to your kids.'

'So many kids grow up in step-families these days. I don't
think they'd even notice the difference. It's normal.'

'Are you saying that you intend to leave Adam and take up
with this man, whoever he is?'

'God knows,' Sasha says, 'but he's on my mind. I can't think
about anything else. I can't sleep. I'd forgotten what it's like.'

Lisa hasn't. It has been almost two months since she last
spoke to Vladimir, but his image is constantly and indelibly
implanted in her mind and heart. In her state, how can she
even consider advising an older – if not wiser – sister who
might be about to make the best, or worst, move of her life?
'I have to get going,' she apologises. 'I'm sorry to rush off, but
I've got an appointment.'

Lisa sits on a leather chair edged with brass studs and fills in
a card with her name, address, email, phone, fax and mobile
numbers, her date of birth, her marital status, her medical
history (operations: appendix, aged eleven) and declares that
she is not diabetic and has never suffered from hypertension.
On the other side of the desk, the doctor glances over what
she's written and ticks some boxes of her own, whose purpose
Lisa doesn't know.

'It's a very simple procedure,' says the doctor, whose eyes seem
unnaturally pale, 'and you can go home the same afternoon,

though you may find it useful to book yourself a few days off work afterwards. Now, would you like to see a counsellor? This is a free service that we offer to all our clients.'

Lisa shakes her head. Her lip is moving of its own accord and she bites it. The doctor's pale eyes are shrewd, but she remains tactfully silent.

'OK, Miss Wood – sorry, *Dr* Wood – we'll see you on Friday at ten.'

'Yes. Thank you,' Lisa says. She gets up to go. Her feet feel weighted down with stones.

At home she ditches the cool, clever detachment of Stravinsky for the better company of Beethoven – excellent for promoting inner strength. Igor jumps on to her lap and begins to press her knees with his front paws. She tries to strike the right balance between cuddling him and stopping him digging his claws into her flesh. Beethoven's last string quartet pleads, entreats and screams: *'Muss es sein?'* And the answer comes at last, joyous and accepting: *'Es muss sein!'* It must be.

On Thursday night at ten o'clock Lisa sits amid the clutter of her living room, passing the time by trying to file papers that have lain about in chaos for weeks. Igor helps by attacking them, singling one out, separating it from its flock, as if it were a gazelle, then moving in for the kill, crunching it up between paws and teeth.

'Igor. I need that.' Lisa tries to remove the miniature black and white lion from his papery prey. In twelve hours, she will go into hospital and be liberated from the spark of life that wants to annex her body. She glances at the phone. It does not ring.

Lisa can't stop herself any longer. She presses out oo, the international code, 33 for France and 1 for Paris, then the eight digits that make up Vladimir's number. Long beeps indicate the French telephone ringing; then comes a click and his recorded voice, a Russian trying to speak fluent French, the same words she's heard a hundred times before. No doubt he's away, giving a concert somewhere. Or perhaps he is there, practising but not answering the phone – at this hour he would just have begun. Perhaps he is at home, but in bed with someone else, or taking a new girlfriend out to La Coupole to eat a platter of iced shellfish.

The beep sounds in her ear and she struggles for words. They won't come. She rings off. Vladimir would hear a message that was not a message but silence. He would dial to find out what number had called, but none would show up, it being international. He would leave it there. He wouldn't phone her and say, 'Did you try to ring me?' He'd never know that she had cheated his only child out of its chance of existence.

Lisa pours herself a brandy; then another. Neither dulls the misery, and she doesn't enjoy them because alcoholic drink doesn't taste as good as usual, thanks to her rampaging hormones. She tries to stroke Igor, but Igor is now in a mood and doesn't want to be stroked, as he advises her with a threatening swing of a paw. She doesn't dare to tell any of her friends what's happening to her – she's avoided all their calls this week and last, pleading exams to mark. Outside, the summer night is fragrant with blossom and sap in Andrew's garden – for such a violent man, he's an astoundingly good gardener.

The sound of a sprinkler and the scents of roses and geraniums and warm, wet leaves drift through Lisa's open bedroom window. Inside her wardrobe, the purple suede shoes stand in their box on the left of the shoe rack, redundant, unused. She goes to bed and lies there, breathing in and out.

On Friday morning Sasha, her mind in Ireland among cool, clear lakes, walks home from the twins' school. Adam is still in bed. In Queen's Park, Lisa and Sasha's mother, Sally, walks a neighbour's dog for a small fee. In Oxford, Gerald reads the *Telegraph* over solitary coffee. In Hammersmith, Liffy is at her desk in school beside Charley, chattering before assembly about what clothes they will take to Greece. In West Hampstead Lisa, with a weekend-sized bag waiting by the door, can't make herself leave her flat. Her feet won't do it. She is due at the clinic at ten and as the minutes tick by it becomes clear to her that she won't be there in time; eventually, that she won't be there at all.

Her mind is an open, grassy field for a battle between two images. First, a struggling single mother, perpetually exhausted by a demanding child and unsympathetic employers, the para-phernalia of washing-machine, high chair, pram, cot, toys, Babygros, jars of pulped vegetables, screams, nappies and guilt scattering through every darkened area of her too-small flat; then another image where nothing is present but a ray of light filled with sunbeams and among them a child – a little girl – with Vladimir's dark curly hair and a stubborn Wood family mouth like Liffy's, her arms raised to the light, breathing in the sunbeams, dancing. The first image, full of chaotic mess and tangible, plastic, disposable items, springs from her mind; the second, pure, clear and imaginary, springs from her heart and none of the other's abrasion can touch its inner truth. He might never know, but she will, and that is enough.

Inner truth, she understands, is the only truth.

The leather chair is vacant; the time ticks by. In the clinic, the pale-eyed doctor glances at the clock, calls the receptionist, confirms her suspicions and smiles.

Nicholas Roerich [Lisa writes] *never forgave Stravinsky for what he saw as a betrayal of trust, friendship and collegial fraternity.* The Great Sacrifice, *or* The Rite of Spring *as it came to be called, was never intended as a work of a single art form, the concert piece as it is known today – taken up by ambitious choreographers yet transcending movement and design with the visceral, primitive power of its sound. Its origins lay in the visions of Serge Diaghilev, their roots going back to the*

Wagnerian concept of the Gesamtkunstwerk, *the Entire Art Work, combining the finest in music, drama, dancing, design and performance. This had rapidly become the standard ideal for Russian artists.*

The impresario Diaghilev was no creative artist himself, but understood the crucial role of the facilitator – a person with the unerring ability to recognise greatness or potential greatness in the arts, the wherewithal to nurture and guide it, and the dynamism to bring together practitioners of different arts and let them stimulate one another's creativity.

Stravinsky was just one part of the Rite. *Roerich's designs – brilliant, folksy, idealised, displaying the earth in riotous spring – carried at least half of the work's message, making palpable the unseen character of the tribe's devotion: the sun god Yarilo, manifest through the image of the flourishing, dependent, grateful* Earth. The Great Sacrifice *is not, perhaps, aiming to propitiate an angry god, but rather to return a child of the earth to the earth in humility as a symbol of fair exchange . . .*

Lisa longs to phone Vladimir and read him the start of the paper, which she has been preparing for presentation at a conference this winter – one that now she may not be able to attend. She used to love talking to him almost as much as sleeping with him. A few months ago they'd have discussed all these ideas, bounced notions backwards and forwards between Paris and London and argued and laughed together. Now there is silence.

I'll have to do it alone, Lisa reflects, and do the best I can. I can do nothing more than that.

11

Adam has forgotten how to relax. Lying in bed at eleven in the morning, too tired to get up because he's been awake since five with what feels like a black elephant slumped on his head, he wonders if he's ever known.

He had no sibling to spread the load of parental expectation. His deep-etched childhood memories don't contain bright balloons and birthday cakes sprinkled with brilliant-hued hundreds and thousands. His inner picture of himself lingers, sober and unsmiling, at the table with his parents on either side, more a man than a boy at the age of twelve. At the weekend he went to Hebrew lessons. At school, at Jewish prayers, he wore a *kippah* – something he hasn't donned for years, at least not until his mother's funeral. On Friday nights his father would say a blessing over a goblet of sweet kosher wine and his mother would light candles and gesture over them and some slices of chollah with her hands, welcoming the light of the Sabbath into their home. We must keep our traditions alive, explained Gerald, because nobody else will do it for us. Ignore them and they will die out. After five thousand years.

'Why?' Adam asked. He didn't understand. All he knew was that he was not allowed to watch television on Friday evenings or Saturday and by Monday the conversation at school would go over his head because he'd missed the latest episode of *Doctor Who* – he could only watch it in the dead of winter when darkness had fallen, ending the Sabbath, by the time it came on. Now, looking back, he couldn't even remember why he'd been so eager to watch *Doctor Who*, or whatever programme it might have been that induced him to become so furious and resentful.

To complicate matters, Martha was never furious or resentful – until Sasha appeared – although she had the most cause to be. Aged thirteen, Martha had been placed on the Kindertransport from Berlin to London. Children, the British government had decided, could reasonably be saved from Nazi persecution – a few, anyway – and it was therefore best to separate from their parents and siblings those neither too young to cope nor old enough to fend for themselves and bring them to England to join relatives or be farmed out to foster-families. To save entire families was deemed impractical and politically dangerous since the electorate were bound to be nervous about a flood of refugees swamping the country. Excuses could be made with hindsight. Nobody knew yet about Auschwitz and Belsen. Nobody could have imagined the fate that awaited Martha's parents and older sister at the end of their later deportation into southern Poland, through an iron gate from which they would never emerge except as smoke and flame and ash through a high brick chimney.

Martha had bidden them farewell at Berlin's Zoo Bahnhof, a solemn little figure in dark coat and hat. She promised to be good. Mutti kissed her on both cheeks and told her to remember to brush her teeth and always say please and thank you. Martha had been taught these words ahead of any other English terms. They'd see her again, Mutti said, as soon as everything had calmed down a little, just as soon as all this was over. Martha leaned right out of the window as the train pulled away and watched them vanish into the distance, until the steam obscured them – Mutti, Vati, Marianne. That was the last time she saw them. Nobody in England ever spoke of them.

She lived in Stanmore with Elisabeth Cohen, a second cousin of Vati's, who, to her credit, made the child welcome, instructing her two sons to treat her as the sister they'd never had (this meant a multitude of things, as brotherless Martha soon found out). Nobody spoke of Berlin. Nobody mentioned her life in Germany. Germans were talked about only as the enemy. At school Martha was taunted from morning to evening, her hair pulled, her Jewish origin mocked and her German accent the target of everything from ridicule to disgust. She brushed her teeth and said please and thank you, because that was all she could do to keep her family's spirit living inside her. Soon she would be home again, she told herself for comfort by night. Soon she'd be back in Berlin, back in the country where people had culture and intelligence and books and pianos, and she'd sing duets with Marianne as if nothing had ever come between them.

The years inched by; the bombs fell; the letters from home stopped with no explanation. Elisabeth Cohen and her husband and sons never asked her about them. She was part of their family now and the past was the past. It was better to forget, Elisabeth decided on Martha's behalf, without consulting her.

When the liberation came and pictures of the camps were shown in the papers and the Pathé newsreels, Martha did not speak for a week. She was already hoarding things in her bedroom cupboard, small things, things that might come in useful, like egg boxes – some day there might not be any – and pieces of string and foil that could tie or wrap things or keep food fresh. But she did well at school and Elisabeth encouraged her to sit an entrance exam for Oxford.

Gerald Levy, the son of a successful British Jewish businessman and now a promising intellectual at Balliol College, Oxford, caught sight of the dark-eyed, quiet girl from St Hilda's across a lecture theatre; and perhaps there was pity mixed with his attraction, or perhaps there was not. She would never know, because she would never ask. She said please and thank you when he took her out to dinner and, later, home to meet his parents. They had a low-key wedding ceremony in front of Gerald's substantial family and the four Cohen cousins who were all that remained of Martha's. She concealed her hoarding tendencies from him when they moved into their first flat; and she never spoke of her childhood, the war years or her parents, or her sister who used to sing.

But Adam, who arrived on the scene some eight years after his parents' marriage, remembered that as a young boy he'd heard disembodied sighs and strange German words as his mother dreamed and called out in her sleep until Gerald's touch brought her back into the present darkness from that of the past.

The immediate effect on Adam was that Gerald and Martha took possibly disproportionate pains to preserve the traditions that the Third Reich had set out to eliminate, although neither had been brought up in homes where such things counted – ironically both sets of parents, German and British alike, had prided themselves on their assimilation. So Adam could not watch television whenever he wanted to. Instead of playing in the park or doing homework on Saturday mornings, he had to traipse to the synagogue and listen to an arcane language that took him years to learn and had to be read and written backwards. The beautiful new bicycle he received for his barmitzvah seemed adequate compensation only for a matter of days. Adam was a child of extremes, with enough intelligence and creativity, if not emotional maturity, to furnish several ordinary children – and with that went a huge dose of stubbornness, self-will and passion, which turned too soon into anger.

One day Adam walked out of Pembroke College, Cambridge, and burned his *kippah*. He grew a beard, took up with some hippies and moved into a squat in east London. A few months later he enrolled at art school and told Cambridge that he was never going back. He didn't stop to think about what effect his actions might have on Gerald and Martha, because as far as he was concerned, it was their fault in the first place. They had placed their world on his shoulders and he was free to reject the task of carrying it, like Sisyphus, up the endless hill of achievement, because his load of anger already weighed too heavily upon him.

As for talking – well, nobody ever talked. Adam could not remember one occasion on which his mother had mentioned her own parents voluntarily. If she felt anything towards them, about them, because of them, she did not say so. She acted, when she acted, out of duty, not desire. For Adam, not talking, not showing your feelings, not expressing your emotions verbally was natural because it was home. The shock – when he entered the National Hall of Psychobabble (as Sasha had called it) and heard the 'team leader' summoning everyone to face right up to their problems and let everything out – hit him with a voltage so high that afterwards he was surprised he could still stand.

Adam's curtains are still closed at midday. Remorse, a black-winged bird with an all-enveloping wing span, flies from the far horizon and settles on his head beside the elephant of grief. He doesn't know where to put the pain, since his heart is too full to hold it all. The children, oblivious, are at school; Sasha, no doubt desperate to get away, has set off to meet Lisa for lunch.

He pictures his days on the Greek island with Sasha, the sun streaming across their young bodies, their limbs tangling together. He's never been as relaxed as he was then.

Adam gets out of bed at last, pulls on some jeans and a creased old black T-shirt and wanders out of the house to the station. Claudia's coffee shop is uncharacteristically closed. He takes a train to Waterloo, then makes his way down the escalators into the bowels of the station, where he catches the Northern Line and trundles up to Camden Town.

He drifts through the crowds of young people and tourists on Camden High Street, browsing in bookshops and through stalls selling leather jackets and logoed tops, and surveying the windows of gift shops filled with useless pieces of expensive pottery, glassware and candlesticks that nobody could ever need but that everybody could be persuaded to want.

Halfway along the High Street, he can't remember how he got there. He knows he must have gone on the train to Waterloo, then taken the Northern Line, but he has absolutely no recollection of doing so. He's in Camden Town and he has no idea why. What is he doing on Camden High Street in the middle of the afternoon? What the fuck is he doing on Camden High Street at all? His palms are clammy and he feels stricken with an irrational chill.

He turns abruptly off the main road and winds his way down a brown-bricked side-street. Someone tall and dread-locked brushes too close to him and he smells a familiar herbal aroma and hears a whisper: 'Want some dope?'

Now Adam knows why he's come to Camden Town. He stops and exchanges a look and an understanding with the passer-by, then follows him round a corner or two. Somewhere discreet, money and a small package change hands. A little later, Adam stops at a newsagent to buy some cigarette papers. Then he heads back to the station.

He can't face smoking a spliff in his family home. He can imagine the twins crying, 'Dad, what's that smell?' and Liffy wrinkling her nose in disgust. Sasha, claiming to support the legalisation of cannabis, shouldn't mind, but he won't take the risk. He walks up to the park and finds his way to a secluded copse of oak trees. Here he sits on the ground, cross-legged as in his hippie days, rolls the joint and, with a private flourish as he strikes the match, sets it alight. Adam recalls, drawing in the smoke and savouring the long-forgotten flavour on his tongue, that prior to her pregnancy Sasha had been none too averse to the stuff herself, and that it might have played no small part in Liffy's conception under an olive tree.

There's a dizzying sensation as the smoke fills his lungs and curls its soft way into his brain, melting the edges of his mind as it goes. While the world blurs, Adam leans his back against a tree, hopes nobody will spot him there, and lets his body grow heavy with numb, weighted solitude, peace and unity. When he rouses himself, some time later – a lot later, to judge by the position of the sun – his legs still feel heavy and his awareness smoothed and cushioned.

At home, there's noise upstairs: the twins are on the PlayStation, involved in the most serious of games. Liffy is sitting on the lounge floor watching the news on television, her face intent, her bony arms clasped around bonier knees. He feels generous, quiet and benevolent. He wants to embrace her. 'Liffs,' he says.

'Ssh,' Liffy says. 'I'm listening to this.'

It's a report about global warming – floods from Africa to York and the threat that as the ice cap melts and world water levels rise the Maldives may be submerged altogether.

'Funny smell,' Liffy remarks.

Her words alert Adam: he's about to make a run for the bathroom to shower, change his clothes, brush his teeth and destroy any traces of his afternoon in the park when Sasha whirls down from the study, looks at him and needs to know nothing more. One glance and one sniff are quite enough for her.

Liffy closes the lounge door. She needs to hear the environmental news, she needs to understand how people are killing the earth and destroying everything that is good and beautiful and peaceful in it out of greed and selfishness; how they could stop it if they were what the reporter calls 'minded to', but they weren't, especially not the Americans who just want cheap petrol and more food than is good for them (genetically modified, too). The Earth Prince is repeating everything in her ear, like an echo of the television. The world is evil; the world is killing the earth and therefore itself. It is killing itself out of its own greed and endless desire. Give it up, Liffy, give it up.

Then she hears Mum's voice as she's never heard it before – high and frantic and despairing, like an animal in pain. Dad's voice is lower – pleading? Comforting? Or is it? She can't make out the words. Just the yells, the screams, the fury that feeds on the air inside the house, the fury and fright that she's breathing in every day, the poison that works into her brain and her blood because she, too, happens to live in its shadow.

'I need space,' she hears her mother shouting. 'I want my life back.'

There's the clomp of a slamming door and footsteps thudding up the stairs, possibly Dad's. She can hear cupboard doors opening and closing, something big being hauled about. She doesn't know what it means. She doesn't want to know. She doesn't want to hear it, any of it. It's all meaningless.

Escape, Liffy, escape.

'I can't escape,' Liffy says. 'I'm thirteen.'

Adam, packing his clothes in the bedroom, feels cold and numb. He's remembering the end of Greece. The message from Sally at the taverna (they had no phone of their own), saying, 'Come home, Sasha, your father's very ill. He's had a heart-attack.' Arriving at Heathrow only to learn that he was not very ill but dead. Sasha's hysterical sobbing, Lisa's sober, fear-filled young face as she tried to be strong for the whole family. The way he had been the one to hunt down the whisky and remove it from Sally's reach, to keep an eye on her and make sure she didn't bring in any more. *I did all that, Sasha*, his heart protests. *I was there for you when you needed me. I held your hand in your grief. I gave up my dreams for you and our children. And now I'm in crisis and you won't stand by me?*

Sasha can't stand by him; she can't help him through; she can't cope. She wants space. She wants her life back. She wants her own company more than she wants his. She needs to be away from him, so he has to go away from her. He takes a shower, brushes his teeth and puts on clean clothes. Case in hand, he goes downstairs and looks at bony little Liffy, his heart breaking under his ribs. 'Liffs,' he begins, 'I'm going to Oxford to see Grandpa for a few days.'

'OK.' Liffy doesn't look round from the news. 'See you when you get back.'

Adam goes to her and gives her a kiss, which she doesn't return. Then he calls up the stairs to the twins.

'We're busy!' comes the furious response – outrage at the notion that saying goodbye to Dad for a few days might be worth interrupting a game for. Maybe just as well, Adam thinks.

'Sasha, I'm going now,' he declares, through the shut kitchen door.

'Take the car if you want,' comes Sasha's voice. 'For the moment. But just go.'

'Sasha?'

There's no reply.

Adam opens the front door, steps outside, closes it behind him. If Sasha says he can take the car, he will. He slings his suitcase on to the back seat of the Honda, starts the engine and drives away from his house. He's oddly calm – whether it's the lingering effect of the cannabis, he can't say, but nothing feels quite real: it's as if a knife blade is piercing his skin under a local anaesthetic. He doesn't know whether to hate Sasha or pity her. She has to be angry, of course. As a columnist it's her role in life: to be angry about matters over which she has no control and for which she offers no constructive solutions. Where would newspapers be without anger for anger's sake?

Perhaps anger is all the pair of them had in common twenty years ago.

Adam drives on, refusing to allow his mind any more leeway until he reaches Davenant Road, opens the gates and sees his father's face, surprised yet not that surprised, troubled but not too troubled, ready to listen first and then, doubtless, to blame him for everything that had just happened. Adam walks towards his father and as he reaches the front door his legs give way under him.

At the dinner table there is a vacuum, a black hole of negative energy where Adam should have been. Dinner is late. Sasha has been working, distracting herself – and the twins are hungry and clamouring for something to eat. Sasha stomps down and makes them baked potatoes, sausages and mixed vegetables. For Liffy she cooks three vegetarian sausages, which look and smell revolting but are all that she will touch. The vacuum in Adam's place pulsates and sucks at the air.

'Where's Dad?' Alex asks.

'He's gone to see Grandpa in Oxford. He did call up to say goodbye.' Nothing new in that: since Martha fell ill, Dad is often in Oxford. She's underestimated the twins, though. Now they say nothing. They just look at each other and then at her with their mirrored dark eyes, just like their father's, and eat on. They understand some things without being told.

Liffy is poking at a vegetarian sausage with her fork. 'Mum, did you cook this with the meat ones?' she asks.

'Of course I did. Do you think I'm a frying machine?'

Liffy pushes the plate away. She's turned white. Normally the twins would have made a joke of the frying machine comment – which Sasha had hoped they would. They'd been enchanted by an old film called *Those Magnificent Men in their Flying Machines* – Sasha's train of thought snips off as Liffy gets up, her food barely touched. 'Liffs, for heaven's sake!'

Light-footed Liffy dashes up the stairs and locks herself into the bathroom.

Sasha slumps back in her chair and puts her hands over her eyes. She expects the little boys to follow their sister's example or laugh at it, but they do neither.

'Mum?' Alex ventures. 'Where's Dad, really?'

'He's gone to Oxford. I told you,' Sasha says, through her hands.

'Why?'

'To see Grandpa. Like I said.'

'Mum?' Matt says. 'Is he coming back?'

She looks up and sees past the demands and desires and homework and past the crass, unformed lust for life that leads to bullied sisters and broken windows. She sees two little humans sitting there suffering in front of her. Their faces are a double vision of uncertainty, two creatures adrift in a fathomless sea. She has driven out the anchor that held them in their harbour because she thought he wasn't strong enough to stay.

Upstairs, she can hear water running in the bathroom and a little Liffy-like cough.

'Mum, is he coming back?' Alex demands.

'I don't know, darlings. I really don't know.'

Perhaps she's been too hasty. Perhaps his transgressions are not deliberate acts of vengeance on her and the children. Perhaps it really is – all of it – his response to all-powerful Martha's death. In which case, by sending him back to Oxford, to the family home, she's just succeeded in doing the one thing she'd vowed never to do, which is to let Martha win. She's sent Adam back to his mother, even though his mother is dead.

The little boys are looking at her with Adam's eyes, brimming with tears of fright.

'I'll phone him,' she tells them at once. 'You can speak to him and we'll decide what to do.'

She finds the portable handset lurking where she's hidden

it, muffled under a green cushion in the lounge, and dials Oxford.

Gerald answers, his manner professorial. 'He's gone to bed.'

'Could you get him, please, Gerald? The boys need to speak to him.'

'As you might understand, if you paused to give the matter a moment's thought, Adam is in no fit state to talk to anybody, let alone his children.'

The line goes dead.

Sasha sits down. Her hands are freezing. Matt opens his mouth and starts to cry.

Upstairs, Liffy takes her mobile and texts her aunt. What comes back is nothing more than: 'Hang in there, darling. L xxxxx'.

Liffy feels let down. She doesn't know what she'd thought Lisa would say, but somehow in times of trouble you expect aunts to have answers. It's nice to know, she reflects, counting her blessings as hard as she can, that there is someone out there who does love her, someone real, not only the Earth Prince. It strikes her that perhaps Lisa has problems of her own, problems she doesn't tell them about.

Sasha lies alone in her empty bed, sweating profusely. Whichever way she turns, she can't get comfortable; there's always a wrist or a hand or a foot in the way of the rest of her. On Adam's side of the bed, the expanse of empty sheet is as endless as the steppes of central Asia.

It's the third night of his absence and she knows she has to go to Oxford to get the car. Life with three children and no car is proving unworkable. Gerald still won't let her talk to him. She has to go: she has no choice. The electronic figures on the bedside clock notch by. One o'clock. One fifteen. One thirty. Two. The moonlight empties itself through the curtains like spilled milk. Just as she is beginning to feel sleepy, something warm and solid lands on the bed and she feels soft fur and whiskers nuzzling close to her – Bill has come to keep her company. Sasha cuddles the purring cat and wonders how he knows.

At six thirty, Sasha gets out of bed and goes to her computer to check the times of trains to Oxford. She'll go as soon as the children are at school. Next she checks her email. Rick has sent her a message: 'Thinking of you. Rx.'

She thinks of him too, with longing, gratitude, despair. It's as if they are on two sets of railway lines, crossing each other at the points but bound to their tracks by too many electric wires carrying them in separate directions. And her train is being diverted now, which way she can't imagine.

The image stays with her as she walks the twins to school, then prepares for her real train journey to Oxford.

From Oxford station, Sasha takes the bus to Banbury Road and walks the last short distance to Gerald's street. Her steps slow as she approaches the gated house. She is not easily frightened, but she is frightened now of what she will find inside. Her car is parked in the driveway. An unnatural stillness hangs like frozen fog over the Victorian gables of the house, its walled garden, its gravel drive; she remembers the stillness from the funeral, when the house had seemed to give up its soul with Martha.

When she rings the bell, it is some time before Gerald comes to the door. Sasha has always found him inscrutable. Today she'd expected at least some sign of emotion – tiredness, sorrow, anger. There is none.

'You'd better come in,' Gerald says.

Sasha wanders into the tiled hallway and looks up the long flight of stairs and the cluttered wall of shelves beside it. The house is weirdly silent.

'Is he . . . ?'

'He's still in bed.'

'Still?' Sasha echoes. It is past one o'clock. She looks into Gerald's cool, dark eyes and the idea strikes her that he's showing no emotion because no emotion can help; perhaps no emotion is appropriate. Or else Adam has a monopoly on emotion now.

'What's happened to him?'

'I don't know yet.'

'What's he been doing?'

'Sleeping.'

'What else?'

'Nothing. He's not been out of bed.'

'For three days?'

'Yes, Sasha. For three days.'

Sasha stares at her father-in-law's impassive expression. No doubt, the words 'physical and mental collapse' wouldn't come easily to him – especially not in relation to his only son. Sasha can imagine him passing judgement on Adam for the un-manliness of daring to feel emotions, daring to admit defeat, daring to fall and keep on falling. She can imagine him passing judgement on her for having allowed any of this to happen – for having made this happen. She imagines her defence: *I never intended this, I don't understand what happened, I never wanted anything to go wrong between us.* How lame, feeble, impossible . . .

'Isn't there something I can do?' she pleads.

Gerald leads the way into the kitchen, where a teapot stands ready beside the kettle. 'Why don't you take him some tea?' he says.

Sasha watches her own hands pouring a mugful, adding the milk, carrying it carefully up the stairs. Adam is in his old room; the door is a slit open and as she approaches she can see the darkness on the other side of it. Gerald lingers in the hall below.

She pauses at Adam's bedroom door and looks in. Adam is a still hump under the duvet.

'Ad. It's me. I've brought you some tea,' she ventures.

'Why?' comes his muffled voice.

'Because we thought you might be thirsty.'

Adam, his mind filled with black fur and feathers and grit in great piles being shovelled from left to right, finds it physically exhausting to lift his head and explain to his wife – he doesn't think to wonder what she's doing there – that drinking tea is pointless, just as everything he has ever done seems ultimately pointless if this is the result. The words, though, will not come out in the right order and when he reaches the end of the sentence he can't remember what the beginning was or even why he had started to say it in the first place.

Sasha listens to Adam's confused words, horror filling her in their wake. She goes to him, puts the tea on the bedside table and reaches out a hand. He flinches away.

Sasha goes downstairs to Gerald, tries to speak and finds that she's crying. 'This is impossible!' she exclaims, through her tears. 'For God's sake, Gerald, can't we do something? Can't we call a doctor?'

Gerald picks up his phone book – Martha's phone book, really, bound in crimson leather. It offers him two suitable numbers. One is the family GP who saw Martha's illness through to its conclusion; the other is Dr Aaron Grunwald, a psychiatrist and psychotherapist whom Gerald has known since his student days.

'Aaron's an admirable man,' Gerald tells Sasha, who is sitting opposite him, weeping, in what had been Martha's armchair. 'When I first met him, I felt intensely guilty in his presence. I knew he was a better person than I was. Why don't you go and get some air in the garden while I see if I can reach him?'

'I will.' Sasha gets to her feet and turns her back. She can hardly believe that Gerald, for all his academic credentials, had not had the sense or sensibility to call a doctor at least a day earlier, if not two. Presumably, in his view, problems of the mind or soul don't merit troubling a medic the way that cancer does. In his case that's forgivable – perhaps.

Like Martha, whom Gerald had not yet met when he got to know him, Aaron was a refugee from the Nazis, though this time from Vienna. He had struggled first for the right to be in England rather than face certain death; later, for the right to acceptance, education and the ability to contribute his considerable brain power to the adoptive country that had so grudgingly granted him those rights.

Beside this, Gerald considered his own life absurd in its ease and luxury. Raised by a wealthy family in an affluent suburb and sent to one of the best boarding-schools in the country, he'd led a life that was almost stereotypically English. His grandfather was related to Disraeli. But at university, this boy with a Viennese roll to his Rs had opened Gerald's eyes because he had lived the true Jewish experience of his day. Like Gerald he was dark-eyed and curly-haired, quick-thinking and alert – the two of them could almost have been brothers. Yet, at that time, Gerald's Jewishness had been swept quietly under a dense-piled carpet and those who stumbled over it expressed, rather tactlessly, their surprise at finding it there at all. First knowing Aaron and then meeting Martha had goaded Gerald's guilt into existence: he had investigated, studied and agonised long and hard before turning at last to orthodox religion and a kosher home. Aaron graduated with every honour that the university could give him and went on in due course to become a professor at the Maudsley Hospital. Now he has retired and is busy writing his memoirs at home in an Oxfordshire village no more than eight miles away.

Gerald, feeling that he could use Aaron's wise words himself at the moment, instead dials his old friend's number to seek advice about his son, while his son's wife waits alone, pacing up and down in the walled garden. Aaron sounds pleased to hear from him, if not ecstatic – psychotherapists, Gerald remembers, often have a brusque phone manner – and not surprised, since the news of Martha's death has travelled with the speed and force of a mortar attack through their networks of mutual acquaintances. Aaron does seem surprised, however, when Gerald describes the turn of events.

'I'm aware,' Gerald says, 'that if I call the GP he'll give Adam some sort of sedation or put him on anti-depressants or send him into a hospital where they'll do the same thing. I'm not sure that that's best for him.'

'There's a good reason for his state of mind,' Aaron says. 'Several good reasons. He's not falling apart for the sake of something irrational. He's suffering and he needs support. I don't see that drugs would necessarily be the long-term solution.'

It is best, the two elders agree, to let Adam feel his pain. To let him make that journey to the bottom of the spirit's ocean rather than suppress his mourning and leave him troubled by its charcoal-black murmurings for years to come. Once he reached the ocean floor, there would be nowhere to swim but up.

'What shall I do?' Sasha demands, when he comes into the garden to tell her.

'Go home, Sasha. Go home and look after the kids.'

At those words, Sasha understands she is doing her husband more harm than good. Perhaps she has brought this upon him. She does the only thing she can: she wipes her eyes, takes out her car key and prepares to drive home.

Lying in bed, Adam hears his father talking to Aaron on the telephone again, late in the evening. He hears the word 'breakdown' and the words 'hospital' and 'drugs'; then, worst of all, 'Olivia and the twins'.

The shadows in the room fall as they have always fallen as long as Adam can remember: the bookshelves striped and grey like prison bars, the moonlight a pale silver far beyond the folds of curtain, a slender river of brightness slithering along the carpet from the hall lamp downstairs. Adam isn't sure how long he's been there, in this bed. It seems like a year since Sasha had appeared before him from the distant past, bringing tea, and disappeared again. It occurs to him that maybe he should find out how long ago it was.

He sits up, switches on his bedside lamp and blinks in its brilliance. He looks at his watch: 22:36, it says. The date it gives is three days after the last one he can remember. He's lost three days. In the grand scheme of things, maybe that's not so bad, but shame crawls through the piles of grit in his mind, scaling their heights and kicking down the shingle as it goes. Oh God, the children.

'Whatever will your children think?' He seems to hear Martha's voice, accusing, judgemental. Who'd have thought that people who are no longer there would simply continue to behave as they always have inside the heads of the living? Still, after fifty years of not changing, Martha isn't going to change now just because she's dead.

'Ach, I don't know what you think you're doing,' he hears her say. 'Who said you had to have a breakdown?'

'I'm not having a breakdown,' Adam argues silently. 'I would if I could, but I don't know how.'

Martha's presence in the room is becoming palpable. He can picture her outline against the moonlight, her stocky, motherly torso, her still dark hair peppered with grey, though he cannot see her features – these have dissolved into the silver shadows. If you don't lean over, expecting support, Adam explains to her internally, you don't fall over. If you think someone is there for you and will prop you up, you lean. When there's nothing there after all, that's when you lose your balance.

'It's true,' his mother's voice in his head says to him. 'I never received support, except from your father, but I never asked for it. I never had those expectations of other people that you seem to have developed.'

'And supposing you did expect support. From me. Supposing we had talked. Talked properly about your life and your family and what happened to them, how it felt when you found out. Wouldn't we have been closer?'

'Ach, Adam. We were as close as I could be to anyone,' is all that Martha says. Adam knows that he is telling himself some truth about her that he had never quite been able to grasp. He imagines her at the Zoo Bahnhof, saying goodbye, not knowing when she would see her parents and sister again, not guessing that she never would. How could she have talked, after year on year of silence? Words don't exist to describe how that feels.

Through the chaos in his head, Adam pictures Auschwitz. Forced out of their rightful lives, dehumanised by their captors and thrown into a furnace like firewood, his grandparents' fate was a greater cataclysm than he or anybody else could comprehend in their safe, cosseted, moderate, modern lives. Whatever he felt about losing his mother, at least her death had been natural. She had died at home in her own bed – suffering, it was true, and from a terrible disease, but nevertheless she had been well cared for and thoroughly medicated until she slipped into oblivion with her husband and son beside her, holding her hands. However abandoned he felt now, how could that possibly compare to what she had experienced as a young teenager in a strange country, trying to understand what had become of her parents and beloved sister, trying to make sense of a fate that decreed she should escape while they could not? As for his own children—

'Adam, don't you see?' He imagines his mother's ghost

speaking gently in his ear, more gently than she would have in life. 'You have what your grandparents didn't have, and what I didn't have in the end. You can choose. You don't have to do this. I know it's hard. But who ever said it would be easy?'

He can let go, fall into the black grit heaps, give up, end up in hospital, put his children through despair and betrayal that at their age might seem only mildly worse than what his own mother has just put him through by dying. Or he can hold on. He doesn't have to let go. That's too easy. He can hold on. One step at a time, one minute at a time, he can get himself back before it's too late. He doesn't know whether the voice he is imagining is really Martha's: perhaps it is Gerald's, or some guardian angel; perhaps it is his own, inner, better self. The voice, wherever it comes from, is growing strong and resilient. 'For God's sake,' it tells him, 'just get the hell out of that bed.'

Adam breathes deeply and musters every ounce of his remaining strength. Then he pushes back the duvet, swings his legs sideways and stands up. His limbs are weak and aching from lying down. His pyjamas smell. His head is spinning, but that's because he hasn't eaten. One step at a time, his mind pushes his body towards the door; next, across the landing; and then, at last, the stairs. One at a time, he goes down eight steps, then twelve, to the hall. The patterned Victorian tiles are cold under his feet. He seems not to have trodden on them for years. Through the lounge door, he can see his father sitting alone with a glass of whisky, watching *Newsnight*.

'Dad?' he hears himself say. His voice still works, then. It's still his own.

'Adam. You're up.'

'I'm going to have a shower. Have you got any eggs?'

'In the fridge,' shrugs Gerald, as if it's the most natural and expected thing in the world. 'Help yourself.'

Now that he's come down, going up again feels easier. In

the bathroom, Adam peels off his pyjamas, pulls the shower curtain to and soon feels warm water streaming across his body, into his eyes, through his hair, down his legs, and as he breathes in the hot, fresh steam and the clean, bright scent of soap, nothing has ever felt so good to him before.

12

Life doesn't stop, Sasha reflects, even if sometimes you'd like it to. Practical things have to be done. People have to be fed.

Sasha feeds her children – the ones who will eat. She feeds her cats. She writes to feed her readers' curiosity. She talks to Cindy to feed their friendship and to her mother and sister to feed their family bond. She talks to Adam on the phone, at last, intending to feed what's left of their relationship.

'Better, thanks,' he says. 'I've bothered Dad long enough. Nick's offered me a room at his place for a while.'

'What does that mean?' she asks.

'All it means is that I'm going to stay at Nick's place until I know what's going on.'

'Until *you* know? What about *me*?'

'You were the one who wanted me to go,' Adam reminds her. 'You said you needed space. Guess what, I need space too.'

'Are you leaving me?'

'I thought you wanted me to,' says Adam.

'But, Adam . . .' Sasha begins. There's a click, and silence.

Sasha aches to talk to Rick to feed their romance – about which she's feeling somewhat less guilty than before – but she waits for him to call her, and he doesn't. As the days pass with no word from him, time goes slower and slower. Why doesn't he phone?

Working her way round Waitrose, she is so distracted that she forgets to swipe the barcodes on four yogurts, a loaf of

Cranks bread, a container of Tuscan bean soup and a tub of reduced-fat guacamole. At the checkout her handset informs her that she needs a re-scan.

Patricia, who is on duty at the Quick Check till, has seen Sasha at least twice a week for more than ten years and sometimes glimpses her on television – although she has scant patience with *The Weekly Review* and usually watches it only long enough to say to her husband, 'She's one of my customers, that one with the curly hair,' then switches off. It is with some embarrassment, therefore, that she has to tell Sasha, 'There's quite a difference between this and what's on the scanner.'

Sasha colours as she makes her excuses and apologies. It's strange to think that she would have saved more than seven pounds if she'd not had to have a re-scan and hadn't declared the unswiped items. No doubt there are plenty of people who take advantage of this trusting system and are never found out. The twins are always trying to think of ways to cheat in Waitrose – wanting to weigh expensive varieties of apple as cheaper ones, or organic broccoli as plain – but luckily they are much too young to be entrusted with a self-scanner.

'It won't happen again,' she assures Patricia.

'I'm sure it won't,' Patricia says.

When she walks through the front door, she hears her mobile phone beeping, alerting her to a message. She's missed a call in the noisy supermarket.

'Sasha, it's me,' says Rick's voice. 'Listen. In August we're going to have a special live edition of the show from Manchester, with audience participation and questions. We'd like you to be on it. You'll get your usual fee plus some, with expenses and a hotel thrown in as well. I *do* hope you'll come. Call me back.'

His meaning could not be clearer. Sasha sits down on the stairs and rubs her eyes. How is she going to do this? It is too perfect an opportunity to miss. It is, however, three days before

Liffy is due to go off on a fortnight's holiday with Charley and family. And the twins aren't going anywhere. She doesn't know where Adam will be by then – home, Gerald's, Nick's or somewhere else? She can't rely on him: she has to have confidence in the arrangements.

Sasha phones Lisa.

Lisa sounds a little troubled at the thought of squeezing three children into her small flat overnight, but she agrees anyway. The twins can sleep on the fold-out sofa bed – they are still young enough to think it's fun – and Liffy can share her large double bed. Lisa will give her a separate duvet to wrap up in so that they don't kick each other. Sasha relaxes. All she has to do now is ask the neighbours to feed Bill and Ben for a night and a day – which they normally agree to do, since Bill and Ben are schmoozy cats once they've worked out where the food is coming from – and she is free to go.

Liffy hovers behind when the other girls pile out to the changing room at the end of the ballet class. Margaret, her teacher, who remembers her mother's days as a dancer, is packing away the CDs and the tray of shoe resin.

'Margaret,' Liffy says, in a small voice, 'can I ask you something? It's just that – the auditions for the ballet school are in November and I'd need to get my application in really soon . . . Do you think . . . I could do it?'

Margaret has been having pains in her left knee and hip, bad enough to make her wince when she puts weight on them. She is only forty-five, but the years of strain she'd inflicted on her limbs, dancing on what were often unsuitable floors, are beginning to demand payback. She fears she has arthritis. She has been trying to pluck up courage to visit her doctor and prepare for an X-ray, but she knows that when she does, she will be put on anti-inflammatory drugs that might soon turn her tendency to heartburn into a stomach ulcer.

And Liffy wants to be a dancer. Does this lovely slip of a girl really want to put herself through all this in thirty years' time? Just today, Margaret is not sure she would advocate dance as a career for any of her charges. It isn't something she'd wish on her worst enemy.

'Oh darling,' she says to Liffy, 'don't you think you should give it all a little more thought first?'

Liffy is silent, wide-eyed and crestfallen.

'Seriously, darling. You're thirteen now. By the time you started there, you'd be fourteen. Wouldn't it make more sense to stay on at your wonderful school and get some good GCSEs first? And then, if you still want to, you could audition for the senior school at sixteen? Otherwise you'll have to adjust to a whole new environment and have different teachers and make different friends just when you need to be concentrating on your exams—'

'Exams! It's always *exams*!' Liffy cries. 'I *hate* exams! I want to dance!'

Margaret is taken aback by her passion – she wouldn't have expected Liffy, this quiet, pale little girl, to express herself so forcefully. 'Darling, nobody likes exams,' she soothes, 'but it's important to do well in them. Then, when you've got them out of the way, you can do what you like and you've got a solid grounding behind you.'

'I'm not good enough, isn't that it? Or am I too fat?'

'Goodness, Liffy, you are certainly not too fat. And it's for the school to decide whether you're good enough. So much depends on what the other applicants are like and how you dance on the day. All I'm trying to say is that you've got to think about what's best for you in the long term.'

'I see.' Liffy's lower lip sets and she turns her eyes downwards.

'Um, Liffy – how are you getting on with your dad not being around at the moment?'

'All right,' Liffy mumbles. 'I'm fine.'

★   ★   ★

Unwinding the ribbons from her ankles and pulling the hairpins out of her bun a few minutes later, Liffy ignores the other girls around her. She is trying not to cry. She *is* too fat, and she is *not* good enough to get into ballet school. That much is obvious. Because if her figure was right and her standard appropriate, they'd let her apply because there'd be no reason not to. And she will never admit out loud in a thousand years how much she misses her father.

It isn't that she saw so much of him when everything had been normal – he worked such long hours and was often not home until well into the evening, when she'd be doing her homework or chatting by phone or computer to Charley and the others. But even if she was busy upstairs, she'd still hear the metallic twitch of his key in the lock and the soft closing of the door behind him, and she'd know he was there.

'He's not coming back, you know,' Alex had insisted, when the three of them had been alone together the other day, messing about in the garden while Mum was on the phone.

'Yes, he is,' Liffy said.

'He's not. They never do.'

'Alex, don't be silly,' Liffy ordered, in her best older-sister voice. 'You don't know that. Dad wouldn't leave us.'

'He would,' Matt said. 'Mum kicked him out.'

'No, she didn't. She wouldn't do that.'

'Did too. I heard her. And you did too – I know cos you said so. They had this blazing row and then he went off to Oxford and Mum had to go all the way there to get the car.'

'Of course he's coming back. That's why he's staying at Nick's place, because he'll be back any minute.'

'Lif-*fy*! Get real,' Alex said. 'We're about the only people in our class at school who have parents who live together.'

'That doesn't mean that they shouldn't or that they can't,' Liffy said, panic in her throat. Around her, the plants that Dad had groomed with such care were already starting to look wild and unkempt.

'But they *probably* can't and they *probably* won't,' Alex said. 'It's all about probability, that's what Julius calls it. He says it's something to do with maths and we'll have to get used to it.'

'Don't cry, Liffy,' Matt said. 'It won't be so bad. Once he's got his own place we'll do like everyone else does. We'll get to see him half the time and Mum half the time. That's what they all do. They fight about it for months and months and *months* and that's what they do in the end, even when you could have told them at the beginning that that's what they'd do. We'll have our own rooms at home and at his new place when he gets one and it'll be good because they'll give us presents the whole time to make us feel better.'

'Mr Worldly-Wise! What makes you think you're so clever?'

Matt gave a very worldly-wise shrug. 'That's what I've seen and that's what people do. All *we* have to do is hope they get sorted soon.'

'It's not fair,' Liffy exclaimed.

'Life *isn't* fair. Get used to it,' Alex said, as their father always did. He used the same inflections as Adam – the two first words broken with a longish pause and a firm falling on to the second word. The sound of it was too much for Liffy and she'd dashed inside and hidden under her duvet.

The Earth Prince is pleased with Liffy. The belt she wears with her jeans is down to its last hole and the scales show that she's lost some weight. But it's not enough, not nearly enough, he warns. And when she lapses and lets herself eat, he won't leave her alone all night, shouting in her inner ear that she's useless, dreadful, impossible, disobedient, out of control.

Liffy has a school assignment, a creative-writing project to complete for the end of term now that the exams are finished. She has been wrangling with herself over whether writing what she has planned might violate her understanding of secrecy with the Earth Prince, but she aches to set down what she has learned from him; it will be nothing like her classmates' stories, that's for certain. She listens for his guidance, but hears nothing. So she decides to go ahead.

Jennie followed the mysterious figure down the road and into the forest. He walked ahead of her, always just a little too far ahead for her to see his face. His skin was a leaflike grey-green. In the middle of the forest he stopped walking and turned to face her.

'Listen,' he said. 'What I'm going to tell you is very important. You must go and tell everybody what I tell you now. You must warn them. You must prevent this happening before it is too late.

'I am the embodiment of the earth,' he said. 'I am the king of the forest, king of all the spirits in the trees and the plants, here and in the rainforest and in the savannah and in the pine-covered mountains. At my command, the earth awakens with all its monstrous power. At my command, volcanoes spew out lava, drowning the villages on their slopes. At my command, trees come to life in the spring and at my touch their blossoms flower. Without me, the daffodils would not bloom, nor the lilacs, nor the roses.

'But you are in grave danger. My subjects are driven from their homes and destroyed under the wheels of bulldozers or in the flames of forest fires. Their health is ruined by the chemicals that are spread on them. Some of their species will never recover and will disappear. The earth has been ruined by mankind, which has forgotten that it is just one more species that cannot live without taking in food from nature. With the earth angry, there will be terrible earthquakes and volcanic eruptions and floods. There will be famine, disease and war. Your people will die in millions, terrible deaths in great pain. This, I swear to you, will come to pass if your people do not give up their greed.'

So Jennie went back to her family and told them, but they laughed at her. She went to her school and told them, and they laughed at her. She wrote to the newspaper and they did not

print her letter. She wrote to the Prime Minister, who never replied.
Time passed. And when Jennie was fifty years old, a great drought
took hold of Europe and Asia and there was no more food and
water. Jennie and her children died of thirst, and as she lay dying,
Jennie remembered her meeting with the king of the earth. With
her last breath she wondered whether anybody would believe her
now, if she still had the strength to tell them.

When the composition comes back to her on the last day
of term, Liffy's teacher has given her a B. 'Rather gloomy and
pessimistic,' she's written. 'Why not think of some possible
solutions instead? Why not have Jennie or her children find a
way to save the world?'

'Because this is what's happening *now*!' Liffy exclaims,
staring at the comments.

'Ssh,' Charley says. 'Leila's going to read hers out.'

Willowy, dark-skinned Leila glides to the front of the classroom and begins to read her composition about an Iranian
girl who has grown up in England but goes to Iran for the
first time, meets family she's never met before and loves them.
Everyone claps except Liffy, who is smouldering with fury.

'Lighten up, Liff,' Charley whispers. 'It's not the end of the
world.'

'That,' Liffy says, in a growl worthy of her mother, 'is *exactly*
what it is.' But Charley isn't listening.

Charley has written a story about a girl who runs away with
a male teacher, but is brought back and humiliated in front of
her schoolmates. She hasn't been asked to read it out and Miss
Carroll has given it a C. Liffy has read it and doesn't like it.
She doesn't understand why Charley should invent the sensations of martyrdom unless it's to imagine some sick romantic
situation in which she'd like to see herself. Robin the flute
teacher has already left for the summer – he's playing in a
festival orchestra somewhere in Germany. Charley doesn't
know how she can live without him. Liffy has told her not to

be ridiculous, but Charley droops about and doodles big flowery Rs across the backs of her exercise books. Liffy wonders how she's going to survive two weeks in Greece with Charley in this frame of mind, but it's much too late to back out now.

Alone in her front room, Sasha listens to the sounds of the house in the school holidays. Electronic clicks, bleeps and thwangs issue from the twins' PlayStation. From the loft come soft thuds and a distant thread of a Bach concerto as Liffy dances. Sasha is making a list of everything she has to do before she goes to Manchester. She is bemused by the quantity of work that is now solely down to her – things that Adam used to do without her even realising it. Spray the rose bushes, wash the car, cook every meal for the children, do all the shopping, washing-up, tidying and laundry, organise the dry cleaning, work out how to set the video recorder (she is not best friends with technology), pay all the bills, get the burglar alarm serviced . . . It seems endless.

Manchester – and meeting Rick – will happen in two days' time. A wave of guilt sweeps over her. In Acton, Adam is renting a room from his old friend and colleague. He's been back now to see the kids; but he wouldn't see her, declaring that he wasn't 'ready'. Rick will be her reward for putting up with this appalling mess, she tells herself – but she can't make herself believe it, not entirely.

She worries about Adam, his state of mind disturbing her like an angry dog awaiting its chance to attack. He seems oddly, frighteningly, in control; and while she knew, had known all along, that Adam had the inner strength and stubbornness to get through his crisis, in some ways she suspects she would almost have found it easier if he hadn't. She doesn't like to think that he's stronger than she is.

Liffy pads in, still wearing her ballet shoes. Her face is flushed and sweaty, her eyes brilliant. 'Mum,' she exclaims, 'I can do triple pirouettes!'

Sasha hugs her. She needs to distract herself, so she begins to wonder whether Liffy is content with her wardrobe for her Greek holiday. 'Liffs, how do you fancy going to the Harrods sale this afternoon?' she says.

The Harrods sale isn't a place Sasha would ever willingly go, but now that she's started thinking about it, she can't remember when she last took her daughter shopping. Liffy tends to go round the shops in Richmond with her friends rather than her mother these days. Perhaps it's escapism, perhaps it's bribery, even corruption, but Sasha goes with the impulse and Liffy's excitement shows her immediately that it's the right thing to do. Sasha calls Julius's mother, dispatches the twins round the corner and waits for Liffy to shower and get ready to go. Soon Liffy springs down the stairs, her gaze more cheerful than Sasha has seen it for some time.

Walking to the bus stop through the sunlight, Liffy chatters about her friends, their families and intrigues, and the ballet steps she's finding difficult. Sasha begins to tell her about her own ballet-school days and the things she and her friends used to get up to in their spare time. Then she finds she has to explain to Liffy what a Sloane Ranger is, or once was. She feels simultaneously ancient and girlish. They sit near the back of the bus to Hammersmith, staring as unobtrusively as they can at the other passengers, poking fun at their mannerisms and laughing together. And all the time Sasha is holding off her own mind and the images it throws at her of where she's going to be on Friday night.

At Hammersmith, they go down into the Underground station to take the Piccadilly Line. To Sasha's horror, the whole world is apparently heading for Knightbridge. Passengers follow each other, lemming-like, into the already overcrowded train at Earl's Court and South Kensington. She and Liffy stand pressed together into a corner by the door with someone's elbow poking into Sasha's ribs; Liffy, thin and big-eyed, looks suddenly very small and young. The train feels like a furnace. When, oh, when, thinks Sasha, will British organisations wake up to the fact that twenty-first-century summers are *hot*, and start prioritising air-conditioning? She feels sweat along her hairline and her heart rate is rising. Liffy glances at her, her eyes concerned.

At last the train pulls into Knightsbridge Station and they are swept along with the crowd that moves as one body towards Harrods. 'There Is Only One Harrods, There Is Only One Sale,' declare the posters. I must be mad, thinks Sasha.

'Why did you suddenly want to go to Harrods, Mum?' Liffy asks. 'I don't think I've ever had anything from there.'

'Yes, you have. You had that lovely soap for your birthday.'

'I didn't know that, did I?'

'Anyway, it's about time you had something decent to wear for a special occasion,' Sasha says, then wishes she hadn't.

'What's wrong with what I'm wearing?' Liffy is in her usual jeans and pink scoop-neck top.

'Nothing at all. Wouldn't you like a party dress to take to Greece? In case you and Charley go out?'

'Hm.' Liffy gazes up at the huge glass doorway. 'I'd have thought Harrods was – like, a bit posh? But it does look – well, exciting . . .'

'Some people object to smart shops because they're so keen to get their hands on what's inside,' Sasha points out. Her daughter lets out a silvery, conspiratorial giggle.

The shop, though, is nearly as hot and busy as the train. They struggle through the throngs on the ground floor towards the escalator. Heat, noise, mayhem – at least, Sasha reflects, it's stopping her thinking too much. Liffy gazes around from the rising escalator, quietly taking in the impressions of wealth suggested by all she sees. Sasha watches the shifting masses. Greedy, grasping, petty, she thinks. She can't tell what Liffy thinks about it: Liffy's way of vanishing into her mysterious inner world is increasingly unsettling. Probably she'll reject anything that isn't a natural fabric made without cruelty to people, animals or plants.

'I'd quite like some trousers – maybe loose linen ones?' Liffy suggests upstairs, back, as it were, in her own body. 'And maybe a black top. Something coolish for Greece?'

'Oh, Liffs, why black? What about something a little prettier? Something blue or lilac?'

Sasha hates the loud music in the section of the shop directed at teenagers. Her head is already throbbing from stress and nerves as she follows Liffy, who drifts at her own pace from rail to rail, browsing through brown broderie anglaise, white petticoat skirts, pink and lilac crossover tops and little black dresses. The clothes are arranged according to colour groups and Liffy, rather than heading for pink and purple, gravitates to the row of black, white and grey. Someone treads on Sasha's foot and passes by without so much as an apology.

'I'll just go and try these, Mum.' Liffy waves a bunch of garments and hangers in her direction.

'OK, love, just give me a call when you want me to come and look,' Sasha says, casting around for a chair.

Liffy slips away behind the changing-room curtain and Sasha, trying to calm her breathing, glances at the other shoppers. Another young girl is going in behind Liffy – a girl with dark, curly hair, a curvaceous shape, a smiling face. She looks relaxed; she looks happy. Somehow she's familiar. Maybe she looks like the daughter Sasha has not had. Maybe she looks as Sasha wishes she could have been at thirteen. Why can't life be simple? Why couldn't she have had a happy home like that girl's? Why can't her own daughter be straightforward, healthily curved, smiley? She spots the girl's mother standing nearby talking into a mobile phone – dark hair, tailored navy jacket, thin legs, designer jeans. And the two girls come out side by side without noticing each other: the stranger in a dusty-pink crossover wrap and full skirt sprinkled with sparkly embroidery; Liffy in the plainest of loose black linen trousers and matching top – beautifully cut and stylish, but hanging off her bony frame in a way that Sasha finds uncomfortably voluminous. She notices how thin Liffy seems beside the other girl, whose bust is ample enough to support the crossover neckline and whose arms are fleshy, gentle, rounded. Liffy looks like a dancer in her black linen, all sinew, tendon and muscle underneath it.

'I do like it, Mum,' she is saying, her tone pleading.

'OK, sweetie, if that's what you want. Wouldn't you like to try something like that as well?' Sasha indicates the girl in the long skirt.

Liffy looks her up and down with a critical eye. 'No, thanks,' she says.

Sasha gets out her credit card to pay for the outfit. It has been reduced from £99.99 to £69.99 – expensive, but a good bargain. She wonders how her credit limit is, wonders how they are going to keep paying for everything they normally have. The children don't seem to understand why this should be a problem. None of it feels real. She's living a nightmare. Harrods lurches and begins to orbit round her head.

She hands Liffy the dark green carrier-bag. 'Liffs, I have to get outside, it's too hot in here,' she hears herself saying as the lights dip and spin.

'Mum? Are you OK?' Liffy grabs her arm and leads her towards the escalator. Sasha is battling nausea. She holds on to her daughter, horrified at the idea of being sick or fainting in the middle of Harrods. Liffy, light-footed, steers her along a quick, ingenious path through the swarming ground floor, and at last the welcoming sunlight bursts upon them on the pavement outside.

'Mum, you don't look well,' Liffy says. 'We shouldn't get back in that train. Have we got enough money for a taxi?'

'A taxi? All the way home? That'll cost a bomb. And I wanted to take you out for tea.'

'I don't need any tea, I'm fine. Why don't we take a taxi to Hammersmith at least, and pick up the bus there?'

Sasha is too frazzled to object. She's faintly aware, as Liffy hails a taxi and virtually drags her into it, that her daughter is suddenly playing the mother and she the child on this bizarre stage, and that this is the wrong way round. But her head is too muzzy right now to present a suitable alternative.

13

On the first Friday of August, Sasha drives Liffy and the boys to West Hampstead.

The car, which needs the wash she doesn't have time to give it, is crammed with stuff: her own smallish leather case for the trip to Manchester, complete with well-concealed condoms; Liffy's rucksack weighed down with books, plus ballet shoes at the top (not that there's an inch of space in Lisa's flat where she could practise); Manchester United holdalls for the boys, full of boots and socks, and a ball in case of trips to Hampstead Heath. Sasha's blood is racing through her in anticipation of this day. She'll head north at once, meeting Rick at the Midland Hotel over the road from the concert hall in the foyer of which the special live broadcast is to take place. Later, she and Rick will sidle off together somewhere for dinner. After that, they'll see what happens.

Lisa's flat is in a Victorian terrace in what her friends call 'the beehive' – a complex of narrow streets tucked away behind West End Lane in which two-way traffic and rationed yet impossible parking make life a noisome, anxiety-provoking business. Lisa's first-floor flat lets her see the sky, which diminishes her sense of claustrophobia. She doesn't have a car, but knows she will have to buy one with the baby on the way. It's one aspect of impending motherhood that doesn't appeal.

Now that she's past the first three months, her abdomen is beginning to balloon and her skin has a new and mysterious glow about it; soon she's going to have to tell people what's happening – including her mother and sister – because they'll notice that she looks unusually well and is gaining weight. Watching from the open window (it's a hot, close day, which she could do without), she sees Sasha's Honda rounding the corner, bursting with children and luggage, and goes down to the front steps to welcome her visitors.

Sasha has left the car in the middle of the road, since there's nowhere to park. She stands in front of Lisa, hair pulled back but escaping in brief, wild curls from its grip; a dark blue linen jacket is slung over her shoulders. The children hang back in a small gaggle behind her. Her dark eyes, for some reason, are burning. 'Thanks, Lee,' Sasha says. 'Honestly, thank you so much. I don't know how to thank you enough.'

Oh, just you wait, Lisa thinks. 'Have you got time for a coffee?' she asks.

'I'd love one, but I've got to dash. I'm meeting Ri – the team at two and I don't know what the traffic will be like.'

'Sure. Well, I'll give these three as good a time as I possibly can. But I hope they like music.'

'Music?' Alex echoes, interested. 'What's happening?'

'My friends Paul and Lindsey, who live up near the Heath, have asked us all to a musical evening at their house. I'm supposed to be playing my cello in it so we have to go – otherwise I'd be letting them down. I'd like you guys to try and enjoy it. How does that sound?'

'Cool,' Matt says, polite but unconvinced.

'Yeah,' Liffy says. She loves music but doesn't like to say so in front of her brothers.

'That'll be an adventure for them.' Sasha wonders where she'll be while the children sit listening to Lisa and her friend.

'Go carefully,' Lisa says, picking up the twins' holdalls and turning to go in. Behind Sasha's car, an irate driver is sitting in a Golf, pressing the horn.

'You too. See you tomorrow.'

Sasha dashes back down the steps, leaps into the car and is off. Lisa smiles at the charade being staged for the children. Sasha is not, absolutely not, going off for a dirty weekend. Adam is not, absolutely not, considering leaving her for good. And she, Lisa, is absolutely not having a baby outside wedlock. Oh, what nonsense it all is. She sighs to herself. Children aren't stupid. Surely they can see what's happening around them.

'How about some orange juice and biscuits?' she says, leading them upstairs. 'And then we can decide what to do today.'

Inside the flat, Igor is lurking, waiting to see what's going on. As soon as he spots the twins, he turns tail and makes for a safe, concealed window-sill behind the lounge curtain.

'Where are we sleeping?' Matt asks, casting a wistful eye after the anti-social cat.

'You two are on the sofa bed. Liffs, you can have half of my bed plus your own duvet.' Lisa pours three glasses of juice and piles some milk chocolate Hobnobs on to a bright green plate.

'Could I have just water, please?' Liffy says, while the twins fall on the biscuits as if they haven't eaten for a week.

Lisa looks at Liffy's pale, drawn face and thin arms and doesn't like what she sees. But she gives her the water.

She explains to the children that she has to practise her cello for an hour; after that they'll go out. Alex and Matt immediately ask if they can use the computer to play games – she agrees reluctantly, aware that they probably know how to work it far better than she does – and Liffy wants to look at her books. Lisa tells her to help herself and retreats to her bedroom with the cello part of the Schumann Piano Quartet.

Liffy leaves her little brothers at the computer – it'll keep them out of trouble – and sits alone in Lisa's cosy yellow kitchen overlooking the back garden. How strange it feels not to know where either of your parents is. Well, she sort of knows. Dad is in Acton; Mum is on her way to Manchester. But she can't picture them at this exact moment. She can't imagine what's going through their minds or why they are doing whatever it is they are doing. She feels alone and adrift, despite her brothers, despite her aunt.

The boys have left two Hobnobs on the green plate. The aroma of chocolate and sweet, oaty biscuit turns Liffy almost faint with longing. She hasn't experienced this level of desperation for food before. She's accustomed herself to doing without. It's relatively easy to avoid temptation at school, as the food is so disgusting; it's the holidays that have proved challenging.

She's invented an elaborate system, which so far nobody has spotted. There are several parts to it. First, it can involve offering to cook dinner, in which case she can make sure the meal contains exactly the ingredients she feels happy eating; or cooking her family the food she would love to eat but won't let herself touch, in which case she gains her pleasure from watching them enjoy it instead and when Mum asks her why she isn't eating, she says she's been snacking too much while cooking and isn't hungry any more. You have to check that the seasoning is right, after all. Their newly fatherless existence places so much pressure on Mum that she's only too happy to let Liffy help.

If she goes to Charley's, she tells Charley's mother that she's eaten at home. When she goes home, she tells them she's eaten at Charley's.

Food is a pleasure. What food she can eat has to be savoured, every bite of it. Each sliver of apple must be thoroughly chewed and every morsel of sweetness drawn out as long as possible. But food can also be a pleasure on the television. She watches every cookery programme she can find – Delia, Nigella, Jamie. Those, plus recipe books and magazines, are the best, full of glorious pictures of exquisite, colourful, perfectly presented dinner-party dishes – pictures that one cannot smell or taste and hence are free of danger.

Now and then Liffy cracks. On the twins' ninth birthday two weeks before, Sasha had bought a cake from Pâtisserie Valérie. It was the most beautiful cake Liffy had ever seen. It was vanilla sponge inside, the layers sandwiched together around heaps of fresh fruit with the creamiest cream imaginable. On top was soft white icing and more cream and HAPPY BIRTHDAY ALEX & MATT in big chocolate letters and a ton of curly shavings of white and dark chocolate dumped over the whole thing. Liffy's innards got the better of her. She realised that if she didn't have some she would break down and cry in front of the twins, then be required to explain why. She ate a piece and it was so good that she had another. Ten minutes later, she felt queasy – she wasn't used to eating anything so rich – and with the queasiness made worse by the appalling guilt that gripped her, she locked herself into the bathroom and stuck her fingers down her throat.

Coming down a bit later, her eyes still watering, she'd spotted Dad walking up the cul-de-sac to take them out to the cinema for the occasion. What a weird sight: Dad coming home, yet just visiting. Before she knew what she was doing, Liffy had shot down the stairs, out of the front door and into his arms. Dad had lost a lot of weight – she could feel his ribs when he hugged her – and he'd grown designer stubble, but he held on to her as hard as ever and she felt a huge tide of relief break over her head. Even if he wasn't there, he was still *there*: he still loved her.

'When are you coming back?' she begged.

'I don't know, sweetheart. Soon, I hope,' he said. His voice sounded thinner too. She could tell that he didn't believe what he'd said any more than she did.

Nothing in this drifting, topsy-turvy world is certain, except one thing: Liffy can choose what to eat and what not to eat. With the Earth Prince's voice in her ear encouraging her, praising her when she is restrained, scolding when she lets herself lapse, it's easy – most of the time.

Lisa has a large and fascinating array of cookery books on

her kitchen shelf. Liffy takes down an armful and begins to leaf through them. There is one in Russian – a strange script crammed with back-to-front letters and printed on poor-quality paper; the pictures, which are fading, are of pickled things, and a big rolled-up pie filled with fish and rice and mushrooms, and purple soup with white swirls in it, and little pancakey blinis topped with creamy stuff and caviar. There's a book about Italian cuisine, with enormous, glossy, full-page pictures of fresh pasta dishes and sun-drenched salads and Tuscan vineyards. There's Jamie with his trendy haircut trying to look ever so cool. There's Nigella, licking her finger. There's *Indian Vegetarian Cookery*, a little paperback with yellowing pages – Lisa hasn't been into such things for a good ten years, it seems. Liffy reads and reads and her stomach rumbles. She's *hungry*. She's desperately, frantically, impossibly hungry. But to eat the last two biscuits on the bright green plate would betray herself, the Earth Prince, her future in ballet and everything she'd been doing to be true to them all for the last few months. The feeling will pass, she knows, if she can only hold out long enough.

In the bedroom, Lisa is playing a most beautiful tune, but keeps stopping and going back over the difficult bits. In the front room, the twins have found a computer game that's keeping them quiet. Liffy picks up the two beckoning circles – like blank, eyeless, evil faces – and takes them to the bin. There she holds the lid open with her right foot on the pedal and rubs the Hobnobs between her fingers into minuscule crumbs. Nobody will ever know they've been destroyed rather than eaten.

'Oh, good,' Lisa says, when she comes back into the kitchen after her hour. 'You've finished the biscuits. Now, what shall we have for lunch?'

They spend the afternoon on Hampstead Heath. The twins charge around with their ball and Liffy strolls, examining the trees, running her hands over the different barks, picking up leaves and inspecting the differences in their outlines and veining or their subtle shadings of green and russet. She'd got out of a pasta lunch by saying she'd eaten the biscuits and wasn't hungry.

'I didn't know you were so into trees,' Lisa remarks.

'I love them.' Liffy's dark eyes are filled with adoration as she goes up to a silver birch and presses her nose to its trunk. 'I love the smell of the wood and the earth and the sap,' she tells Lisa. 'We don't have so many different kinds of tree in Richmond Park,' she adds – in case Lisa thinks she's going mad.

'I love them too,' Lisa says.

Lisa feels enriched by Liffy's enthusiasm: the young girl observes the natural world with such freshness and wonder that it's rubbing off on Lisa's more jaded viewpoint. Lisa has her own natural wonder to worry about, growing within her; her mental space has been occupied with this, rather than the glories of Hampstead Heath.

She can't help wondering why Liffy is so quiet. She seems to hold her head in an attitude of half listening as she meanders through the beech grove near the Kenwood fence, shifting twigs with her toes or picking up a small branch of early beechnuts that's fallen down. She says little, but now and then gives a nearly imperceptible nod. Under her long, loose jeans, her feet stick out like a duck's as she walks; that's what ballet lessons can do for you. The twins are in a world of their own too, but at least they share it – and it involves endless discussion of the latest football results, new models of car and other boys' stuff. They're not interested in hugging trees. To be fair, Liffy doesn't resemble the classic tree-hugger either. She doesn't so much cuddle them as worship them. My niece the pagan, Lisa smiles, wondering what her own child will be like at Liffy's age.

She also wonders what Liffy thinks she's listening to.

*   *   *

Staying with Lisa involves a great deal of walking. The children aren't used to this: they are beginning to flag after their energetic afternoon on the Heath, only to find that they have to walk all the way back to West Hampstead to wash and change and then all the way back up the hill to Lisa's friends' house. Luckily Lindsey and Paul don't live as far away as the Heath, but Alex and Matt, with the mud showered away and their trainers cleaned up, are yawning as their aunt leads them out of her front door at half past six for another twenty-minute hike. Liffy has put on her new black linen trousers and top and walks tall and proud in them, feeling sophisticated. Lisa carries her cello case on a shoulder strap; lugging it uphill makes her pant. On the peaked front of the case is a red sticker declaring the contents FRAGILE and a yellow sticker bearing the words: NO, I DON'T WISH I PLAYED THE FLUTE.

'You should get a car, Auntie Lisa,' Matt protests.

'I might, some time soon,' Lisa says. 'There isn't anywhere to park, but it could be useful.'

'You should get one of those really cool convertibles, so you can put the top down in the summer and we can all go for rides with the sound right up.'

'Dream on, young man!' Lisa says.

'Don't get a car,' Liffy says. 'It's much greener to walk and it's better for you, too.'

'True.'

Lisa doesn't tell her that soon she won't be very comfortable walking such distances. She is wearing a loose cream-coloured linen top and skirt that conceal her shape. She has never had a secret from her best friend before, but the last thing she wants now is for Lindsey to know the truth – since Lindsey's instinct would probably be to pick up the phone to Vladimir on the spot.

'Darling!' Lindsey throws her arms round Lisa and gives each of the children a big kiss. The twins pull faces, but try not to let their hostess notice.

Matt – who plans, when he grows up, to be extremely rich and have a home that will make everybody jealous – thinks Lindsey's house is just what he'll want: a detached villa with two big bay windows to the front and a spacious terrace and garden to the back. There's plenty of room inside for games or table tennis or an outsize TV. The big kitchen contains an enormous silver American fridge that you can almost walk into. The garden is massive. Matt likes life's accessories to be large. He prods Alex and points at the tempting lawn; they beg to be allowed outside, and promptly are.

Liffy looks about, assessing the set-up. There's going to be a big buffet, with around twenty-five people present – she counts the plates. A variety of sofas, chairs and floor cushions have been arranged in a haphazard semi-circle near the piano.

'Can I help you with the food?' she asks.

'That's kind of you, sweetheart.' Lindsey, glancing at Liffy's thin face and lanky, linen-swathed legs, looks surprised but appreciative.

Lisa props herself against a solid wooden counter and folds napkins while Lindsey chatters about the programme for the evening and Liffy arranges home-made sushi on a big earthenware platter, leaving one centimetre of space, no more, no less, between the pieces.

'That's the neatest platter I've ever seen,' Lindsey says. 'You should go into catering, Liffy.'

'I'd quite like to, if I wasn't going to dance.' Liffy takes the platter to the big oblong table where Lindsey's setting up the buffet. It is heavy: Liffy's forearms tremble as she carries it.

'Lisa?' Lindsey says, staring at her friend's stick-like niece.

But Liffy is back now, and smiling: it's too late to say anything.

By seven the guests are assembling. Paul pops the corks off several bottles of champagne. He's a dark, charming man approaching fifty – but, like his wife, he looks ten years younger than he is. He has the strong shoulders of a swimmer and, incongruously, a black beard. 'It's to frighten my colleagues at the bank,' he tells the twins, seeing them staring. 'Not many people in the City have beards, but I'm the boss so I can do what I like!' The twins are impressed by this attitude.

Lisa hugs her friends as they arrive and shakes hands with people she doesn't already know. She's glad to see that Matt and Alex are being fussed over: children are not frequent guests at Paul and Lindsey's chamber-music parties.

'Lisa, I wanted you to meet Chris Spencer. He's lodging with us while he studies singing at Guildhall.' Lindsey propels Lisa towards a personable youngish man with red-brown hair and dark eyes.

Lisa smiles at him and he smiles back. 'You don't look like a student,' she says.

'I'm chasing my dream,' says Chris, looking straight into her eyes. 'I was teaching history in Manchester, but there are other ways I thought I'd prefer to use my voice rather than shouting at schoolkids.'

Lisa looks at the floor. This is pointless. Chris is out of bounds. Everyone is out of bounds now. 'Excuse me,' she says. 'I've brought my niece and nephews. I must make sure they're not getting up to mischief.'

Liffy is thrilled to find that she is being treated as an equal. People who must be at least thirty-five are asking her about her school and its well-known music department. It's not long before she discovers that Lindsey is friendly with St Catherine's head of music. Liffy explains, when Lindsey asks, that she doesn't play an instrument but she does do ballet and her best friend, Charlotte, learns the flute.

'Does she have flute lessons at school?' Lindsey asks. 'Is her teacher Robin Brewster?'

'Yes.' Liffy is amazed.

Lindsey beams under her hairband. 'He's a great friend of mine. He's such a lovely guy.'

'Yes,' Liffy says. 'She really, really likes him.'

'I hope he'll come next time we have a party – we wanted him here today but he's gone away for the summer. He and his wife are playing in a festival orchestra in Germany. She's a terrific oboist, you know.'

His wife? Liffy thinks. Robin is *married*? Charley's never said anything about this. If he's married, what's he doing kissing a fourteen-year-old pupil?

'Excuse me,' she says to Lindsey, and wanders out on to the terrace to be on her own and ponder this. The garden is edged with rose bushes and the air is heavy with their scents. Liffy breathes and something within her shivers and spins.

She's lying to you, the Earth Prince is whispering. *She's been lying all along. Don't trust her.*

Oh my God, thinks Liffy. Oh, dear God, if you exist, please help me.

Lindsey has spent the entire day cooking and has made enough to feed double the number of guests. Nothing in the buffet is predictable. The salad has a special dressing made with Far Eastern condiments like sweet soy and mirin; there's lemon grass sauce instead of dill with the smoked salmon rolls; bright tiger prawns poke out of a light, herby quiche; there are spicy chicken pieces marinated with garlic, coriander and lime; there are deep-fried mini-Camemberts with redcurrant jelly, which fascinate the twins; and a basket full of chunks of different kinds of bread beside a platter of dips.

Lisa takes salad, hummus, tzatziki and olive bread. She does not touch the sushi, the soft cheese, the spicy chicken or the prawn quiche, and she fills her wine glass with water. Lindsey stares first at her plate, then straight into her face. 'No way!' she exclaims.

Lisa looks at her and says nothing.

'Lisa!'

'Ssh! Nobody knows.'

'Oh, my God. Is it Vladimir's?'

Damn, thinks Lisa. _Damn. Damn. Damn._ How silly not to have realised that Lindsey, being clued up on what foods to avoid during pregnancy although she has never been pregnant, would see through her diet straight away. 'Lin,' she hisses. 'This is very important. Don't tell anybody. Nobody knows yet. _He_ doesn't know.'

Lindsey gasps. Lisa reaches out to press her friend's wrist. She can imagine how Lindsey is feeling: she'd wanted a baby and had tried and failed to have one, despite living with a beloved husband in a beautiful home, and now she, Lisa, has come along with this story, so rich in irony . . . 'Please, Lin. Promise me you won't tell.'

'If that's what you want, Lee – if you're absolutely sure – I promise. I don't like it, but it has to be your decision.'

'I'm sure, Lin. Where's Liffy gone?'

The twins haven't seen their sister anywhere. They are talking to Chris Spencer about Man U. Chris grew up near Old Trafford, he tells them.

'The one I like is Giggsy,' Matt is opining. 'He can really _move_.'

'Ah, but do you remember Peter Schmeichel, their old goalie? Now, there was a great player. He had those enormous great paws, didn't he?' Chris says.

Alex wonders when he last felt so happy. Here is a roomful of adults treating him and Matt like real people. Nobody talks down to them. Everyone is hoping they're going to be part of the music, and for the first time he's a bit sorry that he can't be. These are cool people, nice and smiling and relaxed. They aren't boring gits like Mum's TV crowd and those stupid critics who kept saying things like 'piffle' and 'poppycock'. Alex no longer thinks that 'piffle' and 'poppycock' are such exciting words.

The grand piano is the biggest he's ever seen in his life – nine foot long, Auntie Lisa tells him – and he's struck by its air of glamour, something he's never noticed in a piano before. Its keys are shiny and clean, not yellow and filthy like the upright ones at school that get pencils and chewing-gum dropped down the back of them. He goes up to it when nobody is looking; Matt is still chattering with Chris about football. Alex runs a small finger along the surface of the keys. Then he presses one. A soft note comes out. He pulls his hand away as if he's been burned, but nobody tells him off. Instead—

'Do you play?' Paul comes up beside him. Alex shakes his head. 'You should learn. It's fun.'

'It's so difficult, though,' says Alex.

'Have you tried?'

Alex shakes his head.

'Try first,' Paul suggests. 'You might be surprised. It's like learning a language. When you first hear it you think you'll never be able to understand. But once you start practising, once you're immersing yourself in it regularly, then little by little it starts to make sense and before you know what's happened you're speaking it fluently.'

Alex runs a finger up the keys. All sorts of pictures are streaming through his mind. Distant cities full of rivers and old squares and mysterious toyshops, music that he can't play, instruments he's never seen before, people talking unfathomable languages and teaching them to him: a whole world of surprises is just waiting for him to get out into the fresh air and discover it, and however much he finds, he'll never be able to explore it all because he already knows that it is infinite. 'Do you play?' he asks Paul, who, he thinks, is the most interesting-looking person he's ever met. 'Will you show me how to play something?'

Paul, to Alex's astonishment, looks positively flattered. 'Come on,' he says, and gestures Alex towards the piano stool.

★   ★   ★

Lisa, her secret out at last, feels almost delirious with relief. She and Lindsey take a turn round the garden together as the sun sinks towards the treetops. Birds are twittering in the lilac bushes and from the house floats the sound of someone picking out the theme tune of *Match of the Day* on the piano.

'But what are you going to *do*?' Lindsey asks, for the twentieth time.

'The best I can.'

'Are you seriously planning not to tell him? He's bound to find out, you know – even if he doesn't hear it from me. Look, be realistic. It'll be obvious how old the child is. He'll know you would have had to jump into bed with someone else the day you left him, and he'd never believe that of you. He knows you too well.'

'You think?'

'Honey, I know he does. I've heard him talking about you. He thinks the world of you.'

'He did a very good job of hiding it from *me*.'

'I think he still loves you.'

'I don't think he ever did. He liked me, he liked sleeping with me, but as for love . . .'

'But can you imagine how it would feel for him to find out he has a child in London whom he's never seen and who doesn't know him? Do you want to put him through that?'

'Lin, whose side are you on?'

'I'm not taking sides. I'm thinking about what's best for you and the baby.'

'That is exactly why I haven't told anyone.' Lisa sighs.

'You can't hide it for ever, though. Soon it'll be showing – and once the baby's there, and if it turns out to look like him . . .'

Lisa feels boxed in. Lindsey's right: she can't hide a living, breathing, screaming baby, and still less can she hide it when it grows into an enchanting toddler who smiles at people who might say, 'But she looks just like . . .' Perhaps she's being stubborn, as only the Wood family knows how to be. Perhaps she wants to hurt Vladimir in return for the three years of immobile pain he's inflicted on her. Or perhaps she's just been taking the easy way out. She hasn't the foggiest idea what she is going to do, how she is going to cope or how she would break the news to Vladimir. It's easier to do nothing than to answer those questions.

'I'll think about it,' she promises. 'I don't know what I'll do – but I will think about it.'

They're quiet as they stroll back towards the terrace. There, Liffy in her black linen is perching on a bench, her knees bent up and her arms locked round them.

'She's awfully thin,' Lindsey remarks.

'I know. I've been a bit worried, to be honest, but having seen her put away the biscuits this morning, I'm not so concerned now. And she spends so much time on her ballet that she must burn up a lot of energy. Liffy! Are you going to come in and listen to the music?'

'Sure.' Liffy shakes herself out of some kind of dream and trots after them.

The party begins to assemble near the piano: Lisa, Lindsey and some friends with a violin and a viola are going to play Schumann. Liffy, Alex and Matt settle themselves on the big floor cushions, while the adults sit on the chairs and sofas. The piano looms above the children, who discover that Lisa and her cello look larger and more awe-inspiring from the floor. Lisa has brushed out her hair and lets it hang free, released from its usual knot. She finds a tiny crack in the parquet flooring in which to prop her cello on its metal spike, tightens her bow and then checks her tuning, along with the other string players, while people stop talking and take a last sip of their wine. Chris gazes at her long hair, her deep eyes and her lavish figure with an approval that even the twins spot at once. They nudge each other and giggle.

Lindsey leans across and beckons to the surprised Alex, who scrambles up. 'Turn the pages for me?' Lindsey whispers.

'I can't read music!' Alex wails.

'Don't worry, I'll tell you where to turn. Just be ready. OK?' They exchange a conspiratorial glance; and at once Alex feels as alert as Peter Schmeichel in goal at the beginning of an FA Cup final. He notices Lisa beaming at him from behind her cello. And while Lindsey plays, Alex simply can't take his eyes off her fingers, zooming around the keyboard in the second movement, the 'scherzo', faster than he and Matt could ever contemplate on their computer games.

The slow movement of the quartet is so beautiful Liffy can't believe it's real. It's the melody Lisa was practising that morning, but complete and unbroken. The cello sings out into the room, like a low, coppery voice, human yet superhuman. The sun is setting above the garden: it flames its light into Lisa's hair and outlines her body through her ivory linen skirt and loose, shape-concealing shirt. The cello's varnish shines scarlet, reflecting the evening glow around the quietened, listening friends. Lisa's face as she plays is half in sun, half in shadow; her eyes are closed and her head tilts backwards, as if she is merely listening in ecstasy to the music her body is producing through the wood, steel and horsehair under her hands.

Liffy has not heard her aunt perform on the cello before. She vaguely understands that Lisa spends her time in the library or writing weird conference papers on her computer. She knows she plays: she's heard her practising. But now, before her eyes, Lisa is transfigured. Her face is no longer worried or patient, but enchanted, as if given over to angelic visions. Her neck seems longer; her arms are strong and her hands sure.

The music is so beautiful that it wrings Liffy's heart out like waterlogged velvet. It's so beautiful that it silences the Earth Prince. Freed from his insistent voice, Liffy's mind straightens out; the music seems to massage away all its knots. The world seems simpler, less terrifying and a thousand times more exciting. She even feels she could take a little more food than the green salad and plain brown bread she's eaten without feeling too guilty.

After the quartet the music has a break. Champagne corks pop and people graze on the remains of the buffet.

'Is it OK if I have some more?' Liffy asks Lisa.

'Heavens, darling, of course it is!' Lisa says, smiling at her.

Liffy wends her way through to the table and takes a piece of tiger prawn quiche. Salt, herbs, egg and shellfish assault her senses with their guns blazing, and as she eats, her hands grow warmer and her head starts to feel less muzzy. She jokes with her brothers. She and Matt tease Alex about his new job as page turner. She's laughing. She's *happy*. In a corner, Lindsey and Lisa are whispering together: Lindsey seems tearful, Lisa is comforting her. When everyone sits down for some more music, night has fallen and Paul has closed the window against the cooling air.

Chris Spencer has been asked by a small record company to make his first CD, of German songs in English. He jokes about it as he introduces the songs he's going to sing, accompanied on the piano by Paul. He doesn't think that Schubert songs work in English, he says, because Schubert's melodic writing is so connected to the flow of the German language. But, hey, that's what the record company wanted and who is he to argue? Recording opportunities don't grow on trees. So *Lieder* in English it is, and tonight he's chosen a group of four Schubert songs, which translate as: 'Night and Dreams', 'Song in the Greenery', 'Serenade' and 'The King of the Alder'. This seems to be an in-joke, as most people laugh; it passes the children by.

'What's the King of the Alder?' Liffy whispers to Lisa, who is sitting on the sofa behind her cushion.

'You'll see,' Lisa whispers back.

When the last song, 'The King of the Alder', begins, Alex nearly falls off his page-turning chair with shock: Paul pounds at the piano, hammering out a threatening theme in the bass. Chris sings: *'Who rides through the dark, this night so wild? It is a father with his young child . . .'*

The pounding on the piano represents the horse's hoofs. The child is sick; the father is trying to get him home on horseback. Chris changes his voice for each character. First he is the narrator; for the father's words he darkens the tone; for the child's he lightens it; and there's a fourth voice, a ghostly, ingratiating voice, the voice of the King of the Alder, or Erl King, beckoning to the sick child to come with him back to his magic world where all sorts of pleasures await him. Each time the Erl King speaks to him, the terrified child cries out: 'Oh, Father! Oh, Father! And can you not hear Alder King's promises in my ear?' And the father responds, 'My son, you heard only the wind,' until the final time, when the father says nothing, but is filled with dread and spurs his horse to ride faster and faster through the howling storm. And suddenly they're there: the horse, the pounding octaves on the piano, comes to a stop outside their house. *'Within his arms, the child – was dead.'* Two chords; the end. There's a shocked, appalled silence. Then thunderous applause. It is only a story, after all.

On the cushions, a commotion is taking place. Liffy, a hand clamped over her mouth, is struggling to her feet, her body heaving. Lisa grabs her arm and guides her to the toilet under the stairs, where Liffy doubles up over the bowl. Her face is green and her eyes dilated with terror.

Lisa flushes the toilet for her and strokes her hair. 'It's OK, love,' she soothes. 'You're OK now. Take some long breaths. Try and breathe very slowly.'

Liffy reaches for her hand. It's a warm night, but her fingers are freezing.

'You must have eaten something bad,' Lisa comforts her,

rubbing Liffy's chilly hand with both of hers. Liffy nods and says nothing. She kneels down next to the toilet. She is making an effort to steady her breathing but seems to be finding it difficult.

'Hush, sweetheart. Don't cry. Don't worry, nobody's blaming you. These things happen. It could have happened to any of us.'

Liffy shakes her head.

A few minutes pass. Lisa sits on the floor and holds Liffy's hand while her breathing slows. A nagging thought needles at Lisa: this doesn't look like food poisoning to her – it looks like a panic attack.

'You're OK now, aren't you?' she asks Liffy.

'I think so.'

'Come on. We should get you home. A cup of tea and a nice warm bed is what you need.'

Lisa helps Liffy to her feet and they walk back into the party. Liffy is shivering.

'She's not feeling too well,' Lisa tells the concerned Lindsey. 'We'd better get her back down the hill. I'm so sorry.'

'Heavens, don't apologise!' Lindsey exclaims. 'I'll run you home.'

'Are you sure? Right now?'

'Absolutely. She can't walk all that way. Wait a sec while I find my keys . . .'

'No, Lin, let me take them,' Chris intervenes. 'You stay with your guests and lend me the car. I won't crash it, promise. Not even in West Hampstead.'

'Chris, you're an angel,' declares Lindsey, handing him the keys. Lisa averts her gaze.

The twins resign themselves to leaving. Alex embraces Paul and thanks him for teaching him to play *Match of the Day*. Paul hugs him back and tells him that he did well to get the hang of it so fast: he must have a good ear for music. And he's a champion page-turner too.

'Call me tomorrow,' Lindsey says to Lisa, giving her another hug.

'I will,' Lisa promises. 'And remember what I said?'

'Of course. We'll talk. Look after yourself.'

'Auntie Lisa,' Matt says, 'why do you and Lindsey hug each other all the time?'

Liffy is quiet as they follow Chris to Lindsey's Range Rover. Then she says to Lisa, 'You know that song?'

'Which? The last one?'

'Is that – like – a new song?'

'New? Goodness, no! Schubert wrote it in the early nineteenth century.'

'Oh my God,' Liffy says.

'It's powerful, isn't it?'

Liffy nods.

Lisa wonders whether it was sitting too close to a very loud piano that brought on Liffy's attack of nausea, or panic; logically, though, it's more likely to be an impending period. Lisa used to feel sick with her periods when she was Liffy's age. Or it could be that centuries-old children's problem: over-excitement. She wonders if it's her fault for making them do too much in one day.

Chris trundles the Range Rover into Lisa's cramped street. 'Here we are. All part of the service.' He beams. 'Sorry you had to leave.'

'I'm sorry too,' Lisa tells him. 'Thank you so much for the ride. We really appreciate it.'

There's a brief silence.

'It was great meeting you, Lisa. Well . . . You know where we are.'

'Yes. Yes, I do. Thank you. Goodnight.'

Up in the flat, the boys – who are very, very tired – brush their teeth, fall straight into the sofa bed and are asleep at once. Lisa gives Liffy a cup of peppermint tea to soothe her stomach. They sit together in the kitchen.

'Can I just call Mum?' Liffy says. 'I said I'd ring her to say goodnight.'

Lisa brings her the portable phone and Liffy taps out Sasha's number.

Sasha's mobile is off.

'That's funny. Mum never, ever switches off her mobile.'

'Are they still on air?' Lisa looks at her watch. The *Weekly Review Special* will have been over for more than an hour.

'Maybe I dialled wrong.' Liffy tries again, pressing the numbers slowly and deliberately, checking each one as she goes. All that sounds in response is an automated voicemail greeting.

'Oh, well. I'll try her in the morning.'

Liffy goes into the bathroom first, and by the time Lisa is ready for bed, she's tucked under her own duvet, her face lamplit. Lisa is wearing cotton pyjamas. Her abdomen bulges underneath. She notices Liffy giving it a curious glance.

'What was Lindsey crying about?' Liffy asks.

'It's a long story.'

'That guy Chris – he really liked you, didn't he?'

'I think so. It's too bad.'

'I thought you liked him.'

'I do. But it's not so simple.'

'Why not? Can't he just call you and ask you out? Or you call him?'

Lisa takes a deep breath. She has to break the news to them all some time. 'Can you keep a secret?' she says. 'Just for a few weeks – and then everyone will know?'

'Yes, of course I can.'

Lisa sits down on the bed next to her. 'Put your hand here,' she says, motioning to her tummy.

Liffy does. Her hand is still cold.

'Feel anything?'

'It feels – a little – like you've put on weight?'

'Yes, I have. I'm going to put on a lot more very soon.'

'Are you going to have a baby?'

'Yes. I am. He or she is your cousin, Liffs. And he or she is in there right now, growing and growing.'

Liffy, her eyes wide, strokes Lisa's small bulge. 'What about Vladimir?'

'I'll worry about him later.'

'Is that why you don't want to go out with Chris?'

Lisa laughs. 'How can I go on a date with a nice man and tell him I'm about to have someone else's baby?'

'I see,' says Liffy, although she can't quite get her head round it. 'When will the baby be born?'

'January. But I haven't told anyone yet,' Lisa adds. 'I will soon, because people are starting to guess. Lindsey guessed tonight because there are things I'm not allowed to eat. But your mum doesn't know and neither does Granny. So don't say anything to anyone until I have.'

Liffy's eyes are shining. 'Auntie Lisa, it's wonderful, isn't it?'

'It really is. Let's get some sleep now, shall we?'

'Yes, let's. Night night.'

'Night night.'

The lights are out. The twins are silent on their sofa; a sliver of pearly moonlight filters between the curtains. Lisa is drifting in and out of consciousness, her music and her friends and the evening's events circling round and round in her head, when she becomes aware that something is wrong.

Liffy had fallen asleep straight away, but now she is lying rigid on her half of the bed, shaking from head to foot.

'Liffs?'

Liffy does not move. Her eyes are still closed. She is murmuring in her sleep. 'No,' she seems to be saying. 'I don't want to go.'

'Go where?' whispers Lisa.

'No. No! Leave me alone. Earth prints. Leave me alone!'

'Liffy, wake up, sweetheart.' Lisa can't bear it. She takes Liffy's shoulder and shakes until her eyes open.

'You were having a bad dream,' she explains to the upset, disoriented girl. 'It didn't sound like much fun. You were talking in your sleep.'

'Oh God. It was really frightening. I was so scared.'

'What was it? What were you dreaming about?'

'Oh . . . I dunno. Nothing. Just . . . nothing. It's gone now.'

'Would you feel better with the light on?'

'No . . . It doesn't make much difference.'

'Liffy? What were earth prints?'

Liffy's eyes open wider and she freezes – Lisa wonders if she's paralysed by fear. But it passes, and all she says is 'It's . . . it's nothing . . . It's just . . . nothing, really.'

14

A tram rolls by, gleaming in the sunlight on its tidy new rails. Sasha, strolling alone through Manchester, looks on, impressed.

What a perfect way to get around. Faster than buses, more user-friendly than trains, greener than cars, safer than bicycles and more efficient than all four put together. How typical of twentieth-century government that they got rid of them in London, and now the place is gridlocked. She must write something, when she gets home, about how marvellous Manchester is.

She was tired after the long drive, but a good cup of coffee has revived her. That's something else that's changed in Manchester over the last twenty years. Last time she was here, touring with her dance company in 1982, they hadn't been able to get a decent cup of coffee anywhere. The provincial north had left her cringing with horror: dark and dank, grey and grim, the boarding-houses equipped with nylon sheets and ancient blankets with holes in them where anonymous lodgers had dropped cigarette ash. Mostly the rooms had looked out over Victorian railway sidings, from draughty windows that didn't fit properly. What is it about the English, she wonders, that they like to suffer? That they seem to believe it's character-building to live in the cold, that heating a house means you're 'soft', that one mustn't grumble because there's a war on? That must be it, Sasha muses, wandering past yet another Starbucks. The English have never recovered from the fact that the Second World War is over – because nothing half as exciting has happened to them since.

But here everything is moving on. The Royal Exchange, which was black with decades of soot when she last saw it, has been cleaned up. The shopfronts around her hold vast, gleaming, plate-glass windows. Instead of just greasy fish-and-chip shops and plasticky pizza joints, she has been spotting organic juice cafés and sushi bars.

Sasha is glad that Manchester doesn't much resemble her memories of it. It was in Manchester that someone in the audience had laughed at them. They'd been performing a difficult new ballet, made for them by one of the trendiest young choreographers then working in London. It felt difficult and disagreeable to dance and contained many of the movements that in those days were considered rebellious because they were forbidden in classical ballet: flexed ankles and toes, knees turned in, bums sticking out, angular turns – ugliness for the sake of not being beautiful. The music was electronic ambient sound and the choreographer had set out to make sure the movements did not relate to it in any way at any time. None of the audiences on the tour had liked the piece, though most were too polite to say so, especially when the critics were saying how terrific it was. But in Manchester someone had laughed.

He'd laughed so loudly they could hear it from the stage. It began with a great, guffawing snort, followed by a machine-gun explosion of he-haws; then a shout of 'Booo!' and muttering and grumbling from the people nearby as he got up to walk out and clambered as noisily as he could across his neighbours' knees. Sasha, on stage and distracted, had lost her way. She'd never forgotten her movements before. Now she got lost. It lasted only a matter of seconds, but the terrified young dancer she was then had imagined that the horsemen of the apocalypse had come to drag her to hell. It still pains her to think about it. What's past is past; the longer ago it is, the better.

She's never quite got over the idea that Manchester is somehow cursed.

Her journey had been smooth, but she'd arrived to find a message at the hotel that Rick and the TV crew had been held up on the M25 by a puncture. They are on their way, but won't arrive until four, if not later. Sasha has more time to herself than she'd expected.

Without children, without company, Sasha doesn't know where to put herself. All her different roles are, briefly, suspended: mother, wife, daughter, sister, writer, pundit, would-be lover. She has nothing to do except enjoy herself alone. Sasha has never much liked being alone. She has to be solitary to write, but always there has been the certainty that the children are there, that later Adam will be, that the world is part of her and she part of it, even if at the end of a phone line. She doesn't know anyone in Manchester; she is not part of this city and her mind is not in the present but rushing ahead to when she might be alone with Rick. She finds a clean-tabled sandwich bar for lunch, after which she notices a large bookshop across the road and goes inside to lose herself among the shelves.

At three forty-five Sasha buys the paperbacks on the three-for-two offer that she most wants to read, and heads back to the hotel. Her heart misses several beats when she sees the BBC van outside the Bridgewater Hall. Coming and going, setting things up, a gaggle of cameramen, production assistants with clipboards and miscellaneous others are dashing to and fro – what do all these people *do* all day? Sasha wonders – and in the middle of them is a tall, sandy-haired figure in a lavender-blue cotton sweater, talking nineteen to the dozen on his mobile. Sasha lingers, wondering whether to catch his eye from a distance; deciding against it, she marches into the mayhem and touches his arm. Rick jumps, raises both eyebrows, mouths, 'Hello!' at her and brushes one hand against her linen-clad shoulder.

It's soon clear to Sasha that she is (a) early and (b) re-dundant until it is time for the show. She can't get over the complexity of live TV: even today, in this supposed age of high technology, it involves so many trailing black leads, such precision over the placement of the camera, such caution over lighting and microphones. It needs a vanload of equipment, more than a vanload of staff and an endless supply of sandwiches. Watching Rick's substantial shoulders and taut behind, swathed in knitted cotton and light summer trousers, while he darts about like an officious swallow surveying a lake for edible insects, she finds herself half wishing that Cindy could be there too: they'd have gone off for a drink together and talked about books and films and the vagaries of men and had a good laugh.

Instead her fellow guests are people she's heard of but hasn't met before: a composer named Peter Claydon and a gay novelist and critic from Sri Lanka called Vijay Amrasakara. The perfect balance: a white man, a Jewish woman, a gay ethnic minority, reflects Sasha, with some bitterness. Going purely on talent, she reflects, Vijay ought to be there on his own: his writing far outshines anything she's ever done. Her scant attempts at fiction had ended up in the shredder, but for a few pages that the cats had appropriated for their amusement. As for Claydon, he has one piece played every blue moon, by a chamber group in the north of Scotland.

Sasha decides to leave Rick to his job. She goes up to her room, lies on her front on the cream-coloured bedspread with her feet on the pillows and begins to read one of her new books. The silence gets to her. No children; no cats; no Adam. She wonders, a sour taste in her mouth, how he is; she wonders why she feels as she does without him, half relieved, half bereaved. She's in Manchester intending to begin a love affair – a lust affair, anyway. Unlikely, she thinks, but true.

She doesn't mean to fall asleep, but does anyway; and wakes to find that it's nearly seven. Her head is hurting – she should have opened the window for some air – and her eyes feel dry and sore. She puts on her favourite television suit: matching mid-blue linen trousers and jacket, a bright top patterned with a modern, jagged design, and chunky, high-heeled sandals with ankle straps. She runs a large-toothed comb through her hair, dabs on fingertips of pomade to define the curls and pins them back into a silver slide. Then the makeup: deep brown definer and smoky shadow for her eyes, dark bronzed-red lipstick, and some concealer to make herself look less tired, less worried, less fortyish. When she switches on her performing self – a self that radiates to the back of the theatre like white diamonds, as her ballet training taught her – she knows she will look stunning. Nevertheless something inside her feels worn and frayed. She's got to want to be out there; today she doesn't. She should never have gone to sleep.

She's nervous, too. She's not used to audiences being allowed to talk back, as they will this time. They'll be asking questions and she'll have to think of something to say, on the spot, under the lights, in front of the cameras. And she can't get out of her head the incident, twenty years ago, of the man who laughed.

At the bar in the Bridgewater Hall, she can't decide whether she needs caffeine, alcohol or calming herbal tea to get her through this.

'Mineral water,' Rick advises, appearing by her side as if from nowhere. 'You need to be well hydrated to be alert.'

'Mind reader,' Sasha teases him, breathing in the warmth that surrounds him.

'Lots of people feel that way when they're about to be put on the spot like this. I always find them wondering which legal drug they want. Don't worry, it'll be over soon and I've booked this great Italian restaurant for dinner afterwards. We'll have fun.'

'Sounds good to me.'

'So.' Rick's eyes pierce hers. 'See you on the ice. Break a leg.'

'You too.'

Sasha sips her water, half wishing she'd had alcohol instead. Best not to. It's not often that she craves a drink – her mother's experience is warning enough. To stop herself succumbing, she walks away from the bar. Vijay is on the other side of the bright foyer, standing in a golden pool of evening sun: he is both extraordinarily handsome and extraordinarily effete and he's wearing a cream silk Chinese-style jacket. She introduces herself and tells him how much she loves his latest book. As they strike up conversation, Peter Claydon bumbles up to them and butts in. Sasha lets him. None of this, given what she's come here to do, even begins to feel important.

It's time for a sound check. As they take their places and an assistant fixes microphones on to their clothes, Sasha looks at Rick and electricity flashes between them like far-off lightning, its thunder too distant to hear. Now she begins to wake up; to feel glad she's there; to look forward to Later On. She forgets the composer's crummy clothing and pompous voice and smiles at the gathering audience. Rick gazes at her; she notices the creases at the sides of his mouth and wants to kiss them. It's been a couple of weeks since she last had the opportunity. This is her night. The programme is about to begin.

15

Adam takes in the red electronic numbers on the scales, dazed. He's lost more than a stone. His trousers are falling off.

In the mirror, his bearded face looms large as if from a different plane of existence; he hasn't shaved for a month. His old self, the self that was himself – a free spirit, of sorts, who painted – had been bearded. He wonders whether it is emerging from the prison he'd built for it. It wasn't dead – just incarcerated, on a life sentence.

Now that he has a measure of perspective on what has been happening to him, he has begun to feel guilty. At least he is basically all right. He and Nick have reached a modus vivendi, one that involves Nick working long hours – now that he's art director of *Trafalgar* – then coming home for beer and cigarettes with Adam, who has the days to himself. Nick eases Adam's loneliness; Adam eases Nick's.

He's been back to his house, seen his kids, told Liffy he loves her, taken them out to the cinema for the twins' birthday. He's been to Oxford to visit Gerald several times; he's even been to see Aaron to consider psychotherapy. He has taken trips and walks – Kew Gardens, Bushey Park, Osterley, but not Richmond Park, which means home – and tries to force himself to eat, although it doesn't make much difference to his weight. Sometimes he just goes into central London and walks for the sake of walking.

That afternoon, walking through Soho, he meanders half by accident into the art shop where he used to buy all his materials when he was a student, more than two decades ago. The smell of pastels and fresh paper fills him with longing: one whiff and he plummets back twenty years. The longing hurts. He can't bring himself to leave without taking something of the place, and the time, with him. He chooses a large sketch pad and some pastels and pays for them. He never used pastels in the old days – he'd draw with charcoal, or paint with oils; all or nothing. But now he doesn't want the blackness of charcoal, or the fumes of oil paints. It's vital that he tries something new, something undreamed-of. He carries his purchases back to Nick's house, settles himself on a kitchen chair in the box-like patio garden and switches off one side of his brain.

Nick finds him there at seven o'clock, when the sun is slanting over the grey Victorian houses and the neat gardens where roses are donating their evening scents to the warm, beseeching air. Adam is sitting with pad on knee, a box of pastels beside him, eyes lowered and focused, hands working. Nick had been about to offer him a beer, but, seeing what he's doing, keeps quiet. He knows that to interrupt an artist is like distracting someone flying a kite. It takes effort and concentration to catch the current and ride it. Lose that concentration and the kite plunges back to earth; it can shatter on impact.

'You can see if you like,' Adam tells him, without looking up.

Nick peers over his shoulder. 'You always pooh-poohed pastels at college.'

'What did I know?' Adam shrugs.

Nick recognises traces of Adam's old style: imitation-Cézanne blocks of colour, figures in deft, minimalistic, Matisse-inspired lines. Ideally, the whole should exist both as an abstract but aesthetically pleasing collection of lines, colour and form, and as a narrative image, frozen in time. He identifies a mound-like hill; a gnarled branch – an olive tree? A figure lies in the foreground, prostrate, its arms stretched to the sides; two figures loom in the background in attitudes suggesting they're asleep. Perhaps Adam is revisiting that Greek island.

'What is it?' he asks.

'Christ in the garden of Gethsemane.'

'What?'

'What can I draw? I can't draw myself – I wouldn't want to. I can't draw my kids, I miss them too much. And, God knows, I can't draw Sasha.'

'"Could you not watch with me one hour?"' Nick quotes, looking at the blended colours, the acidic flavour in the sharp pinks and purples and greens that Adam has rubbed together into an intense aura around the Christ figure.

'Exactly.'

'I thought you were Jewish.'

'Call me a lapsed orthodox agnostic if you want. I don't care where the image comes from – it's the one I want right now.'

'Can't say I blame you. I feel that way too.' Nick paces across the patio and back again. 'I spoke to Mary today.'

'How's the little one?'

'She's great. I miss her so much. *God*, I miss her. Anyhow. Anyhow, anyhow, do you want a beer?'

Adam, swigging from the can, is absorbed in the thought of his picture. The more he drew, the more he'd wanted to draw, but the more focused the image in his mind, the less satisfactory his rendition felt. He's always kept painting, but it's been strictly amateur for so long that he suspects he's lost his touch. He knows it could take years to build up again to a level that would satisfy him and compare with his work twenty years ago. He can get his old self back, perhaps – but now he understands that rekindling his talent, if talent it had ever been, is a different matter. And still the words whisper over and over in his mind: 'Could you not watch with me one hour?'

'How's work?' he asks Nick.

'I've been airbrushing out a few pubic hairs from our cover girl's bikini line. You'd have loved this job, Ad.' Nick picks up his evening paper and leafs through it to the TV section.

'I can't even remember what pubic hair looks like.'

'Don't worry, Ad, it's like riding a bicycle. You never forget. Or so they tell me. Christ – you know something?' Nick's finger alights on a word in the TV columns. 'Your wife's on the *Review* tonight. Live from Manchester.'

'Manchester?'

'You want to watch?'

'Sure. She can't yell at me if she's on TV.'

All the same, much later, when the *Weekly Review Special* begins, Adam's heart crashes to the floor at the sight of Sasha in her blue linen suit and strappy sandals. She looks ferociously glamorous and fearsomely tired.

The usual adversarial element is missing from the programme tonight, focused as it is on audience questions and responses. Adam wonders who's really interested in what Mrs Bloggs from Didsbury thinks of a new book – isn't the point of these programmes to let people know what the experts think, rather than giving space to anybody who happens to like the sound of their own voice? That's not the direction of TV at the moment, however, so he listens with some interest to the questions sent towards Sasha.

'It's a remarkable achievement,' she's saying, about a new British film set on a housing estate in Tower Hamlets. 'It's a brave, powerful story about the nature of racisim in Britain, and the amateur actors have done a stupendous job at portraying these people's grim lives . . .'

Adam realises that he doesn't miss this aspect of his wife. The stream of judgements that escapes her lips tends to wear him down – so like his mother, sometimes. There is no quiet-ness in Sasha, as there is in him. There is no stillness in her soul; perhaps the capacity for stillness was what had been lacking in her dancing. Endless action means eventual exhaustion in a field where motion is defined by motionlessness. Sasha always has to be on the move, always seeking out life's next thrill, always driven to find expression. All the same, as Adam watches her on screen, love, betrayal, devastation and the pity of it all jostle for space in his fragile spirit. He can never forget the first time he saw her, the first time he spoke to her, the first time they made love. *Could you not watch with me one hour?*

'I don't believe this is a fundamentally racist country,' Vijay is replying, to a question about the film. 'My experience of British society has been that it's remarkably fair. Obviously there are problems, things go wrong. That's what we hear about, those instances where such things happen. But in the main, Britain is less racist than, say, France, where society is much more segregated, and vastly less racist than certain countries in Eastern Europe. It's less class-ridden than India, where the caste system blights people to a desperate degree, and poverty in Britain is nothing compared to poverty in Africa. What we sometimes forget, living in this country, is that we are unbelievably lucky. The biggest problem in the UK is its tendency to insularity. If we played a more positive part in Europe and could lose our self-limiting, myopic island mentality, perhaps people would look further outside these shores and realise that we have much to be proud of and much to build on for the future.'

A mutter of fury goes round the Bridgewater Hall foyer at the mention of Europe, and Sasha rolls her eyes heavenwards. She and Vijay exchange smiles. They are on the same side.

'We're a country of Philistines,' Peter Claydon chimes in. He's an Edwardian-looking fellow in a tweed jacket, streaks of hair pulled sideways across his head to cover the bald area. 'Let's not knock British cinema for the sake of it – it's one of the few areas of the arts that receives any real support in this country. When you look at the level of investment that countries such as France and Germany put into their arts, and the esteem in which artists of all types are held in *Russia*, for God's sake . . .'

Adam watches his estranged wife. Something about her is not the same. He looks at her bright, dark eyes and the shadows under them. She seems restless, which is usual; frazzled – which is not usual, but inevitable since she's coping alone with the kids; and also distracted, which is not at all usual. He wonders what she's thinking. He wonders whether she misses him. And he wonders what she's done with the kids while she's in Manchester. There's no sign of them in the audience. She'd be unlikely to leave them with Sally. The least she could have done was ask to send them to him for the day.

He jumps up and dials Lisa's number. Her answering-machine is on.

When the programme ends and the credits roll, he catches a last glimpse of Sasha in her blue suit, tiny and distant under the churning white letters, and suddenly he misses her so much that he has to sit down and catch his breath. He remembers himself, young, rebellious and idealistic, sitting by her hospital bed; his insistence, quiet but definite, that she would be well again and that he would look after her while she recovered; he could hear his voice telling her how he'd never felt this way about anyone else, that the feeling between them was too special to abandon, that all he wanted was for her to give him a chance, and that if after a while she wasn't happy with him, then she could go, but please, explore the possibilities first – because they could be heroes together. The energy of art, the energy of love – no amount of beard-growing or notions of self-recapturing can bring those back to him once they've gone. *Could you not watch with me one hour?*

16

Rick has booked the restaurant not only for himself and Sasha, it turns out, but also for Vijay, Peter and the production assistant, Marion (thirtyish, blonde, pretty).

Sasha plasters her brightest smile and some extra lipstick over her disappointment before they set off in two cabs, riding out of the city centre towards the suburb of Sale. The restaurant has white-tiled floors, white and green décor and plenty of purple Chianti. Sasha sits next to Vijay and busies herself asking him questions about his creative processes and what Sri Lanka is like. She hardly looks Rick in the eye. The Chianti rasps down her throat, perhaps in greater quantities than she would normally have taken. She doesn't like to admit to herself that she's even more nervous than she was before the show.

She'd expected to spend dinner getting to know Rick that much better, allowing as yet untold confidences to spill out, living for the longed-for moment. Instead she's still in her TV self, discussing the state of arts funding and dwindling audiences and the surge in dross television panel games and how celebrity chefs can have become so popular. Now and then Rick's lilting tenor cuts through the general morass of talk around her, voicing an opinion, making a joke, joining the laughter. Her mind latches on to it and follows it as an angler would the flash of a bright fish. She eats tuna and bean salad, baked sea bass and half a helping of tiramisu – Marion the production assistant has the other half. They order more Chianti. Peter, whose face turns redder with each sip, keeps filling her glass: it's a perfect excuse to refill his own.

When the cabs come to take them back to the hotel, Rick gets into one with Peter and Marion. Vijay and Sasha take the other and amicably swap email addresses. Vijay is gay: they can't threaten one another. Sasha is embarrassed to find that her eyes are closing; images of this long, unfinished day are hurtling through her brain. She doesn't want Vijay, who's been shortlisted for seven literary prizes, to think she's drunk – although she probably is – and she certainly doesn't want to fall asleep.

The five of them say goodnight in the foyer and disperse to their rooms. Sasha has made no arrangement with Rick, but when she reaches her room on the fourth floor – where her book is still open, turned upside-down on the bed – she sits down and waits. She can hardly breathe. In five minutes, the phone rings. She hears his voice and says, 'Come up.' She wishes she hadn't drunk so much: the room is dancing about her like a merry-go-round. She forces herself into the bath-room to brush her teeth and take away the taste of the errant Chianti. She also drinks two large glasses of water. Then she hears the knock.

Rick closes the door behind him and embraces her at once, running his hands up and down her back. Sasha feels queasy. They stand together, fingers interlaced.

'I'd thought we might get to talk over dinner,' Sasha admits.

Rick gives her an astute, blue-lit glance. 'I thought it was best to cover the tracks,' he says.

'I'm sure you're right.'

There's awkwardness in the soundproofed silence. The clocks stop; the universe loiters with intent. The long hiatus could be one second or sixty. Rick finally breaks it, pulling her to him with the unambiguous, well-used phrase: 'Come here, you.'

Next thing she knows, he's kissing her neck and reaching under her bright blouse to her bra fastening, manoeuvring her towards the bed. 'God, you're gorgeous,' he mumbles into her shoulder. 'How come you're so gorgeous?'

Sasha's fingers feel as boneless as wool as she tries to undo his shirt buttons. As Rick unzips her trousers and they slide down, she finds she's worrying like some idiot that her linen clothes are going to be creased. Flat on her back a moment later, she reaches out to the switches to alter the lighting. Rick sits up and pulls off his socks.

'*Wow*,' he says, turning back to her and peeling away her last remaining garments. 'What a body. You're so beautiful. I can see you were a dancer.'

'A dancer who hasn't danced for fourteen years and has had twins!'

'You'd never know that, never. You're so gorgeous. Oooooh!' His skin is against hers, his hands rubbing and exploring. Sasha lies back and tries to luxuriate: nobody has told her she's beautiful for a very long time. If only she hadn't drunk so much: it deadens the response, as Shakespeare noted in *Macbeth* . . .

'What fantastic legs,' Rick grunts, caressing. 'How many minis do you have?'

'What?'

'Mini-skirts. Do you have lots?'

'No.' Sasha hasn't worn a mini-skirt since before her children were born. But this isn't the moment to be talking about such things.

'I've been thinking about you all the time. I've been imagining being in bed with you. I've been jerking myself off thinking about you.' Rick's voice is no longer a lilting tenor: it's become low and frenetic and the words flow, rapid and urgent, into Sasha's ear. 'My cock gets hard every time I think of you.'

Sasha likes the feel of his hands on her body, but wishes he'd stop talking. She tries to distract him with a trick that she knows.

'Oooooh, you sexy bitch! That feels so, so, so, so good. God, I want to put it inside you. I want to put it into your cunt.

But no, no, no, not yet. Not yet. No, wait. Now I'm imagining you in a black mini, one of those tight shiny PVC ones that shows every curve and every line . . .'

Sasha opens her eyes and looks up at the ceiling above Rick's head. It's not that she's shocked – but she's not certain she likes Rick's vociferous approach. It stops her concentrating . . .

'I wanted to undress you on the programme tonight. I wanted to stand up in front of all those people on live TV and pull off all your clothes and say, "Hey, Britain, look at this bloody glorious sexy body, this incredible sexy bitch." I wanted to throw you down on the floor and do it to you right there.'

Then he's on her and inside her and for a few moments it feels as fantastic as she's been hoping. She tilts her body, opening to him, her blood starting to fire up – and then he starts talking again.

She's stopped listening to what he's saying. It's more of the same and she wishes he'd shut up. His body feels good and she wants to lose herself in the sensation, but his incessant stream of words is putting her off.

'Sssh,' she says. 'Be quiet – just feel.'

'I'm feeling, I'm feeling! God, you feel fucking incredible . . .'

She lifts a hand and puts it over his mouth. Rick makes an intensely pleasured noise deep in his throat and sucks at her fingers. That keeps him quiet for around ten seconds, but soon he wants to move on and as his excitement mounts, he talks faster and louder and then, as he comes, he shouts out a staggering stream of ten different expletives. Sasha, underneath, counts them.

She stares up at the ceiling – a fashionable creamy ivory – while he rolls off her and lies back, panting. 'Christ, that was good. *Jesus.* So. It's true, then. I always heard Jewish girls were a good lay.'

'*What?*' Sasha manages.

'Well, aren't you? Look at these hips.' Rick slaps the side of

Sasha's thigh. 'Look at these boobs.' He presses her left breast. 'You're as hot as chilli powder.'

Sasha wonders whether she should make a joke of this, but she doesn't feel like it. All she can think of by way of retaliation is that the Irish are said to have the gift of the gab – which he's just proved beyond reasonable doubt. She wonders whether he talks all the time in bed with his wife. No wonder they're miserable. Or are there some women who like it? Who maybe join in? Is she simply the world's greatest prude? She doesn't think so. She's never been inhibited in bed with Adam. When things went wrong, her sexual inclination certainly wasn't the problem. But Rick's talking, Rick's whole angle on the business, was a profound turn-off. Strange, she considers, that her livelihood and reputation rest on words, but in bed she wants physical expression alone, without speech. That part of her will always be a dancer.

'You're very quiet, aren't you?' Rick says. A second later, he lets out a snore. She looks down at him: he's dead to the world.

Sasha tiptoes to the bathroom, washes and takes a headache pill. Rick doesn't stir when she comes back. She slides under the sheet, keeping well away from him, turns out the light and closes her eyes, longing for an oblivion in which none of this had ever begun to happen.

In the dark, she remembers making love with Adam in the early days. They'd melt together in silence, dissolving the boundaries between them. They'd felt made for each other: two halves of the same person, long lost, reunited. Everything lay in touch and taste, in the surge of blood that wasn't just physical but spiritual too in some obscure way. She misses the darkness, the silence, the depth of Adam's eyes – years ago – locked into hers as they fell together through space and time. Beside her, Rick turns on to his back and begins to snore.

Unable to sleep for the noise, Sasha lies still, knowing she's made the sort of mistake that remorphs the dangers in the world like an earthquake in a zoo. So much for her parallel bloody universes. Her mind had run away with her. She'd pictured an easy transition – trading in the old man for a new model, as Cindy might have put it. Without meaning to, she'd imagined foreshadows of amicable separations for both of them, maybe a new home to furnish together, different routines and intelligent conversations and a trip to Ireland. She'd thought of Basty and the twins getting to know each other and becoming friends – too much to hope that Liffy would too. Oh, please. Per-lease.

She'd been faithful to Adam since the day they'd bumped into each other in the bookshop off Charing Cross Road. She prides herself on her intellect and her reinvented writerish self, she pontificates to the nation on life and love – yet she knows nothing, but *nothing*, of life and love outside her cosy bourgeois marriage, and now that she's trying it, she finds she doesn't like it. How naïve is she? How could she have been so stupid? It's all too humiliating.

Her mind whispering something to her about blue remembered hills and lands of lost content, Sasha slides into an uneasy sleep.

The twins are kneeling side by side on Lisa's window-seat, faces pressed to the glass. They're watching four cars fighting nose to nose at the crossroads.

'Road rage! Road rage!' Matt cries. Down in the street a man in a baseball cap has got out of his car and is demanding that the driver of the car going in the opposite direction gets out of his too. He refuses. Each of the two perpendicular cars is hooting at the other three.

'It's not so great,' Lisa advises, pouring orange juice for Saturday brunch. 'It happens every day. There's two-way traffic on both roads and no space for anyone.'

'We're in a cul-de-sac,' Matt grumbles. 'Nothing exciting ever happens there.'

'When's Mum back?' Liffy asks from the armchair, where she's curled up with a recipe book.

'It depends how long it takes her to get here from Manchester.'

Liffy refuses the orange juice. Lisa had woken at eight to find Liffy gone. She'd got up at seven, she admitted, had some muesli and read her book. She's so used to getting up early, she told Lisa, that it's hard to break the habit in the holidays.

The little flat is ready to burst, holding one owner, one foetus, three children and a seriously displeased cat. Lisa wonders how on earth she will manage here with the baby. She'll have to move. It'll be fine for a year or even two, but the child will need a room of her or his own. She wonders how she will ever be able to afford somewhere bigger.

Liffy glances at her over the top of the cookery book. Lisa gives her a bright smile. Liffy tries to smile back. Lisa's heart twinges. Liffy doesn't look right. She doesn't look well. She's too thin. She must be missing Adam. And perhaps the after-effects of her stomach upset are adding to the problem today.

The four pass a quiet morning with books (the girls) and computer games (the boys), and at one o'clock the doorbell rings.

'That was quick!' Lisa exclaims, letting her sister in in a flurry of blue linen.

'I left early,' says Sasha. Her eyes are red and her face is white. 'I just wanted to get back.'

'Come and have some coffee.'

'Thanks. As I've actually managed to park in this idiotic street, I ought to take advantage of it.'

'Mum! Mum!' The twins and Liffy run up to hug Sasha, who embraces each one in turn. Lisa smiles: this will be her, soon.

Lisa and Sasha make small-talk about the programme over coffee and Sasha sniffs pointedly at the faint pong of cat litter. Neither can say the things they want to say because of the children. Sasha tells Lisa about Vijay and Peter and how much

Manchester has changed. She can't say that the vegetation of her world view has lost its leaves overnight. Lisa can't say, 'What's wrong with Liffy? Why is she frightened of earth prints?'

There is one thing she can say, however. Liffy knows now; so does Lindsey. What's the point of keeping it secret any longer? People know – and it doesn't feel as bad as she'd expected.

'Sash, I've got some news. Can you guess what it is?'

Sasha's eyes travel up and down Lisa's blossoming body. 'You have got to be joking.'

'Not a bit.'

'When?'

'January.'

'Vladimir?'

'Naturally.'

'Oh, God. What's he going to do?'

'I'm more worried about what I'm going to do.'

'Jesus, Lee. Is it too late for an abortion?'

'I want it, Sash.'

Liffy smiles for the first time all morning. The twins, who hadn't been privy to the secret, are wide-eyed.

'What are you talking about?' Alex demands.

'Auntie Lisa's having a baby,' Liffy tells them. Their mouths fall open.

'Lee, you're either very brave or completely crazy,' Sasha says. 'Possibly both.'

'I think – I think – small people are a good thing,' Liffy chimes in.

'Of course they are, Liffs,' Sasha says, 'but there's a time and a place for everything. This, Lee, doesn't look like either.'

'It has to be both.'

'Of course,' Sasha muses, 'there are plenty of women who would love the chance to adopt . . .'

'I'm not giving it up for adoption! How can you even think of that?' Lisa's cheeks have turned carmine.

'You'll have to move.'

'At some point, yes.'

'You might have to get the Child Support Agency on to Vladimir.'

'I don't want Vladimir bothered.'

'You don't want him *bothered*? He's the father of your child! You've got to involve him. You can't just pretend he doesn't exist.'

'Sasha, it's my baby, it's my problem. I'll handle it in my own way. All right?'

'You're being unbelievably obtuse about this. It's crazy.'

'One thing, Sash.' Lisa diverts the subject, which is sometimes the only option. 'I haven't told Mum yet.'

'Oh no. Oh my God. What's she going to say?'

'That's her problem, not mine. I've got enough to worry about. But I will tell her, very soon.'

'Oh God. Poor Mum.'

Sasha, to Lisa's astonishment, flops back on the sofa and puts a hand over her eyes. Lisa has never seen her look so stressed. For the first time in years she feels sorry for her sister.

Out in the street there's more hooting and shouting. The twins leap up from the computer and run to the window to watch the fun.

'We should hit the road,' Sasha says, behind her hand. 'Come on, guys, get your stuff together. Time to go home.'

Liffy drifts towards the bathroom while the twins dive about picking up yesterday's discarded T-shirts. Matt has lost a Homer Simpson sock.

'Sasha, I'm slightly worried about Liffy,' Lisa whispers, while the children are out of the room. 'She's so thin.'

'It's been a hard time for all of us.' Sasha's personality balloon, usually flown so high, has flopped to earth; it's as if someone has let out all the hydrogen. Lisa wonders who.

'Liffy's the lucky one – she's getting a holiday,' Sasha adds. 'She's off to Greece with Charley and family.'

'Is she *eating*?'

'Eating? Why? Didn't she eat here?'

'Well, she had a tummy upset last night at the party and I wouldn't blame her if she hadn't wanted to eat this morning . . .'

'Buffet food, was it? Always dangerous. Oh, how was the playing?'

'Good, thanks. Alex wants to learn the piano.'

And in the surprise of this unexpected piece of information, in asking Alex whether it's true (it is) and why (he explains), Liffy's upset stomach is forgotten. Liffy packs up her rucksack and asks Lisa if she can borrow the Jamie Oliver cookbook.

Then they're all gone, piling out of the front door and walking, running or trailing (respectively, Sasha, twins and Liffy) up the road to their car. Lisa waves to them from the window. Igor comes out of his hiding-place, stretches his legs and body and gives a contented cat yawn. Silence descends on the flat, which now feels larger and emptier than ever before.

17

Liffy is drowning in Aegean sunlight. It's as if someone has pulled a scarf off the sky to reveal, underneath, the glorious blaze that is the real summer, not the bloodless British photocopy of it. She stands on the veranda of Charley's parents' villa, eyes closed, and feels the heat seeping into her skin. She wants to turn herself inside out to absorb it, be one with it, let it bake her alive. Even her hands and feet, normally so chilly, feel warm here.

Charley runs up and takes her arm. She's wearing a white bikini patterned with red cherries, a matching sarong round her long legs. She's put up her dark hair in a high pony-tail and perched some designer sunglasses above her forehead. She's carrying a bag marked FCUK in which she's put towels, sunscreen, two bottles of water and some fruit. 'Let's go to the beach!' she says. 'Why don't you get into your gear?'

Liffy doesn't really have beach gear, not the way Charley does. She has a black swimsuit that goes well with her dark-gold hair, but nothing glamorous or designer. She nods, says, 'I'll just be five minutes,' and slinks into the back bedroom she and Charley are sharing. It's late afternoon – they've been travelling nearly all day. The shutters are closed against the heat; under them, the window edges shimmer as the sun bleeds light through the cracks.

Liffy puts on her swimsuit and stares dubiously at herself in the mirror while she winds her long hair into a knot. Other people might think she's become skinny, but she can't stand the sight of the bulging flesh on her thighs and breasts, which she's sure have been filling out over the past months despite her care over what she eats. She's not sure what Charley's parents would say about her shape – they're sunning themselves on the terrace at the back of the house – so she pulls on a grey T-shirt and a short denim skirt as well and tries to make herself skip as she goes back outside.

The two girls make swift progress along a steep, winding track that leads from the white complex of villas through groves of olive trees and cypress down to the beach, less than fifteen minutes away. They stop to pat a grey donkey that stands alone looking out over an old stone wall; Liffy strokes its soft ears while it noses hopefully at Charley's bag, which contains apples. Round the next corner, the small beach spreads in front of them, a semicircle of sand around a little cove bordered by smooth boulders.

Liffy flinches. The beach is black.

'The island's volcanic,' Charley tells her. 'That big hill in the middle was a volcano once, but Dad says it doesn't ever go off any more. It's extinct or something. That's why the sand's black – it's got ash in it.'

Liffy feels cold again. She doesn't like the idea of black sand, although she couldn't have told Charley why. Sand ought to be white or gold. Black sand suggests disease and decay. It's been harmed, perverted. She's not sure she wants to sit on it.

Charley throws down her bag, unties her sarong and dashes into the lapping water. 'Come on, Liffy!'

Liffy is worried about taking off her clothes – there are quite a number of people on the beach, mostly families with toddlers, plus two youths playing with a frisbee and a few retired couples snoozing in deck-chairs. But the water is tempting. It's been such a long day – they'd got up at five o'clock in the morning to go to Stansted Airport, then the plane had been delayed an hour, and after the flight to Athens they'd taken two ferries to get to the island. It had been hot and exhausting and Liffy had realised that her eating standards were going to be difficult to maintain in a different family. After all this, the sea looks as cool and inviting as fresh lemonade. Liffy kicks off her plastic flip-flops, bites her lip and strips; she runs to the water to conceal herself below it as quickly as possible. It's colder than she expects as it creeps up her body, but it doesn't take her long to get used to it. Last summer she'd learned how to float, at last, so she puts it into practice, lies on her back on the waves and closes her eyes. Sea water fills her ears with a magnified, echoing roar. The sun smells of salt and fish and oxygen.

A splash nearby and Charley surfaces next to her.

'Oh my God, isn't this wicked? Liffs, you don't have any sunglasses, do you?'

'Somewhere. I don't know where I put them.'

'We'll have to buy you some proper ones, like mine. We'll go shopping tomorrow. Those boys are cool, aren't they?'

'Which boys?' Liffy says, looking the other way. The island's shoreline is hilly, blue and green and volcano-dark beside the sparkling sea.

'The ones over there. With the orange frisbee. I wonder if they're here for long.'

'Charley, they must be at least eighteen.'

'So what? We're sixteen!'

'No, we're not! I'm thirteen and you're only just fourteen.'

'We don't have to be. We can be whatever we like. You're as old as you feel. And I certainly feel sixteen.'

'You look sixteen,' Liffy admits. 'I don't, though.'

'We could always say you look young for your age. I think you look *great*. You've lost loads of weight, haven't you?'

'A little.' Liffy lowers her body further into the water, immersing herself down to her shoulders.

'Seriously, you look fantastic. All you need is some decent clothes and a bit of makeup and you'll pass for sixteen anywhere. Leave it to me, I'll sort you out.'

Liffy isn't keen on makeup – most of it stings her eyes, which are often red and sore these days. Mum says it's conjunctivitis, whatever that is, and makes her put nasty yellow ointment on them. As for clothes, she's been abandoning her favourite pinks and purples in favour of grey and black, which are less conspicuous. It's a relief, now, having decided that the Earth Prince is protecting her, knowing she is his and cannot be threatened by anyone else.

'Liffy! Hello-o!' Charley is waving a hand in front of her face. 'Is there life on Mars? Which do you like? I like the fair-haired one, with the silly Bermuda shorts. I could sort him out with something better and then he'd be quite a pin-up. You can have the other one.'

'I don't like either of them much,' Liffy mumbles.

The girls wade up on to the beach and dry themselves. Liffy hates the black sand between her toes: it looks like sprouting mould on her flesh. Sitting down, she brushes her feet until they are free of every last grain.

Charley pulls off her bikini bra and lies back on her towel, topless.

'Charley, don't!'

'Why not?' Charley shrugs, eyes closed.

Liffy thanks heaven that she's had the sense to wear a one-piece swimsuit, so Charley can't order her to do the same.

'Want an apple?' Charley says.

'Thanks.'

Charley turns on to her front and crunches into her own apple, glancing sideways at the frisbee game. Liffy usually eats apples by cutting them up, but she can't as she hasn't a knife. Instead she shaves it into tiny, fine slivers with her teeth, sucking out the juice, crunching up minute morsels of the icy texture. Charley is too distracted by the boys to notice.

'Charley, what about Robin?' Liffy ventures. She doesn't trust Charley over Robin, but it might serve as a good deterrent.

'What about Robin? He's not here, is he? I won't see him again until September. Look, they're coming this way! Quick! Pretend you haven't noticed them.' She pulls a magazine out of her FCUK bag and fixes her gaze on a horoscope. Liffy lies on her back with her eyes closed.

If they'd hoped the boys would speak an interesting language, they're wrong. As they walk nearer, across the black sand, it's quickly apparent that they're English too, from somewhere in the north. Charley studiously ignores them and they lope on by without comment. As soon as they've gone, Charley throws down the magazine.

'They noticed us!' she says, triumphant.

'Did they?' Liffy tries to sound bored rather than frightened.

'Of course they did. Why wouldn't they? That's why they didn't say anything to us. I bet you anything that we'll see them here again and they'll talk to us.'

Liffy doesn't understand Charley's logic, but is willing to take her word for it.

At the villa, Charley's mother, Anna, has been to the little local supermarket and is preparing dinner on the veranda. She's made the ultimate Greek salad with lumps of fresh feta and shiny, luscious kalamata olives, and fresh bread and tara-masalata and hummus, rounded off with outsized, bulging purple figs.

'Hi, girls,' says Charley's dad. He has told Liffy to call him Jonty, which, she thinks, is a too-youthful disguise for a forty-something Jonathan. 'Having fun?'

He talks to them in a tone that Liffy thinks should be reserved for the under-tens, but when they sit down to eat he offers both of them a little white wine if they want it. Charley accepts at once. Liffy hesitates. Her parents don't offer her wine and, if they did, she'd refuse. But she doesn't want to look totally pathetic, clueless and uncool, however much she feels that's exactly what she is. 'Just half a glass, please?' she ventures.

A few minutes later, her head is spinning. She's not certain she likes the flavour, although she can taste the grapes in it. It's an amusing local something that they've found in the village shop, Jonty tells her.

'Do have some more food, Liffy,' Anna encourages. 'You've hardly eaten anything.'

'A little more salad would be lovely,' Liffy lies. She helps herself but, when Anna is looking the other way, slips back into the bowl as much of the feta and as many olives as she can. She eats up all the leaves, tomato, cucumber and spring onion, which help to calm the burning longing in her stomach. She avoids the dips – she knows how high their fat content is. Charley is eating everything, but in small quantities.

But Anna doesn't leave it there.

'Liffy, please, have some bread and hummus. It'll do you good. You look so pale.'

'The sun will sort me out,' Liffy says. 'I'm not that hungry. It's been such a long day and I'm really tired.'

'Er, yes, it has, hasn't it?' Anna's eyes are too sharp for Liffy's liking. Anna works for a building society and deals with people all day – unlike Mum, who sits in her study and talks constantly on the phone but hardly ever *sees* anyone except on the TV show. Mum is therefore much more wrapped up in herself than Anna is: she's less likely to notice other people's problems.

After supper Jonty channel-hops on the satellite TV, looking for some news. Anna reads a magazine and Charley offers to paint Liffy's nails for her – 'I'll do yours, then you can do mine.' Liffy doesn't like the bright blue that Charley wants on hers, and insists on a plainish, pearly grey for herself. Outside are soft, unfamiliar sounds: the high-pitched rasping of crickets, the whine of mosquitoes around the veranda lights (Anna soon decides to turn them off, saying, 'We don't want to get eaten alive') and the rustle of a breeze in the olive branches. There are no aeroplanes and the island has only one real road. The atmosphere is eerie with quietness.

When they go to bed, Charley falls instantly asleep. Liffy lies awake. She's worried that she might talk in her sleep again, as she had at Auntie Lisa's. At least Lisa had got the wrong end of the stick about the Earth Prince. Perhaps she should stay awake, just to be on the safe side. Liffy tries, but she's too tired. Hoping desperately that Charley will sleep as soundly all night as she is now, she closes her eyes.

The days pass in a blur of sunshine and water. In the mornings Anna and Jonty plaster themselves with sunscreen and lie on the sunbeds on the terrace, reading. They're tired out from working so hard for the past months and they want to do Absolutely Nothing. The girls go out and explore. Anna and Jonty give them water, fruit, organic muesli bars and some money and wave them goodbye.

On the first morning, they stop at the best beachwear shop they can find and Charley picks out some sunglasses and a bikini for Liffy. They're not as beautiful or expensive as her own, but they will do, she says. Liffy tries them on. The bikini is sea-green, too bright for her liking, and the sunglasses have gold rims, which she finds too flashy. She swaps them for others: plain black for the bikini, tortoiseshell frames for the sunglasses.

'Liffs, I told you to leave it to me!' Charley exclaims, offended. Liffy calmly sticks to her own choice, but she agrees to the sarong that Charley selects for her, which she likes: it's white, patterned with big, smoky-grey flowers.

In the afternoons they lie on the beach and swim in the sea or in the pool that belongs communally to the villas. Charley reads a magazine called *Seventeen*. Liffy, wrapped in her new sarong (she doesn't want to risk heavy sunburn), reads a book about global warming and, when she's finished it three days later, a book about the evils of the fast-food industry. Charley keeps an eye open for male talent, but insists that the English frisbee-playing boys are the most fanciable.

One morning the girls walk through the rising heat towards the little whitewashed town that spreads across the steep slopes down to the sea. An occasional donkey cart or moped passes them; people greet them in Greek or in English. Charley looks out for the boys, but they're nowhere to be seen.

They sit in a café, drink orange juice and watch people, which Charley seems to think is fun. Liffy has managed as usual to avoid eating breakfast by getting up before everyone else, then telling them she's helped herself already. She'd succumbed, however, to two of the irresistible figs, which are fruit and therefore good: they tasted indecently delicious. She spins out the joy of the orange juice for as long as she can.

She's been debating with herself whether to tell Charley about Lisa's baby; now she decides in favour of it. Charley thinks it's amazing and rather terrifying. 'She'll be a single mum,' she exclaims. 'How awful!'

'She really wants it,' Liffy says.

'Well, she's not so young any more – didn't you say she's thirty-three? There's this thing called the biological clock that aunts talk about now and then and I guess hers must be going off.'

'I think it was an accident, actually. But she says she's happy.'

'Unbelievable. Oh my God, Liffy, imagine being thirty-three!'

'Robin must be not so far off that.'

'Robin's twenty-six. That's nothing!'

Liffy suspects that Robin is older. If he's friendly with Lisa's friends, he's probably a similar age to them. And most men don't get married as young as twenty-six. How exactly had Charley decided he was twenty-six? Had she hazarded a wild guess – or just made it up?

They while away the morning poking around in souvenir shops and clothes shops and accessory shops and chemists where different brands of makeup are sold. They sit on a bench in the shade and send text messages to their schoolfriends. Liffy wants to send one to Sophie, but Charley says Sophie's stupid and she's only at the school because her parents are filthy rich and she doesn't think they should hang around with her. Liffy feels sorry for Sophie, but doesn't argue. They send a message to Leila instead.

On the beach later on, there's no sign of the boys yet. They usually emerge around four o'clock, play frisbee, swim and then disappear towards the seafront bars. Liffy and Charley spread out on the sand, on the patch they've decided is 'theirs', and bask and read and doze.

Then they hear, across the little beach, the sound of English voices. Charley is at once alert and watchful. 'They're coming towards us! Put on your sunglasses, Liffs – they make you look older.'

They also help to hide her face and her terror. Liffy does as she's told. The boys are approaching fast – making a beeline for them.

'Hello there, girls,' the fair-haired boy says. He's got spots, Liffy notices, and a big smile. Charley presumably likes the smile more than the spots.

'Hi,' Charley says, blinking.

'Mind if we sit down?'

The lads land heavily on the black sand – to Liffy, they're big, hulking presences carrying an unfamiliar smell of aggressive male sweat that makes something inside her cringe.

'Where you from? Down south?'

'London.' Charley smiles, poised. The boys are northerners. *Oh God, they're going to get at us for having posh voices*, Liffy thinks. But it doesn't seem to bother them.

'Which team d'you support, then? Chelsea?'

'Liverpool,' Charley says, without a moment's hesitation. 'They're the best. I like Michael Owen.'

The boys give a Liverpudlian football-fannish roar of approval – 'Wal*lop*!' Liffy keeps quiet.

'Fancy a beer? We were going to have one from the beach caff,' the dark boy says. 'What can we get you?'

'Thanks,' Charley says. 'I'll have half a lager.'

The dark boy looks at Liffy. 'Mineral water, please,' she says. The words come out as a squeak.

'Water? Nothing stronger?'

'Just water, thanks.'

He shrugs but seems to accept it.

The spotty boy grins at them. 'What it is,' he says, 'is we keep seeing you here and we had this bet on whether you was English! I'm Mark and this here's Gary. Gaz.'

'I'm Charlotte, but everyone calls me Charley. And she's Liffy.'

The brown-eyed boy, Gary, or Gaz, looks into Liffy's face. 'You Irish, then?' he asks her.

Liffy's about to say no, she was conceived under an olive tree, but thinks better of it. 'Kind of,' she says instead.

Gaz and Mark go up to the beach café and bring the drinks back. Charley watches them, Liffy notices, appraising their strong legs, their muscular arms, their short haircuts. At least they don't have beer bellies. Yet.

Liffy wonders what on earth they're going to talk to them about over the drinks, but Charley doesn't seem worried – and in the event the lads do most of the talking. They like the sound of their own voices. They're at college, Mark says. He's going to be a roofer. He likes being high up and doing things that other people think are dangerous. 'Oooh,' Charley says, as he obviously intends her to.

Gaz says he doesn't know what he really wants to do yet, but he's learning carpentry because it could be useful. 'Bet you go to some dead posh London school,' he adds.

'Only the best!' Charley jokes. 'We like a laugh, though. Don't we, Liffy?'

'We're going to go clubbing tonight,' Gaz says. Liffy prefers him to Mark, the appropriately named spotty one. His skin is clear and his eyes are brown and kind. For some un-accountable reason, she likes his broad shoulders. 'Do you want to come with us?' he says.

'That'd be cool. Wouldn't it, Liffy?'

'If . . .' Liffy says, then wonders whether she ought to be mentioning that they need to ask Charley's parents first.

'Yeah. It'll be fine,' Charley says.

'Well, then. We'll meet you at half ten, shall we? There's a bar opposite, with a garden – we'll see you in there.' Mark tells Charley how to find the club, which is one of only three on the island, and adds, 'See ya later,' with a wink.

'Later,' Charley says. Liffy gives a brief nod.

They watch the boys saunter away.

'I don't think we should go,' Liffy says, as soon as they're out of earshot.

'Why not? Liffs, what are you so scared of? They like us. They want to take us out.'

'Do they?'

'Course they do. What's wrong with that? They're OK.'

'Charley, I don't want to go.'

'Well, I'm not going without you. What's up? Haven't you ever been on a date?'

Liffy shakes her head, mute. Charley rolls her eyes heaven-wards. 'It's about time you did, then. Look, it'll be fun, and there's four of us – it's not like you'll be all on your own with a strange bloke.'

'What are your mum and dad going to say?'

'We don't ask them, we *tell* them. It'll be all right. They know I'm a responsible person.'

Are you? Liffy thinks. *Are you really?*

At the villa they find Anna and Jonty in much the same place that they'd left them that morning. Beside Jonty stand several empty beer bottles and beside Anna two much depleted ones of wine and sparkling mineral water. They appear drowsy and content. Since leaving home, their skin has changed colour from pallid pink to lobster puce and is now veering towards mahogany.

'We're going out tonight,' Charley announces.

'All right, darling,' Anna mumbles into her lounger. 'Don't be back too late, will you?'

'We won't,' Charley says. Liffy knows that they're meeting Gaz and Mark at ten thirty, which sounds as if it should be on the late side already as far as parents are concerned.

'Let's go and have a kip,' Charley suggests. 'We want to be awake later, don't we?'

That at least sounds sensible. Liffy follows her, praying to high heaven that she knows what she's doing.

18

Sasha closes her eyes tighter and tries to go back to sleep. She doesn't want to be awake.

A layer of skin seems to have been peeled away from her and the London air on her face is hard and grating and raw. She feels exposed and unprotected, a tiny speck in the impossibly large universe of south-west London. The planes overhead roar into her ears, placed in the sky specifically to disturb her. The twins, resentful that Liffy has gone on holiday without them, are more than usually quarrelsome. They want their father. He is phoning them every other day, but now he's started to say that he wants to speak to her too and she's never felt less like speaking to him in all her life. She's never felt less like speaking, period.

She takes a train into Waterloo and meets Cindy for coffee in an Italian espresso bar in Soho. It's crowded and smoky and the air swarms with a heady mixture of languages, some West European, others Slavically unidentifiable. Sasha is surprised to see that even now there are people in the café who glance twice at her and Cindy because one of them is white and the other black.

Cindy is writing a play – the first time she's crossed back over the fence between critic and creative – and Sasha is envious of her resolve.

'But let's talk about you,' Cindy says eventually, pressing Sasha's wrist. 'How are things?'

Sasha gives her friend a quick résumé of the developments in her life. She doesn't tell Cindy who her fling was with, but she does say she's had a fling and found it a deeply depressing experience.

'Oh honey,' motherly Cindy says, 'welcome to the real world. Thousands of women go through this the whole damn time.'

If that's supposed to help, it doesn't. Christ, thinks Sasha, is *this* what lies in store for the next few years? She wants life. She wants sensation. She wants passion. Not the anaesthesia of family routine. But is this the life that waits for her? Life, sensation and passion can also mean death, sensational disappointment and passionate revulsion. It crosses her mind that Adam's bereavement and collapse were as much an expression of life, sensation and passion as anything she has ever experienced – but one sensation she seriously doesn't want to experience is regret. She slams a mental door on the mischievous idea that's prodding her with a red-hot miniature trident, and gives her attention back to Cindy.

'Don't go there. Don't get into that trap,' Cindy is exhorting her. 'Don't look outside. You need to look within yourself. You need to do something that's yours. You've spent all these years giving and giving to other people – your husband, your kids, the TV people – and not doing anything for yourself. Do some writing. Get on with your new book. Go to ballet class. Try writing some poetry.'

'I can't dance any more and I certainly can't write poetry. Cin, it's like the whole earth just tipped over to one side. Like those camera angles you see in films when everything's going wrong. Everything's falling over.'

'Then turn it the right way up again, with your own two hands! Come on, Sasha, you're a powerful woman! You can do it! If you can't, then who can?'

Sasha is afraid to tell Cindy, who is so confident, so charismatic, so articulate and positive, that she's begun to lose faith. Women, she's realised, aren't *so* powerful. They're merely – well, more powerful than they used to be. Power as such involves all kinds of subclauses, small print and side-effects.

And this particular woman has given what power she'd had to the wrong person: a television producer who doesn't know when to stop talking.

The bottom line, she's realised too late, is that bedding the producer is not a good idea.

He is not the least significant person of those who choose the guests for the programme.

He is on the BBC's monthly payroll. The guests are not.

If she tells him it's over and he doesn't want it to be, if she falls out with him, the first casualty will be her appearances on the show.

With Adam gone, and unemployed, her children are entirely dependent on her, as is the mortgage, and the council tax, which is rumoured to be about to go up, and OK, Gerald may be paying the school fees but the children still have to go to birthday parties where expensive presents are expected and on school trips abroad that cost the earth, and her book still sells, but not as well as it used to, and her column brings some regular income, but losing the show would mean a huge reduction not only in ready money but in her general exposure to public view, which in turn might hinder the sales of her existing book, never mind the one she is now embarking upon at long last. She hopes that her publisher will follow her newly signed contract with the cheque for the advance before they realise she's out of favour with the BBC.

Women are powerful. But the balance of power between the salaried employer and the freelance employee has nothing much to do with that. Bedding the producer is still not a good idea.

On her way home from meeting Cindy, Sasha goes into Waitrose and buys food for herself and the twins for dinner. She has a craving for some heavy-duty protein and chooses organic mince for spaghetti bolognese (they should make the most of red meat while Liffy is away), with tomatoes, onions and mushrooms, Parmesan and a bottle of not-too-cheap

Rioja for herself. Her mind is not on her shopping: she forgets to weigh, barcode and self-scan the onions and mushrooms, and although the meat has not registered on the scanner she has forgotten about it by the time she gets to the checkout and puts her Waitrose account card into the machine.

'Hello, Mrs Wood,' says Patricia, who's manning the Quick Check counter. 'How are you?'

'Fine, thanks. And you?' Sasha is only half present, despite a nagging sensation in the back of her mind telling her that something isn't right.

'Saw you on the box the other day.'

Sasha's account card comes out of the machine, having registered her shopping and provided the total price. She puts in her debit card in its place.

'Do you like the show?'

'It's all right. I don't always know what you're talking about – it's things like these plays that most people don't actually go and see.'

'We don't choose them,' Sasha says. 'The producer does. And then he lets us tear each other to pieces over them. It's all very odd.'

'You can say that again.'

Sasha takes her debit card back, says, 'See you later,' to Patricia and walks out of the shop. A minute later she remembers that she has not paid for much of her shopping. She effectively has a bag full of free bolognese-to-be. Nobody's noticed. An uneasy self-satisfaction zips through her veins.

A little later the twins hammer on the front door, while Sasha is sitting in front of her computer gazing impotently at the chapter headings to which her new editor has agreed. Her title is good – *Making Dances*; the book, when she starts writing it in earnest, will be about how women must learn to choreograph their own lives, according to their strengths, to enable their spirits to grow, just as a dancer's technique does through choreography that uses her body in new ways.

The boys have been round the corner at Julius's. She lets them in: the quiet house is jolted awake by their zoo-like noise. They're fighting over something – she's given up trying to understand what – and are soon charging around on the ground floor chasing and thumping at each other and yelling, without regard for furniture, paintwork, ornaments or world peace. Sasha presses her hands over her ears, trying to concentrate. Then, distantly, she hears a crash. Dashing out of her study, she nearly falls over Ben the cat, who is running for his life, ears well back. 'What the hell is going on?' she shouts.

There, in a thousand porcelain pieces on the living-room floor, is Martha's favourite vase, donated by Gerald to Adam. Martha used to keep it on the hall table in Oxford, filled constantly with roses, lilies or orchids. The twins bite their lips and turn their eyes downward.

A fury wells up in Sasha that she knows is the same fury that floored Adam. She screams at them, she doesn't even know what words she's using, and it is only with the biggest effort of will she has ever applied that she marches them to the kitchen, gives Matt a dustpan and brush and Alex the electric Dustbuster and tells them that their punishment is to clean up the mess themselves, every last splinter of it.

After starting them off and making sure they avoid anything too sharp, she leaves them to do the remainder, wisely or not, and closes the study door behind her. All she wants is quiet and she won't have any for another ten years, and only then if the boys really do leave home and go to university somewhere away from London. Sasha feels her life has been stolen from her. Her feet are becoming mired in a fatal, muddy suction. The earth below her is pulling her down into itself and will consume her and spit out her remains.

And she knows how easy it would be – how abominably easy – to tip over that edge, as Adam had. It's just an incline of the body and mind a few degrees either way, backwards or forwards, off their precarious equilibrium. If she'd been less geared to staying strong – if she'd been mourning the death of a parent – the fury might have got the better of her and she, too, might have seized a twin and punished him with blows. She remembers Gerald's equanimity – 'A good hiding never did anybody any harm' – and Adam's shame and distress at his own memories, confessed years ago on a dark Greek beach, of being punished for the slightest transgression: a cane on the hand or a belt on the backside (from Gerald) and a bruised cheek more than once (from Martha). He had not even broken a kitchen window or an heirloom vase to earn those blows.

Maybe every generation gets parenting wrong in its own way, Sasha considers. She notes this down as a possible topic for her column and makes a list of media people and psychologists with whom to discuss the idea before writing it.

The phone rings.

'Darling!' comes a breathy Irish whisper. 'I can't talk for long – I'm in the office. Wondering when we can see each other again.'

'Let's have a drink after the show on Friday.'

'Oh, a drink! Sasha, it's you I'm thirsty for.'

'Christ, Rick – it's so difficult. I can't ask you round, really, not at the moment . . . I've got the twins here all summer . . .'

'Send them to their dad for a bit. That's what dads are for.'

'Let's talk later,' she says. 'Rick, I've got to dash – they've had some kind of accident.'

She runs from the phone as if from a smouldering furnace. Downstairs, Matt has done his level best with his dustpan and brush and Alex is running the Dustbuster over every inch of carpet around where the vase had shattered. Twins on one hand, Rick on the other. At least the twins are hers. At least she knows she belongs with them. She misses Liffy, which surprises her. Even with her sulks and her silences and her ballet and her stubborn lower lip, Liffy is part of her and it's hard to do without her delicate, intense little presence.

Much later, when the twins have gone to bed, Sasha opens her Rioja and puts on a video of a French film to keep the silence at bay. If there's one thing worse than racket, it's silence.

When Nick clears his throat one evening and says, 'Listen, Ad, Mary and I have been talking . . .' Adam isn't particularly surprised. 'We have to give it another go,' Nick goes on, without meeting his gaze. 'I don't seem to do too well without my daughter.'

'I understand,' Adam says. 'I don't do too well without mine either.'

It's come sooner than he expected, but after the initial distress he knows that it's no bad thing that he will be forced to move on. In any case, Nick's tales of life at Forrest & Burns are too depressing. Adam trusts his old mate to be the soul of discretion, but he doesn't want Henrietta, Clarissa and the rest attempting to snoop into his new life, such as it is, via encounters with Nick at the Coca-Cola machine.

Gerald has been encouraging him to come and stay; this is the last thing on earth Adam wants to do. But Oxford – yes, Oxford is another matter. Oxford is home, really, more than the London suburbs could ever be. Adam has long been suppressing his artist's urge towards having beauty around him, rather than suburban greyness. When he boards the train at Paddington, he notices that he feels strangely light.

Swallowing his pride, he makes several trips to and from the dreaming spires, hunting through the lettings for small flats and bedsits. Most turn out to be so miserable that they send him scurrying straight back to Acton. On the third day, he finds something that will do: a short-term let, but that is all he wants, at least for now. It's a large studio, with kitchen and shower room, above a shop on a side-street; it's the only residential part of the building and is self-contained, not requiring him to meet anyone on the stairs, and the shop, a delicatessen, closes at five thirty each day so his nights will be undisturbed. The shop isn't doing well – probably because it's too close to the supermarket – and the estate agent explains that if the shop closes, the freeholder may decide to sell the entire building, flat and all; hence the cheap rate at which Adam can rent it. For the time being, the gentle, permeating smell of olive oil, roasted peppers and Italian garlic sausage is something he can learn to live with. He needs a space that is his own, not just a spare part of someone else's; then he can start to think about what to do for employment.

'Good idea,' Nick says. 'You know, if it doesn't work out, you can come back whenever . . .'

'Thanks, mate. But I hope you'll have better company again very soon. It's been fun, I've really appreciated this, and the best I can wish you is that I don't ever have to do the same for you. Good luck. Go for it.'

Nick shakes Adam's hand, looking away.

In the street Adam, hoisting his rucksack on to his back, spots Mary getting out of a car and unloading a small girl complete with pink cardigan and toy rabbit. He hears the child say, 'Daddy!' and his heart hurts so much that all he can do is march away as fast as he can without turning back.

In his new studio, there isn't much to encumber him. His art materials go with him; so do some books and papers and files, and the clothes he's brought away from Somerset Road, which don't include his suits. That's all. Standing in the middle of the room, surrounded by his few boxes and the rucksack, he experiences an odd sensation of floating. He can't quite believe how easy it has been to make a decision, act on it, take charge. It's too easy. Something must be wrong. He makes himself his first dinner – an Italian feast from the deli downstairs – and later sleeps fitfully, aware of the unfamiliar colour of the night and the strange, haunted sounds in the water pipes.

In the morning, quietly ecstatic, he sets off for a walk. It's easy to slip back into loving Oxford as much as he used to as a child; and walking through the town does him good, as it always has. It gets his blood moving again, which unfreezes his brain. He reclaims his territories; he reminds himself of the geography; he notices which shops have changed, which are the same, which are closest to his new home. Browsing among the books in Blackwell's or finding organic produce of which Liffy would undoubtedly approve in the covered market helps to engage him with the world outside his own mind. Now he needs to think ahead; most immediately, about how to earn some money.

Adam has visited Gerald's old friend Aaron several times, sessions for which Aaron refused to charge him. Aaron, Adam soon discovered, understands a soul in crisis. Pain is best when you feel it, he tells Adam. It's the pain that you refuse to feel that harms you. Pain passes through the body if you allow it its right of way; if you don't, it seeps into your tissues and stays there like a stagnant lake, unseen for years, perhaps to emerge one day as a tumour or immune deficiency or arthritis. What neither of them wonders aloud is whether this was what had happened to Martha, who buried her own childhood pain under her adult possessiveness, both personal and material, for more than fifty years.

What you need, Aaron advised, is work. Not necessarily a job, but work: something productive; something that gives you a sense of achievement in a small way on a daily basis. Adam has few ideas on the subject. Prodded by Aaron, he agrees that he understands art and design; that he has natural intelligence, communicates well, gets along fine with most people and has more of a head for figures than he's permitted himself to admit. But since he has not the slightest intention of going back into a publishing house, none of these qualities are going to do him much good unless he can come up with some positive suggestions.

In the centre of Oxford, he turns down a cobbled side-street not unlike the one in which he now lives, lined with intriguing small shops: a bookshop that specialises in comics, where young men in anoraks and glasses congregate; a New Age boutique dripping with crystals and dreamcatchers, stinking of incense; an accessory outlet with a selection of faintly eccentric hats and scarves in the window; and a bright, attractive little gallery. The walls are white, the spot-lighting tasteful, the space hung gracefully with black-and-white photographs by a journalist whose name Adam recognises from a newspaper or two. He opens the glass door and goes in.

The photos on one side of the room tell the story of the journalist's visit to the war zones of Kosovo. Adam's heart twists inside him as he sees the children with huge, dark, hungry eyes, the shattered houses, women in headscarves in attitudes of despair amid the rubble. The opposite wall displays a selection of cityscapes in different lights, capturing the atmosphere of rain, of sunshine, of nightfall in London, New York and Florence. The plain white walls and the light – ample but not direct – give the gallery an atmosphere of calm: a space where people can gaze and dream and think.

The labels of many of the pictures are adorned with small red dots, indicating that they've been sold. Adam peers more closely at them. Each of these prints sells for £300, or £400 framed. The photographer has made available ten prints of each. Adam's mind kicks into action. That means that from each picture, assuming all the prints are sold, it's possible to have an income of as much as £4000. Even minus the costs of producing the prints and the frames, that's not bad for one photo. There are ten pictures in this half of the gallery – a potential £40,000. The gallery, no doubt, takes a big cut of this – fifty per cent, if Adam remembers correctly from his days trying to sell his own work.

The gallery is staffed by a dark-haired young woman at a desk near the door. Adam hangs back as a pair of egg-shaped American tourists quiz her about the cost of the pictures. She is being polite but firm: 'This price is final, but you can claim the duty back at the airport if you spend more than—'

'Over in Istanbul,' the woman interrupts, 'the shop halved the price of the carpets we bought, they were so happy to have our custom.'

Adam stifles a smile. The assistant sees him and smiles back while her customers are looking the other way. He notices her big brown eyes. A wing twitches inside him.

Eventually the tourists leave, muttering to each other about the ridiculous prices in Europe but having arranged for their purchase to be shipped to Ohio. Adam goes up to talk to the assistant.

The girl, whose name is Bronwyn, offers Adam a cup of tea and some useful information. She's just finished a degree in history of art and this is her first job. A retired photographer owns the gallery and she deals with the admin for him. They advertise in local papers, tourist brochures and the magazine of the Royal Academy of Arts. Business is a little unpredictable; of course, some things sell better than others.

'The cityscapes are going like hot cakes,' she tells him. 'The war-zone pictures aren't.' But Oxford is such a hotspot for tourism, and for the intelligentsia who are interested in unusual photography, that sales are remaining reasonable even in economically tricky times.

'Nice place you've got here,' Adam says, casting an eye round it. The gallery consists of a ground-floor showroom, with a small office and a storeroom at the back. Upstairs there is a privately owned flat. His mind begins to whir: a pleasant sensation, which he has forgotten during the past months.

'Drop in any time,' Bronwyn suggests, smiling up at him. 'Come and say hi.'

'I will. Thanks.'

Adam pockets a business card and walks on, absorbed in calculations.

           *   *   *

Lisa is dusting her mother's living room in Queen's Park. The house is near a school populated mainly by Muslim children; a mosque has gone up round the corner, complete with a small dome and minaret. Girls flock past the house after school in the afternoon, chattering like any teenagers but wearing headscarves that conceal their beautiful black hair. Sally watches them from her front room. She doesn't like them, she tells Lisa. Lisa asks her why not – they're only kids. Sally shrugs.

'You must get out and about more, Mum,' Lisa says. The Dresden china ornaments on the mantelpiece had once belonged to Sally's mother. Lisa wipes the dust carefully off each one with a yellow cloth. Really they all need a good bath, but she's terrified of breaking them: their filigree work is fine and brittle and Sally loves them so.

'Where should I go?' Sally says. 'Since your father died, there's not been much point in being here at all.'

'Dad died fifteen years ago,' Lisa says gently. 'It's a long time, Mum.'

'Time. What does it mean anyway?'

'Oh, Mum, I know it still feels like yesterday. It does to me too. But you've got your own life to live. You're in good health, you can get around fine, you've got a free bus pass and you live in London. You could be out at exhibitions and theatres and seeing friends.'

Sally looks at her from large, sad eyes. Lisa's heart aches for her. At least she's not drinking, not the way she used to. But even now, neither Lisa nor Sasha spends enough time with her. Life takes over – work, teaching, practising – and sometimes it's easier to cope with guilt than with the sense of emotional drain that visits to Sally usually bring on. Lisa, who lives closest to her, tries to go round once a week; Sasha sometimes manages twice a month, but sometimes doesn't.

Lisa knows, deep down, that Sally had not been that much happier when her husband was alive. Dave Wood had been not alcoholic but workaholic: an entrepreneur, born in the East

End, he'd started his own building company and made a lot of money, having begun from nothing; occasionally a venture took him back to nothing. He was out all the time. He got up before six a.m. and came home frequently after eight in the evening. The girls, growing up, hardly ever saw him; when they did, his perfectionism caused them no end of trouble. They felt they could do nothing without him criticising them for weakness, carelessness or general incompetence. He rowed frequently with Sally; their shouting matches could be heard right down the street. No doubt, Lisa had reflected many times – remembering how she had tried to ignore the noise and the alarm it caused while trying to finish her harmony and counterpoint exercises – the tyrannical personality of her father had a lot to answer for: Sally's alcohol problem, Sasha's various difficulties over the years, Lisa's own relationship disasters – her tendency to fall for men who were physically or emotionally absent, or who otherwise put her down or let her down; sometimes all of the above.

On the other hand, it's not fair to blame your continuing troubles on someone who's been dead for fifteen years. Lisa coughs over her dusting.

'You look tired, love,' her mother says. 'Come and sit down and have a cup of tea.'

Lisa is looking at a photo on a shelf of Sally with her charges: several neighbourhood dogs that she walks for their owners.

'He's lovely, the retriever. Prince, he's called.' Sally points at the biggest, yellowest dog. 'He's my favourite.'

'Prints?' says Lisa, absently. 'Paw prints?'

'No, love, like Prince William. I'll put the kettle on and there are some biscuits for you. Though I hope you don't mind my saying, dear, you've put on weight.'

Lisa says nothing. She hasn't made any decisions about how to break her news.

'Lisa?' Sally turns round from the kettle in the kitchen as Lisa lingers, silent, in the doorway. 'You're not . . . ?'

'I've been meaning to tell you . . .'

'Oh God. No. No! Tell me it's not true!'

'Mum!'

Sally shakes her head, covers her eyes, lets out a wail. Lisa looks on, feeling redundant and guilty. Inside her, she can feel a fluttery sensation: the foetus has grown into a living, moving creature. 'Mum. Please don't cry.'

'All I ever wanted was for you girls to be happy! Oh Lord, where did I go wrong? Was I such a bad mother?'

'Hush, Mum. I *am* happy. I'm having this baby because I want to. It's Vladimir's, but he doesn't know about it. I really want it and I'll love it just as much on my own as I would have with him. Please don't cry, Mum. Please don't see it as a bad thing. It's my child. It's your grandchild. I'd be so happy if you could love it too.'

Sally wipes her eyes with a teatowel. Lisa has a flash of inspiration.

'You know,' she says, 'that when it's born, I'm going to need all the help I can get.'

In the dim kitchen light (why won't she use anything brighter than forty watts?), Lisa notices that Sally's eyes are drying. Her mother is looking interested for the first time. 'Would you be able to come round lots and help me?' Lisa encourages.

'Hmm. I suppose I will. Yes. A child. Another grandchild! And you, with all your books and lectures. It's good to be needed.' Sally is musing aloud, but Lisa detects, at last, at the lined corners of her mouth, the flicker of a smile.

19

Charley is concentrating, lips curled under. She's brushing out Liffy's long, shining hair. It gleams a tantalising shade of dark gold in the lamplight; it is fine and thick and filled with a tremulous, pervasive wave that is hard to subdue into fashionable straightness.

'You've got such incredible hair,' Charley says. She winds it into a golden rope, then up into a chignon, which she begins to pin.

'I'd prefer it down,' Liffy says.

'No, you'll want it up in the club. It'll be hot, you'll be more comfortable. There, that looks cool. Yeah?'

'Yeah.'

'Now, your eyes . . .' Charley starts on the makeup. She blends three different shades of eyeshadow across Liffy's lids and under her brows. The effect complete, she adds the mascara. Liffy blinks and the black stuff smudges under her eyes.

'Hold still!' Charley wipes it away and starts again.

The Liffy in the mirror is not Liffy as she knows herself. This is a Liffy who looks, if not quite sixteen, then certainly older and more sophisticated than she is. She's wearing her new black linen, but under protest – Charley had refused to allow her to go in a T-shirt and jeans. At least the black linen is more restrained than Charley's gear: a cherry-pink top with a plunging V neck and exposed midriff, a short, tight skirt and high-heeled sandals.

'We're off out, Mum,' she calls.

'Have fun, darlings, don't be back too late,' Anna says, from the living room where she and Jonty are watching satellite TV over the remnants of the evening's second bottle of wine.

'They're drunk,' Charley declares, as the two girls set out into the night. 'They wouldn't care if we went home to London for the evening!'

Her heart sinking, Liffy suspects she's right.

Gaz and Mark are waiting for them in the bar opposite the club. The boys have grabbed a table on the pavement and are ready with a big jugful of a frothy, deep pink cocktail. Liffy isn't sure she likes the look of it.

'Your mum and dad didn't mind, then?' Mark teases Charley, as she downs her first glass.

'They're too drunk to notice!' Charley giggles. Liffy's skin crawls. She senses that Charley shouldn't be telling the boys this.

'Go on, Irish,' Gaz encourages. 'Try a bit. It won't poison you. It's just wine and fruit juice and a bit of vodka.'

'Half a glass, please.'

She sips. The drink is delicious; pieces of fresh fruit float about in it. There's something strong in it too, some sort of medicinal kick that makes her screw up her eyes.

The jug of punch diminishes quickly – the boys drink most of it, Charley does her best to keep up and Liffy has more than she'd meant to because she hasn't noticed Gaz refilling her glass. She can't understand half the things the boys say because of their northern accents. She's managed to switch off part of her mind, the part that is terrified, and pretend that this evening is happening to someone else, that she's only there watching it. She holds the image of the Earth Prince close to her for protection when Mark pushes back his chair and says, 'Let's get in there.'

Charley dances, eyes half closed, body swaying from side to side. Her slender young hips lift in turn and her shoulders, exposed by her sleeveless top, look smooth and fresh and lovely.

Her hair has come out of its pony-tail and hangs, wild and free, around her shoulders.

The music – not music to Liffy but noise – is so loud that when they try to talk they can't hear anything. It's so loud that it's impossible to think: nothing exists except the frenetic thumping of the beat, the technically generated wails above it, the clips of words repeated again and again because that's what recording technology can do. The coloured lights flash so fast out of the darkness that the eyes are soon as boggled as the ears. It's airless and Liffy's body is drenched with sweat. She can't hear, see or breathe, except in desperate snatches between the flashes, the beat, the stench of sweat. Reality fragments around her. She looks at the other kids in the club – many of them not much older than she is – and wonders at the ecstasy on their faces. They seriously believe that this is heaven, when she knows that it's really hell. She sees a girl nearby swallow something tiny and round, then turn to fling her arms round the nearest boy, screaming with laughter.

Mark, on the dance-floor with Charley, has put both hands on her waist.

'Come on, Irish,' Gaz shouts in Liffy's ear. 'Try it. Just five minutes.'

'Water,' the Earth Prince whispers in her inner ear. 'Drink water. Plenty of water.'

'Can I just have some water first?' Liffy shouts back at Gaz. 'It's so hot and I'm so thirsty.'

Gaz fetches her a glass from the bar and Liffy downs it in one. It's good, pure, healing. Then Gaz takes her hand and pulls her on to the dance-floor.

As Liffy makes the effort, as she lets her well-developed dancing instinct take her over and automatically settles into graceful ballet-trained movements, Gaz's eyes widen. She understands that she's impressed him without even trying.

'You can't half dance,' he mouths at her.

Liffy can feel the beat from the top of her head right down

to her toes. It sounds different when she moves with it. Like swimming in deep water, the prospect is more alarming than the reality. Like the sea, it holds her up and carries her along. The current is turquoise and emerald and translucent violet, glinting under the lights, and Liffy remembers the story of the little mermaid who turned into foam and blended back into her own element.

Gaz is watching her, his face bemused and thrilled. 'Where did you learn to dance like that?'

'Ballet school!' Liffy shouts back – it's half true – pleased to see his astonishment. Her brain switches off, dancing with him to the beat. They try to copy each other's movements and the lights flashing in her eyes dazzle her. They don't talk until they run out of breath – the dance music is so fast – and totter to the bar to recuperate.

'Irish?' Gaz says.

'Yeah?'

'How old are you?'

'I can't hear you!'

'I said, how old are you?'

'Sixteen,' Liffy shouts.

'No. How old are you *really*?'

Liffy hesitates. She's not a good liar. She's OK at being economical with the truth, but telling straight lies doesn't work, unless they concern her eating habits.

'Come on, Irish. You're not sixteen, are you?'

'Well, not yet.'

'And her? Your fire-breathing friend?'

'Um, well, she's nearer sixteen than I am.' That was technically true, at least.

Gaz is trying to catch Mark's eye, but on the far side of the dance-floor Mark is so entwined with Charley that he doesn't notice.

'I do lots of ballet,' Liffy says, to change the subject. 'I want to be a dancer.'

'You *are* a dancer. You're fab.'

Gaz orders a beer for himself and more water for Liffy. Liffy wonders what he normally does on holiday. He and Mark are probably the kind of lads who go off in groups with their other friends – clubbing all night, sleeping until afternoon, going to the beach, drinking as much as possible, pulling girls, having sex. Is that what they're expecting now? Of course it is. It has to be. But she feels safe. The Earth Prince is protecting her, keeping her clear of the drink, the noise, the drugs, the heat. She's lightheaded with the dancing and the lack of air, but she knows she's safe. Gaz is nice enough to be concerned that she's a bit too young. A lot too young. She looks up at him and wishes she wasn't.

She casts around, biting her lip. There's no sign of Charley or Mark anywhere.

'Where's Charley?'

'Don't worry, Irish. She'll not have gone far.'

'I can't breathe in here. Can we go outside?'

Away from the high of dancing, with the air rushing to meet her and quietness with it, the music's volume leaving a ringing, rushing sound in her assaulted ears, Liffy's confidence drains away. She's becoming afraid and her head is hammering with pain.

The street is quiet and empty. Straight ahead lies the sea; a golden crescent moon dips over the dark water.

'Charley!' Liffy shouts.

'Ssh . . .' Gaz takes her hand; she lets him, because she likes the way it feels. 'Like I said, they won't be far off. Let's sit here and wait for them.'

They stroll together back past the bar, which is closed. Beside it, encircling the beer garden, is a stone wall, the height of Liffy's head and Gaz's chest. Gaz lifts Liffy on to it and hauls himself up beside her. He turns her hand over and strokes the palm. 'Out with it,' he says. 'Real age?'

'Thirteen.'

'Charley?'

'She's fourteen.'

'Christ.'

'D'you think Mark knows?'

'Dunno if he's asked. He thinks she's up for it.'

There's silence in the street. Liffy is starting to shiver: it's not cold, but the contrast with the furnace that was the night-club is making her chilly.

'You're all right, Irish,' Gaz says. He's still holding her hand. 'You know, I can't help wishing you weren't so young.'

'Sorry!' Liffy wants to laugh, but isn't sure she won't cry instead.

'Don't be sorry. You're a special girl. I don't think I've ever met anyone like you. You're not like most of those posh girls. You're not all spoilt and little-madamish.'

'Please don't.' The tears are going to win over the laughs any moment. Her teeth, unaccountably, are chattering.

'Cold?' Gaz puts an arm round her. His body, close to hers, is softer than she'd expected, and warmer too. It's hard not to accept it – it's hard not to cuddle up and like it. It's impossible. One finger is soon under her chin, lifting her face towards him. And the kiss, when it comes, is more than she had dreamed, if she had dreamed, more than she'd hoped, if she had hoped: a flushed flower of tenderness, a whole un-suspected, undiscovered world waiting for her. Her body contracts with longing for more; she parts her lips and leans towards him. She feels as light as a bird.

Gaz pulls back. She suspects he's not used to resisting girls. She imagines that some other physical presence is pushing him away from her; *she* certainly isn't.

'Come on,' he says. 'We should stop this. I'll get the car and run you home.'

'Where's Charley?'

'Mark's probably seen her back already.'

Liffy wonders if he's lying. She can't bear to think of where Charley might be.

'I shouldn't go without her.' She hesitates on the wall, looking around in the bronze haze of the setting moon. Perhaps if she holds on long enough, Charley will appear – magically – and everything will be OK. It's a frantic hope, but it's all she's got.

'Let's wait a few minutes, then.' Gaz doesn't seem too disappointed. He moves his head towards her to kiss her again and Liffy raises her mouth to meet him.

As she does, her ability to balance evaporates abruptly, almost as if something or someone has pushed her. She tumbles backwards, right off the wall, letting out a cry as she falls. The drop isn't far, but the shock is such that she slumps where she's landed – in the bar's back garden – gulping for breath and ready to die of embarrassment.

'Liffy! You OK?'

'I'm fine,' Liffy says. But she doesn't budge. She feels frozen alive. Because she knows it was the Earth Prince who made her overbalance and pushed her off the wall away from Gaz. She can't believe it. The Earth Prince wouldn't let someone kiss her, even when she wanted him to. *Oh God*, thinks Liffy, sitting paralysed on the grass. *Oh my God.* Then she hears a cry, somewhere nearby, in the depths of the dark garden.

'Liffy! *Liffy!* Help!'

'Gaz, it's Charley!'

Gaz jumps down beside her and pulls her to her feet.

Before they can move, a figure staggers out of the bushes. It's a frayed, tattered figure, weaving around dazed, drunk, drugged or all three, her top unbuttoned and loose around her shoulders, her short skirt ripped at the side.

'Mark! What the fuck's going on?' Gaz careers past the ailing Charley.

Liffy rushes to her friend, who clings to her: she can hardly stand. 'Liffy,' she howls. She's crying and her makeup has leached into purple and black streaks around her eyes. She is blind drunk – her breath stinks – and the wild, unfocused look in her eyes reminds Liffy of the girl in the club who'd swallowed the pill.

'Let's go home.' Liffy puts an arm round her. Charley staggers a few paces, sways and nearly falls.

'What happened? Please, Charley, you've got to tell me.'

'You fucking moron,' Liffy hears Gaz saying to someone in the shadows. 'She's fourteen. Fourbloodyteen! Are you off your rocker?'

Mark comes out into the moonlight. His flies are undone. 'Jeez . . .' he says.

'Get away from me, you filthy bastard!' Charley shrieks.

'Fucking hell,' Gaz says, looking at them both. 'Mark, go home, fat-head. I'll run them back.'

'Gaz's OK,' Liffy soothes Charley. 'We'll be fine. You're going to be fine.'

'But she was gagging for it, mate,' Liffy hears Mark say to Gaz.

Charley stands still and wails like a baby.

When they're on the right side of the garden wall at last, when Gaz comes by with the car after what feels like a millennium, Liffy shoves Charley into the back, where she keels over and falls asleep. Liffy is stone-cold sober as she jumps into the front. 'Thanks, Gaz,' she says, pressing his arm. His face is set and angry while he drives them along the road out of town.

At the gate of the villa complex he pulls up and hauls Charley out. He looks into Liffy's face for a minute. And turns, and drives away. Liffy wonders whether she'll ever see him again. Her first kiss still lingers on her lips like strawberry juice.

She supports the semi-conscious Charley, lurching past the pool to their house. On the far horizon are the first straw-coloured streaks of breaking dawn.

Inside, Charley stumbles into the bathroom. Liffy can hear her being sick and thanks heaven or nature that she's been able to hang on long enough to get there. When she doesn't come out again, Liffy goes in and finds her slumped on the floor, unconscious.

Liffy tries to pull Charley to her feet. She can't. Charley is bigger and heavier than she is and she's out cold. Liffy has two choices: she can wake Jonty and Anna and get them to help; or she can leave Charley where she is and hope that she wakes up in the morning before her parents do.

Liffy decides on the latter. She doesn't know whether it's right or not, but if she stays awake herself, she might be able to wake Charley in good time, once she's recovered a little, then Jonty and Anna might never have to know anything about it. She goes back to the kitchen to make herself a cup of tea. Waiting for the kettle to boil, she's surprised to find that she's crying.

20

Lisa is on her back, eyes searching the pattern of green and grey dots on the screen beside her. The jelly and the ultrasound monitor are clammy on her bare abdomen. The doctor, an Indian woman younger than she is, moves the probe from side to side across her bulge and watches the screen.

'Look . . . there's the head. That's a little foot, just there . . .'

Lisa can't take it in. It feels too unreal. 'Everything looks OK, doesn't it?' she asks.

'Oh yes, very much as we'd expect, very healthy, moving around a lot. Do you want me to tell you whether it's likely to be a boy or a girl?'

Lisa hasn't been able to make up her mind about this but, put on the spot, she says, 'All right, go on.'

'I think it's a girl. I could be wrong, but that's how it looks.'

Lisa can hardly speak.

'Look.' The doctor points. 'There's her little heart, beating away.' She flicks a switch on the ultrasound machine and Lisa hears a frenetic thudding that is within her but not her own.

Dazed, she gets dressed and finds her way out through the hospital corridors and into the muggy afternoon. She doesn't feel like going home yet. She longs to have someone to tell about the experience, someone to share it with. Every other woman in the waiting room seems to have brought a man, and some have brought children too, all of whom will be looking at the scans with her . . .

She calls Lindsey from her mobile phone and is duly invited up to Redington Road for the afternoon, but when she gets there she's too embarrassed to say more than that everything looks healthy and normal. To show her excitement wouldn't be fair on Lindsey, who seems unlikely ever to experience it for herself. They spend the afternoon in the garden talking about other things, drinking Lindsey's home-made lemonade, and before they know what's happened it is half past six. Lindsey offers to run Lisa home, but Lisa says, 'Thanks, but don't worry – I fancy a walk.'

She sets off down the hill and takes her time, lingering in the corner shop to buy some pasta, orange juice and apricot yoghurt, gazing at the newest releases in the window of West End Lane Books, putting off going home. She knows that she will walk into her flat and, but for a nagging, hungry cat, find herself entirely alone yet again.

She thinks of her sister engaging in an affair with some mysterious man, of Adam making his way alone in Oxford – twenty years together, and now look! And the children, bemused and probably more destabilised than they know, Liffy, thinner than ever, needing attention she's not getting. Thinking of them all, especially Liffy, she could weep. Maybe her own situation, alone and pregnant, is the preferable one in this emotional hot-pot of silly, crazy, irresponsible people who really should know better, but never do.

Sasha stands in Rick's office, her back against the door. He's pouring whiskey, his back in its habitual blue sweater turned to her. He's humming the programme's signature tune and hasn't seen the look on her face.

She hasn't acquitted herself as well as usual on the show. Everyone has been surprised today by her uncharacteristically non-confrontational manner. She won't admit even to Cindy, whose spirited discourse carried the show pretty much single-handed, that she doesn't have any appetite for fighting.

Rick turns, goblets of golden liquor in his hands. His blue

eyes, which had followed Sasha hungrily all evening, register surprise, then a question.

'Rick,' Sasha says. 'Listen. I can't do this.'

'What do you mean?'

'I can't. It's all too sudden. I need time. I need some space of my own – emotional space. I mean, it was great – Manchester – but I can't go on.'

'Darling! I don't understand!'

Sasha doesn't really know what she's saying. She just knows that she had been desperate to sleep with Rick and the next morning she had been filled with revulsion at him, at herself, at the entire situation. She'd built up a mental construct about a man she hardly knew and, however much she'd desired him, actually sleeping with him had told her that there is more to knowing someone than you can gather in a few Friday-night office snogs that may be interrupted by the cleaning lady. He's neither what she'd thought he was, nor what she'd wanted him to be, and having got to know him this much, she doesn't want to know him any better. She can't tell him this. She can't tell him that the amount he talked in bed, and the words he used, let her know him too well. Instead, she simply says, 'Rick, it's got to stop.'

'Come on, Sasha, sweetie. You don't mean that. I know you don't. Drink your whiskey – you'll feel more relaxed.'

'I do mean it. It's over.'

'But it's barely begun!'

'All the better to stop it now. Rick, I'm going home.'

Rick puts down the glasses and Sasha watches a cloud of understanding billow into his face. 'My God . . . Sasha . . . you unbelievable bitch! You led me on! You made me think . . .'

Sasha wishes she could block up her ears with a mixture of wool, wax and superglue. She pulls the door open, slams it behind her and strides, head high, along the deserted BBC corridor. She doesn't look back. Her dignity intact, at least on the surface, she asks the front desk to call a taxi for her. Waiting for it to arrive, she closes her eyes and tries to pretend she is somebody else, anybody rather than herself. Then she thinks of Adam, to whom she was never unfaithful in twenty years; that only makes it worse.

In her handbag, her mobile phone beeps. She whips it out, frightened that Rick is going to abuse her by text message. But no: this message is from Liffy, who should be sunning herself on a Greek island, the lucky little so-and-so. She wonders when she'll bump into Rick in the supermarket again. Then she looks down at the message.

As Liffy is coming home early, because things are not as they should be and Anna is insisting they have to talk privately as soon as possible, it looks as if there is about to be serious trouble. Sasha decides that she must pack the twins off somewhere for an afternoon so that she can deal with the situation in peace. She and Anna fix on the following Saturday. Julius and his mother have gone on holiday. She tries to phone Lisa, but Lisa is out and hasn't switched on her mobile. She tries Oxford – there's no reason why Adam should not come and take them out – but nobody answers the phone and Adam's mobile is also off. She knows that he's up to something: some new venture has spurred him into action, she has no idea what. She can't help wondering whether it's another woman. She pushes away the idea: it turns her stomach.

Alex and Matt whine, 'Why can't we just stay *here*? We won't get in the way.'

'Because you can't. Now, who else can we try?'

Alex has a brainwave. 'What about Paul and Lindsey?'

'Your new musical mentors?' Sasha teases him. 'Darling, Paul and Lindsey live in Hampstead. It takes ages to get there and back.'

'You could take us somewhere to meet them, though. Please, Mum, phone them and see?'

Sasha is bemused by her son's decision to make friends with

a pair of adults, let alone musical ones, but she phones Lindsey anyway to explain the predicament, and is astonished when Lindsey exclaims that of course they'd love to have the twins for an afternoon. Saturday would be ideal for them; Sasha mustn't worry about anything, they'll meet them at Waterloo and take them out and bring them home again and she won't have to go anywhere near Hampstead. How bizarre. Sasha is aware that most of her friends would rather go to Aberdeen for the day than take her twins out. Why should Lisa's friends suddenly decide they love their company?

She wonders whether she needs to suspect Paul and Lindsey's motives. She wonders what on earth really happened in Greece – Liffy has been monosyllabic about it. She wonders why her children are suddenly not so young any more.

At Waterloo, Paul and Lindsey – a pair of smiling people with a soft, sparkly atmosphere around them – are waiting outside WH Smith's. Sasha takes one look at them and relaxes. There's nothing to worry about. Lindsey, in her Sloaney hairband, has the semi-childlike air that so many of Lisa's musical friends have: naïve, perhaps, but never dangerous. Paul looks eminently respectable, but for his beard. And Alex hurtles across the station concourse and throws his arms round Paul's waist.

Drawing closer, with the more reticent Matt, Sasha is struck by Paul's physical resemblance to Adam. Six foot tall, dark, almond-shaped eyes, beard, which Adam has grown again after all these years. The jigsaw pieces fall into place. Sasha fiddles with her hair, which is coming loose from its grip. She calls up an emergency smile, shakes Paul's hand, kisses Lindsey and thanks them both profusely.

'What shall we do?' Alex asks, jumping from foot to foot. Matt stands by, saying nothing.

'Well, I thought we could go for tea and cake at Gabriel's Wharf or Tate Modern,' Lindsey suggests, 'and at four we'd like to take you to a children's concert in the Purcell Room, which a friend of ours is playing in. He's offered us free tickets. It should be fun – you'll like it.'

'Will I like it too?' Matt says.

'You could try!' Paul winks at him. He pulls a crumpled concert flyer out of his corduroy jacket pocket and shows it to Sasha.

She looks at the names of the players. 'Oh my God,' she says.

'What do you think?' Lindsey asks. 'Should we?'

'I don't know.' Sasha doesn't want to think about this problem as well. 'It's up to you.'

Now she understands their eagerness to meet the twins on this particular day. She's not certain that it's a good idea, but Lindsey, being Lisa's best friend, maybe knows Lisa even better than Sasha does. Sasha leaves them to it and wanders back to her train.

Paul, Lindsey, Alex and Matt leave Waterloo by the front steps, aim for the river beside the Royal Festival Hall and stroll east along the South Bank. It's a humid day, full of greys and golds and greens. The twins run around and chase each other. Paul and Lindsey saunter along hand in hand, keeping half an eye on the boys, past the concrete bunker of the National Theatre, the contemporary brick and glass under the Oxo Tower and the tiled Victorian tunnel beneath Blackfriars Bridge, towards the vast brown hulk that is Tate Modern.

Under its dusty plane trees, the Embankment is heaving with tourists. Paul and Lindsey encourage the twins to play Spot the Language: they identify French, Italian, Japanese and something that Lindsey insists is Hungarian. London, these days, is full of strange and fantastical word-worlds. A paddle-steamer on the river booms out music with a deep bass beat; on board, people are celebrating some mystery milestone. Matt wonders how much it costs to hire the boat for the day, while

Alex chatters about all the different sounds they can hear. At the gallery, they make for the café and the grown-ups drink espresso; the boys each eat a gigantic piece of chocolate cake with cream, which makes Matt feel happier with life than he has for most of the day.

After tea they turn back towards the South Bank Centre; here they go through heavy glass doors into a wide black and white lobby, and from there into the Purcell Room, where the rest of the audience consists of adults with children just like them.

Matt wishes he wasn't the only one who thinks it's boring to sit and listen to music for an hour – he's used to feeling and thinking the same things as Alex. He doesn't much like Alex's music, while in return Alex doesn't really like him enjoying maths and money. Thinking that they don't see completely eye to eye makes him feel miserable. It's only now that he looks down at the programme and spots what Sasha had seen earlier. At once he doesn't feel so bored any more.

'Vla-di-mir Va-si-lev-sky,' Matt reads. 'Hey.' He nudges his brother. 'Isn't that Auntie Lisa's boyfriend's name?' He notices Paul and Lindsey exchange a glance.

'Auntie Lisa's boyfriend's *name*?' Alex echoes. 'It's not only his name. It's him.'

Alex makes his twin understand that Paul and Lindsey know this too; that that's why they're here; that all this has been planned and is the reason that Paul and Lindsey were so keen to take them out today; that the two of them are part of some grand scheme that hasn't much to do with them but in which they may play a crucial role. Matt takes it all in solemnly, in the split second that is all they need to conduct their inaudible communication.

They shuffle in their seats as the three musicians walk out on to the platform and take their positions. The bespectacled violinist stands up and starts talking. 'Hello, boys and girls!' he says. 'Are you all having a lovely holiday?' The children, with one mind, fidget, glare and don't respond. He carries on in an over-jaunty tone; Alex and Matt wonder how he could be so clueless. They turn their attention to the other musicians. They half expect to see Auntie Lisa holding the cello – but the cellist is a plump, wide-faced Russian man. And at the piano is the great Vladimir Vasilevsky, doing his bit for musical accessibility, outreach and education.

The boys have never seen Vladimir before. None of the family has. As far as they're concerned, he might have been a figment of Lisa's imagination. Vladimir doesn't even look real. On display on the concert platform, he reminds them of some exotic animal: his legs are long and gangly like a giraffe's, his arms wide and strong like an ape's. He has large, round, darkish eyes, curly dark hair, designer stubble. He is, the boys are happy to see, wearing leather trousers – cool! How unexpected that is in somebody who by rights should be their uncle. They signal approval to each other.

Alex's attention is fixed on Vladimir's hands as he plays the music, but Matt can't get comfortable in his chair, which is the wrong height and width for someone of his size. He wriggles and Alex kicks him when Paul is looking the other way. The musicians play short pieces and the violinist makes lousy jokes in between. He probably makes the same bad jokes at every concert. To Matt, this doesn't look like good business practice. He's convinced that a trio is a brand and if you want a good brand you don't do pathetic things that spoil its image. But Vladimir doesn't talk: he just looks cool and plays the piano, which is his job. Matt decides he likes Vladimir.

The concert is over after an hour. While the other families meander out into the foyer for drinks and sandwiches, the twins follow Paul and Lindsey up on to the stage and through the door at the back. A second later they are in what Lindsey calls the green room (odd, Matt thinks, since it isn't green) and there, talking to their friends and wiping white dust from their instruments and sweat from their faces, are the musicians.

Vladimir is holding forth in Russian to a well-dressed young woman on the other side of the room.

The twins glance at each other.

Lindsey goes up to Vladimir and interrupts his conversation. First she hugs him; then she says something that makes him turn, startled, in the twins' direction. They inch forward.

'These are Alex and Matt Levy,' she says. The twins are surprised that she's identified each of them correctly. Most people get it wrong a few times first, if less often now than they used to.

Vladimir raises his eyebrows. Then he shakes their hands. Close to, Matt wonders why the whites of his eyes are so large. His upper lids look top-heavy, as if it must be a tremendous effort to keep them open. The shape of his face is astonishing: he looks as if someone has carved him out of wood.

'Alex and Matt,' he says, his accent as heavy as his eyelids. 'You are Lisa's nephews?'

The boys nod.

'Did you enjoy the concert?'

They nod again.

'I like your trousers,' Matt says. From the corner of one eye, he sees Lindsey and Paul hovering a little way off. They are waiting for something. They are waiting for the twins to do what they want the twins to do. He takes a deep breath. 'Aren't you our Auntie Lisa's boyfriend?' he says.

'I was.' Vladimir's strange, too-large eyes seem dimmer for a second. 'She didn't want me to be her boyfriend any more. I haven't seen her for several months. How is she? Is she well?'

'She's . . .' Matt trails off, his nerve failing. Part of him, a part that he doesn't quite understand, is telling him that it's very odd indeed that the pair of them should be the ones trying to explain this to Vladimir.

'She's not ill?' Vladimir's face is concerned.

Matt wonders if it's only Russian people whose faces are so

expressive, or only English people whose faces are not. 'She's – um, she's fine,' he says, chickening out.

'She's having a baby,' Alex says. The twins look up at the pianist, their eyes more serious than they realise.

He stares back, speechless, for a few seconds. 'When?' he asks.

'January,' Matt squeaks.

Vladimir lowers his eyes to the floor, apparently counting something. To their left, Paul puts a hand on Lindsey's shoulder.

'Why didn't she tell me?' Vladimir turns to Paul and Lindsey and his eyes widen even further with new understanding. 'You knew? You *knew*! And you didn't tell me? My God. Am I the only person who doesn't know about this?'

'Vovka—'

'This is unbelievable! This is crazy! This is insane!'

Alex and Matt reach for each other's hands. Matt has a lump in his throat.

'Alex? Matt? Where is she? Is she in the same flat?'

They nod, shrinking back from this large, suddenly desperate leather-clad man.

'Um, Vovka, er, do you still want to come out for a drink?' the violinist asks him – now mercifully unaffected.

Vladimir shakes his head. 'There's something I have to do,' he says.

'Alex,' Matt hisses, 'she's going to kill us.'

Liffy and Charley have been sent into the garden while Anna talks to Sasha inside. Liffy sits on the grass close to her father's neglected rose bushes. The blooms are half their usual size because he hadn't been there to give them their midsummer feed. Round black spots have appeared on some of the leaves. She picks up five fallen petals and shunts them from hand to hand. How silky and fine they are; how tragic is their short lifespan, their inevitable fading. Her eyes are making her miserable: they feel hot and itchy from the conjunctivitis, which is back in force, made worse by exhaustion and too much makeup.

Charley sits nearby, pulling the petals off a daisy.

'I don't understand it,' she grumbles. 'Why did we have to come home? I'm fine, really. It was bad at the time, but I'm fine now. I told you not to say anything! Why did you have to go and *tell* them?'

Liffy shrugs. In the event she hadn't had much choice, and now her heart is a muddle of anger, misery, disappointment and fright. She doesn't want to talk about what had happened to Charley. It had been a no-win situation. She'd tried so hard to stay awake, but she was so tired – and she hadn't known that Anna would get up to go to the loo only an hour after Liffy and Charley had got back, and that she would trip over the prostrate Charley in the dark, and that Charley would have been sick again without even being conscious. And Liffy hadn't known that Charley had taken any kind of drug at the club, or anything about what she'd been doing with Mark, or what Mark had been trying to do with her, in the garden behind the wall. But Liffy – who hadn't drunk much and was fully conscious – had had to be the one to explain. Charley had been so pissed that she has only a sketchy idea of what happened. She insists that she didn't let Mark have sex with her, but Liffy doesn't know whether to believe her.

Inside the house, Sasha puts down her coffee cup and folds her hands as she listens to Anna.

'I'm not convinced,' Anna says, 'that Liffy and Charlotte should continue being friends. After all, if Liffy leads Charlotte astray like this . . .'

'*Liffy?*'

'She's clearly got some problems of her own that she needs to work out.' Anna is thin-lipped.

'How can you blame Liffy? Charley's always been the more mature of the two.'

'Which is precisely why she would never do a thing like this.'

'When you say Liffy has some problems . . .'

'She doesn't eat, does she? All she ever ate was fruit and a little salad. Her bikini's falling off her, she looks like a concentration-camp victim. Don't tell me you haven't noticed that she doesn't eat.'

'Liffy's still a little girl. She's much too young to get into the not-eating thing and, what's more, she'd be far too scared to go to a club. All she's interested in is ballet, vegetarianism and global warming.'

'Sasha, I wonder how much you really know about your daughter,' Anna says. 'I think I should take Charlotte home now.'

'Please do.' Sasha gets up and opens the back door.

Anna goes into the garden, takes her daughter's arm and marches her away. Liffy just has time to scramble to her feet and call her name; Charley turns back and gives Liffy a last, bewildered glance. Then she's gone. Liffy hears the clonk of doors closing and the rumble of a car engine. The grass seems to fall away under her feet, leaving her suspended over a granite precipice.

She forces herself to walk into the house and up to her mother, who is in the conservatory collecting half-empty mugs of coffee. Liffy puts a hand on her elbow. She knows that what's coming won't be good.

'Liffs, I know this isn't fair,' says Sasha. 'The thing is, they don't want you and Charley to spend so much time together.'

'Thought so . . .' Liffy says. 'Mum, I know I shouldn't have let her out of my sight, but it just happened – I couldn't, like, do anything, cos when I looked for her—'

'It's OK, sweetie. I know it wasn't your fault. You don't need to tell me that.'

'Thanks, Mum.'

'It'll all blow over, you know. These things usually do.'

'Yeah. It's all right. I'm cool.'

Somehow Liffy gets up the stairs to her room. Once there, she lies down and gazes at her blue frosted-glass vase, which holds a fresh bunch of anemones. She calls inwardly to the Earth Prince because he's the only person she can ask to come to her now. He's there at once, inside her eyelids, whispering comfort, holding her close to him.

That makes her think of Gaz and her first kiss: both of them vanished without saying goodbye. She'd feared the Earth Prince then; now she can see he's the only one she can trust.

'It's good,' the Earth Prince whispers. 'It's best. You'll see.'

'Why?'

'You're not ready yet. But it won't be long now, Liffy.'

The words are so distinct that Liffy sits up. Her head is spinning: she hasn't eaten today. She hasn't even wanted to. She looks down and thinks she sees a smear of earth on her right arm, where the Earth Prince's hand had rested a moment ago. And even this doesn't seem so extraordinary any more.

Lisa has spent the later part of Saturday afternoon sitting in her favourite café in West End Lane, sipping herbal tea and indulging in an almond croissant – if she can't enjoy pâtisserie while pregnant, when can she? She smiles at neighbours who pass by, chats to one or two people she has got to know who, like her, are regulars here, and passes the time as best she can, reading a novel about musicians that presents such a romanticised view of their lives that it almost makes her laugh aloud. At seven, the café closes and she has to head home.

Approaching her house, she sees a dark shape by the front door. There, sitting on the top step with his head bowed, is a lanky figure with curly hair. For a moment Lisa thinks it's a mugger waiting to ambush her. Then she wonders whether it is one of Andrew and Melanie's peculiar contacts who appear at unearthly times of night – though not usually at seven. And then the figure raises his head and she knows exactly who it is, as she's really known all along.

Lisa and Vladimir hold each other's gaze, motionless. Vladimir's eyes travel down Lisa's body and fix on the bump.

Lisa spots Melanie behind the ground-floor window, watching them.

'Vovka,' she says, pushing past him to unlock the door, motioning him to come in. He follows her up the stairs. In the flat, still silent, he bends to stroke Igor, who chirrups a feline greeting. 'Do you want a drink?' Lisa says.

'No. Thanks.'

'Something to eat?'

'No.'

'Well. What do you want, then?'

'Lisa, for God's sake!'

She backs away.

'Is it mine?'

'Yes. Of course it's yours.'

'I don't understand.' Vladimir doesn't shout at her – she'd been afraid he might. Instead he speaks quietly. In some ways this is worse. 'Why didn't you tell me?' he says.

Lisa sits down on the sofa and looks away. 'I think,' she ventures, 'because I didn't know how.'

'Well, I tell you how. You pick up the telephone and you say, "Vovka, I'm having your baby."'

'And then? If I do that, what do you say?'

'What do you mean?'

'Vovka, we'd broken up. You made it so clear you didn't want anything more than we had. How could I spring this on you?'

'Lisa, this is unbelievable.'

'Why? That's what you said.'

'That was before.'

'Vovka, in my experience you're nothing if not consistent.'

He doesn't respond. Instead, he says, 'What do you mean to do?'

'Have the baby. Live here for a bit, then move somewhere else – maybe further out of town, maybe somewhere with a bit of a garden for her to run around in—'

'Her?'

Lisa looks him between the eyes, fainting inwardly, pulling reserves of courage out of heaven knows where. 'I went for a scan yesterday and they said it's probably a girl. Not definitely. But probably.'

Vladimir's eyes burn with pain. 'Lisa, it wasn't your intention to tell me? Or to ask me to support you and the child? Or to let me have any part in her life? Were you intending to tell *her* who she really is?'

'I meant to tell you. I didn't want to ask you for help. I didn't want to burden you with this – you're so busy—'

'So you let me find out by accident, when Lindsey brings your nephews to see me! For God's sake, this is my child too. This is my daughter! Do you really believe I'd want nothing to do with her? Did you think I'd want nothing to do with you? Lisa, maybe you forget: you left me. I never left you. What do you take me for? You think I'm some kind of tyrant, a dictator – like your father was to you. Am I some kind of monster? Whatever did I do to you that makes you think I'm such a monster?'

'Nothing. You did *nothing*. That was the trouble.'

'I don't understand you. I don't know what I've done to make you want to hurt me like this.'

'Of course you don't know. How could you? You've never taken any notice of my needs, you've never let my feelings impinge on you in any way – so why should I expect you to start now? Vovka, we're finished. We always were.'

'Then if it's all the same to you, I will leave now, because I have work to do.'

'Fine,' Lisa says, without moving. 'Goodbye.'

Igor, oblivious to what's going on, winds around Vladimir's ankles. Vladimir bends and picks up the cat. Lisa senses his great forest-coloured eyes fixed on her across the animal, which he holds close to his chest. She looks at him standing in the middle of the room: a tall, pained man cradling a small, purring cat.

'Are you seriously saying goodbye?' Vladimir says. 'It's not necessary.'

'It is. I tried, Vovka, I tried so hard for you. But I can't live like that.'

'You are determined, then, not to let me share this with you?'

'Why should I?'

'Because, Lisa, this is my family. You know I've never had family, not really . . .'

'I don't care, Vovka. That's not a good enough reason.'

'Then what the fuck *is* a good enough reason?' Vladimir explodes. Igor's paws flail and his fur bristles as he decants himself away.

Lisa bows her head, shakes it from side to side. 'If you don't know,' she says, 'then I can't tell you.'

Vladimir strides out of the flat and slams the door.

Lisa tips over on to the sofa, racked with sobs. At the same time she tells herself to get a grip. Come on, girl. Be sensible. Don't get so upset, it's bad for the baby. She makes herself get up and go to the kitchen for a glass of water. Her throat feels skinned alive. Her soul feels skinned alive. Stop crying, she orders herself. Crying won't help.

21

'Liffy, please eat your dinner.' Sasha, her heart in her mouth, challenges her pale, peaky daughter.

'I had tea earlier . . .' says Liffy, trailing off – she had almost forgotten that she can no longer use Charley as an excuse.

'Well, I didn't see you,' Sasha snaps. 'As far as I know, you might have eaten nothing since breakfast. And why are you wearing that big jersey?' September sun is pouring into the kitchen and Sasha is sweating in a sleeveless top.

'I'm a bit cold.'

Sasha looks at Liffy's fingertips. They are white, so white they verge on blue. She begins to feel chilly herself. Questions and doubts shoot about her mind like rubber bullets. 'Eat up and you'll feel warmer,' she tries.

'I'm not hungry, Mum. Can I go and do my homework?'

Sasha waits, searches for words, her brain silently splitting open. Each day it's the same: Liffy refuses to eat. She'll put away a plateful of green salad, she'll eat brown rice, fruit and organic vegetables – only organic, though – but the twins have to eat too, they're hungry little boys, they need meat and potatoes and chocolate ice-cream and every evening it's the same battle, the same horror, the same thumbscrew that Liffy is tightening around her day by day, week by week.

Sasha caves in and lets her go: there is nothing else she can do. Liffy slips away up the stairs and, while the twins devour their sister's leftovers, Sasha sits at the kitchen table, puts her head into her hands and tries not to howl aloud. How can Liffy do this to her – to all of them? And how can she, Liffy's mother, be so powerless to stop her? She knows that she is watching her daughter starve herself. Yet the resulting stress is not goading her into action but paralysing her with fright. She simply doesn't know what to do. Worst of all is that when she knows she should feel worried, she feels furious instead.

This isn't all. A month has gone by and she has not heard from *The Weekly Review.*

Normally the phone rings, or an email arrives from a researcher booking the guests, confirming her invitation. Now, after one glum return in which Sasha and Rick had managed not to speak more than two words to one another ('Hello' and 'Goodnight'), there is nothing but silence.

Sasha can't believe it. She can't understand how Rick can be so small-minded. She can't understand why men are ready to go to such lengths for – basically – a shag; or why a miserable damp squib of a one-night stand should make anyone so vindictive. Admittedly, he's the last person on earth she feels like seeing just now – perhaps he feels the same. One shouldn't mix business with pleasure.

That had been exactly her mistake.

The phone rings and Sasha, on automatic pilot, answers. It's Adam.

'Ad? How's things?' she says.

'I'm busy.' His voice has gone up by an octave; it's almost at its old pitch. It has energy in it, too: the dragged-down depression has mysteriously lifted. 'I think I'm on to something,' he says. 'If it comes through, I'll tell you more.'

'Good.'

'How are the kids?'

'Fine. When can you take them out?' This is all she really wants to know. She wants time to herself now, time to ponder and reflect, time that she doesn't have even with the children going back to school. Time to write. Space. Air. Peace. All she really wants is peace.

What she really wants, besides that, is to tell him of her anxiety about Liffy, but Adam has enough problems of his own, too many to be able to help, and it would make him feel worse. Anyway, perhaps it's just that she's 'projecting', reading too much into it. Perhaps it's just that bloody Anna and her bloody daughter have put the wind up her. Liffy has always been so sensible. Charley's a liar, Sasha has deduced that much, so there's no reason to suppose that her mother is any better . . .

'OK,' Adam is saying. 'If that's what you want I'll come on Saturday and take them out. I won't get in your way.' He doesn't say goodbye before he hangs up. Sasha's innards smart abruptly as if he had struck her. No blow has ever passed between them in twenty years.

Does she want peace? Or does she want passion? She wants both, but they don't go together. If she has one, the other will have evaporated. She'd been teetering on the edge of obsession with Rick. Now that it's finished she understands, obliquely, that maybe what she'd wanted to feel was desire itself, not its appeasement. She doesn't want to live without passion. But to live with passion means to be driven by it, and probably to be driven back into another house of cards, one that can topple as easily as the first – although there weren't enough cards in Rick to build a house in the first place.

But that's the nature of illusion: even when you recognise it for what it is, you still work day and night to preserve it, in case repeating it often enough makes it real. She misses that illusory, luminous, seductive state of mind. She misses being obsessed. She needs adrenaline. She needs to feel her blood racing through her arteries, she needs to be aware of her aliveness in every moment of every day. At peace, if she's honest with herself, she feels half dead.

And so the next morning, while the children are at school, she goes in search of an adrenaline rush in Waitrose.

She takes two shopping bags with her and self-scans most

of her items. The barcode on her bag of fresh cod fillets won't scan, though; neither will the one on the mature Cheddar; and the piece of root ginger she takes is so small that it costs only three pence and there's simply no point. She trundles up to the Quick Check counter, pays by debit card at the machine and wanders out of the shop with free fish, cheese and ginger, wondering whether she'll be spotted and stopped. Nothing happens. Nobody notices. Sasha experiences her adrenaline rush. She's become a successful criminal.

Liffy's new classroom overlooks the grey asphalt playground at the back of the school and a few poplar trees beyond. Charley is sitting on the other side of the room. They've been ordered to keep apart and Liffy finds she doesn't mind too much. She sits next to Sophie, whom Charley doesn't like. Charley, for her part, has manoeuvred herself into a place next to Leila. Liffy's heart hurts a little when she sees Charley's high ponytail beside Leila's blue-black mane. But her heart often hurts – it's a stress problem, Margaret told her at ballet class. It's not a heart-attack, just a muscular pain. Nothing to worry about. Breathe deeply and it'll go away.

It's been the hottest summer for five hundred years, or so she'd heard on the news. Now, after the blistering heat of August, an Indian summer has set in. The leaves look as if they've been brushed with pale gold paint, the sun slants down at sharper angles, casting the world into lurid brilliance offset by lengthening, distorted shadows; and near the river the air carries the scent of early fruit and dry earth. At break, Liffy strikes out alone.

They're not supposed to leave the school premises, but she leaves anyway and walks for ten minutes to the riverside at Chiswick Mall. The grey Thames glistens beside her and seagulls shout overhead. Solitude, says the Earth Prince, is good. Solitude is vital now, at this stage of Liffy's purification. She mustn't waste her time with those silly chattering girls and their stupid games. The time of reckoning is near.

She doesn't really miss Charley. Not really. Of course, you always miss someone you've been close to, even if you didn't much like them at the time. But she must strive for clarity of mind and purity of body, and Charley did neither of those any good.

Knowing this, however, doesn't help Liffy's sense of abandonment. First Dad. Now Charley. And even if Mum is physically in the house, her mind is somewhere else. Liffy can't help feeling that Mum would prefer not to be in the house at all, given the option. Meanwhile, the twins are so busy being the twins, obsessing respectively about music and money-oriented maths, that they don't notice anything around them. Liffy is alone. She sometimes wonders what she's done wrong.

She always gets up early and misses breakfast, telling Mum she's eaten already – these days, Mum has to get up in time to walk the boys to school. She gestures at her lunch – just enough to stop herself becoming hypoglycaemic. At supper she eats salad with wholemeal pasta or brown rice. Mum argues and tells her to eat more, but Liffy always wins because Mum is either too tired to fight or too busy calming the twins, who nag and scrap and punch. After supper, Liffy works her way through pyramids of homework; and every spare minute she spends in her loft studio, practising, burning off calories and fat, aiming for the audition in November. Mum, dark circles under her eyes that make her look like a panda, barely noticed when Liffy asked her to sign the application form.

Walking along Chiswick Mall, she's missing lunch, but she doesn't care: she has no appetite anyway. She loves Chiswick Mall: a long, car-free stretch beside the river, lined with Georgian houses with long gardens, it's the sort of place where you can imagine yourself back into the nineteenth century, living in a world free of traffic and chemicals and gaps in the ozone layer, free from the frightening population, with its baggy clothes, baseball caps and concealed knives, of Hammersmith's busy shopping streets.

Later that afternoon, she goes to ballet straight from school. In the middle of the class, taking her turn to dance the *enchaînements*, she begins to see spots in front of her eyes. They leap about and turn grey, filling up her vision from bottom to top, obliterating it.

When she comes round, she's on the couch in Margaret's studio waiting room, with her classmates fussing round her and Margaret making a phone call nearby. The idea that she might call an ambulance brings Liffy back to consciousness at once.

'I'm fine,' she says. 'Could I just have a drink, perhaps? Or a spoon of honey?'

'Honey?' echoes Margaret.

'I'll be fine – really. I just need some sugar, I think.'

'I still want to get hold of your mother.'

Mum is out, her mobile is off and the twins have gone to Julius's house until she gets back. Liffy doesn't know where she goes or why. It's probably a library, like Auntie Lisa, because she says she's writing another book. Liffy had thought that writing a book meant you sat in your study and wrote. That's not what Mum does. She's out more than ever.

Margaret sits down beside Liffy, takes her hand and squeezes it. One of the girls brings her a glass of orange juice with a spoonful of honey stirred into it. Liffy swallows it almost in one gulp. She feels less dizzy at once, although she's not sure she can stand up, let alone dance, and her hands and feet are so cold that they hurt.

'Liffy,' Margaret says, 'this really worries me. You've lost a lot of weight since last term and you shouldn't need to be bundled up in all these leg-warmers and crossovers while the weather's so warm. Are you eating properly?'

'Yes. I'm fine. I just fainted. It's nothing.'

'You don't look fine to me. Will you promise me something? Get your mother to take you to the doctor and have a proper check-up. Fainting isn't a good idea, you know.'

'I'm probably getting my period,' says Liffy, who hasn't had a period for two months. She's heard at school that if you lose enough weight your periods stop: it's a mark of her success that she has reached that stage. And what a relief it is. No blood; no pain. It's like being a child again. She can see, in Margaret's shrewd gaze, that she doesn't believe her, but to Liffy, end has come to justify means. The scales told her this morning that she had dropped another pound.

When Dad comes down from Oxford on Saturday and takes them out to Richmond for the afternoon, she finds that, strangely, part of her wants him to see how miserable she is. On the other hand, part of her is terrified of what will happen if he does. Will he scream at her? Will he punish her, as he punished the twins? Won't he blame her? She adopts a contingency plan. She pulls leg-warmers on under her jeans, to make sure she doesn't feel too cold and to pad out the shape of her legs, which she knows he'll think are emaciated, even though she knows they aren't. She puts on a sweater and over it a big grey sweatshirt several sizes too big, together, the garments swathe her bony frame, disguising it. She puts on makeup, including a dab of rose-based liquid rouge, which makes her cheeks pinker but looks natural.

Dad embraces her and doesn't seem to notice a thing. She doesn't quite recognise him. He's wearing jeans and a black top and smells of cigarette smoke. She can't get used to the beard. She still imagines she'll see him in his work clothes, clean-shaven, smokeless. She wonders where her real father has gone. Then she wonders whether this is her real father: this is who he was all along, only he never noticed and neither did she. That man with the demanding job, the long hours, the late evenings in print week, was never real. He was a phantom that she'd grown up thinking was her father when all the time he wasn't. He was a fake; perhaps he was never there at all. And if he was fictional, perhaps the rest of it is fictional too. Nothing in the world is real. Nothing lasts. She can't get her head round it.

'Come on, Liffs, wakey wakey,' Dad interrupts. They are sitting in a café on Richmond Hill, choosing lunch. 'What would you like in your baked potato?'

Dad, Dad, Dad, wails something inside Liffy.

'Plain salad, please,' she says. 'And no potato.' Alex kicks her under the table and she kicks him back. The impact hurts her foot more than it hurts him. Her bones feel like the fragile stalks of a plant, she doesn't know why.

'Come on, sweetie. Do have something else.'

'No, thanks, this is all I want. I'm not really hungry.'

'God!' groans Alex. 'Dad, this happens every time we have a meal. It's really, really boring.' Liffy notices Dad glance quickly into Alex's face, then into her own.

On the way back, Dad takes her aside while the twins are being distracted by a toyshop. 'Liffs,' he says, arm around her shoulders, 'are you eating properly?'

'Yes, of course I am,' Liffy says. 'They're just picking on me, Dad. They always do.'

'Hm.' He looks at her long and hard; she sees him assessing her shape. She's glad she's had the sense to pad herself up. Perhaps she'll start doing it for school too, just to be sure.

Liffy has to prepare a solo for her audition. Margaret keeps her behind after the others have gone, having ascertained that she is feeling well (she is: she's brought her jar of honey with her and swallowed some in the changing room before class, and she has put on an extra wrap to distract her teacher from her boniness). Margaret plays her a piece of music on CD. It's a flute solo – high and haunting, backed by whispering strings and harp, full of wild, lonely harmonies and fluttering breezes.

'It's from *Daphnis and Chloë* by Ravel,' Margaret tells her. 'It's a dance for Chloë in the final scene. The ballet is set in ancient Greece and Chloë, who's been rescued from pirates by the god Pan, is paying tribute to him in a dance. She tells the story of how Pan fell in love with a nymph called Syrinx. But she didn't love him and to escape from him she turned herself into river reeds. Pan picked some of the reeds and made them into the musical instrument that we now call the Pan pipes. If you like it, we could choreograph it together. We'll show off all your best qualities – lots of spins and little jumps and you could wear your hair down. What do you think?'

Liffy nods, bright-eyed. She loves it. It feels like part of her already. She tells Margaret she's happy to stay late at each lesson and work on it. She takes the music home and improvises to it in her studio, imagining how it feels to turn into a reed.

She looks up the god Pan in an encyclopedia of mythology that she finds on the Internet. Pan, it says, is the god of wild nature. She reads the story of *Daphnis and Chloë* and laughs to herself. How strange that Margaret should pick that story for her. Not that Gaz had much resembled a pirate, but the Earth Prince, her own personal god of wild nature, had come to save her from him, even when she didn't want to be saved. The flute melody lifts her up and she interprets it, curling and spiralling, introducing the light jumps and spins that she likes. Pan is the second Earth Prince she's found; the first was the Erl King, King of the Alder, which had been a terrible shock – but all this proves, at least, that he existed in ancient Greece and in nineteenth-century Vienna and he could still exist now. It comforts her to know that others have seen him too, even if they called him by different names.

At night, though, the ideas that comforted her during the day turn round and lance her mind like a razor. Because now she suspects that the Earth Prince isn't only her imagination.

He could be real. Countless people have seen him and named him. And he would have more power than she had given him credit for. He'd be no imaginary friend: he'd be a god. He'd be no companion to chat with: instead he'd hold her in his power. Half asleep, she has a vision of him grown vast, the size of Mount Olympus, cupping her in the palm of one hand while she performs Chloë's dance of the river reeds to honour him. He has plans for her and she doesn't know what they are.

Liffy opens her eyes. Her pyjamas are soaked with sweat and she can't control her breathing. She flings away her duvet and goes downstairs. Around her, the house is sound asleep. Feeling her way into the lounge in the tobacco-brown darkness, she persuades Ben to talk to her. This cat used to sleep on her bed every night. He used to settle down beside her and purr. Now he's suspicious and distrustful. Is it the green-brown touch of the Earth Prince that has frightened him away? Liffy feels as if she's going to choke. Then she feels faint. Clutching at objects along her way, she manages to get to the kitchen and find her honey. Her hand shakes as she unscrews the top and plunges in a teaspoon. The thick sweetness is almost unbearable on her tongue, but she knows it will help her. She can't pass out again.

She sits in the lounge for a while, honey in front of her, playing with the Ceefax button on the TV remote. That's what Dad always used to do. She looks at his chair. Bill the ginger cat is curled up in it now. And she thinks of Dad's difference, Dad's pain, his distance from all of them, and she can't stop the tears that well up like the river in which her reeds would grow. In the fug of misery that envelops her, her bones are becoming reeds and her eyes a river and her heart given away to the unreachable to save her from all the pain of being human. Her skin, she fancies, is turning green. Her fingers will lengthen into leaves and her mouth soften into a flower.

Hours later, she wakes up on the sofa. Mum is shaking her

shoulder gently. 'Liffs,' Mum whispers, 'wake up, darling. What are you doing here? What's going on?'

Liffy glances at the floor around her but sees no trace of leaf or petal. 'Oh, nothing,' she mumbles. 'I got up for something to eat and I guess I fell asleep.'

Mum looks at the open jar of honey on the coffee table, then puts a hand flat on Liffy's forehead, which is no longer burning but cool as the morning air.

After seeing Liffy off towards the school bus Sasha, numb with misery, picks up the telephone. She can't leave this any longer: she can't keep pretending that in another day or two Liffy will eat again and be well. But she doesn't know who to call. She can't bring herself to phone Adam for help. She won't try Sally, who she's sure would be worse than useless. Lisa has left her machine permanently on since her bust-up with Vladimir. Cindy would storm in, indomitable as ever, and make her take Liffy to A and E, which would be the worst idea in the world. And who else is there?

Sasha dials the GP's surgery. The line is engaged. She gets through after ten minutes.

'We have no appointments with Dr Matthews until a week on Monday,' says the receptionist, impassive. 'What time would you like?'

Sasha submits to an appointment in almost two weeks' time. She can't face booking Liffy in as an emergency, which is the turn-up-and-wait alternative, because she doesn't want to frighten her. But she wishes to God above, and Tony Blair in Downing Street, that the NHS could be less log-jammed than it currently is.

There is someone else – entirely unrelated – whom Sasha needs to call; and, having done all she's allowed to do for Liffy, she decides to tackle the other problem next.

The thing she hates most about the big organisations she deals with – television, publishing, newspapers – is having to read between their lines. The veneer is smooth, polished rose-wood; what happens underneath is not the privilege of guest speakers or freelance writers to observe. Nothing is direct: that wouldn't be tactful; that wouldn't be cricket. Perhaps the English Establishment is not so different from its old self despite successive changes of government, not to mention century.

Sasha thinks of herself as English rather than Jewish. She observes no festivals, speaks no Hebrew, has been to Israel only once, a long time ago, to visit some of Adam's distant relations. But part of her wants up-front honesty in day-to-day dealings – simple, direct truth, even if it has to be blunt, even if it might hurt – and this is where she begins to feel like a foreigner. It's not the English way of doing things. Sasha thinks of the various schemes and logos and policies that have run through the television world in the time she's known it and peels them away one by one, like outer leaves on a jungle plant concealing a core that may or may not leach poison.

'Oh – Sasha – how nice to hear from you,' says Marion, the blonde production assistant. 'Can I call you back later today? I'm about to go into a meeting.'

'Is Rick available?' Sasha asks.

'He's just gone into the same meeting . . . I'll leave a message for him to call you back, shall I?'

'Thanks.'

Sasha hangs up, clenching her teeth. Her jaw hurts with the pressure. *If they want to boot me out, the least they could do is tell me to my face.* Oh, the underhandedness, the two-facedness, the slipperiness! The falsehoods, the judgements, the mis-judgements. And all she's done is refuse to continue an affair with a married producer!

Sasha gives them one last chance: she waits for the call. She waits until two in the afternoon. Nothing. She waits until five. Silence. She wonders whether to write a letter, and instead of working on her book, she spends her mental energy on wording it: 'Dear Rick' . . . no, 'Dear Richard . . . I am a little distressed' . . . no, 'I am slightly perplexed to find that I have not been invited back to *The Weekly Review* . . . Am I to infer from this that I am no longer welcome?' . . . No, that won't do at all, it's much too honest . . .

There's commotion in school. Huddled groups are whispering around the classroom and skulking in the corridors. Leila is dabbing at her beautiful dark eyes with a linen handkerchief. Charley has vanished. Liffy asks Sophie what's going on, but Sophie doesn't know and hasn't noticed anything wrong. Liffy wonders how anyone could be so insensitive to the jangling of nerve-endings in the air that day.

But it's Sophie who breaks the news eventually, though without connecting the whispering groups, the invisible Charley and that there was nobody to give her her flute lesson.

'I went along to the music block and there's this notice on Mr Brewster's door saying all lessons are suspended until further notice and the school will make them up later or refund the money. There isn't anything about why.'

'He's gone?' Liffy says.

'I dunno about gone, but he's not there.'

Liffy's mind juggles the pieces and throws them into place. She jumps up and runs to the toilets, where she shuts herself in a cubicle and sends a text message to her aunt: 'Auntie Lisa, something strange happnd 2 Robin, plse cn u ask some 1 where he is? Lol Lif x'.

Lisa is in IKEA when her phone bleeps. Lindsey – feeling desperately guilty over her role in the Vladimir débâcle – has driven her there in the Range Rover to buy some furniture that she'll need when the baby arrives. Lisa now has a small purple car of her own, as of two days ago, but Lindsey had insisted on taking the capacious 4WD instead. So Lisa's new car sits in the residents' parking site down the road, gathering its first dust and enjoying its first scratches from the local schoolboys. Now the two young women are standing in the vortex of the store's windowless labyrinth in Neasden, gazing at a display of cots veneered in plain white and light beech.

Lisa looks up from the phone, shows Lindsey the message and says, 'What on earth—'

'Oh God,' Lindsey says. 'It's horrible. I meant to tell you about it, but I didn't want to upset you seeing as Liffy's friend is studying with him . . . But what happened is, one of the girls accused him of trying to rape her.'

'*What?*'

'Of course it's madness. Robin would never hurt a fly. There's no way he would ever put a hand on a pupil when he's teaching – he's so aware of all the trouble there can be. But it's her word against his and the headmistress decided to believe the kid. How is Liffy, by the way?'

'Thin. Too thin. She fainted in her ballet class and nobody's doing a bloody thing about it.'

'Can't *you* make them?'

'I asked Sasha and she said she'd booked an appointment with the GP, but it's almost two weeks away still. Christ, I'm just being mean to Sasha – it's not as if she's not trying . . . But it's all so unfair, Lin.'

'Tell me about it.' Lindsey nods, glancing at Lisa's swelling abdomen.

A bickering family pushes past them – a fat mother, a beer-bellied father, two squalling under-threes. There but for the grace of God, Lisa thinks. She would rather be herself; she would rather be alone than be them. She texts her niece back: 'Call me 18r.' Then she says to Lindsey, 'I think the beech, don't you?'

'Lee, are you sure you're doing the right thing?'

'Yes. I prefer it to the white. Now, what else do I need? A cupboard, a set of shelves . . .'

'I meant – about Vladimir.'

Lisa pushes her hair out of her eyes. She wishes IKEA had windows. She always loses her bearings in there – she almost loses her sense of gravity: she never knows where the way out is. 'He can't do that,' she tells her friend, sweat trembling on her nose. 'He can't just turn up on my doorstep and say he wants to be part of a family. Not after the way he behaved towards me.'

'I've got a theory.'

'Which is?'

'You're punishing him.'

'Why? Because I don't want to live with a man who doesn't want to live with me? It's not *me* he wants, Lin. It's the baby. And even then, it's *a* baby, in abstract. It's the fact of having someone to call family, not the baby for the sake of who that baby is going to become and not because it's him and me having a baby together. He can't see anything except in relation to how it affects him.'

Lindsey presses her lips together and casts a sideways look at Lisa. 'Sometimes, Lee,' she says, 'I think you can't either.'

'What?' says Lisa. She is watching another family go past – a single mother this time, with an infant and a four-year-old. The baby is crying, the four-year-old is whimpering, the mother – who looks ten years younger than Lisa – is screaming at them both. She's wearing grubby jeans and a grey T-shirt stained at the shoulder with something orange. She looks as if she hasn't slept in seven months; probably, thinks Lisa, she hasn't. She looks miserable, desperate and half mad. Lisa watches and waits as they make their way past; she almost expects the mother to break down and strike the four-year-old. Instead, when she stops walking, she gathers the whinging child into her arms in an abrupt gesture of total security and protection.

Lisa feels tears prickling in her eyes. She is watching love – diamond-strong mother-love – in the middle of IKEA. What does Vladimir know of this kind of love? What will he ever?

Is it not his right to have the chance to sample it, even if its moments of joy are few, its sorrows many, its anxieties infinite? Or is she rationalising because she's wondering how in the name of heaven she is going to cope on her own?

'Where *is* Vovka?' she asks, swallowing.

'Somewhere,' Lindsey says. 'Probably at a piano. But somewhere.'

That night, after talking to Lisa for twenty minutes, Liffy shuts herself into her bedroom. The twins next door are playing a noisy war game on their PlayStation. Liffy puts her fingers into her ears and screws up her eyes.

A voice in her inner ear is saying that Charley is lying. It's the voice of logic. It's something she knows already. Robin is being wronged. Lisa is sure of it; Lindsey, who knows everyone, has no doubt either. But she, Liffy, is the only person at school who can say so. Talking to Lisa has strengthened her resolve and her confidence. She has to tell someone.

But the disloyalty gnaws at her still childish sense of fairness to a friend. One has to trust one's friends, one has to be loyal and faithful to them.

On the other hand . . . She can still see Charley in Greece, her makeup and tears blended into a purple mess, her clothes torn, her eyes wild. Was that a loyal way for Charley to behave to her? She tries next to think of how Charley must have felt when Mark began to do – whatever it was that Mark had done. She'd have been scared shitless. So if she'd been upset in her flute lesson – her crush on Robin being so innocent by comparison – and if perhaps Robin had given her a tissue, perhaps had tried to comfort her with a pat on the shoulder, would it not have been easy for her to mistake the pat for, well, something else?

The twins have fallen silent, told off by Mum for playing instead of sleeping. Liffy can hear the television in the lounge. She pulls on her dressing-gown and goes down.

Much to Liffy's surprise, Mum is watching a horror movie. 'Don't watch this, Liffs, it'll give you bad dreams,' she says, without taking her eyes off the screen. Liffy sits down and looks.

It's an old black-and-white film, with creepy, threatening music. A beautiful girl is asleep in an ancient-looking bed, a wreath of white blossom round her neck. An older woman, presumably her mother, comes in. Her nose wrinkles: it appears that she doesn't like the smell of the flowers. She lifts the wreath off the girl, opens a window and leaves. The camera pans on to a very artificial-looking giant bat flapping around outside. A moment later, the bat is in the room and turns into a tall, thin man with terrible, terrible eyes. He draws back his lips and reveals long, fang-like teeth.

Liffy gets up again. 'I think you're right, Mum,' she says. Her knees are shaking.

'It's only a story, Liffs. But I don't think you'll like it.'

'I wouldn't have thought you'd like it either.'

'I don't. But it's better than lying awake thinking about the BBC.'

Liffy thinks better of unloading her worries about Charley on to her mother. Mum is stressed out enough as it is. She trots up to her and gives her a kiss on the cheek. 'Don't worry, Mum. We'll be OK,' she says. 'You don't have to do that silly programme, do you? I mean, it's just talk, isn't it? I don't think anybody really listens to it anyway.'

'Yes, darling. Go on, get some sleep. You need it.'

'Night night, Mum.'

On the screen, the man with the long teeth is bending over the young girl in the bed. With a great build-up from the music, he lowers his head towards her and sinks his teeth into her neck.

Liffy wobbles on her feet. She can feel the fangs poised against her own jugular. She thinks she's going to faint again. She picks up Bill, the ginger cat, who is washing his paws nearby and takes him upstairs with her for company, half climbing, half collapsing back into bed. Bill, thank goodness, though he's not her usual cat, curls up companionably next to her. He's less sensitive than his colleague, Ben. Liffy leaves the lamp on.

In the morning, when Charley gets on to the bus, Liffy pulls together all her courage. She waves at Charley and motions to the seat beside her – where Charley always used to sit, but no longer does. Charley looks at her as if in outrage, but comes and sits with her anyway. 'I'm not supposed to see you,' she says.

'How can you not? We're in the same form. We get the same bus.'

'My mum says you're a bad influence.'

'Your mum should know what really happened, and so should mine.'

'Your mum never notices anything.'

'Charley, don't be horrible about my mum, it's not her fault. I don't like us not talking to each other.'

'Neither do I,' Charley admits.

'Charley, what happened with Robin? I keep hearing people whispering, but I don't know what really happened.'

'I got him what he deserved. The sack. He's out.'

'But why? What did he do?'

'Oh, wouldn't *you* like to know?'

'I would, actually.'

'He touched me where he shouldn't have.' Charley shrugs.

'And he got the sack for it?'

'Of course. He's my teacher. And I'm under age.'

Liffy thinks again of spotty Mark in Greece, flies undone in the beer garden. She remembers Charley's composition, the one about the schoolgirl who ran away with a teacher and was caught in a sick, humiliating conclusion. She thinks of Charley batting her lashes at the boys on the black beach. Something turns over in her stomach.

At lunchtime she escapes to Chiswick Mall. She sits on a

wooden bench in front of the row of rose-bedecked, ample-balconied houses fronting on to the river and considers her decision. She doesn't know how she's going to tell the headmistress that Charley is lying. She has no proof, other than her aunt's friend's view that Robin's character is sound, which may not be enough. It will be her word against Charley's. And she doesn't even know Robin, not officially. She knows him by sight – he looks like a robin, a bouncy, bright-eyed fellow who doesn't so much walk to the music block as jog, saying good morning to everyone he sees on the way.

After half an hour she wanders back to school, takes several deep breaths and goes up to the headmistress's office to make an appointment via the secretary. But when she explains what it's about, the secretary fetches Miss Murray straight away. Liffy likes Miss Murray, who is a fair-haired woman in her forties: there's something energetic about her kindness when she welcomes Liffy into her office that gives her the confidence she needs.

'These are very serious allegations, Olivia,' Miss Murray says, a few minutes later.

Liffy is perching on the edge of a chair at the far side of the desk. 'Thing is, my aunt knows him – she has friends who are friends of his – and they all say he'd never, ever, ever do anything like that.'

'One's friends usually do say things like that, Olivia. Everyone wants to have confidence in their friends. Speaking of which, I understand that there's some problem between you and Charlotte.'

'Charley's mum doesn't want us going around together any more,' Liffy says, crestfallen. 'We got into trouble with some boys on holiday. I promise it wasn't my fault, Miss Murray. I didn't want to go in the first place.'

Miss Murray looks her up and down and gives a gentle nod. 'I can believe that,' she says.

'Charley's had a crush on Mr Brewster for months. I think

that maybe she really wanted him to – touch her and then he didn't and she's angry. Or something. I don't know. I don't really understand any of it. But I am sure it's not true and I am sure he shouldn't be sacked.'

Miss Murray's face is inscrutable. 'I've interviewed him,' she says, 'and that's what he told me. But it's his word against Charley's. And I can't be sure that you aren't in some way trying to get your own back on Charley for what happened in Greece, which sounds very regrettable. You know, Liffy, a real friendship can always withstand its troubles. All sorts of things come between people, but when you learn to forgive somebody your friendship can be strengthened in the end.'

'Yes . . .'

'There is one more thing I can do before we decide whether to take it up with the board of governors. We had a break-in last term in the music block and some of the music-technology equipment was taken so we've installed CCTV there. It covers the corridor where Mr Brewster has his room. I could have the tape analysed to see if it tells us anything more. What do you think?'

'I think that would be good.'

'Right. We'll have it done.'

Liffy is relieved when she's allowed to go. Her conscience is clear – relatively, at least.

She doesn't know how to explain adolescence to an adult. Presumably they've all been through it, but presumably they've forgotten what it's like. She doesn't know how to explain to the headmistress of one of London's finest girls' schools that Charley wants to have sex, just to know what it's really like – and yet at the same time is nine hundred per cent terrified by the idea. Her own abdomen still aches with the ghost of Gaz's kiss on the pub wall.

Lisa is trying to prepare a lecture about Debussy, but she's feeling nauseous and exhausted. She can't remember ever feeling so tired in her nearly thirty-four years. Outside the window, she can see the West Hampstead madwoman, swathed in red robes, carrying a wooden walking-stick in one hand and an orange in the other, making her way up the street, muttering to herself and tapping the stick in a quirky rhythm on the pavement. She sits on the front wall below Lisa's window, plays with the orange, taps her stick, mutters curses at the passers-by. Lisa closes the window to cut out the sound and the woman looks up and swears at her. Lisa beats a retreat to her kitchen with a notebook and the cat to get away from her.

Concentrating is hard enough already. Is it true that she is punishing Vladimir for reasons of her own? How can she be certain that Lindsey's right? How can anyone ever tell what's right? She distrusts men; she always has. That's because of her father's violent temper, her unreliable boyfriends, her intellectual training that makes her question everything that comes her way. She looks gift horses in the mouth; that's how she is, that's how she's always been. She has to put everything under a microscope, explore every pore, find every genetic weakness, every hairline fault that could lead to an earthquake. It's got to be perfect. But what's ever perfect? Can she settle for something that's less than ideal to stop herself settling for a situation that ultimately could do her, and her child, more damage?

What's perfect? She thinks of Adam and Sasha. She thinks of her own parents. She thinks of Gerald and Martha. Even Lindsey and Paul, on the surface a perfect couple with a perfect home, have their problems – how wrong it seems that she should have a baby on her own, while they, ideally situated to raise a child, can't have one. By her feet, Igor rolls on to his back and waits for her to stroke the soft white fur of his underbelly. Cats are so simple. It's so easy to love a cat.

Lisa picks up the telephone and presses out 00-33-1. Then she puts it down again.

* * *

The next day, home from giving her Debussy lecture, to which only half of her students had turned up, she meets Melanie on the stairs.

'How's you, Lisa?' Melanie asks, taking in Lisa's figure. Melanie is tall and her waist resembles a hornet's. Fresh from a yoga class, she is wearing a blue catsuit, five necklaces and multiple studs in her ears. Her hair, which hangs nearly to her waist, is plaited into a Caribbean cornfield of tiny braids.

'Fine,' says Lisa.

'You know,' Melanie bites her lip, 'I couldn't help hearing your lovely man, um, going out a few weeks ago. What's – I mean – like, is he coming back?'

'Oh, God. I don't know. I don't know what to think. I made him go.'

'No way!'

'He doesn't love me. He just wants to be a dad.' There's no point hiding it: the bump's getting bigger every day.

'Je-*sus*. He *wants* to be a dad? He actually wants it?'

'So he says.'

'And you threw him out?'

'Kind of.'

Melanie shakes her head and avoids Lisa's gaze. 'Well,' she says, 'it's your decision.'

While Melanie's face is turned half away, light from the front door reaches her and Lisa sees a bruise on the girl's cheek, subtly purple against her dark brown skin. 'Melanie, what happened to you?' she asks quietly, pointing.

'That? Oh, nothing.' Melanie doesn't look Lisa in the eye. 'I tripped over on the patio the other day.'

Later that evening, Lisa hears Melanie and Andrew rowing in their kitchen, and the crash of the front door when Andrew walks out, and the tinkle of glass on the hall floor as the pane next to the lock shatters with the force of his rage. Then comes silence, but for a soft sobbing at the back of the house, accompanied by a pungent curl of cigarette smoke. Lisa peers out of her front window and sees Andrew's bulky form, clad in jeans and topped with a baseball cap that ill suits him, striding away up the street towards West End Lane.

She tries to push aside her own feelings by going down and offering to call an emergency glazier. Melanie, her hands shaking, is drinking whisky, too upset, and possibly too drunk, to do anything practical or sensible. She gets up, puts her arms round Lisa and holds on. Lisa strokes her plaits and offers her some arnica ointment for her bruises.

Upstairs again, around midnight, Lisa's heart smashes itself against her ribs. In Paris it is one o'clock in the morning. She pictures the quiet house in the courtyard – her refuge, her paradise lost, sitting empty without her, without him. He's away somewhere, playing. He's always away somewhere, playing. That's his job. That's his life. It always will be: she can't change it and he won't.

On the other hand, he comes back. He does come back.

She closes her eyes and agonises and argues and clenches her fists until they hurt. She won't call him. She won't.

She gets out of bed, opens her wardrobe, reaches to the back. There she finds a shoebox, untouched for months. She blows off a little dust, lifts the lid and takes out the purple suede shoes. She hasn't put them on since the night her child was conceived. They are as beautiful and silly as ever, soft, luxurious, the surface gleaming like the ghost of crystallised violets. After a moment she turns back to her bed, places the left shoe on the empty pillow beside her and lies down, one hand resting on its finely shaped lilac toe.

Three days after Liffy's little chat with the headmistress, a new notice goes up on the music-block board. Mr Brewster's flute lessons will resume on Monday.

Charley glares across the classroom and Liffy feels her scalp prickle. She'd never imagined that her best friend could look at her with such hatred.

At break Charley comes and stands in front of Liffy and stops her leaving. The room empties around them.

'You scum,' Charley says. 'You disgusting little bitch.'

'Charley—'

'My mum was right all along. I should never have been your friend. You're mad, you are. You're a piece of shit.'

'For telling them Robin didn't do anything? When he didn't?'

'How do you know what happened? You weren't even fucking well there.'

'Charley, I know you and I know about Robin. I know there's no way—'

'You know, you know, you know, you fucking know-it-all. You don't know shit.'

'Charley—'

'I'm going to show you what you're worth, Liffy Levy.'

'Get off me!'

Charley has grabbed Liffy's pony-tail and is pulling it hard. Liffy can't believe the pain. 'Charley!' she screams. Then she screams louder, hoping someone will come in, because Charley has grabbed a pair of scissors from a nearby desk and is coming at her with them, pressing a knee into her lap to hold her down. Liffy, wailing, expects the cold blade on her neck, the scissors turning into Dracula fangs, sucking out her blood. But instead Charley dives behind her. There's a sickening crunch of blades on thick hair and Liffy's long, luxuriant pony-tail plummets to the floor, still in its slide.

Charley flings down the scissors and strides out.

Liffy, trembling, is on her own. In disbelief she runs a hand over the shorn stump of hair behind her neck. She'll never be able to hold up her head in the classroom again.

She barely has time to gather her thoughts before her classmates start coming back.

'Liffy! What happened to your hair?'

'The lawnmower won then, did it, Liff?'

'Liffy's lost her hair! Liffy's lost her hair!'

Liffy is shaking from head to foot, because she's suddenly understood that it's not only her class who will taunt her now, but the whole school. By lunchtime everyone will know what happened to her, and why. Charley will make certain of that. And at home she'll have the twins to deal with, beastly little boys who haven't a clue what a girl's hair means to her, and she'll have to explain it to Mum . . .

The entire class of thirty girls seems to be gathered around her, screeching like a flock of seagulls on a rubbish dump, gearing up to peck her to death. Liffy has only one idea: to get out. She scrambles up, grabs her rucksack as ammunition and makes a nose-dive at the crowd of green-clad gannets around her, propelling herself towards the classroom door. She's almost surprised when she finds herself on the other side of it unscathed, tearing down the empty corridor towards the back stairs.

She half fancies someone is behind her, running, and she summons the wings everyone has always told her she has on her heels: her feet move faster and faster, round and down the twisting staircase, until she finds herself at the bottom by a door marked EMERGENCY EXIT. This is an emergency, so she exits.

She's now on the passage that skirts one side of the main school building and, as there's nobody around, she keeps going. Without being challenged, she sprints out into the street and round a few corners until she finds herself on Shepherd's Bush Road. She has never in her life been so glad to see Shepherd's Bush Road.

It's not long before she arrives opposite the blocks of beige stone that house the Hammersmith Underground and bus stations. She pauses and digs in her rucksack for her purse – thank heavens she'd had the presence of mind to bring it with her. She has twenty pounds. Twenty pounds should probably get her where she wants to go. She crosses the road at the traffic lights, goes into the older annexe of the Underground station and takes the eastbound Hammersmith and City Line to Paddington.

Here, the mainline station thronging and echoing under its arch around her, she uses a ticket machine. She doesn't want to speak to anyone as she is the only young person in a school uniform on the concourse. She presses OXFORD, then CHILD SINGLE. Happily her remaining money more than covers it. She puts a note into the slot. Five minutes later she is on a train, pulling westwards out of London.

Settling in for the ride, she reflects that she should perhaps alert her mother to the fact that she's not going to be home at the usual time. She takes out her phone and calls Sasha's mobile. It rings and rings; there is no answer. Liffy leaves a short message: 'Mum, it's me, I'll try you later. Don't worry.' She hangs up, wondering which library her mother has buried herself in this time.

Sasha isn't in the library. She is in Waitrose, apprehended on her way out by the store detective. In her bag are items whose barcodes she has not even tried to scan: bananas, apples, a cauliflower, potatoes and an extra large pack of green salad leaves. The detective had noticed the distinctive-looking Sasha putting some of these into her bags without scanning them, then happened to spot her going to the Quick Check counter and not declaring them to Patricia. A quick word with Patricia ascertained that she had found Sasha with excess items before.

The more Sasha protests that it was a mistake, that she was distracted, thinking about something else, the less good it seems to do. The store detective speaks into a walkie-talkie and indicates that she must follow him through the side door into the offices. The gaze of every shopper in the supermarket follows them. Sasha wonders how this can possibly be happening to her.

22

When Adam takes Bronwyn from the photographic gallery out for lunch, he has no idea that this exquisite, sun-ripened September afternoon is about to become one of the most frightening days of his life.

Bronwyn comes from south Wales. She's five foot one and has a lilting accent and long, sleek dark hair. She's twenty years younger than him, but she has information he needs and a beautiful, petite body. She has recently finished her degree and doesn't want to leave Oxford. Adam takes her to Brown's, where they order vegetarian rissoles, a large salad and two glasses of white wine to speed the discussion.

Adam is aware that poaching other people's employees is frowned on, but his years with Forrest & Burns Magazines have left him with limited scruples about this. Indeed, he's realised in the last few weeks that he'd learned some useful tricks in the world he'd hated. He knows how to say the right thing to a lot of different people, including bank managers. He knows how to bargain and barter, how not to take no for an answer. He knows how to get what he wants – around ninety per cent of the time. But, best of all, he's found that knowing what he wants, at least workwise, gives him something to live for.

He needs to employ someone who has more experience than him in the day-to-day running of a private gallery. He's done the sums, thrown himself into business plans, trawled every gallery and magazine in Oxford to discover the good local artists and worked out that if he can save money by doing the decorating himself, once the delicatessen has moved out, and living at least for a while in the studio upstairs, he could possibly afford to offer Bronwyn a slice more than her photographic employer, plus increased responsibility. They will open at the end of October with a Best of Oxford Artists exhibition that he's planning to advertise in the Royal Academy magazine, the Tourist Office, the *Independent* and every local paper. It's soon; it's a lot of work; and it's tiring, and Adam is furious with himself for still getting very tired very easily. But the gallery project has provided him with some impetus, some energy and, best of all, hope. Since the bank manager said yes, the freeholder agreed to his proposals and a large sign saying CLOSING DOWN went up in the delicatessen's window, Adam has felt for the first time that his new life is beginning in earnest.

As they eat, Adam watches Bronwyn's slender young arms and her soft, shining hair and wonders whether it's sensible to employ someone so attractive. He is glad, though, to find that he can feel attracted to anyone: it means he's still alive; it means there's hope here too. Especially when Bronwyn runs her fingers through her hair, lifts her chin and tells him, 'My boyfriend went off with my best friend two months ago.'

When they leave the restaurant, he shakes her hand and gives her a kiss on one cheek. She insists that he kisses the other as well and says that she has to give a month's notice but will do so on 29 September, in time to start work for Adam on 30 October. Adam watches her pacing away down the road, her handbag swinging on one shoulder, then turns to walk home.

His thoughts circumnavigate the situation. He is aware that, sooner or later, assuming he and Sasha are separating permanently, he's going to have to get a flat of his own where he can have his children to stay regularly. He knows now that he will have an inheritance from his mother that should enable him to buy something suitable in due course. Thinking of Sasha fills him with a difficult admixture of anguish, anxiety and fury.

He wonders what she will do when he tells her about Bronwyn – assuming something good happens between him and Bronwyn, which it may not: his mind is racing way ahead of reality. He wonders what the children will say.

It's just as he's picturing Liffy, Alex and Matt that his mobile phone begins to play the James Bond music. 'Adam Levy,' he says automatically.

'Dad?'

'Liffs! Is that you?'

'Dad, I'm at the station.'

'What station?'

'Oxford. Can you come and get me?'

'Heavens, Liffy, what—'

'I'll tell you all about it, but please, can you come and get me?'

Her voice is thin and strained and Adam's innards lurch with fright. 'I'll be right there. I'll be on the bus,' he exclaims. 'Stay where you are, I won't be long.'

He dashes across the road with scant heed to the braking cars around him and doesn't pause until he reaches the bus stop two hundred yards away.

Liffy is waiting on a red metal bench in front of Oxford station, a forlorn little figure in green school uniform. Adam notices, for the first time, how thin she has become. Her cheekbones stand out like twigs and her eyes are enormous in her shrunken face. Something peculiar has happened to her hair. She is sitting with hunched, rounded shoulders, her arms crossed about her midriff as if comforting herself. Adam leaps off the bus and runs towards her. Her arms fly round him and he holds her tight, trying to give her some of his own warmth and energy because she seems to have none of her own.

'What happened?' he demands, appalled. Almost nothing is left of her arms but bone, sinew and skin.

'Charley cut off my hair,' Liffy says into his shoulder.

'Charley?'

'I couldn't stay at school. I couldn't go home. I couldn't do anything else. I had to come here. I look such a mess . . .'

'Darling, you'll look fine in no time. I've got a friend who knows a good hairdresser. We'll take you to him and you'll look super-trendy half an hour later. Short hair is the in thing, I promise. You wait and see.'

Liffy looks up at him with the great, dark saucers that are now her eyes. Adam's nerves shudder. It's not a hairdresser that Liffy needs. It's a doctor.

'Let's get you home first,' he says, his mind working fast. His studio is in such a state, full of cigarette smoke, unwashed beer glasses and unwashed washing, that he decides, with a stab of shame, that he can't possibly take her there. 'We'll go up to Grandpa's and you can have something to eat and a rest. Then we'll sort out everything else. All right? Because school will be worried and Mum will be worried too.'

'I tried Mum. She's not answering her phone.'

Adam and Liffy climb aboard the next bus north. Adam looks at Liffy's skeletal hands clinging to the rail above the seat in front and his brain fizzes with fury and fright. What is Sasha thinking of? What is that school thinking of? What – for that matter – has he been thinking of? Something is horribly wrong with his daughter. He looks at her and sees a child who is only half there, only half what she should be, barely half alive. Fear pounds in his temples.

Gerald, thank heavens, has gone to his old college for the day to have lunch with some former colleagues and use the library. The house is still and empty. Liffy sits at the kitchen table, staring blank-eyed into the walled garden.

'Just black tea, please, Dad,' she says. Adam presses biscuits towards her, but she refuses them. 'I'm not hungry.'

'You look hungry. You look very hungry. Liffy, you're *impossibly* thin. What the hell is going on?'

Liffy smiles for a moment as he says she looks thin. She actually smiles. It's the first time she's smiled since he spotted her on the bench.

'I'm auditioning for ballet school soon,' she says. 'I've got to look right.'

'Ballet, schmallet! Liffy, you don't look right. You look ill. You're not going to audition for anything if it makes you ill.'

'Dad, I'm fine. I feel great – apart from . . .' Liffy touches her violated hair with her fingertips, as if afraid to put her palms too close to it.

'I'm taking you straight to the doctor.'

'No! Please, no, Dad. I don't need a doctor.'

'That,' Adam says, 'is something I've heard before. I'm going to insist someone sees you right away.'

'Please, Dad,' Liffy wails, 'couldn't you call school first? Just to let them know where I am? And try Mum again?'

Adam feels trapped. He does have to call the school. That's vital. 'OK. You'd better tell me exactly what happened,' he says, sitting down opposite her.

Liffy tells him, and as she describes Charley's behaviour in Greece, Adam reaches over to take her hand. It's so cold that he nearly drops it with fright.

He phones school and speaks to Miss Murray in person. Liffy wanders out into the garden; he watches her cropped head bending over a late golden rose, sniffing its perfume. He explains everything to the headmistress, who tells him how helpful Liffy has been and says that Charley's behaviour was evidently a revenge attack. Adam says he will call again in the morning and is meanwhile going to get Liffy's hair tidied up and take her to the GP. Next he phones Sasha, whose mobile rings but is not answered. He tries the house, but only the answering-machine is working, playing his own voice back at him; Sasha has not bothered to record over his old message. He wonders why not. He tries the mobile yet again – it goes unanswered for a third time.

'Sasha, call me on my mobile urgently,' he barks at her voice-mail. 'Liffy's here. I need to speak to you, fast.'

Liffy is still outside. It's a beautiful day: she should enjoy the sunshine. No doubt it beats the hell out of being stuck inside that dreadful school building with its grey playground and its hours and hours of homework and its mad atmosphere – bright, privileged girls cooped up together, cramming themselves with knowledge while starving themselves of nourishment. Adam lifts his eyes to the window.

Liffy is stretched out on the lawn by the bench, apparently asleep. In her green uniform she looks as fragile and fragmentary as a heap of mown grass. She's lying on her side, knees drawn up, head on one wiry arm. Around her, Martha's cherry tree is shedding the first of its red-gold autumn leaves. Adam watches one spin slowly through the air and land like a drop of blood on Liffy's cheek. She doesn't stir.

He flings open the back door. 'Liffy!'

No response comes from the motionless form on the ground. Adam rushes to her and lifts one limp hand. He can feel her pulse, but it seems weak and slow. He brushes her hair back from her face and now he sees, on one side of her brow, a red gash and a developing bump. She's hit her head on something – the wrought-iron arm of Martha's bench, he realises. She's fallen – maybe fainted – and concussed herself in the process.

As he plunges back inside towards the telephone, memories flood him and he damns his soul to hell for ever with the idea that he should have noticed, he should have been seeing her more often, he should have been less absorbed in his grief and more aware of her. He should never have allowed Sasha to throw him out. He should have been there for Liffy and he wasn't. This is the price.

When the ambulance comes, he rides in it with her unconscious form, holding her soft, chilly hand, unable to draw his eyes from her face.

★   ★   ★

Sasha is in an office in Waitrose, attempting to explain herself. Inwardly she is trying to calm down and count her blessings. At least they haven't called the police. At least the children weren't with her. At least she's not late for fetching the twins (yet). It's only a few stupid items from a supermarket. She's not a film star in Hollywood, arrested for carrying off thousands of dollars' worth of clothes. 'I really didn't mean . . .' she says. 'There was never any intention of shoplifting.'

'But you don't deny,' says the polite store detective, 'that when I stopped you, you had a number of items in your bag that you had not paid for.'

Sasha says nothing for a moment. It's pretty indisputable. 'No,' she says. Then: 'It was an oversight on my part.'

Outside the office, there's the sound of raised voices.

'Is that Sasha Wood in there?' a strange male voice demands. 'I'm Dan Merry, *Riverside Reporter*.'

Sasha closes her eyes. *Oh God, this is all I need – a story in the press saying Sasha Wood has been caught shoplifting in Waitrose.* 'Please,' she says, her mouth dry as desert sand, 'can't you get rid of him?'

The store detective looks straight at her. He won't smile. 'We'll do our best,' is all he says. 'We'll be taking this up with the magistrates' court, Ms Wood.'

There is no way they're going to put me in prison for this, Sasha thinks. They've got more important people to put in Holloway. Child murderers, for instance. Five items from Waitrose can't carry a prison sentence. No, the problem isn't prison. The problem is public disgrace. If she was a plain housewife, the disgrace would be present but short-lived. But Sasha is a media personality and that means the five items of food she put unpaid-for into her shopping bag, just to gain a tiny rush of excitement, are an embarrassment that will blight her for a year, maybe two years, maybe for ever. Because once it's in a newspaper, it's permanent. You think newspapers are here today and gone tomorrow, but Sasha knows they are not. They are there for years, decades, centuries, preserved in excellent condition in the British Library and many other distinguished outlets in the world's great cities of learning.

She's informed enough about the world of law to know that it doesn't function on intuition or understanding. It's interested only in bald facts. It matters not a jot why you did something, it only matters what you did. It won't help her to say that she was worried, distracted, in need of – well, not even she knows exactly what she was in need of. All that will concern the law is that she was caught leaving a shop without paying for something she had in her bag. There's no way round it. *What am I going to tell the children? What am I going to tell the schools? What will their friends say in the playground? What will their friends' parents say? Just how much press interest is this going to get?*

She slinks home the back way. She wonders when she will dare to walk along the main road again.

To her relief, the man from the *Riverside Reporter* is not yet loitering outside her house. Inside, she notices her mobile beeping quietly, indicating a new voicemail message. She dials and listens.

*

She is asleep yet awake, conscious in a parallel world that she had suspected exists but into which she could never step before. She is pure spirit, her body left behind on a hospital bed wired up to drips and monitors. She is as pure and beautiful as she has always wanted to be: her hair is long and natural, undefiled, her body cleansed of all contaminants, her eyes seeing as clearly as if she had opened them for the first time. The veil of illusion has gone. All that is left is the brightness in which she stands, alone and waiting. She is unaware of time: she recognises at last that the past, the present and the future are all one.

She raises her arms to the sides, palms upwards, drawing light into her hands. She turns her face to the rays of the dawn and feels its power flood through her body where blood used to be. The centres of her palms grow hot; the heat concentrates, fierce and irresistible, in a central spot that burns until it grows almost painful. Her hands shine first red, then gold, beaming out their light to the sky. She is connected now, part of this celestial electricity, channelling its radiance.

A shining figure kneels before her. He looks up into her face and she knows him. He rises to his full height and extends his arms, mirroring her movement. He places his own palms over hers and they stand conjoined, the green against the white, exchanging their energy through the stigmata. Joy engulfs her. She has never known rapture before. Her head tips back, her eyes close, her soul flies out, his electricity shoots through her purified self and from her back into him.

They stand together, facing the sunrise.

'The earth, my realm, seeks renewal,' the Earth Prince says. 'This is my plan for you. Are you ready to hear it?'

'I am.'

'You will leave your world to join mine. You will not return. By leaving your world, you repay the debt that your species owes. Your human form will be left behind – dead – while your spirit joins itself to me. Together our energy will renew the bond of humanity and nature, without which there can be no more life.'

'Is this what I must do?' Liffy asks.

'It is not my decision. It is yours. I don't demand of you, Liffy. I ask you. I am asking you for your soul. Do you understand?'

An unfamiliar sensation is moving through Liffy, from her ankles upwards. She is trembling.

She is going to die.

23

Sasha sits desolate by Liffy's hospital bed. She feels as if someone has torn out her heart.

Sunshine filters through Venetian blinds and casts bands of brightness across Liffy's still, white face. A monitor bleeps softly beside her; a drip filters a transparent solution into her veins; a catheter has been fitted, trailing out into a bag propped on the floor near the foot of the bed. Tubes and plastic and dripping fluids surround the unconscious girl.

'Unless we get some nourishment into this child right now,' the doctor had told Sasha, when she burst into the ward, 'she is in very serious danger.'

Sasha moans aloud. She strokes her daughter's skeletal fingers, lifts them to her mouth, kisses them one by one. Her beautiful daughter. What has happened to her beautiful daughter? How can it have happened right in front of her? She closes her eyes, presses her hands to her face. She remembers how terrified she felt waiting for the plane home from Greece, knowing her father might die, not knowing he was already dead. The fear floods back from the distant past, but compared to the terror that her own daughter may die, it seems no more than a flimsy plaster-cast of fright. The fear that fills her now crushes her mind with the force of a Pacific tsunami.

'Liffy,' she moans aloud. 'Liffs, darling, can you hear me?'

The door opens a fraction and Adam comes in. He meets her gaze.

'Sash,' he whispers.

Sasha bends double and buries her face on her knees. Adam

crosses the room and sits next to her. Automatically, she reaches for his hand.

'I sat with you like this,' he says, his fingers curling round hers. 'Do you remember?'

'Ad, why didn't I see what was happening to her? Of all people, I should have known. I should have stopped it. I saw it, I recognised it, but I didn't do anything, I kept putting it off, I kept not wanting to believe it was really happening – and now—'

'Sash. It's not your fault. Nobody's blaming you. I'm not blaming you. I understand.'

'But I don't! My own daughter goes into the same condition I once had, and I don't do anything to stop it. And people tried to warn me. I know they did. I didn't listen to them, not even Lisa. Am I going crazy?'

'Don't make it worse, Sash. It's bad enough already.'

Liffy lies still and insubstantial under the white sheet, the tubes and the wires. Her eyelashes are long, her hair mussed in its brutal cut. She looks as pale and pure as a wax effigy. To Sasha, she looks holy. The sun through the Venetian blinds gives a bright edge to her hair against the pillow case. Sasha watches the light moving and shifting as the minutes slip away. Adam sits holding Liffy's hand to one side and Sasha's to the other.

Sasha can't bear the impersonality of the hospital, or the idea that for the doctors they are just another family suffering from the effects of a case of anorexia – if a more complicated one than usual, because of Martha's bench.

Oh yes, says the eating-disorders consultant, who looks like a recovered anorectic herself. All the signs are there. Sasha describes Liffy's behaviour over the past few months and the doctor nods, nods and nods again. She reassures Sasha: Liffy has done an exceptional job in concealing her condition. Nobody noticed how bad it was because Liffy didn't want anybody to notice, at least not directly. Times of stress; the onset of adolescence; family instability and bad atmospheres; bereavement; bullies at school; astronomical academic standards and school expectations of perfection, not to mention peer pressure, which can be the worst thing. Ballet lessons. Ballet-school auditions! Oh yes, Liffy was a prime candidate for anorexia.

It is with all the pain buried deep in the forgotten spaces of her mind that Sasha says, 'The dreadful thing is, you know, that I once had it myself.'

'That's not unusual,' the doctor replies. 'Are there any addictions in the family?'

Sasha glances sharply at the breast pocket of Adam's denim jacket where a packet of cigarettes is ill concealed. Adam says, 'Sasha's mother has had an alcohol problem from time to time.'

The doctor makes some notes.

'Is she going to be OK?' Adam asks, his voice cracking.

The doctor looks up at them and is quiet for a second that feels like an hour.

The floor plunges away from Sasha's feet. 'Well?' she snaps.

'I hope so,' says the doctor. 'We're doing everything we can, Mrs Levy. We don't really understand why she hasn't come round yet. It could be because she's so weak, but I think we ought to send her down for a brain scan, just to be on the safe side, to rule out the possibility that it's a brain haemorrhage.'

Sasha wants to scream. She wants to lift up this pussy-footing wimp of a doctor by the scruff of the neck and shake her until she makes Liffy well. But that's not going to do any good. Adam touches her shoulder; he knows what's going through her mind, as he always did at times of crisis. His touch calms her – out of sheer force of habit – and she lowers her head and nods.

Adam and Sasha walk side by side up the hospital corridor to Liffy's room and resume their chairs, waiting for news of when their daughter's brain can be scanned. A little later, Sasha goes outside to phone Julius's mother to see if the twins can spend the night at their house. Eventually the news comes: the scanning department is so busy that Liffy can't be 'done' until the morning. Sasha, in agony, phones Lisa and leaves a long, rambling message on the answering-machine, which she knows makes little or no sense but mirrors her state of mind.

In Liffy's room, the hours pass. Eventually it starts to get dark. The evenings are drawing in and growing colder.

'Mrs Levy,' the doctor says, stopping by on her ward round, 'go and get some rest. We'll take good care of her.'

'But if something – happens . . .'

'We'll call you immediately if there's any change. All right?'

'I don't need to go home. I've put the boys with a neighbour for the night and the cats are being fed too . . .' Sasha knows it sounds inane to mention the cats, but everything in the world sounds inane right now. How can it be that everyday life continues when Liffy may be hanging between life and death?

'Come to Dad's,' Adam encourages her. 'You need some sleep. We both do. He'll be happy for us to stay there.' He rests one hand on her arm and its warmth surprises her. She hadn't realised how cold she feels.

Adam bounds up to a taxi waiting in front of the hospital and opens the door for her. Sitting beside him on the way to Davenant Road, her teeth start to chatter. She knows she must be a forlorn sight when Gerald greets them at the house. Perhaps this new Sasha – standing on the step frozen with fright, weeping and shivering – is in the only condition in which Martha, had she been there, would have shown her compassion.

Gerald, too, is generous to her. He kisses her cheek, takes her coat from her and pours her a large brandy. He is as ravaged by emotion as Sasha and Adam but, unlike them, not accustomed to admitting it.

Sasha declines the offer of dinner and says she will go straight to bed; ironically, in the circumstances, she can't face food.

*   *   *

Adam installs Sasha in the spare bedroom. Then, weary and headachy, he goes back downstairs to Gerald. He casts a long look at the spot where he last saw Liffy standing conscious, smelling a rose. The imprint of her outline seems to hover in the twilight at the edge of the lawn. Martha's cherry tree is weeping leaves like tears of blood on to the tidy green grass.

Gerald clears his throat, lecture-like. 'I find it hard to understand how anyone managed not to see this coming,' he begins. 'The girl's been fading away, thinner every time I've seen her. It should have been obvious, especially after what you'd been through with Sasha all those years ago. Shouldn't it?'

'Dad,' Adam says, 'I didn't notice you spotting it any earlier either.'

'Your generation.' Gerald sits back in his leather armchair and sips his drink. He isn't listening to Adam. 'Your generation. You were all taught at an impressionable age by our own prime minister to think of yourselves only. My generation grew up with ideals. We had a war and its legacy to deal with. We wanted a fresh start, a new country with justice and fairness and a decent life for everybody. In a few short years Margaret Thatcher put paid to that. Be greedy, want more money, want material things, let everyone else go and jump in the lake if they get in your way. Unfortunate, isn't it, that she didn't remember to say that none of this should apply within the family?'

'Dad, this is no time for one of your lectures,' Adam says.

Gerald ignores him. 'Your generation only ever thinks of itself. We old people – we, the ones who can teach you the important lessons of life – we're a nuisance, an irrelevance to a world that's obsessed by youth and looks instead of intelligence, experience and hard-earned wisdom. You get married, you make vows and if you find you're not living happily ever after, but instead just *living*, as people do, you chuck out your partner, start all over again and make the same mistakes.'

'I never wanted to leave. None of this was meant to happen.'

'You think of yourselves ahead of your children. God alone knows what you want out of life, but nobody seems to have told you you have actively to look after your children to bring them up decently.'

'Dad, one more word and I'm walking out of this house,' Adam explodes.

Gerald looks at him, impassive. 'It's nothing personal,' he says. 'I'm not accusing you. Just the state of this insane inside-out world. If any of you had lived through a real war, not just the antiseptic TV pictures of them, you'd have your heads and your values screwed on the right way round. As it is, you put money before love, and everyone talks about rights but nobody has heard the word "duty". You've got everything, and I mean *everything*, upside-down. And that goes also for young girls who think it's *cool* to starve themselves to death. How about a refill?'

'Dad, my daughter is very, very sick. I need to try and sleep. And so do you.'

In bed, Adam closes his eyes, but his father's crashing insensitivity has left him at boiling point, with nowhere to put down his anger. He thinks of Sasha, asleep in the next room, her dark hair spreading over the pillow, and hears the Oxford bells strike eleven; then midnight. Oblivion, the coiled serpent that will not release Liffy, eludes him. He hasn't eaten and as the night deepens he has to acknowledge that he should have. He can't accept that even when the heart is so overloaded with grief, the stomach still needs to be filled. Eventually he gives in and goes down to the kitchen for a bowl of muesli.

A dark shape sits at the table where Liffy had sat earlier that day. It takes him a confused second to realise that it is not Liffy, or her ghost, but her mother.

Sasha has got to the muesli box before him.

'Great minds,' Adam remarks, as he helps himself.

Sasha makes a noise in response that is half grunt, half laugh and more of a sob than either. 'I heard some of your dad's little lecture,' she says. 'Ad, how can you stand it?'

'You're a fine one to talk about lectures.'

'Don't. Not now. I can't handle it.'

'OK. I'll go to the lounge and you can sit here and then we don't have to talk.' He makes for the door.

'Ad, don't go.'

He looks at her silhouette.

'Please don't go. That's not what I meant.'

He turns, walks back to the table and sits opposite her. 'No,' he says, 'I don't suppose it was.'

Adam and Sasha link gazes across their bowls. Even now – perhaps especially now – the past twenty years linger upon them like a silken membrane.

'So,' says Adam, 'what did you mean?'

'I think we should talk.'

'Talk? What is there to talk about?'

'Don't be obtuse, Adam. We can't go on like this.'

'Don't use that schoolmarmy voice on me. I don't like pretentious words. I never did. And as you were the one who wanted me out of the house, I don't know what you mean by "we" can't go on like this.'

'Ad, look . . . it all got too much. I know it's been difficult, but I never meant for you to move out – I just needed some – some—'

'Space. *You* needed space when *my* mother died. You couldn't just be there for me. You had to be jealous. You could only think about how it affected *you*. My mother died, I had to watch her dying by inches, suffering the way nobody would let a dog suffer, and all you could think about was that you weren't getting enough sex! That's great, Sasha, that's a sign of a bloody great marriage.'

'How am I supposed to tell my children that their father is a nervous wreck who smokes dope and can't be bothered to hold down a job?'

'How am I supposed to tell my children that their mother used to be fun and lively and exciting to be with? They won't believe it in a month of Sundays!'

'Exciting? How about living with you? How's that for draining the excitement fresh out of life?'

'Damn you, Sasha, everything I did was for you and the children!'

'Well, if that's all the integrity you've got, how can you expect your children to grow up with any? You're a pathetic idiot!'

'And you? You should have been looking after Liffy. You didn't see what was happening to our daughter right under your nose, you're so damned self-absorbed!'

'You could have been looking after her too if you'd bothered to come home!'

'That's right, Sasha, pass the buck. Just pass it on. Don't even think of taking responsibility for your own mistakes. You're the cultural critic, you're the one who's always right. It's all someone else's fault, every single time—'

'Adam, shut up.'

'Shut up yourself. If you stopped talking for once in your life, you might start listening.'

'Adam, *shut up!*'

'You shut up and try listening to your daughter!'

Sasha presses her fists to her temples. She goes to the kitchen wall and leans her forehead against it. 'Adam – stop it! Please just stop it! I can't stand it! Don't do this to me!'

'And how about what *you*'ve been doing to *me*?'

'Adam, this isn't you. This isn't me.'

'It bloody is now. When did you last listen to Liffy? When did you last even look at Liffy?'

At her daughter's name, something inside Sasha gives way. Someone who doesn't seem to be her sees the kitchen floor coming to meet her, sees her knees buckle and hears a wail that seems to emanate from a tunnel of her heart long buried and forgotten – *I wish I were dead.*' There's nothing she can do to stop the tears, however hard she thumps her fists against the floor, however desperately she wills herself to emerge from this horror of a night, however tender her husband's hands feel in her hair as he comes to her to try to calm her.

Gerald, roused by the noise, finds them there a few minutes later, sitting together on the kitchen floor like two children, holding on to each other as if to the last splintered plank of a shipwreck.

24

Two minutes after phoning Sasha in the morning, Lisa flies out of her front door and runs down the street to her new car. For the first time, she's glad it's there: it will get her to her mother's house and both of them to Oxford fast.

The sight is dreadful: Liffy lying still and skeletal and unconscious under wires and tubing, Sasha slumped in a green plastic chair in a corner, head in hand, Adam pacing up and down in the corridor. Lisa hugs them both, long and hard, then goes up to her niece and kisses her forehead. The electronic machine makes cold electronic noises beside them. Sally stands frozen with shock in the doorway, her eyes brimming with tears.

Sasha looks up and says, 'Oh, Mum.'

'Darling,' says Sally, her voice choked. Sasha half stumbles out of her chair and throws herself into her mother's arms. She hasn't wept on her mother's shoulder since she was fourteen years old.

'What I can't believe,' she says, into Sally's moss-green blouse, 'is that I did this to you, and when I was going through it, I never thought once about how you would feel. I only ever thought about myself and how fat I thought I was. Could you ever forgive me?'

'There's nothing to forgive, darling,' Sally says quietly. 'There never was anything to forgive. It's ancient history now. Did they do the scan already?'

'Yes.' Sasha tries to compose herself.

'And?'

'There doesn't seem to be a haemorrhage, which is good news. But they don't know why she isn't awake. Apparently it doesn't make medical sense. They said something about indications of intense brain activity in the dream state, which I don't even begin to understand, but they can't bring her round and they don't know what's going on.'

'What can I do to help?' Sally asks, pressing her hand.

'Just be here, Mum,' Sasha pleads. 'Just so we can all be together. I'm so glad you came.'

Lisa bends over the bed. 'Liffy,' she whispers.

In the bed, arms spread out and pierced with medical tubing, Liffy appears almost trapped on a crucifix, her family in poses of distress and dejection beside her. Something nags at Lisa's thoughts, an image, a thread of sound, a violent, uneven rhythm. A young girl dancing herself to death for the sake of her tribe.

All her research papers rise in her mind and flare into flame. Is Liffy the Chosen One, the victim who must take upon her innocent shoulders the full burden of the tribe's fears and insecurities? Sacrificed for the return of spring? Is that how Liffy sees it, without knowing that she does? Was she trying, by making herself ill, to force some kind of emotional spring to return to her family? And, watching Sasha and Adam, who are moving in unison, echoing each other's movements, consciousness locked together for the first time in months if not years, Lisa wonders whether Liffy's mission has met with success, at a fearful price.

But who, then, is the god to whom the sacrifice is being made? Lisa shakes herself. Her mind is out of control. Or is it? A vase of orange lilies stands, still and glowing, by the window; beyond it, Lisa spots people walking by in the street. A large yellow Labrador is padding along below, led by an elderly woman. Lisa glances at her mother, remembers the words 'prince' and 'prints' and looks at the flowers in the vase and the tranquil autumnal world outside, remembers herself dreaming away the days at thirteen and knows that she needs to go and do some reading, quickly, to get to the bottom of this.

The images taking shape in her mind make no rational sense, but that doesn't mean they can't be real. She needs to read and to double check her facts. It may not help. Nothing may help: it may be too late for that. But still, an insight into Liffy's mind, a way of tapping into the force that has been holding her in thrall while she refuses to eat, might not do any harm either.

She doesn't need to check, because she can still see it so clearly, that it was the Schubert song 'Erlkönig' that had catapulted Liffy into a panic attack so powerful it had made her sick; and that it was that night she had cried out in her sleep the words 'earth prints' or, as Lisa now knows instinctively is correct, 'Earth Prince'. She wants to look up the name in every dictionary of mythology she can find in the British Library. She needs Sasha to go home, ransack Liffy's room and explore the inner depths of her computer looking for clues. Lisa thinks of Erlkönig, Schubert's King of the Alder, whispering temptations to the dying child, waiting to carry its soul away, and she presses her hands to her belly in some desperate prayer that such creatures of darkness might never touch her unborn baby.

Lisa tells Sally, Sasha and Adam that she'll be back very soon, leaves her car in the hospital car park and jumps into a taxi. She's too anxious as it is to want to worry about parking and one-way systems.

In the calm, paper-scented surroundings of Blackwell's, Lisa makes straight for the health section. There, on a shelf well above her head, sits an entire row of books about anorexia nervosa. Lisa borrows a set of steps, climbs up and pulls out the most promising titles. Sitting alone in her flat, while the baby grows inside her, she has been practising her speed-reading and she's made some progress. She takes out her pencil and uses it to help her skim through the pages as rapidly as she can . . .

And before long she finds what she's looking for. Lisa runs her pencil over the sentences.

> The young anorexia victim in the broken or breaking family may be consciously or subconsciously apportioning the blame upon herself, especially in those family units that have mistakenly placed the burden of adulthood upon her in the process of dealing with their own problems. It is all too easy, under these distressing circumstances, for the child to develop a self-hate that urges her to recognise that if she ceased to exist, so would, perhaps, the problems that are driving her obsessive-compulsive behaviour. In some cases we have noted that the adolescent girl views herself in a quasi-romantic light as sacrificing her own happiness in order mystically to obtain that of her family. To put it bluntly, however, the end result, in these rare but pertinent cases, can be that she sacrifices not merely her happiness but her life.

Lisa sits down on the steps and reads the paragraph again. If only academics and medical people wrote clearly, she fumes. If only she were allowed to write clearly herself. If you write too clearly, too readably, other academics turn up their noses at your research, or so she feels. But the idea she can shape amid all these qualifications chimes in tune with the one that had begun to ring out to her in Liffy's hospital room.

A young virgin, the Chosen One, compelled to dance herself to death for the sake of her tribe. Her death means their life, because it will guarantee the return of spring. It will pacify the sun god, Yarilo.

When I was thirteen, Lisa muses, I used to invent fantasy characters, fairies and goblins with magic powers, and I'd make up stories about them and pretend, when I was being bullied at school, that they were there to protect me. The worse things got at home, the more I retreated into my own world . . . And if I'd been as precocious as girls are these days and I'd invented a nature god, what would I have called him? I certainly wouldn't call him Yarilo. I wouldn't call him anything that I found in mythology, because that's too official, too impersonal. But I might not be able to think of anything especially thrilling . . . so I might very well decide to call him the Earth Prince.

This is ridiculous. There's no way she can know what is going on in Liffy's mind. Adam and Sasha will never swallow one word of something so irrational. But the child inside her twists and flips, like the burnished flash of a fish in an underwater cavern, and Lisa silently asks her unborn daughter – with whom she's started holding long internal conversations – if any of this makes sense to her. She's a sensible girl, Lisa's daughter-to-be: she beams back the answer that her mother should trust her instinct. If we trusted our instincts more and 'rationality' less, says the spirit girl, we'd all be happier. Trust me, she says, because I trust you. We're in this together.

Lisa asks an assistant where the folklore section is. When she finds it, she settles down in a corner for an hour with a pile of ten or twelve books. What she finds is more interesting than she'd anticipated. Before she leaves, she buys several, as well as the volume on anorexia.

Out in the street after more than two hours, she is desperate to find a readily available toilet. It's the thing she dislikes most about pregnancy – constant pressure on her bladder. She goes into a café full of wooden tables and newspapers, heads straight for the loo, then settles herself and her bump at a corner table to order hot chocolate.

Sipping it – the most consoling drink in the world – Lisa remembers the glow that suffused her sister, at least some of the time, when she was pregnant with Liffy; she remembers the love Sasha used to tell her about, the unity of heart and mind that was Sasha-and-Adam, and she thinks of where they are now, on opposite sides of the bed in which their daughter is neither dead nor truly alive, in which perhaps she is pursuing in her dreams the love she can't find outside.

Strip away the nonsense and the love is there – the love will always be there – but it's in battle, trapped among the land-mines of needs, demands, hormones and expectations, with nothing but its own integrity to support it while the explo-sives blast apart its shining spirit.

She knows that the future she longs for with Vladimir and their daughter could be beautiful, but would be nothing like her dreams. She knows her hopes would be thwarted, she knows how frustrated she would be, how lonely when he travels without her, how scared of those women in every country who admire a great pianist and fling themselves willingly at his feet. She wonders what the earth and its ruling spirits have in store for her and she is grateful that she's no clairvoyant, because in the end she thinks she'd rather not know.

*

She feels her soul leave her body and rise into the green and silver woods. She is blending with nature. Her hands are melting away and in their place new-born, burgeoning leaves are pressing their way towards the sky. Her hair flows around her and becomes one with the wind and the water below. Her skin is changing into the soft petals of the first spring blossoms and her bones into branches. As for her flesh, what's left of it will nourish the roots and the soil and feed the earth back into health and vigour. Her spirit floats, transfigured.

The Earth Prince draws her to him, green on white, spirit body to spirit body. She is encircled as if by the branches of a great oak. Soon there will be no division between them. Soon he will possess her. The sacrifice will be made. As her soul swoops above them, free, in ecstasy, he anoints her with his kiss.

*

The day draws to a slow and agonising end, with no change in Liffy's state either for better or worse. Reluctantly, the four of them part. Lisa and her mother head back to north London; Adam stays entrenched in the green plastic chair by Liffy's bedside; Sasha has to go home to take care of the twins. Leaving Liffy is such a wrench that she can't let herself stop to think about it.

Driving down the M40, she finds herself bemused by the ordinariness outside her car: lorries hogging the middle lane, drivers taking stupid risks as they overtake while talking on their mobiles, St George's flags adorning the white vans. How can the world around her go on as if nothing has happened? If Liffy dies, she will die too. She'll inhabit her body, she'll go about her daily duties, she'll care for the twins, but a section of her spirit will leave her for ever.

She rings Julius's mother's doorbell and at once the twins stampede out and fling themselves at her; she takes comfort in their coltish warmth, pressing her cheek to their still babyish hair and luring them home with promises of sausages and chips. When they charge up to their room and she hears the PlayStation starting up, she goes to the answering-machine and presses 'play'.

Into the empty front hall comes the voice of an official, impersonal-sounding woman who could equally well have been a robot, informing her that she is expected to report to the magistrates' court at ten o'clock on Monday morning. Next, an over-friendly male voice that she seems to have heard somewhere before announces himself as Dan Merry of the *Riverside Reporter*, wanting to talk to her about one or two little matters.

'Fuck,' Sasha says aloud. A third message follows: the *News of the World*, it seems, has got wind of Sasha's exploit in Waitrose.

'Mum,' one of the twins yells down the stairs, '*when* can we get new trainers? Please? *Please*, Mum? Julius has just got these really cool—'

Sasha thumps her way up to them. 'Boys,' she says, 'your sister is very, very ill. Nobody is going to have any new anything until she's better, because frankly, my dears, you need to learn to think about someone other than yourselves for once.'

Alex and Matt stare at her with dark, serious, uncomprehending eyes, then turn back to their game. Sasha trails back to the kitchen, feeling as alone as she has ever felt in her life.

The clock ticks softly above the sink; a plane drones low overhead on its approach to the airport. The house has been freshly cleaned, that morning, by Sasha's golden girl, a language student from Poland who scours the place from top to bottom once a week. Now it is sterile, empty of Liffy's delicate energy. It is also empty of Adam's more colourful aura, the musky smell of his T-shirts, the complex reds and purples that seem to swirl in the air around him. Sasha's heart is aching. Since their screaming match in Oxford, something inside her seems to have come loose and she's started, perversely, to miss him. She misses his warm eyes, his usual tolerance, his one-time calm, the way he hugs the kids.

When the telephone leaps into action, she grabs at the receiver, dreading the voice that will speak to her – the hospital? A reporter? But the voice is her sister's.

'Sash.' Pregnant Lisa sounds even more tired than Sasha feels. 'I'm at Mum's. I'm going to stay here tonight – she's very upset. Now, listen. Can you get into Liffy's computer?'

'Why?' Sasha says, feeling stupid.

'You'll think I'm crazy, but I bought some interesting books.'

'Lee, Liffy is at death's door and you expect me to be interested in your books? What the hell—'

'Sash, hear me out. I think Liffy has created a sort of mental universe for herself – the anorexia may be part of it – and invented a character she calls the Earth Prince. Now, because of what happened when she came to stay with me, I think this imaginary character has developed some kind of hold over her—'

'Since when are you a child psychologist?' Sasha snaps at her little sister.

'Just listen to me. Please. It may not help, but then again it might. Can you get into her computer and see if she's written anything – a diary, essays for school, stories, anything at all – referring to some kind of Green Man character?'

'Are you trying to tell me that my daughter is obsessed by little green men from Mars? Are you crazy?'

'No. I'm not.'

Lisa sounds so tired, so crestfallen, so desperately miserable that Sasha immediately regrets her words. 'Sorry, Lee,' she says. 'I'm stressed out.'

'Aren't we all? But the Green Man I mean is the one the pubs are named after – the one you see carved into gargoyles in medieval churches. He's a symbol of nature. He's frightening and powerful, but he's also positive. He symbolises ongoing life. I'm not sure that Liffy knows that.'

'You think the image she's created of him is trying to kill her? Is that what you're saying?'

'I don't know. I suspect she's frightened of him, in thrall to him. I need to know more.'

'How exactly is this going to help?'

'I don't know,' Lisa admits. 'But I do know that I'd do anything under the sun to help Liffy and beginning to understand this a little – might – just might—'

There's a crash upstairs in the twins' room.

'I have to go and deal with the monsters,' Sasha tells Lisa, as gently as she can. She doesn't feel gentle, but she fights to bring her fury under control. 'I'm far too tired to wonder about esoteric symbols today, but if I do come across anything I'll let you know. All right?'

'Whatever,' says Lisa, and hangs up.

The twins have pulled out one of their drawers too far and it's fallen on to the floor, spilling socks and pants in all directions and splitting the chipboard sides. Sasha lets off steam by yelling at the boys while she tidies up. In her temples, Lisa's words are humming. The Green Man? She thinks of the pubs, the pictures with the terrifying face garlanded in leaves, the gargoyles, Robin of the Greenwood, pictures being sucked through the vacuum of her memory in headlong free association. Why would Liffy think of such a thing?

Then again, why would she not?

Sasha wants desperately to have a drink and go to bed. Instead she decides to have a drink and investigate Liffy's computer. Her hackles rise at the thought of following up Lisa's idea, but her curiosity is too strong. She has to do it. She opens a bottle of Rioja and carries a glass of it upstairs, past the sign that says OLIVIA'S ROOM, NO ENTRY ON PAIN OF DEATH.

The empty room – still adorned with the Pooh and Piglet poster, the blue frosted-glass vase, which now contains a withered bunch of dahlias, and a photo of Liffy with her schoolfriends, Charley included (oh dear!) – makes her heart ache even more.

She goes to Liffy's bed and lifts up the pillow. She presses it to her face: it still smells of her daughter, faintly sweet, oddly floral. Across its soft white surface lie several long, honey-coloured hairs.

Sasha switches on the computer, cradling the pillow on her lap. How extraordinary it is, she reflects, opening and assessing the folders on the screen desktop, that Liffy must be the person on earth to whom she is closest and yet this girl, born of her body and Adam's, has a soul that is hers alone, that springs from elsewhere, that has nothing to do with either parent. She opens Liffy's email and looks at the SENT folder – schoolgirl messages to her friends, talking about boys and homework and makeup and hated teachers. She searches fruitlessly for a diary – Liffy is too private to risk such a potential giveaway – but in the DOWNLOADS file she is aghast to find reams of pages containing calorie counts, diet ideas and exercise plans, which turn her stomach. Then she opens the HOMEWORK file and investigates English composition. Here she discovers Liffy's end-of-term essay.

He walked ahead of her, always just a little too far ahead for her to see his face. His skin was a leaflike grey-green . . . 'I am the embodiment of the earth,' he said. 'I am the king of the forest, king of all the spirits in the trees and the plants, here and in the rain-forest and in the savannah and in the pine-covered mountains. At my command, the earth awakens with all its monstrous power . . .

Sasha reads on. It sheds no light on Liffy's collapse, but she can see, without a shadow of a doubt, that Lisa is right. How on earth can her sister see such a thing when she, Liffy's mother, can't? Is she, as mums go, really that deficient? She remembers that Liffy is bright, beautiful and gifted, that the boys are healthy, normal and down to earth, that all three do well at school. She must be doing something right. But is it enough? How can it happen that a girl like Liffy, give or take a hormone or two, can create a mental world so powerful that it takes possession of her? Is the only truth the inner truth? Can it be that the life of the imagination is stronger than external reality? Sasha, thinking of her mother, goes down to pour herself another glass of Spanish wine.

Lisa makes up the bed in her old room at her mother's house. It's years since she last stayed there. The room is silent and fossilised; Lisa's files of notes from her university undergraduate course and master's degree are perched on top of the bookshelf. Once there had been a time when Lisa did not know Vladimir, a time when her father was alive, a time when Sasha was twenty years old and starved herself, terrified that her appearance on stage was not sylph-like enough. Standing in her room, Lisa feels as if that time is still the present, while she and her bump and her beloved niece exist as futuristic shadows, projecting themselves backwards. Her mother has gone to bed and even though she is, for once, not alone, Lisa feels lonelier than she ever does in her flat.

Lisa tiptoes downstairs to the lounge where, in the dark, she fumbles for the phone and dials 00-33-1. Next she dials the rest of Vovka's number. The answering-machine – as usual – is on. Lisa takes a breath.

'Vovka,' she says, through the tumult in her mind and the lump that chokes her throat, 'Vovka, it's me. Are you there? If you're there – please pick up the phone? Please?'

Nothing reaches her ears except the turning of the tape in the machine. She pictures the empty room, its muslin curtains motionless, the piano closed and waiting.

By eleven the next day Sasha is sitting outside the hospital on a bench, talking on her mobile. She has never wanted less to talk. She has never wanted to be free of her work the way she does now. Rick's production assistant, Marion, has seen the *News of the World* and, being upfront with Sasha at long last, has rung to say they can't consider inviting her back on to the programme until the fuss has died down.

'Fine,' snaps Sasha.

'But, Sasha,' the girl says from White City, her voice as embarrassed as any Sasha has ever heard, 'is it *true*?'

'I don't know. I haven't seen it. I don't know what it says.'

'It says SASHA'S SHOPLIFTING HELL.'

'Does it? Does it really? Do I care? No, I don't.'

'But—'

'Listen. My Liffy, my daughter, my angel, my little girl, is lying unconscious in bloody hospital. Do you think I care about the *News of the* fucking *World*? Do you think I care about rabbiting away on television about some bloody pretentious film that nobody is ever going to watch? You tell Rick from me that the lot of you can rot in hell for all I care. Have a nice life.' Sasha wishes she could slam a door

in the BBC's face: all she can do is press the red button on
her phone.

As soon as she has done so, it rings again.

'Sasha Wood? *News of the World.*'

'Fuck off,' Sasha says. An electric fury is simmering within her
as she presses out the phone number of her publisher and hears
herself calmly cancelling her own book contract – to her editor's
spoken concern and distress but, no doubt, unspoken relief.

There's a swirl of ivory linen and long hair nearby and she
sees her sister walking towards her out of the sunshine.

'You're right,' Sasha says, by way of greeting. 'You're
absolutely right. I don't know how you knew, but it looks like
you're right.' She waves in front of Lisa's nose a printout of
Liffy's school essay.

Lisa sits down beside her and reads it, nodding.

'What do you think it means?' Sasha asks.

'I don't know. It depends how much she knows.'

'What do you mean?'

'The Green Man,' says Lisa, 'is supposed to be about life,
not death. He's frightening – but so is life. The richness, the
verdant growth of life, can be terrifying, especially when
you're about thirteen. Don't you think?'

'Just a bit.'

Lisa pulls a book out of her bag and points at a paragraph
that Sasha is almost too frightened to read. 'Traditionally,' she
says, 'the Green Man is about continuing life, not forthcoming
death. He stands for the cycle of birth and death on which
the whole of nature depends.'

'Maybe that's so. But all I've found in Liffy's room is this
ghastly essay predicting doom, gloom and despair.'

There's silence for a while.

'God, Sash,' Lisa exclaims at last, 'I feel so awful. I feel
responsible. I should have jumped up and down and screamed
about her state months ago. I should have seen, when she came
to stay—'

'Hush, Lee. Of course it's not your fault. If it's anyone's fault, it's mine.'

Lisa says nothing. In thirty-four years she's never known Sasha admit that she's in the wrong.

Sasha is trying to remember something. Somewhere she has heard that people in a coma may be able to hear what's being said to them. 'Perhaps we should tell her. Perhaps she can hear us,' she says. 'Who knows? It can't hurt, can it? Shall we try?'

Sasha stands up and holds out her hands to Lisa. The sisters entwine their fingers, then turn to walk side by side back into the hospital.

In Liffy's room, the monitor emits an occasional faint bleep. Sally is in the chair in the corner, turning the pages of a tabloid newspaper without seeing its words; Adam sits on the side of the bed, holding Liffy's hand. Neither even registers surprise when Sasha tells them about Lisa's discovery.

Sasha takes Adam's hand in her left hand and Liffy's in her right. 'Liffs,' she whispers, 'I hope you can hear me. Listen. We've found the Earth Prince. We know who he is. We know what you're going through.' Sasha cannot believe she is saying these words, but the sight of Liffy's green-white, waxlike face compels her to go on. 'Liffy, listen to me. The Earth Prince is not there to kill you. The Earth Prince is an ancient symbol of ongoing life. He's there not to kill you but to make you live. He's positive. He's there to help you. Not to kill you,' she repeats. 'Life. Not death. Life. Not death. Life. Spring comes back, you know. It always comes back. It's not down to you.'

The monitor bleeps. Liffy does not stir. Sasha, Adam and Lisa watch and wait. Everything is stillness. Outside, the first leaves of autumn drift towards the ground.

★

Love is light, light is love. The brilliance pulses through her until she is radiant with it, luminescence rising from her palms and feet, bolts of energy shaking her like electricity. Love makes her weight-less. Now she can soar, unlimited by gravity. Love has taken her into itself. And the surprise is that the love is also flowing out of her, pouring itself like the blood of stars into the universe – the more she gives, the more it surges up inside her. It directs itself to the Earth Prince: she can almost see the phosphorescence of her love for him flowing outward and garlanding him. In her mind, far, far away, she can see her family – and there is refulgent love within her for them too, a sensation that is pure and free, full of forgiveness. She remembers Gaz and to him, wherever he is, she can send out shafts of the same love, unconditional, demanding nothing; an end in itself. Her breath fills her lungs with the air that fuels the love, because love is the energy that binds atom to atom, heart to heart, soul to soul, soul to universe.

Her heart is free. The Earth Prince has freed her. To be freed is not what she had expected. She had waited for death, for sacrifice. It did not come.

The Earth Prince's hand passes across her forehead. 'Oh, my dear,' he says – and she hears, astonished, a hint of regret. 'I feared that this might happen.'

She had waited for the sacrifice, for the dagger poised by her throat and the spear at her heart. Instead her spirit has come back into her body. She is mystified. New energy is coursing through her. An energy that is fresh and fiery, an energy that reminds her of her old days, learning to dance. Perhaps she is his now – but also he is hers and his energy has entered her and given her renewal.

The Earth Prince takes both her hands and raises her to him. 'Tell me. What is your decision? Will you leave your world for me, Liffy?'

'I will,' says Liffy.

But even as she speaks, she knows it's not true. The hope she feels is hope for life. She doesn't want to die. She doesn't want to leave her world, her family, the possibility of finding on earth the love she has experienced in spirit. But she has given her pledge. Terror begins to take hold of her – until she looks at the Earth Prince and sees in him an infinite sadness.

'No, Liffy, I have to let you go. You thought you were willing to give your life for the sake of the earth. But giving means loving and the risk was that the love within you would awaken, and this came to pass. Had that not happened, the sacrifice would have been complete. Yet now you are too alive, too loving, too human. Your new-found love is so strong that I cannot keep you here. You are free. Go now. Live well for me.'

'But what will happen now? What will happen to the earth, you, all of us?'

'That isn't for you to determine.'

'I love you,' Liffy says.

'It is not me you love. It is simply that you love.'

She doesn't want to leave him, but feels her fingers slip from his grasp as the light takes her up into the air and whirls and shakes her and she feels something annoying invading her wrist and hears an insistent electronic bleep in her right ear until she has to turn and see what it is and finds herself looking into her mother's eyes.

25

Waking Liffy is one hurdle. Getting her to eat is quite another.

The eating-disorders consultant comes to talk to her, banishing Adam and Sasha from the room. Nurses bring her food and replace her drip. She's distressed; she cries a lot. Gerald comes to visit and walks up and down the corridor muttering about the evils of fashion magazines. Liffy begs to be left alone.

'Don't cry, darling,' Sasha pleads. 'You're going to get better now.'

But Liffy, sobbing, can hardly speak. She doesn't know how to put into words the idea that she's seen something so beautiful that no earthly experience will ever be able to match it. She can't remember in detail, still less explain, the dream that was more than a dream; nor does she want to.

Sasha organises the twins into staying at Julius's house so that she can remain in Oxford. The next morning, Julius's mother phones Sasha in exasperation, wanting to know when the twins can go home because they are driving her crazy. Sasha snaps at her that Liffy has nearly died and she's not going to leave her yet. As a measure of last resort, she phones her mother and begs her to look after them for a couple of days, to which – to Sasha's astonishment – Sally agrees at once and with apparent enthusiasm. Sasha wonders whether she's understimated her mother's place in the family circle for all these years.

The doctors tell Liffy that she'll be staying in hospital until she weighs eight stone.

'Eight stone?' howls Liffy, who currently weighs less than six. 'I'll be an elephant!'

'No, you won't. You'll be a healthy adolescent girl.' The doctors explain to her the damage that such severe malnourishment can leave behind – brittle bones, vitamin and mineral deficiencies, fertility problems. It may mean two months in the eating-disorders unit.

'I can't have anorexia,' Liffy protests. 'I'm too fat! What about school? What about my ballet-school audition?'

Her school is being kept informed and the audition has been cancelled. Liffy begins to howl again. Inwardly she calls to the Earth Prince to come back to her. He does not respond.

At the weekend, Sasha goes home and brings her mother and sons back with her. The twins are solemn and tongue-tied in the hospital, distressed to see their sister confined to the unit, puzzled that she is being effectively forced to eat ice-cream.

'We could help you with that!' Matt exclaims, looking wistfully at Liffy's lunch. 'I'll give you 50p for it, Liffs.' Sally ushers them hurriedly out of the room. Liffy eats painfully, miserably, mouthful by slow mouthful. The nurses watch her with the surreptitious yet hawkish eyes of probation officers.

'Anorexia is a form of painful, slow-motion suicide,' the consultant tells her. 'You don't want to die, do you?'

Liffy won't talk about what she dreamed during her coma. She tells everybody that she doesn't remember, which is partly true. When Lisa asks her what the Earth Prince really was, some time in her second week in hospital, Liffy says she doesn't know what she means.

Adam has to go back to work: he has to finish the decorating, organise the fittings and phone the artists, while Bronwyn has undertaken to set up the computer and filing systems in her spare time. The show has to go ahead.

'Sasha,' he says, 'will you come and see the gallery? I'd like to show it to you.'

'Are you sure?'

'Absolutely sure. Please come.'

Where the delicatessen's counter used to house jars of anchovies and pitted olives, where the chiller cabinet had displayed buffalo mozzarella and marinated grilled artichokes, there is now a peaceful white rectangle in two parts; in the ceiling are wooden beams, beside which Adam has arranged careful, discreet yet vivid lighting. The gallery faces north, which minimises the potential glare from direct sunlight on the glass that will one day protect paintings on the wall. 'This was all deli shelves,' Adam tells Sasha, unlocking the door. 'It's opened up so beautifully – it's even better than I thought it would be.'

Sasha walks into the empty space and gazes upward. She pictures the place full of new creations, the room stirring gently with people appreciating them: an idealised vision, perhaps, but one that she likes. 'It's nice. Calming, somehow,' she tells him. 'The light's good, too.'

In the office, which still stinks of new paint, she notices the neat desk, the ordered filing cabinets, the clear, unfamiliar, feminine handwriting on the paperwork. She wonders who Adam's second in command is.

They stroll from the gallery and walk together as far as Merton and Christchurch Meadow, relieved to have a few minutes' release from the airless hospital with its chemical smells and atmosphere of sickness, tension and dread.

Sasha begins to talk. She hasn't talked to her husband for months, if not years. She hasn't told him her fears or her hopes, because with Liffy and the twins to worry about her feelings seemed insignificant; and nobody ever had the time to sit and talk in any case. She confesses to her idiotic exploit in Waitrose and that five unpaid-for items of shopping have scuppered her TV, literary and journalistic career, at least for the time being. She'd shown up at the magistrates' court, held her head high and been duly fined, cautioned and released, dodging several reporters as she left the building. Then she went home and had a cup of tea. Beside Liffy's illness, the incident seems trivial.

To her delight, Adam listens to everything she has to tell him and begins to laugh.

'Oh God,' he says, 'shoplifting five things from Waitrose? Haven't they got anything better to write about?'

'It's so silly.' Sasha's load feels lightened by his laughter and she joins in. 'It's so bloody ridiculous! But, in a way, I'm almost glad. I don't want things to feel as they did before. I don't want life to be the same.'

'What do you want, Sash?'

'I want things – to improve. I want to change the way I – we – live, possibly.'

'We?'

'I know we can't go backwards.' Sasha moistens her lips.

'I know that too.' Adam strokes her wrist with one finger, but won't meet her gaze.

Sasha senses him wrestling internally. 'I can live without my column,' she says. 'I can live without that stupid TV show. I don't miss it. I can probably live without my book, and it could be that they'll let me resuscitate it once all this has blown over. But I couldn't live without the kids and I don't know whether . . .' She can't finish the sentence.

'You've lived without me very well for four months,' Adam points out.

'I haven't. What a mess this is.'

A couple of students ride by on bicycles, laughing together over a private joke. The girl's long hair blows around her shoulders as she pedals. Her boyfriend, riding behind, can't take his eyes off her. She glances back over her shoulder, beckoning to him with her gaze, warm and open and trusting. Their laughter fades into the blend of traffic and birdsong.

'Adam,' Sasha says in a rush, 'maybe we can put something right – maybe it isn't too late. You can't fix anything between yourself and your mother now, but *we*'re both still here. Do you think you can forgive me?'

Adam lifts her hand and kisses the palm, but he still doesn't look at her as he says, 'I'll think about it.'

She decides against telling Adam about her other miserable episode, the one featuring a certain TV producer: admitting to an affair, however pathetic its outcome, isn't going to help heal any rifts. Rick rankles in her mind like a block of mouldy cheese at the back of a fridge. The best thing she can do is throw it out and scrub down the shelf with something antibacterial. Perhaps the affair, short though it was, will become a skeleton in the cupboard, perhaps it will come out one day – that's a risk she has to take – but for the time being she must erase it as thoroughly as she can. How peculiar, she thinks, that her feelings for that man had been so powerful that they'd occupied part of her every waking minute for nearly two months – and now they'd vanished, as insubstantial and useless as cobwebs.

'Life is still full of surprises,' is all she tells Cindy.

'You bet it is,' says her friend.

In Davenant Road, the twins, parked on their other grand-parent for the weekend, chase each other round the walled garden and play ball well away from the windows. They're frustrated that they have to keep their voices down and not run inside the house, but Alex has been playing the piano and is surprised by the number of Grandpa Brownie points he's accumulated for it.

Gerald, closeting himself in his study to read in peace, is bothered at first by the racket from the garden; but when the family goes out to see Liffy and the house falls silent, he finds himself wishing they'd come back.

Now he watches his grandsons shouting and leaping outside. He is thrilled and bemused by Alex's absorption at the keyboard. He's bemused by the whole thing. Children, new little people, filled with the blind energy and mindless life that keeps the world going. All he'd wanted was to be alone with his memories of Martha, but now he is beginning to feel that maybe, after all, that is the last thing he really wants.

He's grateful that his house is big enough to accommodate the family at the moment, but when they go home it's going to feel huge, heartless and full of ghosts. Something will have to be done.

Gerald gets out the telephone directory, finds the phone number of a reputable estate agent in Summertown and makes an appointment for someone to come round the next day to give him a valuation. He can feel Martha's unheard cry of protest as he says into the receiver, 'I'm thinking of selling my house.' But it doesn't stop him. Hanging on to the house can't bring Martha back. Life has to go on; and if it is to benefit the living, not the dead, he reflects, then sacrifices have to be made. Perhaps it's time for him to give up the fantasies that sustain him – lest that sustenance proves poison instead.

Liffy sits in the eating-disorders unit, pondering how on earth she has ended up there. She wonders why people keep asking her about the Earth Prince. She wonders how they knew. Even if she'd told nobody about him, somehow they had found out; and, as he'd told her on the day he first appeared, once someone discovers that she has seen him, he cannot come back. Since she woke up, she hasn't been able to summon him to her. She knows she will never see him again.

A blanket seems to have been thrown back from her brain. The too-thin doctor says that that's because she's eating: her blood sugar had been disastrously low and this was why she'd been confused – this was why she'd had moods of elation, terror and despair in such quick exchange, this was why she had had some trouble telling the difference between what was real and what her own mind had created. Liffy doesn't believe her, but she can't deny that, one way or another, she is starting to feel better.

Admitting it is horrible. The patterns mapped out in her brain like tramlines don't want to change. To eat an apple in a few big, crunching bites instead of the fine slivers she's learned to love feels wrong: sinful, greedy, appalling. To put food into her mouth that contains sugar, fat or both sometimes makes her gag; a doctor or nurse stands over her while she eats to make sure she swallows. It's torture, agony, surely against all regulations about human rights. And yet the relief – the overwhelming, oxygenous relief – not to feel hungry!

Giving up the dream of ballet school has been the worst thing of all. Sasha at last tells her the bald facts straight up: 'If you get through the audition, they measure you and check your proportions. You're a lovely little dancer, but your legs are short for your body – not so that anyone except a ballet school would notice, but notice they will. They also need to make sure that your knees reach the ground when you bend them out to the sides. Liffs, darling, yours don't. They never did and they never will.'

'So however well I danced, they weren't ever going to take me?' Liffy says, eyes filling.

'No, sweetheart. They weren't.'

'But I was all set! I had my lovely Chloë dance.'

'You still have it. You'll still have it once you're better. There's no reason you can't keep dancing. It just doesn't have to be the be-all and end-all of life, does it?'

Liffy says nothing. She hasn't considered this before.

When Sasha leaves, Liffy closes her eyes and tries again to call the Earth Prince. But he doesn't come; he never does. Instead when she looks up she sees her father standing in front of her, holding a huge bunch of stargazer lilies.

She's astonished at the way everyone is paying her so much attention. She hasn't had this much attention in all her life. Her brothers have never been so nice to her – perhaps they're still hoping she'll give them her ice-cream. Her mother has never called her 'darling' or 'sweetheart' so often before. Her father has never spent so much time with her.

He comes in smiling from work on his gallery, his old jeans splattered with white paint, bringing postcards for her to look at of pictures by some of the artists he's going to display in the first show. Bronwyn recommends a hairdresser; Dad persuades him to come to the hospital and tidy up the mess in which Charley had left Liffy's hair, since Liffy is not permitted to go out; when he's finished, Liffy has the trendiest cut in Oxford. He brings her flowers, books, a miniature CD player with headphones and some of her favourite CDs to listen to. Best of all, she can hug him all she wants. As she does, she notices the threads of silver that lace the curls around his temples.

'If you wanted attention, you've certainly got it,' the psychiatrist remarks, in one of Liffy's plentiful sessions. 'Was that what you wanted?'

'I dunno. But, yeah, I like it.'

'Did you maybe feel nobody was giving you enough before?'

'I dunno. You don't think about it, really. You just live. You don't realise what you didn't have until you have it, sometimes, and other times you don't know what you have until it's gone. Mostly you just do the best you can with what you've got.'

The psychiatrist's eyebrows rise briefly.

The next weekend, a parcel arrives. It contains a hefty box of Lindt fondants. Sasha opens it for Liffy and says, 'It's from Charley.'

'What? More chocolates?' Liffy gestures at her white Formica cupboard, on top of which are piled a box of Marks and Spencer's truffles, a sealed gold cardboard carton from Godiva Chocolates, a row of Bendicks Bittermints and an enormous tin of Quality Street.

Each box tells a story of its own. The truffles are from Robin Brewster, the flute teacher, to say thank you and get well soon. The Godiva box is from Grandpa, who seems to have clocked into caring about her in an entirely new way – unless it's just that, for the first time, he's determined to show it. The Quality Street is from her entire class at school. The Bendicks are from Margaret, her ballet teacher, to commiserate over the audition but to tell her it's much for the best. Charley's contribution sits beside them, taking up the last available surface.

Liffy, remembering a TV series about India that had held her riveted, thinks of the food offerings that are left by suppli- cants at the temples, small sacrifices that their bearers hope will make their luck change. With the exception of Robin's gift – he is sweet enough simply to say thank you – all the other chocolate boxes are sacrifices to her, pleas for forgiveness. All these people are blaming themselves, whether rightly or wrongly, for what's happened to her. In addition, she's had hundreds of cards – from schoolfriends, distant relations she barely remembers, Lindsey and Paul, Bronwyn and some of her mother's colleagues like Cindy Smith and Vijay, the writer with the unspellable surname. Liffy sits back against her pillow, satisfied: perhaps the Earth Prince has turned her into a minor deity after all.

> *Dear Liffy,*
>
> *I wanted to say I'm sorry.*
>
> *I got suspended for two weeks. Nobody wants to talk to me. Mum sold my flute. Not that that matters, I was useless at it anyway. I hope you're not still mad at me and I promise I'll never do anything like that again as long as I live. Please forgive me, please let's be friends again.*
>
> *Please read the enclosed. I hope it helps make up for every- thing.*
>
> *Your friend,*
> *Charley.*

Liffy takes the envelope that falls out of Charley's letter and looks at it, surprised.

'What's that?' Mum asks.

'Dunno.'

The writing on the envelope is square and slightly childish, and Liffy's surname has been spelled wrong. But she can hardly believe her eyes when she takes out the card, which has an olive branch on the front.

> *Dear Irish,*
>
> *Sorry to hear you've been ill. Charley wrote and told me. Please get yourself better very soon. I am back at college now doing carpentry and I am enjoying it. I like learning to do inlaid work – that's when you put contrasting pieces of wood or mother-of-pearl or other things in patterns inside your basic wood. When I'm a bit better at it I'll make you a box for your jewllrey. I hope we can meet again one day soon. I'd like that if you would.*
>
> *Please get well soon Irish and take good care of yourself. Mark and me are sorry about what happened in Greece, you and Charley are great girls and we want you to know that.*
>
> *Love,*
>
> *Gary (Gaz)*

Liffy's mind spins. Charley must have tracked down the boys – how on earth? Maybe through the apartments on the island? Maybe she'd known where they were staying? She must have written to Gaz, told him Liffy was ill . . . Oh my God, thinks Liffy, by writing to Gaz, Charley would have had to relive the horror of that last night in Greece . . . all for her sake.

'Liffs?' says the bemused Sasha.

'Oh Mum,' Liffy bursts out, 'I'm so glad I didn't die!'

Sasha looks at her transformed features, too surprised to say anything.

'And you know something?' Liffy adds, her eyes sparkling.

'What, darling?'
'I really, really like my haircut.'

Later, back at home, Sasha pours herself a glass of Rioja and logs on to the Internet.

They don't need such a huge house. They need enough space for the kids' bedrooms and for her study, but they don't need a big conservatory, or a dining room as well as an eat-in kitchen, or – any longer – a ballet studio. If she isn't going to Television Centre any more, she doesn't need to be in London. Attending a different school might help Liffy get over her problem; her school may be harming her, overflowing as it is with stick-insect teenagers under endless pressure to do well. The boys would have time to settle into a new primary school and they could explore which secondary school will suit them in a couple of years' time, if she and the kids were to sell up and move and lower their mortgage . . . If she and the kids and Adam, too, were to sell up and move to Oxford . . .

Sasha, who is an expert at Internet research, doesn't take long to discover that North Oxford is a tad pricey and isn't a realistic option for 'downshifting', as she reluctantly admits she has to call it. Around Oxford, however, there are villages. Pretty, Oxfordshire countryside villages within easy reach of the city. There, for the price of their Sheen house, they could buy a detached home with four bedrooms and a large garden, with no flight path and no South Circular and a hefty chunk knocked off the mortgage.

At least if she moves to Oxfordshire with the children, they can have a fresh start and be close to their father, whether or not he moves back in. She and Adam can find their own way now: they no longer have to live, instead, a life that Martha had chosen for them. It is up to Adam, ultimately: if he wants to come home to her, she will be ready to take him back. She knows better than to expect complete forgiveness: her betrayal was too extreme, and however intense her regret, she can't undo the damage. All she can do now is try to find the best thing to do for the children, especially while Liffy is recovering. For herself, she'll do the best she can with what she's got.

With the new academic year under way, Lisa slides easily into a hollow imitation of her old life: giving her lectures, marking students' work, coaxing her mother out of the house whenever possible and meeting Lindsey for coffee in West End Lane, or Louis Pâtisserie when she feels able to drag herself up the hill to Hampstead village. On Saturdays she and Sally go to Oxford to see Liffy; apart from that, her car sits almost unused. She still can't believe she has one.

Coming in from work one afternoon, she meets Melanie in the hall.

'How are you doing?' Melanie exclaims, staring at Lisa's bump.

'Fine, thanks,' Lisa says. 'What about you?'

'Yeah, I'm fine too, I guess. Do you want to come in for coffee?'

Lisa accepts out of sheer curiosity. She's only ever been into Andrew and Melanie's flat in emergencies, or to ask Melanie to feed her cat while she's away.

Andrew, rather to Lisa's relief, isn't home. Melanie, piling coffee into a percolator for herself and a peppermint teabag into a mug for Lisa, says that he's working. 'For once in his life,' she adds. 'He can't hold a steady job. He always walks out or gets himself sacked.'

Lisa wonders, not for the first time, what Melanie sees in him. Melanie claims to have been a model once upon a time: she's long-legged and curvaceous and her exotic looks were, no doubt, what drew Andrew to her. In the six years since Lisa bought her flat, Andrew has lived with a succession of three or four stunning-figured, well-dressed black or mixed-race women. Andrew is fiftyish, overweight, violent.

Each relationship starts with music, flowers and long, loud love-making, but ends sooner or later in screaming matches and broken windows.

'Would you like a *drink* drink?' Melanie leaves her coffee untouched. Lisa declines politely. 'Oh, the baby,' says Melanie. 'You are good. I couldn't do that.' She takes a tumbler from the side of the sink and pours a large quantity of Martini into it.

A few sips later, Melanie has begun to talk and she won't stop. Andrew, she declares, is feckless, useless, impossible, stupid, incompetent, not even much good in bed. 'I was so fooled by him,' she rambles, refilling her glass ten minutes later. 'When I moved in here, I was being so much the little housewife. I didn't want to move in, but he begged me, he really pleaded, he sent me flowers and bought me sexy underwear and he just wouldn't take no for an answer. And I was busy getting nice ready-made dinners from Marks and Spencer and putting fresh flowers on the table every week. Can you believe it?'

'I can't help hearing you fighting,' Lisa tells her.

'I'm sure. I'm sure. I always wonder, oh God, Lisa upstairs, she's such a nice girl, what can she be thinking?'

Lisa says nothing.

'Lisa, I just don't know what I'm going to do,' Melanie goes on. 'He always says sorry, he always says he won't do it again, but he always does. And sometimes he really hurts me, but then it's sweetness and light again the next morning and he acts like nothing happened. I go off to work and everything seems, like, normal, and I manage to convince myself that he really won't do it again, until it happens the next time. And he's got this thing about black girls, he thinks we're glamorous or something . . .'

Lisa listens. She wants to leave – the place stinks of cigarette smoke and she doesn't want to breathe it in more than she already has to upstairs. But Melanie, on her third Martini

Rosso, is going on and on, and Lisa feels desperately sorry for her. Christ, and I think I've got problems, she reflects.

'Melanie,' she says, after half an hour, when the girl lets her get a word in edgeways, 'you don't have to live like this. You're young, you're fantastic looking, you've got all that experience modelling. You could be out there doing something else with your life. You could find a man who'd be good to you. You could have kids, if you want.'

'I've got a kid,' says Melanie, to Lisa's astonishment. 'I've got a boy who's twelve. He lives with my mum. Andrew won't have him to stay here.'

Lisa doesn't know exactly how old Melanie is, but is certain she's under thirty. The words hit home. She tries to imagine herself in Melanie's position. Smarting with shame, she remembers complaining to Melanie that Vladimir 'only' wanted to be a dad.

'So,' she says, 'he beats you up and he won't let you have your son with you. If you're that unhappy, why do you stay with him?'

Melanie sips. She takes in Lisa's words in silence. 'That's interesting,' she says eventually. 'I've never thought of it like that. My friends are always saying, "Oh, leave him, leave him," and all I do is dig my heels in.'

She looks up at Lisa, her dark eyes filled with the most extraordinary expression, as if a lightbulb has switched on inside her head. 'You're right. *Why* do I *stay*? . . . It must be something in me that's making me.'

'Melanie, I'm sorry, I've really got to go,' Lisa says. 'Thanks for the tea. Let me know what happens?'

'I will,' says Melanie, her eyes still bright. 'Lisa, thank you so much.'

'You just take care of yourself. OK?' Lisa gives her a hug.

Four days later Lisa hears shouting in the hall and suitcases bumping down the front stairs. Melanie has packed her stuff and is moving out.

Lisa lies awake most of the night. Her unborn daughter seems to be practising ballet inside her womb. Lisa half dreams, half daydreams, about what she will look like, wondering what to name her, wondering whether her surname should be Wood or Vasilevsky. Vladimir has never returned her call – or, if he has, he left no message and she'll never know.

Adam and Bronwyn have been working late into the evening at the gallery. Adam had never suspected how much paperwork would be involved; how many hours on the phone, how many unsolicited calls from artists desperate to be exhibited – how strange it is to be on the receiving end of this, he reflects, rubbing his eyes. Around seven, Bronwyn had nipped out to buy a bottle of wine and they've drunk their way through two thirds of it as they ploughed through the to-do list. Now it's nearly ten thirty.

'Aren't you hungry?' Adam asks her. 'I can make some pasta upstairs, if you like.'

Bronwyn, half hidden behind the computer and forests of papers, tries to say no; but her eyes say yes and Adam can hear her stomach rumbling. He sprints up the stairs, boils a kettle and chops onion, garlic and a red chilli. A little tuna, a little white wine, some fresh basil, a single candle on what passes for his dining-room table . . .

'This is the most delicious pasta I've ever had,' declares Bronwyn, a few minutes later. Adam looks over at her and drinks in the sight: the firm young breasts, the shining hair, the deep chestnut of her eyes. Outside, autumn rain is battering on his windows. 'I always liked cooking,' he remarks. 'I never got to do enough of it in the old days.'

Bronwyn lowers her eyes to her pasta and eats. Adam has already finished. He's got into the habit of eating too quickly – with terminal messiness, it's a symptom of bachelordom. He's too old to live like that, he reminds himself. He must do something about it.

Bronwyn's plate is empty and the chime of cutlery on china is stilled. A long and rapidly thickening silence sinks on to them, one of those silences that happen not because there's too little to say but because there's too much; one of those silences that Adam hasn't experienced for many years. Their eyes don't meet. Adam gets up and starts pottering about, putting away mugs to defuse a little of the tension.

Bronwyn pushes back her chair and stands up. 'I should get going,' she says.

Adam, at the sink, feels her eyes boring into his back. 'Thanks for everything, Bronwyn,' he says.

'It's a pleasure.' He senses a brief, choking strain in her voice and turns round. Before he knows what he's doing, he has crossed the room, the pot-scourer still in one hand, and reached out for her. Her body against his is warm and fresh and adorable.

'Adam, don't.' Her voice is muffled in his shoulder.

'Bronwyn, you're so lovely I can't stand it,' Adam hears himself say.

'You too,' says Bronwyn.

Holding her, Adam thinks he's hearing things. Can it be that this lovely girl twenty years younger than him actually finds him attractive and desirable? Is this possible? Surely not? As if to experiment, almost merely to check, he tips her face towards him and kisses her lips. There is no mistaking the heat of the kiss she returns. He tries again, just to be certain. He knows he ought to let go of her, but it's not so easy. Instead, he lobs the pot-scourer back into the sink.

An hour later, lying under a blanket in the lamplight, Adam and Bronwyn breathe together in silence. Adam can't believe what he's just done. Everything worked, almost too well. Not once did he think of his mother's illness and death; not once did he stop to worry whether his body was still his own, whether it would obey the desires of his mind and spirit. Bronwyn, half asleep, is lying with her back to his stomach, their curves folding together in experimental parallel. His fingers run across her soft, unblemished skin and his nose rests in the dark locks of her hair – the same colour as Sasha's, though the texture is different. Oh God, he thinks, drifting towards sleep despite himself. Sasha.

In the morning Bronwyn, brushing out her hair, turns her big brown eyes to him and says, 'Are you going to see Liffy before work?'

'Yes, of course.' Adam is pulling on his trainers.

'Adam?'

He peers towards her – is he imagining it or are there tears in those eyes? 'Bronwyn? Are you OK?'

'I think . . . Oh, shit. Adam, last night was so beautiful. But . . .'

'Did I do something wrong?'

'Of course you didn't. But I could really fall in love with you . . . and I don't want to because I think you'll hurt me if I do. I think you'll go back to your family. I told you what happened to me earlier this year. I don't want to get hurt again.'

'What makes you think that? Supposing I want to be with you?'

'Well, do you?'

Adam feels abruptly paralysed. He wonders why she has to challenge him like this. He wants to get along to see Liffy; he doesn't want to have to make life-changing decisions right now. Reality butts against him and, with it, a sneaking and inappropriate resentment. How can she ask such a thing at all, after one night? But then, he reflects, she's only twenty-three. She's only ten years older than Liffy. She's younger than he was when he met Sasha for the first time. She's putting him on the spot simply because she doesn't know any better.

'That's what I think,' says Bronwyn. 'Look. I'm here for you if you want me. But I'd rather you decided now than in six months' time.'

'Bronwyn. You're so sweet.' He reaches out an arm. She stands still in front of the mirror, hairbrush in her hand, watching him. He feels as if she and her reflection are a vision from a different, better planet. Does he love her – or her youth, her freshness, her newness? Or, even worse, that she was there when he needed someone?

'You're sweet too,' she says. 'But I don't want to get hurt. Can you promise that you won't hurt me?'

Adam goes up to her and kisses her. 'Bronwyn . . .' he begins, but doesn't know how to continue.

'You've got to decide this one,' Bronwyn whispers into his ear. 'You're the only one who can.'

Sacrifices need to be made, Sasha tells the twins on a chilly evening at home, just after the for-sale sign has gone up outside the house. Liffy's illness can't carry the can for everyone's selfishness any longer. Alex and Matt don't understand what's come over her. 'Why do we have to move just because Liffy's ill?'

'Because we're going to help her get better if it's the last thing we do. You two are going to stop being revolting to her, starting *now*. I won't answer for the consequences if you don't. Get it? Got it? Good.'

'What do we get in return?' Matt demands.

'Alex, we'll find you a good piano teacher in Oxford. Matt, you can have lessons in anything you like – football, tennis or whatever.'

'Can we have new trainers?' Matt bargains.

'Yes. You need some. Your feet are getting too big for the ones you've got.'

The doorbell rings.

'Expecting anyone?' she asks the boys. They shake their heads.

'Probably someone collecting.' Sasha finds her purse and goes to the door ready to give a pound to Scope or Cancer Research.

In the pool of light on the doorstep stands the bearded, bejeaned Adam. Sasha stops in her tracks as the images of Adam as she had known him twenty years ago, Adam clean-shaven and commuting, Adam unemployed and depressed and the new Adam – two decades older, yet closest to the Adam she knew in the beginning – fold into one another and merge.

At the sound of his voice, the boys fling themselves at him from both sides. Adam tries to pick them both up at once, but they've grown too much. 'It doesn't seem so long since I could tuck one of you under each arm,' he tells them. 'Not any more, I can't.'

The twins pull at him, wanting to show him their homework, their PlayStation, their paintings, Alex's piano-playing. Sasha has retrieved her parents' piano from its home at Martha's friend's house. She had met some surprise and some recalcitrance, but the piano is hers (with Lisa's consent) and its rightful home is with the twin who wants to play it.

'In a few minutes,' Adam says, hugging them. 'Come on, guys, I need to talk to your mother first.'

'Let's go into the kitchen,' Sasha says. 'Boys, go up now and finish your homework.' Her heart is racing. Adam would normally have phoned to say he was coming.

'I spent this afternoon with Liffs,' he says, sitting at the table, automatically in his old place. 'She's looking forward to seeing you on Friday and she's dying to come home.'

'As long as she's eating.'

'She is. She really is, she isn't bluffing. I don't know what those psychiatrists say to her or get her to say to them, but she understands what's going on and she seems to know what she has to do. It's hard going, but I'm sure she'll get there in the end. She's going to be fine.'

Sasha pours herbal tea for them both. 'How's the gallery?'

'Almost ready. You'll be there for the opening, won't you?'

'How would I not be?'

Sasha looks at Adam. He looks at the floor. Sasha draws in

her breath – it strikes her abruptly that he may not be there for the reason she'd thought.

He is quiet for a long time. In his eyes, Sasha can see a struggle knotting up their lines of communication. 'Is there something you want to tell me?' she asks.

'No, no,' Adam says, too quickly.

'Are you sure?' Sasha's voice cracks.

'It's hard, facing things alone,' Adam ventures. 'It's so easy to make mistakes. Really stupid mistakes.'

'Like shoplifting from Waitrose.' Sasha knows she's putting off the moment of facing whatever stupid mistake Adam is trying to tell her about – and the longer she can put it off, the better. 'I've been such an idiot,' she says. 'The whole thing's ridiculous. But I've worked out what matters to me, so it can't be all bad.'

'OK. What does matter to you?'

'The kids. Getting my feet back on the ground. And – you. Ad, I want us to try again. Maybe I can help with the gallery while we wait for all the bloody fuss to simmer down. I'd like to. I know you still need more rest than you're getting. What do you think?'

Adam gets up and puts his arms round her shoulders from behind. 'Oh, Sash, I don't know. The last weeks have brought us closer because of Liffy, and I think that's what Liffy wanted all along. But it's so easy to assume a new home means a new start. You know, we'd still be us. We'd just take all our problems with us. What the children want and what's best for us in the long run aren't necessarily going to be the same thing.'

'I'm not sure what you mean.'

'Sash, I met a girl . . .'

'I know. I knew it. Are you in love with her?'

'It'll never work,' says Adam.

Sasha isn't sure whether he's referring to the girl or to herself.

'She likes me too,' he goes on. 'That seemed so amazing to me, that she could think I was desirable, that she could want to be with me. I'd lost so much confidence. I felt – useless. Redundant. You could say emasculated. Spare and old and dreadful. And you know something? Just as I've realised I can be myself, just as I've stopped feeling like a tree that's been hollowed out by lightning, she thinks I'm going to come back to you.'

'And?'

'She's lovely. She's frightened. She's been badly hurt before and doesn't want to get hurt again. She wanted me to promise that I wouldn't hurt her – by coming back to you and the kids. And I discovered I can't make that promise. That told me more than I knew.'

Sasha, sitting with her hands over her face, pictures to herself the foundations of their house, lying in the London clay where they have always lain; the bricks are chipped and worn, but the house is still standing.

'I can't make you any promises either,' Adam goes on. 'It's a leap of faith. But if we don't make that leap, we'll never find out whether we could have. What I don't want to happen is for Liffy to think she's won. If her anorexia is about her thinking she can bring us back together, I don't want her deciding that it's worked. She can't be allowed to blackmail us.'

'We'll tell her the truth. She'll know the score exactly.'

'Yes. These things are going to get talked about. It was only my mother who couldn't talk about important issues. We're going to be different now. Aren't we?'

Sasha lowers her hands and gazes at Adam, her heart spilling over. Her lip is trembling. She doesn't want to cry. She isn't the kind of woman who cries. At least, she wasn't until recently. 'I'd like that,' she says. 'We owe it to ourselves at least to give it a go.'

'There's one thing more you can say to convince me.'

'What's that?'

'Think about it.'

Sasha thinks and when the answer comes to her she almost

shouts with frustration at her own stupidity. 'I still love you, Adam.'

'I still love you too, Sasha.'

Sasha holds him, wondering with a distant sense of dread what will become of them; but for the moment all she wants is to have him there with her. The twins charge in, screech to a halt at the sight – and cheer.

26

The Christmas lights are still up and the early-morning sun gleams through translucent frost when Liffy and Sasha walk into the Royal Free Hospital and take the lift to the maternity ward.

Lisa is sitting up in a bed near the window, her hair loose and messy, her face wet with tears. She's had a bad time: twenty-six hours in labour. The pain was so violent that she almost thought she was dying.

'I just couldn't believe it,' she tells Sasha. The tears are pouring from her eyes – she can't stop them. She's in shock, she tells her sister, and her hormones have gone berserk. 'I never knew what it would feel like. I've never been so frightened in my life. It's this force that just takes you over – your body has a rhythm to it that you know nothing about until it's there. It's something so – my God, it's primitive, I don't know what else to call it, it's just pure, brutal, appalling nature and you belong to it and you can't do anything to stop it until they tell you you can have the epidural. I've never screamed like that before! My throat's sore now.'

Lisa doesn't tell Sasha that she has inadvertently found the answer to her question about where *The Rite of Spring* came from. Racked with pain, her body forcing her through moves far beyond her control in the middle of the night, she recognised the force through the fug of agony and terror and remembered reading somewhere that Stravinsky had been present at the birth of one of his children not long before he wrote the piece. She'd forgotten at once, because at that moment her mind wasn't her own. But now, in the clear morning, the first of her daughter's life, she feels that she understands something she had never grasped before.

'So here you are, on the other side,' Sasha says. 'Aren't you glad?'

'I can't believe it.' Lisa blows her nose, her hand shaking almost too much to hold her tissue. 'I've got a daughter. Look at her, Sash. Isn't she wonderful? Isn't it incredible – here is a perfect little person who is totally innocent. I can't believe it.'

Sasha gazes at the small pink creature in the crib at the foot of Lisa's bed. She looks just like Liffy did on her first day in the world.

Liffy bends over the crib. 'Can I pick her up?' she asks Lisa.

'Of course you can. Be very careful and support her head.'

Liffy reaches down and takes into her arms the warm bundle of white blanket and pink flesh topped with a tuft of soft hair.

There's the sound of footsteps coming to a halt, a sense of a new presence nearby. Liffy turns round. A tall, dark man is standing beside them, his arms full of flowers and his deep grey-green eyes full of tears.

Lisa looks up at him over her sister and niece and baby, speechless.

'Lindsey called me,' he says, with a thick, exotic accent.

The entire ward seems to have quietened around them. Vladimir goes to Lisa's side and reaches for her hand. Lisa, her face blank, lets him take it.

'Did you really think I wouldn't come?' he asks.

'I didn't think anything. I was too busy screaming blue murder.' She looks down at her fingers, interlacing with his. She's already cried so much that she can hardly cry any more.

'I tried to phone you,' she says. 'Months ago. In September. Where were you?'

'Brazil,' says Vladimir.

Liffy can't take her eyes off Vladimir. His dark hair, his

grey-green eyes, his swarthy skin, those incredible cheekbones. Everything about him is green and brown; even his clothes are in earth colours, brown and olive and cream. Vladimir, for all his elemental talent and his fame, is a creature of the earth.

Her steps silent, she goes slowly up to him, the baby in her arms, head supported carefully as Lisa had told her. Without asking Lisa first – in case she says no – Liffy extends Vladimir's new-born daughter towards him.

Vladimir says, 'Liffy?' Then he reaches out, takes the baby from her and sinks into a chair, transfixed.

'Liffs,' Sasha hisses. 'Let's go and have a cup of tea.'

When they return half an hour later, which Sasha thinks should be long enough to do the trick, Vladimir is sitting close to Lisa, his cheek against the top of her head. Lisa sees them coming back, closes her eyes and smiles. There is nothing more to say, nothing more to be done.

The baby is now in Lisa's arms, engaged in some heavy-duty sleeping, making unconscious little snuffly noises under her blanket. Sasha reaches out one finger and strokes her soft, silky forehead. 'She's so pretty, Lee,' she says. 'I know everyone always says that about new babies, but she really is! What long eyelashes she has. Have you decided what to call her?'

'We were just talking about that,' says Lisa. 'We were just talking about what to do, where to go, what to call her. We want a name that is – maybe – as good in France as it is in England. We might live there – in the end – perhaps.'

'We wondered,' Vladimir says, 'if you have any ideas for names, Liffy?'

Liffy looks at Vladimir's face and can hardly speak. She knows those eyes so well. 'There are some names I like,' she says, in a whisper.

'Such as?'

'Chloë? After *Daphnis and Chloë*?' The part she would never play now; the dance she would never perform. Perhaps this new little girl will have the chances she's never going to have.

'That's pretty.' Lisa nods. 'Chloë. Maybe she could be a Chloë.'

'Don't take it just because Liffy happens to like it, Vladimir,' Sasha says.

'I do like it,' says Vladimir. 'And you know, Sasha, you don't need to call me Vladimir – in Russia this is very formal and we use diminutives all the time. My Russian friends and Lisa always call me Vovka, but in Britain most people call me Bob.'

Liffy begins to laugh. The baby stirs and gives a gurgle. Liffy laughs louder. The mysterious, magical Vladimir of the photos in Lisa's flat, the unconscious prototype for her Earth Prince, has turned into plain old Uncle Bob.

'What's so funny?' Lisa asks, drying her eyes.

'Oh . . . I'll tell you some time,' Liffy says.

'Bob' and Lisa lower their voices and talk in Russian – a dusky waterfall of sound that seems oddly familiar to Liffy, but of which she can't understand a word. She wonders if Lisa will teach it to her; after all, as of fifteen minutes ago they're planning to raise the baby – Chloë – to be bilingual.

Lisa is telling Vladimir about her new theory of *The Rite of Spring*. 'Its power comes from birth. It's really about life and its renewal. Not death.'

'Most likely,' says Vladimir, 'it's both.'

'But you know what would happen if I presented that as an academic theory behind *The Rite*? I'd be laughed out of town.'

'Of course. But we know – and perhaps only we should. Shall we keep it to ourselves?'

'Let's,' says Lisa. She gives Liffy the baby to hold again while Vladimir – who, fifteen minutes ago, admitted at last that he loves her – embraces her and lets her admit it back.

Silver light pours through the windows on to Liffy and Chloë. It illumines Chloë's tiny new hands, her long eyelashes, her intent, screwed-up pink face. Liffy has a new love in her life. From now on, everything is going to be different. Life is strong, renewing, heedless of the hearts it heals. Liffy takes her cousin and lifts her towards the sun.